Bander's Keep

By

Paul Amdahl

Bander's Keep
by Paul Amdahl

Copyright 2017

Published by London and Stout Publishers

londonandstout.com

Cover stock art Vaughn Mir

This book is dedicated to my brother Scott

Prologue

The smell of sulfur oozed from the hot-water spring. Tan algae fluttered along the rock walls of the bath. Bander slid his frame slowly into the slimy pit. Chills from the heat rippled up his body while he acclimated to the temperature. Here, and only here, could he relax and allow the minerals to sooth his arthritic frame. He had spent years abusing his body in his quest for more power. How he relished these moments! Outside this chamber he maintained a facade of strength and vitality. Although no one could challenge him, he didn't want to waste his time dealing with fools. Better to rule the masses through inferences of strength.

The hot water worked on his bones and he let out a long sigh. Tensions evaporated. His journey to the witch's circle had tired him. He needed this.

"My Lord," the words hesitantly echoed from the caverns that led to his relaxation pool.

Bander's eyes opened with disgust; disgust at the disruption, disgust at his self-imposed duties. He ignored the voice, allowing himself the luxury of another moment in the water.

"We caught one."

He eased himself out of the pool, careful with each handhold and careful to avoid the slippery moss. He moved cautiously to where his clothes lay. Every item of clothing he wore was black. He didn't care for black especially but he knew that it fed the aura of power. He dressed and tied his black cloak around his neck. The cloak would inspire subconscious fear and cover the frailty of his body and any weapons he wanted to conceal.

He knew that Quid would not call for him again. Repeated information annoyed him. His servants were careful never to bother him.

He took his time arranging his necklace. The silver complimented the black cloak. A severed lizard head hung from the chain. The eyes stared blankly and the bloody flesh disgusted and unnerved all who looked upon it. He wore the trinket to create fear, but also because it served to distract anyone he engaged face to face. Distracted people were easier to read.

Now, properly dressed, Bander towered like a king.

"Approach," he commanded.

A skinny man quickly emerged from the cavern's entrance. The man was insignificant. His balding head and pointy nose made him look pathetic, as if he was about to sneeze.

"Lord, I have prepared your laboratory as you ordered," said Quid. "I would have done it earlier, but the nature of your request demanded prudence. My messengers returned with highly unacceptable inventory. I dispatched them twice to find a specimen of the size you wanted. Plus I sought an intangible predatory look in the eyes, a hard concept to convey. The first and second specimens though vicious, lacked a certain quality, not at all what your lordship requested."

"Enough of this rambling. Show me what you caught."

"This way sir, I have him in a big glass case with a velvet blanket covering it up. I thought you might enjoy some of the trappings of my showmanship experience. As you recall, before you recruited me to your gracious service, I wanted to be a magician. You know with all the hoopla and mirrors and glitter and smoke. To personify the impossible."

Bander walked through the chamber and down the passageway. His lapdog followed at his heels and continued to clamor on about details beneath concern. Bander heard every inane comment but his mind wondered lonely chambers. They continued past several closed doors that lined the hall, finally arriving at a nondescript wood door. It opened to a room with a large square box in its center. The velvet covering hid the box's contents.

"Shall I unveil the creat..."

Bander ignored him and simply walked over to the case and ripped the covering off. A flash of movement came from inside the glass as a giant snake struck at Bander. Only the thick glass prevented this cold fury from sinking its frothing fangs deep into Bander's flesh. Bander didn't flinch at the savage attacks as the beast continually lashed out against the glass beating its face. Venom and blood obscured the view. Quid looked on. His pleasure at the ferocious display his captive put on for his master almost made him forget not being able to 'unveil' the terror.

"Do you see? What did I say? Isn't this impressive? He stretches three times the size of any of the others my men caught. Sixteen feet long and thick with muscle, this rare species inspired the most fear of any snake. A particularly nasty breed, this one killed two men before we saw it. It lived in the porous rocks on a volcano's edge. We tied a goat up and when the snake launched itself out its hole we pulled it in with the goat carcass. It was still pumping poison into it. We slid the whole bloody scene into the bags. His attention to his meal allowed his capture. Ferocious but stupid, Lord."

"Perfect," said Bander. The movement of the snake reflected in the gleam of Bander's eyes. "Leave me."

Quid looked hurt but he moved quickly out of the room. Bander turned his back on the snake. He moved to a cluttered shelf. Pushing aside several bundles he found a small wood statue. It fit in the palm of his hand. "Tock. Hello my old friend," Bander spoke to the relic.

He set the carving down on a table and then gathered kindling and built a small fire near the snake cage. The fire crackled as it fed on the bits of fuel. Its flickering light cast eerie shadows and

7

reflected in the glass of the cage as well as the reptile's eyes. The snake stared transfixed at the movement of the flame. The firelight on snake's skin recalled the history of things sliming their way out of the primordial goo. Of the first time a sea-beast braved the land to sink its fangs into an unaware animal. To drag it down to the depths, a place where dark intentions hid and railed against the barrier.

Bander's pupils cast off an even more vile light, light not tempered and dulled by the innocence of animal nature. Freewill curled its rancid lips in the reflection in those eyes. Bander picked up the relic. "Time to serve." He cast the carving into the flames. The fire welcomed this addition. As it burned, a noxious black smoke curled upward like the probing tendrils of a serpent. Bander kept his distance and watched with satisfaction as the emanations drifted gently into the cage. As soon as the creeping black-smoke found the snake's nostrils the snake reacted. Its huge oily body rolled and thrashed. Bander's breath caught in his throat while he watched. Then the snake went still.

Bander kicked dirt onto the fire. He opened the cage and watched as the length of black nightmare slowly slid into the room. The eyes of the creature radiated a new intelligence.

"Welcome, to your new prison, Tock," said Bander. "My great enemy, I have a purpose for you."

Chapter One

The cow looked back, concerned, while Larry swooshed the soapy sponge over the bovine's ass. Cow-ass-washing was not glamorous work but it offered the reward, often not present in other jobs, of taking a dirty ass and cleaning it of infection and fecal matter until it gleamed of health and cleanliness. The end of a long day left one's soul content. The meals tasted better and the beer, colder. Larry ignored the cow's trepidation. He learned a long time ago to take charge when tending to an animal's backside.

The morning grew whiskers and Larry's bucket was a tepid mess. He worked without complaint. Larry liked working with animals. He felt more comfortable around them than people. Animals didn't make fun of his stutter. His shy, quiet ways calmed the creatures he cared for. When he occasionally laughed it looked awkward, but that made it all the more contagious.

Larry's vocational partner, Bob, was also his brother. Bob and Larry both had crew cuts. Bob stood slightly taller than Larry. Bob always carried an assortment of small tools with him. If anyone needed anything cut or measured Bob was quick to help. He wore a special vest that he made, to keep all of his tools in. Although they were twins they didn't look that similar, except for their haircuts and their eyes.

They each had one blue eye and one eye without color. The unusual eye housed no iris. Everyone in Agea Hills accepted the brother's birth defect. Folks originally regarded the babies as either blessings or curses. Now, the brothers had outlived their novelty and were nothing more than a couple of 4-leaf-clovers amongst a field of 3-leaf-clovers when no one is looking for luck.

"D,d,d, did you manage to f,f,fi, fix the leak in your roof?" stammered Larry.

"Well, 'fixed' might be too strong a word," said Bob smiling. "I managed to climb that tree next to my house last night. From there I could survey the work site and devise a plan of action."

"And?"

"Well I concluded that I needed to make some mud-cement out of the creek-clay and sand. I don't have the proper tools for mudding so I figured I could make a spackling knife out of a broken plate I have at my house, but when I climbed out of the tree I scraped my hand up pretty bad on the rough bark. So there you have it."

"H, h, have what? Did you fix the hole or not?"

"I can't be expected to mix up a batch of roofing cement with a scraped-up hand. It could get infected. No, it's better to wait until the scrape heals and then I can attack that leaky roof properly."

"Yeah, 'fixed' might have been too strong a word," noted Larry.

The brothers worked through the day. The smell of cattle made their work a visceral experience. In addition to the cows, farmers also brought sheep, goats and even dogs. Animals need to be clean to be healthy. This grooming business had been in the family for years. At some price, people would rather pay to have certain jobs done. Luckily for the brothers everyone would rather pay them, than do it themselves. This gave them a strange sort of power.

Agea Hills is the kind of place where it rains on schedule. Bob's scraped up hand would make for a pretty good story. Of course it would be exaggerated. Bob looked forward to telling it.

The taverns would be full of tales tonight; of romance, jealousy, and scandal. Most would involve farm animals in one way or another.

Larry and Bob conducted their usual ritual after work. They put the tools away and walked wearily toward the river to bathe. The waters were fresh and cold, a stern cold. Larry washed himself quickly and efficiently in a hurry to get out.

Bob prefered to jump and splash, fighting the water the whole time. "Holy crap! This is freezing. Dang it. Brrr. Clean enough!"

They both got the job done. Although tired, they trotted anxiously toward the bar. The end of their menial day meant the beginning of their personal day.

The tavern smelled of meat and beer. People from different lifestyles and vocations shared jokes and laughter. A boisterous game of darts occupied one wall. The stools around the bar were filling up. The bar contained mostly men but there were women too. The workday done, now they could get drunk and live.

Once inside, Bob and Larry went their separate ways. After having spent the day together they needed a little space.

Larry walked back to the darts. His friend Jim greeted him with a big smile. "Larry, come on. What took you so long? I have been stalling these guys."

"S,s,s,sorry J,J,Ji Jim," said Larry, looking down. He always stuttered more around other people. His hands got sweaty as he tried to relax.

"That's okay, now that you're here we can make them wish that they never challenged us to darts," said Jim throwing a dart into the board.

Larry was good at darts. Everyone in town knew it. Bob had built a dartboard on the back of Larry's house where Larry practiced all the time.

Jim handed the darts to Larry with a flourish as if he was bestowing a king with his sword. A waitress brought Larry his usual drink while he sank a bull's eye.

"This is going to be easy!" said Jim.

On the other side of the room Bob sat at a table with some older fellows. He had gotten them interested in some project that he was working on and they watched him scratch a diagram into the wood table they surrounded. Bob face was animated and excited as he described how he planned to mix the mudding compound for his roof.

At the bar an old man started singing some raunchy song. The pretty young woman sitting near him started to sing harmony and for a verse they sounded great.

"I didn't know that she could sing like that," said Bob.

"Yeah, I think she used to sing with her father at home," said Nick, a big fat guy sitting with Bob.

"It sure is a shame about her dad," said Joe, a skinny bald guy at the table.

"Do you think that there is any chance he is still alive?" asked Bob.

"Are you kidding?" said Nick. "You know that anything that wanders into the wasteland is as good as hamburger."

"I lost another sheep to the wasteland last week," said Joe.

"Well at least it was a stupid one," said Bob. "Any animal with half of a brain knows instinctively not to wander outside of the town. You can almost feel the evil things that live in the wasteland around Agea Hills."

"All sheep are stupid," said Joe.

The air changed. A stranger walked in. He caught everyone's attention like a big nose. A stranger hadn't visited Agea Hills for 40 years. There was no trade between villages in this part of the world. It was too dangerous to travel between towns. The woods hid horrible things. Animals that wandered off were forgotten.

The stranger was tall and lean. His shoulder-length hair grew as unkempt as his graying beard. The dark blue cloak he wore looked to be wool. He could have stepped out of a forest or out of a cave or climbed down off of a horse. This man seemed wild, like an animal.

12

He walked over to the bar. "I would like to try your wine," the stranger said. The bartender got right to getting the man's order, grateful of something to do to still his nerves. The rest of the people in the room acted as if nothing out of the ordinary was going on. No one wanted the stranger's attention. They were a group of water buffalo using their anonymity to stay the lion's rush.

The stranger paid for the wine with a small gold sphere. The sphere was perfect. "Surely this is enough for a glass of wine," he made a face when he said wine.

"Yeah, that's plenty. I've never seen gold in that shape before," the bartender said. "Where did you get it?"

"That, my bartender, is standard currency in Snaigor Hills," replied the stranger.

A palpable uneasiness settled over the eavesdroppers around the bar. How could this man have traveled between the towns?

As the bartender took the sphere to the back room to store it safely the stranger turned to the men sitting to his left. "How are things in Agea Hills? Is there any news?"

"Who wants to know?" said a young man who had obviously had too much to drink.

The stranger turned to face the young man. The indigo cloak slid off of the bar as the stranger stood up. The tavern was completely silent now. The young man's pulse quickened. The stranger towered over him. There could be any sort of weapon hidden in that cloak. Every one could tell that something bad was about to happen.

Another man at the bar spoke up, "Not much happens here, the weather has been mild lately."

"We did have some bad storms last year though," another man interjected.

The stranger turned his attention to the two men who spoke. The young man took this chance and quickly walked to the other side of the tavern.

"No, I'm not concerned with the rainfall in Agea Hills. I'm talking about news. Has anything interesting happened lately?" said the stranger settling back down to the bar.

The two townspeople looked at each other confused.

"You walking in here was the most interesting thing that I think has ever happened here."

"Yeah," the other one agreed.

"Oh," the stranger sighed. "Well maybe you men can help me get my bearings in this town."

The two guys looked at each other. "Yeah sure."

"For instance," the stranger said. "Who is that man tending bar?"

"That's Fred."

"Yeah, Fred is a great guy," the other man interjected.

The stranger looked around the room nonchalantly, "How about that guy?"

"That's William, he's a tailor."

"Yes, he has a very nice jacket on," agreed the stranger.

"And what about that guy," the stranger pointed at Bob.

"That's Bob, he and his brother run a grooming business. Mostly they clean up diseased livestock for the ranchers."

"Interesting."

"Tell me more about this bartender. What makes the wine so bad?"

"Well sir I don't think we can help you with that, see, we don't drink wine."

With that the stranger finished his glass in one final swig. "I can't say as I blame you gentlemen." The stranger got up off of the barstool, turned and walked briskly out of the bar into the night.

Both men were immediately besieged with questions from the rest of the people in the bar. Everyone crowded around them to hear their responses.

"Well Buford, what was the stranger doing in Agea Hills?" someone in the crowd asked.

"I don't know, he didn't say."

"How did he get here? Is he planning on staying?" someone else asked.

"He didn't tell us that either."

"What was his name?" the bartender asked Buford.

"He didn't say."

"Well we all saw you two sitting over here talking up a storm with him. What were you talking about?"

"He was interested in the town, general news, that sort of thing."

"He wanted to know about the people of the town."

"What about the people of the town?"

"Well, he asked about Fred and he liked George's jacket; we told him about Bob washing cow butts," Buford said smiling.

The night in the tavern continued, with laughter. The stranger's appearance whet the imaginations of the revelers. Various pockets of story telling and bravado broke out in parts of the bar.

Larry listened intently to the drunken ramblings of one

townsman. "I bet that the stranger is a spirit. That he is here as a warning to us. We have lived isolated from the rest of the world for so long and now the demon's messenger has found us. Oh woe unto our land. For his coming here can only bring death."

"If he was a spirit, how come he came to a bar and drank a glass of wine? That sounds like the sort of thing a man would do after a long day of travel," replied the bartender.

"He didn't come here for the wine, he came to look us over. He looked all around the bar probably caught a glimpse of every one of us."

"So," said the bartender.

"So, our demon knows us now and we know nothing of him."

"You have had too much to drink yourself. Your demons are born of drink and not hellfire."

"I could use more to drink."

Bob found his way over to Larry as brothers often do when there is trouble. "Larry, what do you make of the man in the cloak?"

"Well, I..." stammered Larry; "I say he's a traveler from another town just like he says."

"Yeah, but why would he come here? Even if he knows how to get through the forests safely why come to a boring town like Agea Hills?"

"Maybe he doesn't know how boring it is," answered Larry.

"Well he soon will, it's not a good idea to start at the town's hotspot and work your way down from there. He should have started at our barn and then made his way over to the gardens and then maybe to the store and then to the mayor's office and then he could have ended up here at the bar, a couple of hours from now after everyone is a little tipsy."

"Yeah, that, that would have been the way to do it. But he probably just walked over to the noisiest part of town when he got here."

"Well it's a shame. Now he's got nowhere to go but down," said Bob.

Larry and Bob made their way out of the bar with pleasant good-byes to all their friends. As they closed the door they shut out the lunatic tales of evil spun by various drunkards.

The coolness of night energized their skin. Evenings in Agea Hills crawled black as spiders. The two made their way with the help of strategically placed candles in various town windows. When there is no other light, a candle burns like the sun.

The brother's houses sat next door to each other. Neither was fancy. Shelter against the weather and a little privacy was all they provided.

As they lay in their respective homes readying themselves for sleep, the mystery of the stranger played with their imaginations. Bob's train of consciousness, although it started with the stranger at union station, jumped the tracks and ended up veering into which type of wood stain would he use on his perfectly repaired roof. He fell asleep proud of the job he would eventually do on that leak. A big warm smile playing across his lumberjack face.

Larry looked uncomfortable. His eyes stared straight up at his ceiling. The presence of a stranger in town made him feel like he had eaten a bug. Sleep would not come easy for Larry tonight.

*   *   *

The stranger made his way around the town. He had seen what he was looking for. Now he must prepare himself. He had time, maybe several hours. He slid into a dark spot next to some trees and sat on the ground to make his plans.

*   *   *

Quid accessed the lever to his secret chambers. The secret passageway revealed itself. Quid stormed into the hallway muttering to himself. He carefully navigated between the trip wires and loose floor rock that would have dropped him into a man-made pit lined with spikes. He maintained contact with one of the walls with his hand to stabilize the poison darts that would have been released if he hadn't.

Bander allowed him this office. He could create any sort of space he wanted. This was in exchange for unquestionable authority. He was Bander's slave. To the rest of the world he was a powerful man. The ruler of the army. But Quid grew to loathe his office. At first it was everything he ever dreamed of. Executing Bander's orders was an honor. He couldn't jump to attention fast enough. He laid awake at night thinking on how he had done that day and what he could do tomorrow to please his master. But the winds had shifted somewhere along the course.

Quid unrolled a map on his desk. He set various books on the corners to hold it open. The map showed Bander's kingdom. Sixteen towns that paid taxes and swore allegiance to him. Bander's Keep was roughly centered between the towns. It had taken Bander four years to conquer the towns. It was not too hard to defeat the citizens but it was very difficult to move an army through the wasteland. Gelks had to be used and they were tough to come by and often chose death before service.

Quid never understood why Bander chose to stop conquering. Quid hadn't been in his service then. That was too long ago, before he was born. But it didn't seem that anyone could stand up to him. He squinted at the map. Bander's defensive position was strong, nothing could get to Bander's Keep that he didn't want there. Perhaps the old wizard was getting conservative in his old age. Maybe he was building a nest in which to die.

Quid wouldn't make that mistake once he attained power. He would push for more land, more cities, and more money. There was a virtually unexplored wilderness in seven days ride in any direction. Surely there were more towns to take. The old books talk of hundreds of societies. If that was true, the world was huge and ripe for the picking. Quid knew that the Gelks had a city but so far none of them would divulge its whereabouts. The other species of man that shared Bander's main town all came from somewhere. But they would never tell for fear of Quid's soldiers.

Bander was getting old and focused all of his attentions on his quest for a special champion. Some creature so foul that nothing could stand up to its fury. Quid wondered what exactly Bander planned on using the creature for. So far Quid had devoted way too much time to ferreting out these beasts and then with the help of the soldiers, capturing and bringing them to Bander. He always was there to pass judgment. Why did he get to decide that this was good and that was bad? Quid had grown to resent his position.

Here in his chambers he was completely safe. The hallway was lined with poisoned darts, booby traps, and false floors. He settled himself into his plush chair. He didn't kid himself about Bander's power though; so far, every creature that he had brought to his master the master had killed. Quid had no idea the extent of Bander's power. He must bide his time. For now he would jump. But somewhere down the road Bander would be gone. And then he would be ready.

Chapter Two

Larry awoke to the sound of a match being struck in the room in which he slept. The glare from the fire filled the room and temporarily blinded him. The light quickly died down as it was sucked into a pipe only to flame up again as the smoker exhaled. The sound of the pipe being stoked created an eerie world in which to awaken.

"Who is there!" Larry blurted out, more from adrenaline-coated fear than from bravado. Still half asleep and wide-eyed in a silent room, Larry saw the figure's location by the glow of the pipe.

"Calm down, I didn't mean to frighten you."

"Who are you?" demanded Larry.

"My name is Grento."

"The s, st, stranger," Larry rasped. Larry's mind raced to grasp this moment. The voice in his house emanated like a wraith from the grave.

"Yes, I guess so," Grento replied.

"What are you doing here? How did you get into my house? What do you want?" Larry struggled for information anything to fix his situation and allow him to proceed.

"Ah, all good questions. But the answer you seek is no, I am not going to hurt you," Grento responded.

Larry was not reassured. Grento's voice sounded too re-laxed. He obviously wasn't worried about trespassing or anything that Larry could possibly do to him. That sort of confidence is unsettling.

"Welcome," Larry choked out trying to sound inviting. Grento merely stared at him intensely. "Is there anything I can get... or eh you must be tired..." Grento cocked his head to the right, still silent.

"Can you at least hand m, m, me my pants?" Larry said.

Grento burst into hugely loud laughter. Larry looked scared and tried to smile but couldn't quite pull it off. Grento's laughter filled the little room as only a noise in silence can. As Grento finished he said, "Get your pants on, we must wake up your brother."

Larry didn't want to get his brother involved. It was bad enough that he was involved. Larry made a move to lead Grento in the opposite direction from his brothers home.

"Bob's house is back over this way, Larry," corrected Grento grabbing Larry's sleeve. Larry's momentum stopped cold as the stranger's grip was as unforgiving as ice.

"Eh, oh yes, of c, c, course," Larry stuttered.

Larry turned the correct way. Then, together, they walked through the night to Bob's house. Larry knocked on Bob's door. There was no answer. Larry knocked again. He looked over at Grento as if to say, "Not my fault, he doesn't appear to be home," when the groggy voice of Bob called out, "Who is it?"

"It's me, Larry. Open up Bob."

The door opened and there stood Bob in his red and orange pajamas wiping the sleep out of his eyes. "Larry what is it? Do you know how late it is?"

"Bob this is Grento, Grento, Bob."

"Hello."

"Well, let me light some candles," Bob said as he turned back into his house. Larry and Grento followed him. Bob's house was simple, two chairs and a bed and a table all arranged around a cooking-fireplace. The table was covered with drawings and bits of rope and all sorts of small objects. It looked like Bob used this area to create new inventions.

Bob lit the candles on the table and sat down on the bed. Grento and Larry each settled into the chairs. Bob looked to Larry for assurance, none was forthcoming. Larry wore a brave mask as if going along with Grento would make everything all right. Grento's face was the face of authority. His stern eyes regarded the brothers like a drill sergeant scrutinizes a fresh batch of recruits. He looked unforgiving. Bob and Larry found themselves squirming in their skin.

"What can we do for you?" Larry asked.

"Ah, it begins..." Grento sighed. "It's not what you can do for me it is what I have come to do for you."

"For us? How could you even know us? You obviously come from outside of our town and we have never been outside of Agea Hills," said Larry.

"This is of course quite true," said Grento. "I have come searching for you. I knew only of your birth defect."

"You mean our eyes?" said Bob.

"Yes," said Grento.

"Why would you care about a couple of guys with eyes that don't match?" asked Larry.

"It's not that I care about it," said Grento. "Listen, let me tell you a story. Maybe that will answer your questions."

And so Grento began his tale.

"This world is much bigger than you can imagine. Your lives have been spent in virtual solitude. Let me start with generalities. Have you noticed how there is a boundary to your town? How there is a natural meadow that is where you and your friends live and work and grow food that is surrounded by shrubs and then forest. You never venture out into the shrubs or forest do you? Have you even tried? Well, no matter. You know that creatures live around your village that will kill anything they catch. And you are right. The things that live in the woods are more horrible than any nightmare you could possibly have with your limited point of reference.

23

Your brains don't even contain the required concepts to imagine the sheer terror that lies waiting right outside your little town.

Most of you never even think of leaving. This knowledge has been passed down through the generations and has allowed you to live relatively safe, if somewhat dreary, lives. What you don't know is that the world is made up of many towns just like yours. Each one an island unto itself surrounded by the wasteland. Each village thinking it's alone in the world and content in this knowledge. Not all of the villagers are the same though. Evolution has had a nice time with the isolated species. There is a even larger picture to think about one that my species is uniquely aware of..."

"Your, your species?" stammered Larry.

"Ah, yes, my species. Of course, you assumed that I am human, like you. You were quite mistaken. I am a Gelk. Anyway, back to my explanation. The world is divided into various city-states or towns. This division is not strictly due to physical environmental structures. If it were, then the various creatures that live in the wasteland in between cities would simply enter the cities and gorge on the inhabitants whenever they wanted to. They are unable to do this. The world is governed by many opposing energies...gravity, inertia, radiant energy etc. One energy field keeps the monsters at bay. It divides the world into places inhabited by demons and places inhabited by you and species like you. This force is like the light of a campfire. The wolves will keep a certain distance from the burning heath. As long as you keep feeding the fire and stay near you are safe, but venture into the darkness and you will be gobbled up.

"But you said that you have come from another town," said Bob.

"That is true. I have come from far away and I have walked through the wasteland," replied Grento.

"How did you do that?" asked Larry

"I am a Gelk," replied Grento.

Larry and Bob turned to share an expression of confusion. Grento took a deep drag off of his pipe. The embers inside the bowl created a circle of light around Grento's face. With the drag concluded, his face faded into the dim candlelight. As he exhaled it sounded like steam escaping a tomb.

"Gelks are similar to humans. We don't have magic that protects us if that's what you think." Larry and Bob both shook their heads and mumbled incoherently as if to say, "No, of course not."

"We are travelers, as a species, I mean. Gelks wander through the wasteland. It's a little hard to describe, if you or one of your friends wandered out of the town's boundaries you would indubitably walk into the waiting lair of one of the beasts and get killed. Gelks, how should I put this, know the way. An invisible path runs through the wastelands. Gelks sense it and can move through without stumbling into any webs or holes or what not. It's as if the force that keeps your little town safe extends like tributaries from village to town to city. Gelks simply follow the path."

"Amazing," said Larry. "So, there are other t, t, town, towns like Agea Hills?"

"Yes, many, many towns. And not all of them contain humans."

"What?" said Bob.

"What, what do, do they contain?" stuttered Larry trying to act mildly curious.

"Oh many species, all different shapes and sizes with various attributes. One nice thing about this world is that there must have been a time when the species could communicate because the languages are basically the same wherever you go. There are variations of course. But a Gelk can get by in any town."

"Surely you have much better p, p, places to visit than Agea Hills? I am afraid we don't have much to offer a w, w, world traveler here. You have already been to the bar," said Larry.

"We could take him to the sitting rock," said Bob. "We got a rock just over on the other side of town just perfect for sitting on. I ain't kidding, you would think someone made it. But no one did, it's just like that. Sometimes I like to go over there in the evening and just sit and think about what a great rock for sitting that is. Course there is usually a line. But most folks don't sit too long as they have got lots of stuff to tend to. Not me. I just love sitting on that rock," said Bob.

Larry was looking a bit sheepish listening to Bob and added, "Of course we have other stuff to do."

Grento stared at the brothers while they rambled on. He looked like someone just told him that he had eaten some crap by accident.

"I know what you have in this little town. I have been here before," said Grento raising his voice.

"You have b, b, been here before?" said Larry. "When? I can't imagine no one mentioning a stranger."

"It was a long time ago, when you two were just babies."

"You remember us from when we were babies?" asked Bob.

"Yes I do," said Grento. "I was traveling the wasteland about eh, it must be about 16 years ago. I was going to visit a cloak-weaver, the very best in the land. Man, he could make a cloak that no wind would blow through. The wool was so perfectly spun and wound that you could feel comfortable in any weather." Grento trailed off and stared into the fire.

"Grento?" prodded Bob.

"Anyway, I thought that I should stop and enjoy some of the trappings of civilization at a small town called Fanto, but when I got near I could smell it burning. When I got there I saw the vilest sight I have seen in my many travels. An army had swept through this gentle village and killed everyone in it. They set the homes on fire. It looked like hell. Everyone was dead. I strode through the town like the conqueror must have, surveying the complete destruction. The smell of death was intense, masked only by the smoke. Bodies lay sprawled like so much carrion. And then I saw something move. It was near the edge of the forest. It hesitated for a minute and then ran for the trees. Well I don't know what force was guiding me at that point but I ran after it. I was filled with fury and wanted vengeance on whoever was left over of the raiding party. Into the trees I raced, the figure not more than twenty yards ahead. And then I heard the gentle crying of a baby. I stopped running and looking down at a tree stump saw the two of you. Two little babies crying in the wasteland. The figure I was chasing stopped and watched me for a moment. It was all wrapped in rags. I couldn't see its face hidden in the cowl. I looked from you to the figure and then as I prepared to give chase again, the figure's body ripped apart and formed three wraiths, which ran in different directions. I couldn't chase all of them and I was stopped by a cold shiver as I realized that whatever I had been chasing would have easily killed me. It wasn't human. It wasn't of this world. It struck me that I might have interrupted the grim reaper coming for you. It slunk amongst the fire and the dead and tried to carry you away. But I was there to stop it.

I took you both, you were so tiny. I took you to Agea Hills and left you with your new parents. I didn't want to leave you in a town nearby to Fanto for fear that whatever army was marching would burn it too. Agea Hills I knew to be in a quiet valley with gentle farm people who wouldn't judge your unusual eyes. It was lucky that it was me that found you as I am a Gelk and able to navigate the wasteland. You have providence on your side."

"Our parents told us that we were adopted but they made it sound like our parents died in a farming accident," said Bob.

"Our eyes..." said Larry. "Are we, you know, human?"

"Oh yes, no question. There isn't any race of people with eyes like yours. That is nothing to worry about. There was something spooky about a couple of babies with one blue eye and one black eye. You know how big baby's eyes look. Well that only made the mutation that much more out of the ordinary. Some folks call your black eye the 'dead eye'. I guess because it doesn't share the life-full color of normal eyes."

"But only one of my eyes is black," said Bob.

"I guess they would say that you are half-dead," Grento said.

"That is funny," said Larry sarcastically.

"An optimist would say that I am half-alive," said Bob. Grento stared at Bob, shaking his head.

Grento said, "There are serious matters to discuss." His eyes looked like an animal's, wild with focused attention. He set his pipe to the side and continued. As if on cue, a gust of wind blew outside the small house. "I came to Agea Hills to find you. I think that you two are in great danger."

"Danger?" asked Bob.

"Well, that is just it. I'm not quite sure. I am a member of group that gets together periodically to consult each other on our various travels. Gelks are a wandering folk and we each usually choose separate paths. At the last meeting — 'meeting' might be too strong a word — usually we get together and have some drink and exchange stories. Six days ago I met with my friends and man after man told similar stories of death. That along their paths they had visited towns or villages where a pair of brothers had been murdered."

"M,m,m, murdered, you say?" said Larry.

"Quite. And each pair of the brothers shared some form of birth defect."

"Like our eyes," said Bob quietly.

"Yes," said Grento quietly.

The brothers sat in the hut and felt their world changing. Larry thought about what Grento was telling them. He felt abstracted from the information he was receiving. This wasn't about him, this was a story.

"How were they murdered?" asked Bob. "Maybe it is just a coincidence."

"They were all bitten by a special kind of snake. The breed is called a Nacoona, which means 'black poison'. They are very rare. They usually live in the porous rocks of volcanoes far from any people."

"If all of the folks in these towns where these tragedies occurred are isolated like us, how do they all know what a Nacoona snake is?" asked Bob.

"You are right to be wary of me and my story, Bob so I won't take that as an insult."

Bob heart sped up and sweat broke out on his forehead as Grento leaned towards him. During the short pauses in their conversation the quiet of the night stole quickly in to remind them they alone were awake.

"There is a myth about this snake, well maybe more of a ghost story. You see even though most towns are completely separate entities many of the folk stories and legends are the same. Curious really. Anyway, there is the story of an ancient shaman who lived all alone by the sea."

Larry and Bob both noted the term sea and looked at each other.

"You have heard stories about the sea. That is a perfect example of what I am talking about. You have never seen the vast expanses of water. But you have heard the stories."

"Yeah, but those are just stories?" said Larry.

"Let me continue; there is too much to talk about to get sidetracked. The old shaman had powerful magic, real magic. He captured the soul of a man and put it into a Nakoona snake. He sent the snake to kill his enemies. And it did, with clock-like precision."

"The people that were killed were killed by a shaman?" asked Larry.

"No, that is just a legend. That shaman would have died long ago. Most think that the old legends are metaphors for life. In this case it would be something to do with combining the animal part of man with his evolved self. Or something about inevitable death. But my friends seem to think that someone has discovered the art of the old shaman and sent a Nakoona snake out to kill. Through the various rumors there is even a name for the soul trapped in the snake, Tock.

Grento's words echoed through the space of the house like the eclipse of the sun. They eliminated all light and warmth. Larry and Bob were obviously shaken by these words. Larry's hands were trembling and he looked like he was going to get sick. Bob fell off of the bed in a girlish spasm when he hit the floor he made a whimper noise.

"To..To..Tock you say?" asked Larry with all the confidence of a librarian in a fight.

"Yes," said Grento firmly.

"Where, where is T..to..Tock, right now?" asked Larry.

"I don't know," replied Grento.

"You don't know," echoed Larry. Bob climbed back onto the bed.

"I don't know, but I know he is after you and you both must leave Agea Hills," said Grento.

"Why would he be after us? This doesn't make any sense," said Bob.

"It is a long story, one that I can relate to you during the course of our travels," said Grento. "Now get packed for a journey, we haven't much time."

"Sorry, Grento is it? But we are not about to go into the wasteland because some stranger shows up with some spooky story," said Bob.

Larry nodded agreement to his brother.

"The wasteland is a dangerous place. No one goes there. Well, except you apparently," said Larry.

"Have you seen anything unusual lately?" asked Grento changing the subject.

"No, aside from you, it has pretty calm around here."

"W, Wh, what do mean, un, un, unusual?" asked Larry coyly.

"I mean, has anyone seen anything supernatural, ghosts, demons, things of that sort especially at night," said Grento.

"No, I think we would have heard about that," said Bob.

"W,W, Why do y, y, you ask?" said Larry.

"I wondered if anyone had seen a Thumper yet," replied Grento.

"What is a Thumper?" asked Bob.

"Oh, I don't think you fellas should worry about that. You don't believe my story," said Grento.

"Well, just for the sake of the story, what are they?" asked Bob.

"The shaman who controlled the souls of his victims used a creature called a Thumper to locate his enemies. People are saying that they have seen Thumpers all over the place. I am sure that most of that is nothing more than folks imaginations but if they are back..."

"What do they look like?" asked Bob.

"Oh, Thumpers are creatures that only sort of exist. They can get into anywhere. Doors can't stop them for they pass right through. In the daylight they are invisible but at night... well, you don't want to know. Anyway they are used to find people. Distances mean nothing to a Thumper. They can climb out of your floor-boards and then sink back to the other side of the world."

Bob and Larry listened. Grento's story sucked the warmth out of the room. Larry looked around and realized that all the objects seemed foreign or distant or dead. He was suddenly aware that he was one of only three living objects in the room and that made him feel self-conscious.

"Whoever sent Tock to kill you will surely use a Thumper to find you. Once they locate you two, it won't take Tock long to get here."

"You're mad," said Bob.

"Perhaps," said Grento. "But mad or not, friend or foe, if you do not leave with me, the Thumpers will come and then Tock will kill you."

Grento saw the impact of his words on the brothers. He anticipated their reluctance to blindly follow him. His decision to persuade them with fear was a gamble but he knew that he wouldn't get far away very fast if he had resorted to taking them by force. He watched his words act like creaking doors or the howl of coyotes on a lonesome night as the young men went from confident to questioning to scared. He would leave them to think.

"I have warned you. I offered my help and you refused. I have done what I can."

Then he stood and he walked out of Bob's house into the darkness.

"W, w, w, what a nut," said Larry trying to figure out how he felt.

"Why would a killer snake be after us?" said Bob.

"I hope he leaves town tomorrow," said Larry.

"Do you want me to make some tea?" offered Bob.

"Yeah, that would be good. I would rather hang out in here than go back over to my house with that lunatic out there," said Larry.

"I wonder what his motive is?" said Bob. "I mean, why would he make up this story about a giant snake named Tock? Is he trying to lure us away from the town?"

"Because he is coo-coo. That's why," said Larry. The flames from the little fire lapped around the base of the teakettle like eels darting out of their caves. Bob looked over at the door wondering if the man was standing right behind it or if he was far away by now.

"What if he is telling the truth?" asked Bob. Bob always looked at a problem from all sides.

"What you mean? That there really is a possessed serpent slithering through the night towards us?" said Larry sarcastically.

"Yeah," said Bob. "I mean why would this guy, Grento, travel through the wasteland risking his own life to come to Agea Hills a place that he has already been so he knows that there is nothing going on here, to tell us a story to get us to go with him into the waste? It doesn't make any sense."

"Of course it doesn't make any sense, the guy is crazy." said Larry.

"Obviously," said Bob. "I am just trying to make sense of it."

The tea tasted bitter but warm and comforting. The brothers both enjoyed letting their imaginations run all over this incident.

"What if we would have gone with him?" asked Larry grinning. "I wonder what sort of things we would have seen in the waste?"

"Who knows, probably a lot of ghosts and things that eat farmers. Or maybe there isn't that much out there. Maybe all the stories about people disappearing into the trees are made up," said Bob.

"I doubt it," said Larry. "Think of all the livestock we've lost, something had to have eaten them."

"That is a point, but maybe they just found better grazing ground."

"I bet we could have handled anything that came after us," said Larry imagining himself in battle.

"Yeah, it sure would be cool to see what is out there. We'd be the first. Real explorers. Every one would talk about us."

"Do you remember when we were kids and we went into the fringe of the trees that time?" asked Larry.

"Of course, remember how it got real quiet as soon as we got out of sight of the town?"

"How could I forget? I don't think we've ever run that fast since."

"In some ways I wish that this was real. That you and me would be forced into a grand adventure battling the unknown."

"I know, it would be sweet. But I think it's probably one of those things that's better to think about than it is to do."

"Maybe if the crazy-guy is still here in the morning we can talk to him some more. We know he came from the wasteland so at least part of what he is telling us is true. I wish I could figure out why he would make up a story like that. Did he want to rob us?"

"He could have done that here, plus we have nothing any-one would particularly want."

"What if he was telling the truth and now he left and the snake shows up? We should take precautions."

"Naw, now you are letting your imagination get the best of you."

"Oh really, then why don't you go back to your house and get some sleep. Maybe you could sleep with the door open to let in a gentle summer breeze," said Bob.

"To tell the truth, I am not all that tired tonight. All t, t, th, this talk about Tock and Grento has g, g, got my energy up."

"I notice that your stutter is back. That usually happens when you get nervous," said Bob.

"Or when I g, g, get excited," corrected Larry. "You've got to admit that sneaking into the wasteland at night is a little more interesting than washing livestock."

"I can't think of anything worse than the wasteland at night," said Bob. That time when they were kids had affected Bob more than he let on. He had nightmares for months after that day. Something had been watching them. He was sure of it. Something horrible. "Well, we had better try to get some sleep. Why don't you stay here tonight Larry. It will be like old times when we used to have sleep outs. I could really use the company." Bob made this request more for Larry's benefit than his own. Larry was younger and Bob felt a responsibility to look out for the little guy. Bob never told Larry about the thing in the wasteland that day. He protected his brother in subtle ways that only he knew.

"I guess I could sleep over," said Larry. Larry was glad to have the excuse not to go home. Grento's tales of Thumpers and snakes had left him feeling a bit vulnerable.

The brothers fell asleep side by side talking about adventure and each secretly glad for the others company.

The morning found them energized and they hurried to the inn to eagerly-anticipated bacon with eggs scrambled in the grease. The smell of breakfast greeted them as they swung open the door. Inside men were engaged in conversation while they dunked their

35

bread in coffee and licked runny egg yoke off of their plates.

"If it isn't the Masefield brothers. What, you weren't hungry this morning?" said Sally the waitress.

"We were up late last night," said Larry.

"Can we get our usual?" asked Bob.

"Goose a couple of birds and sizzle a pig, the Masefields want their usual," shouted Sally towards the kitchen.

"Thanks," said Bob and Larry.

Bob and Larry sat down at a large square table of faded gray wood with two men. Both wore plaid shirts like Bob.

"So has anyone seen the stranger this morning?" asked Bob of the group.

"Nope, I think he was probably just passing through. The kind of man who can survive in the wasteland probably doesn't take to town life too well," said Sam, a fat friend of Bob's since childhood.

"I heard that he spent the night in Joe's barn with the horses," said Noel, a short man with dark hair.

"How are the eggs today?" asked Larry.

"They are really good but I wish they would serve a bigger portion," said Sam. "It is embarrassing to have to order two servings."

"There is nothing wrong with the amount of food, it is the size of the belly that is your problem," said Bob smiling.

"Yeah, well Bob, we can't all have the appetites of a little girl, can we?" retorted Sam.

"That stranger wasn't the only weird thing to happen last night," said Noel.

"What do you mean," asked Larry.

"John Clearwater came pounding on my door in the middle of the night. He was frightened like a child. I figure it was all the excitement of the stranger showing up and the talk afterwards in the bar that got his imagination going. I think he had the dream to scare the gods."

"What did he say?" asked Bob.

"It was hard to understand him at first. He was so out of his mind. He made me and my wife bar the door and he backed into a corner of my house like a crawdad. Well you know that Molly is good with people. She can be very comforting when she wants to. We made some tea and finally got old John calmed down. He never went to sleep though."

"What was his dream?" asked Larry.

"I guess the reason it took him so hard was it was one of those dreams that seem real, you know like you are awake. He had just lain down for the night and he was about to blow out the candle he keeps at his bedside when he heard a scratching at his window. He said that he thought it might be a mouse. He said that the noise didn't bother him he is used to life in Agea Hills used to the bugs and the mice and whatnot. But he sat up in bed and stared at the window to try and see the culprit when the noise stopped. Again he was about to blow out his last candle for the night when the scratching started up again but this time it was at his door. This unnerved him as a mouse wouldn't try the window first and then try to get in through the door. It was just a little scratching, hardly anything to notice at all but in the quiet of the night it sounded much louder than it probably was."

"What was it?" asked Bob interested.

"I bet it was a cat," said Sam. "Old lady Marlowe's cat is always on the prowl at night.

"He got up and went to his door but just as he was about to

37

open it the noise stopped. He waited a moment and then opened the door anyway. But as the light from his candle illuminated his front step there was nothing to see. He went back to bed and then he heard the scratching start up again but this time it came from directly under his bed."

"Holy cow! What did he do?" asked Bob.

"Ask him yourself," said Noel pointing to a disheveled man entering the inn.

"John," called Bob. "Come sit with us."

The man approached the table. He was jittery and obviously still a little shaken from the dream. He wore a large knife in his belt and he kept his hand on the hilt.

"Noel was just telling us about your dream but he didn't finish. What was under your bed?" asked Bob.

John took some coffee from Sally and took a moment to take a sip before responding. His eyes bulged wide and his hands shook so that the coffee dribbled onto the hungry wood of the table.

"I leapt off of my bed when I first heard the noise. It continued while I got my candle in hand. I stood there in my own house, a grown man, unnerved by what probably was the sound of a mole trying to dig through my floorboards trying to gather my courage and still my shaking hand. I had to use both hands on the candle as I was trembling so violently I feared the candle would be extinguished. And then I saw it."

"What," asked Sam quietly. Some of the other folks in the inn had quieted down to listen to John's story.

"I don't know what it was but it climbed right out of my bed," said John.

"You mean 'out from under your bed' don't you John," said Sam.

"No, I stared in horror as a little demon the size of a dog

38

clawed its way up through my bed. First I saw its hand rising out of the center of my mattress. I didn't know what it was, I didn't recognize it. Then I saw it for a clawed appendage and then another burst forth and then the snout ascended through the very spot I had laid moments before. I couldn't move, I couldn't scream, I was paralyzed, forced to watch this apparition rise from hell into my room. It was covered in black hair. Its snout was longer than a dog's and ended with large nostrils, which were snorting and testing the air. It leapt from the bed onto my chest knocking me to the floor. Its little human like hand grabbed at my candle. It seized the tallow and held it up to my face. This completely illuminated the things face and I stared into its little pink eyes. It looked at me for a moment and I could almost imagine it deciding that I wasn't worth the trouble. Then it dropped the candle onto my chest and bounded off of me. I heard it scratching at the floor. The candle had gone out and now I regained the use of my faculties and I ran out of there. I have never been so scared in my life."

"Wow, that is some nightmare," said Sam.

"This morning me and John went back to his place to have a look around. You know, check under the bed," said Noel smiling. "There was nothing there, there was no hole in the bed or the floorboards or anything. It was just a bad dream."

Larry looked over at Bob and the two shared a moment of understanding. The two wolfed down their breakfasts and left the inn to talk in private.

"I don't like the sound of this one bit," said Bob.

"You don't think it was one of Grento's Thumpers, do you?"

"I see the thought crossed your mind too," said Bob.

"It was just a dream, it is a coincidence," said Larry.

"We need to find Grento. He is the only one who knows about this stuff. If he is crazy or not, I want to talk to him," said Bob.

39

Larry and Bob searched all over town but there was no sign of the mysterious traveler. Finally as they had practically talked themselves calm and no longer thought they needed to find him. They found him. He was sitting on the town's famous 'sitting rock'.

"You were right, Bob, this is real comfortable," Grento said. "What are you guys up to? Aren't there any smelly cow butts to wash?"

"Very funny, we wanted to talk to you," said Bob.

"Be my guest," said Grento.

"Last night John Clearwater had a dream that a little demon creature clawed its way through his floorboards," said Bob.

Grento sat up and stared at the two with a stern face. "Did it look into his face?" asked Grento.

"Yes, it did, it held him down and then looked him over and then left," said Bob.

"And there was no trace of the way it got into the house, was there?" asked Grento.

"No, there wasn't. But like I said it was a dream," said Bob.

"That was a Thumper. It looked into his face to see his eyes. It was looking for you. There is no time left. Tonight there will be more of them. They come on like locusts. At first there are one or two then they are everywhere. You will be found in a matter of days unless we leave now."

"It was a dream," said Larry.

"Even John said it was a dream and he was there," added Bob.

"I hope you realize the truth before it is too late," said Grento lying back onto the rock.

Bob and Larry looked at each other and shrugged. They

headed back towards their houses. It had already been a long day and they still had work to do.

That night the brothers were awakened by the shouts of various people in their town. Candles lit up everywhere as Bob wiped the sleep out of his eyes and Larry pulled on his big cloak. A big fellow came running up to them. It was Sam.

"Noel saw one!" he said.

"What?" said Larry.

"He saw the same thing John saw. Only this one climbed out of his cupboard. It grabbed onto his head and pulled him into the shelving before letting him go and then it disappeared too."

"B, b, b, but this is im, im, impossible," stammered Larry.

"Molly's husband says he saw one too," said Sam. "It looks like whatever it is, it's real!"

Sam went on his way to go tell more people about the events and Larry and Bob walked as quickly as they could towards the barn where Grento slept.

Grento was up. All his gear was in his pack and he wore the heavy blue cloak that he had arrived in. "There is no time left for discussion. Go pack some supplies and I will meet you at your houses."

"B, b, b..." Larry started to say.

"Go!" shouted Grento.

Bob and Larry turned and went back to their houses. They had chills and began to pack stuff in Bob's house. They were utterly terrified and couldn't stand up to Grento's authority. So they did as they were told.

Larry felt numb and confused as he sorted through the trunk he kept at the foot of his bed. He never believed that there were really monsters living in the wasteland. He didn't think that there were people outside of Agea Hills. All the stories of travelers from other towns he thought were part of some folk heritage. Metaphors not reality. He could understand Grento, maybe, a lone traveler. That seemed at least possible but the idea of actual Thumpers, that was pure nonsense.

He didn't know what he was supposed to be packing so he grabbed his knife and looked over his warm clothes. His rugged boots were probably on the list so he put those on. He picked up his big pack, the one he used when he would camp out with Bob. It felt heavy and was still full of junk from his last campout. He turned it over to dump it out onto the floor. Out spilled another pair of boots and a Thumper.

The Thumper landed on its side and it took a moment of flailing legs and raking claws before it righted itself. Larry stared in shocked amazement at the beast. For a split second they both stared at each other through amber-frozen time and then it attacked.

Larry was forced backwards into the corner of his room. The Thumper came on incessantly, quickly, with purpose. It swiped Larry's legs out from under him and as Larry fell it sprang onto his chest. Larry felt the little hairy hands grab the sides of his head and then he was staring into the horrible pink eyes of the thing. It's eyes narrowed as it surveyed Larry, it looked from one of his eyes to the other and then back again. Its twisted mouth curled up at the edges in an evil grin and then it jumped backwards off of Larry and as it landed on the floor it disappeared into the wood.

Larry lay sprawled in the corner his breath coming in gasps like he had the wind knocked out of him and now it was trying to come back. Sweat poured down from his armpits and his hands were clenched in fists.

"H, h, h, help," he meekly said to the room though not loud enough for anyone to hear. "Help," he managed to get out, this time more forcefully. In a moment Bob and Grento were standing in his doorway surveying the mess in his room and found Larry in the corner.

"What is wrong?" asked Bob.

Grento and Bob offered their hands and helped Larry to his feet.

"Why aren't you packed yet?" asked Grento sternly.

"I s, s, s, saw one," said Larry.

"What?" asked Bob.

"Right here, it was in my bag," said Larry.

Bob looked over to Larry's bag on the floor. It was obviously empty.

"It was a Thumper," said Larry.

"Did it see you?" asked Grento obviously concerned.

"It stared right into my eyes and then it smiled," said Larry. "It disappeared right into the floor."

"There is no time," said Grento "The Thumpers will tell Tock where to find you. Finish packing."

As they fiddled with packing supplies a realization came to Larry. It spread across his face like a mudslide down a mountain.

"Grento," said Larry. Grento turned his attention from the window to the man.

"Where are we g, g, g, going?" the words caught in Larry's throat.

"Into the wasteland of course," came the reply.

"How can we do that?" asked Larry.

"I will guide us, do not worry. Now let us finish packing and we will go," said Grento.

They finished gathering their respective supplies and followed Grento to the edge of the town on the south side. They stood there for a moment realizing what they were doing. This moment, whether they were cognizant of it or not was the flesh of life, the symbolic event that makes cowards of most men. Anyone that steps into that unknown forest is affirming life. Most of humanity is content to read about guys like Bob and Larry.

Larry could barely see the edge of the forest in the dark. It was quiet and big. They waited a few moments for their eyes to adjust to the darkness and then, following Grento like a mother duck, the brothers left their home and entered the wasteland.

Chapter Three

Bob remembered his youthful excursion into the edge of the waste. Something watched him then. Something that he was sure was still waiting for him. Now he stared at the same beckoning darkness and he felt eight years old. Larry stood at his side and looked at him for reassurance. He smiled at his brother.

They snuck into the trees. The starlight from years past alone witnessed the brothers embark on a journey that had been started 1000 times before.

After about an hour of walking Grento stopped.

"We will sleep here until morning light," said Grento.

"What about Tock the snake? Or the things that live in the wasteland?" asked Bob.

"This is a safe spot. As for Tock, he is quite a ways behind us. He will have to scout the entire perimeter of your town to find where we entered the wasteland. Unless he gets lucky," said Grento.

"What do you mean, unless he gets lucky?" asked Larry.

"Well, when he gets to your town he will have to figure out where to find you. Then when he discovers that you are gone, he will have to methodically search the perimeter of your town for evidence of our passage into the wasteland."

"Oh," said Larry relieved.

"But Tock is very smart," continued Grento. "Since no one in your town ever goes into the wasteland he could be reasonably sure that the one pair of tracks that head into the wilderness are none other than our own. In which case he may be much closer than I am counting on. There is also the possibility that he climbed aboard a Gelk wagon and got a ride to near your town which would also increase the speed in which he will catch us."

"Well that is just great," said Larry obviously annoyed. "You seem rather unperturbed that Tock might bite us at any moment killing us in a horrible way."

"Well, Larry, we simply don't have any choice. We were dealt a certain hand of cards and now we are playing that hand as well as we can," answered Grento.

"A hand of cards?" said Larry.

"Plus," added Grento, "Tock is not after me."

Sleep didn't come easy for Bob and Larry. The stillness of the forest settled around them like a coffin. The ground was relatively soft and accommodating but not so when one is used to the particular lumps and indents of their own mattress. Sometimes one decision changes many little things in our lives.

Larry woke up slowly, sleep tugged at him with heavy hands. Grento sat, deep in meditation with his legs folded in front of him. His face was completely relaxed and his breathing was slow and rhythmic. Grento looked at one with the forest. Larry sat up and felt a sharp pain in his neck. The forest floor had given him a sore neck to remember it by. Larry stood up and walked over to Bob. Bob was sleeping soundly. Much to Larry's surprise Bob's head rested on a big fluffy pillow. Bob wore a smile of contentment equal to any dope junkie. Larry gave Bob's legs a little irritated kick. "Yoo hoo, sleeping beauty, time to wake up. There is a crazy poisonous snake after us. Sorry to disturb you, I will have the maid make up your room."

Bob woke up and rubbed his eyes. Grento too, had been roused from his thoughts and walked over to join the brothers. "How did you two sleep? Wonderful weather we had, don't get used to it."

Larry snatched the pillow from Bob's camp area and held it up like the head of some demon.

"And where did you get this?" Larry asked accusingly.

"I packed it from home of course," replied Bob.

Grento swiped the pillow out of Larry's hand and looked at it as if it were the very heart of his lifelong enemy. "What the hell do you mean? Packed it from home? This is not some summer walk to gather flowers. You are in the wasteland. There are two animals within earshot of us that could tear the flesh from your bones. You waste my time packing luxuries?" Grento's nostrils flared and spittle shot out from between his clenched teeth with his words. His anger held like a dog is held back by its sled. Larry didn't want to think what would happen if that tether ever broke.

"Gather your provisions, we must break camp. There is a long way to go today," said Grento.

Grento walked over to his cloak and busied himself amongst his belongings. Larry just shook his head at Bob. Bob didn't see what the big deal was. He picked up his pillow where Grento had dropped it and stuffed it into his pack. The group began walking in complete silence. The mood of the morning was one of irritation. The less said, the better.

"Hey Larry, how is your neck?" asked Bob.

"Why you son of a bitch! You know perfectly well..." said Larry.

"Enough!" shouted Grento.

The party got quiet once more but Bob had a sheepish smile on his face. Larry just shook his head.

The terrain was easy going. The trees grew spaced out and the ground was made even by years of pine needles quietly decomposing. No sounds harassed the travelers as they made their way through the morning. The air was crisp like dried leaves. Grento now had calmed down sufficiently and began to instruct them. "You must remember to keep your heads up when walking through the wasteland. You are so entranced with where you put your feet

47

you could walk right off of a cliff."

"Yes Grento," said Bob. "But since we have a deadly snake after us I want to be careful where I step."

"You don't have to worry about stepping on Tock. He's more likely to drop out of a tree onto your soft necks than risk getting stepped upon," said Grento. This instantly brought both Larry and Bob's heads and eyes up off of the ground and they looked into the trees.

"Oh would you both quit fooling around?" said Grento. "Tock is a ways behind us and he will not make as good of time as us. He cannot hunt you until the sun has sufficiently warmed his skin. Right now he is helplessly lethargic. Cold blood you see. But what lives in these woods can easily kill you so it's best to keep your head up so you can see what's coming but more importantly and I cannot stress this enough, so you don't get lost."

The brothers agreed to try and continued on with their heads up.

The morning turned into midday and Grento called for the party to stop for a quick lunch and rest. Everyone found a rock and sat down to their thoughts. Mostly the thoughts were of how their feet were tired and they were hungry.

Grento opened up his traveling cloak. Around his neck he wore a necklace of woven roots. He twisted it around until he found an end of the strange plant and broke off a couple of inches. Larry wandered over to him to inquire about the strange jewelry.

"It's Mako root," explained Grento. "It grows very quickly and is quite nutritious." He broke the piece of root in his hand in half and handed a half to Larry. Larry took the food and with Gren-to's encouragement put it in his mouth. It tasted like the inside of a leather shoe. "From the look on your face you are not pleased with the root," laughed Grento. "I know it's not what one would call a 'good tasting food' but it is food. You see the Mako root cannot live in the ground like other plants. It requires a near constant amount of moisture and certain minerals. The plant lives in a symbiotic relationship with a host animal. In this case, me. The reason it tastes so foul is because this plant drinks its life from my sweat."

Larry looked a little upset.

"If you don't eat that entire root you could grow your own Mako root necklace," said Grento. Larry walked over to Bob trying to keep from throwing up. Bob was fiddling with his pack.

"Bob, you are never going to believe what Grento eats," said Larry.

"What?" asked Bob.

"It's called a Mako root. He grows it around his neck on the inside of his tunic."

"No thank you," said Bob. "If you don't mind I will stick to my sweet cakes."

Just then Bob pulled a lovely little cake out of his pack. He wiped up the little bit of powdered sugar that dusted his hand and licked his fingers. Larry stared in disbelief. The bitter salty taste of the Mako root was still on his tongue. "Where did you get that?" asked Larry.

"I brought it from home of course," answered Bob matter of factly. "I swear, I don't know why you and Grento thought that it's only important to bring unpleasant things on a great adventure."

Larry quieted the desire in himself to yell at Bob instead he tried to share in the fortune.

"May I have some of your cake?" asked Larry.

"Sure," Bob handed Larry some cake.

Grento joined the brothers and shook his head in amazement at the site of the cake. Just then a high-pitched horrified scream filled the air. It sounded for about five seconds and then went quiet. Something had just died in a bad way. Bob looked at

Larry as if to say, "What the hell was that?" Grento looked serious but not overly concerned. "That was the sound of nature in the wasteland. Some animal stumbled upon another animal. That is all."

Larry and Bob's faces were wide eyed and puzzled. They looked as if they wanted to ask a thousand questions but were inclined to remain silent lest their voices attract something.

"That is the way of the world. Something gives up its life so that something else may live," said Grento. "We had better move out."

The brothers gathered their supplies quietly and quickly. They kept their eyes focused on the surroundings and scanned for signs of movement. The sun's light finally crested the hills and its warmth was pleasant. Grento set the pace in a southwestern direction.

The morning hike was without incident. They made good time while the effects of sleep were still in their bones. The brothers shuffled along behind Grento. After a couple of hours the trees gave way to a clearing. Grento surveyed the meadow for a few moments before changing direction to go around it. Bob and Larry followed him. As they made their way around the meadow, the trees became denser. Grento led them in serpentine patterns between the timbers. The little branches tore at them like cognizant hooks leaving little scrapes here and scratches there. Signs of passage. The trees got so dense that they had to search for ways through. At times they had to crawl on their hands and knees under twisted branches. Bob and Larry looked longingly at the wide-open space of the flowered meadow. Of course both were smart enough to intuit that Grento probably knew that there was a reason not to go through it. After a particularly difficult spot through the trees the party stopped. "We are through the worst of the trees now," Grento said. "Let's rest."

"Just out of curiosity," asked Larry. "What lives in the meadow?"

"I don't know," replied Grento.

"If you don't know why didn't we go straight across the field instead of wasting our energy to claw our way through these blasted trees?" asked Bob.

"Because, Bob, that's not the way. I can tell which way we can go and that meadow is not the way. I'm not sure of what specific danger that field holds but I am sure we don't want to know. Trust a Gelk on this one," said Grento.

"What about Tock?" asked Bob. "Do you think he is anywhere near us?"

"Oh, I hope I have not overly frightened you. Tock is probably quite far from us. For one thing, he is not a Gelk and does not know his way through the wasteland. He is quite dangerous enough himself to handle some of the dangers that lay in wait among the trees but he is no fool and he will proceed with caution. He will take his time, but he will never stop searching for you. Only by delivering his deadly bite can he be free. He is very intelligent but he has no idea where you are going or why."

"Then why was it so important for us to leave with you?" asked Larry.

"Because if you had stayed where he knew you to be he would have surely killed you," answered Grento matter of factly. "Tock will continue to search for you but how could he find you?"

"So what are we going to do? Are we to wander the wasteland forever with you?" asked Bob.

"I have been thinking about that. I think we should find out why Tock's master sent him after you."

"I have so many questions..." Larry was cut off by a look of warning from Grento. He followed Grento's eyes towards the clearing. At first he didn't see anything, then he caught some movement by the trees where they first encountered the meadow. An enormous animal, bigger than a cow, and like nothing he had ever seen before shook its thick head. Its fur was long and stringy. It smelled the air and started moving towards them.

51

"What is that?" said Bob.

"It looks like a huge hairy cow," said Larry.

"Look at its feet, those aren't hooves, they're claws!" said Bob.

"It is all the way on the other side of the clearing and I think that I can see its teeth. That can't be good," said Larry.

Grento noted its route as well. "We will have to kill it," Grento whispered.

"What?!" asked Larry perplexed at the notion. Bob started to tremble.

"That is a Dungeen. Do exactly what I say. The only chance we have is to attack it as a group from all sides. We will wait for it to get to us and then we will have it out with it."

"A, a, are you sure?" Larry stammered.

"No time for debate. Get behind that tree. Bob, you get by that tree. I will try to draw its attention," said Grento.

The Dungeen was getting closer. It appeared to be moving faster the closer it got. It smelled food and didn't want it to get away. Larry tried to ready himself. He could feel the adrenaline pumping through his veins and his heart thumped against his chest in a primordial war beat. Bob was completely immobilized. He was a cricket in front of a tarantula. He wasn't going to move and that was that.

The Dungeen was having problems getting through the thick vegetation. The sound of the trees breaking and cracking under its awesome weight reverberated through the forest. Grento had taken a position right where the beast would emerge through the trees, a large knife in his hand. For a moment it looked as if the density of the forest might stop the beast but it had smelled warm blood and was coming on in determined frenzy. The trees became too much for the creatures bulk and in a burst the beast turned and lumbered into the meadow to circumvent the forest. Larry's heart leaped up as he had been hoping that the beast would veer into the meadow and some unseen killer would take care of it for them. Nothing happened to the Dungeen however and Larry prepared to die in violent fashion. The creature charged through the meadow towards the party. The Dungeen was close enough to see clearly now. Its chin was wet with drool, which foamed with every breath. Its long stringy hair appeared to be alive.

It stopped just shy of where they waited and looked down and at itself. It shook its giant head and then it shook its entire frame like a dog does to dry off. As it shook, dirt flew off in all directions. But then the dirt appeared to be sucked back on. The creature shook again and more dirt was shaken off and again was sucked back on. It wasn't dirt; it was some sort of bugs. At first Larry thought that the creature maintained a symbiotic relationship with these black beetle things but the trepidation the creature exhibited laid this suspicion to rest. More black insects climbed the creature covering its legs and then its entire body. The Dungeen shook and shook but there were too many bugs. It tried to stumble to the forest but appeared to be held in place by the multitudes of insects. Its face was covered its eyes its mouth its nostrils all swarmed with these horrid little devils. Suddenly the Dungeen let out a horrible scream as if its tormentors had chewed through its thick hide and now were hurting it. The screaming and thrashing went on for twenty minutes until the Dungeen was dead, an unrecognizable lump under a swarming black hill of death.

The field of flowers must have been completely covered with the bugs all hidden by the grass and plants.

Larry and Bob came out of their respective fighting positions and stood with Grento watching the Dungeen's body being chewed apart by a million tiny teeth.

"I'm glad we didn't walk through that meadow," said Bob.

"Don't be dumb, Bob," said Larry.

"Well aren't you?" asked Bob.

"Of course I am but you don't have to point it out. Don't you think that is a little obvious? That we would be glad not to have been eaten by those things," said Larry.

"I realize that that was quite a traumatic experience for you guys so I am going to tolerate a little nervous banter but get it out of your system. There are things that are a lot worse than that Dungeen, things that hunt in the wasteland between the cells."

Larry and Bob turned their stunned expressions from Grento towards each other and then back to Grento. "What do you mean? You said you could lead us through, in between all the nastys that would eat us. You said this very clearly."

"I can lead you through and help to avoid the pitfalls but of course there are things that wander about. What did you think the wasteland creatures ate? I admit that a meadow of voracious carnivorous insects was a new one to me," said Grento.

"We had better get moving. The walking will calm your systems," said Grento. He turned and began walking. Bob and Larry followed him in disbelief. The trees were no longer so constricting and the walk was rather pleasant. Larry and Bob talked back and forth as they made their way. "Can you believe the size of that thing? It was huge," said Bob.

"Yeah, it was big alright," said Larry. "And mean looking," said Bob.

"Yeah, not too friendly," said Larry.

"Do you think it would have eaten us?" asked Bob.

"It sure looked like it wanted to," said Larry. "I wonder if there are any more of those wandering around these parts. I bet old Grento up there wouldn't tell us if there were."

"I would have clobbered that Dungeen real good if it had made it across the field," said Bob.

"Yeah, I bet it feels lucky that the knats of death chewed it up alive instead of it having to face your wrath," said Larry.

"I didn't see you..." Bob was cut off by Grento.

"Will you fools give it a rest? That Dungeen was hunting us by scent but it might as well have been simply following the pointless bickering," said Grento.

"Are there more of those beasts out there?" asked Larry.

"You bet," said Grento. "There are all sorts of things out here."

"That is, that is great," said Larry.

"Do you see that rock outcropping?" asked Grento pointing toward a rock outcropping.

"Yes," answered Bob and Larry.

"At the bottom of that rock formation is a small lake. If we hurry I think we can make it there to camp tonight," said Grento.

Chapter Four

The farm-boy stood on the shore, fishing. He waved a light reed fishing pole back and forth over his head. The little speckled trout in the stream went about their usual feeding. The boy must have been stealthy in his approach to the water; the fish had no idea that he was there. The carefully hand-tied fly drifted through the air and landed upstream with not the slightest of ripples in the water's surface. It looked more natural than many of the clumsy living mayflies and mosquitoes haphazardly zigzagging above the water.

The boy, an eleven year old, had forearms tan from numerous days spent fishing followed the drift of his fly with the attention of a eagle marking a fish in a lake. The trout were completely fooled and three of them raced to rise to the fly. The winner hit the artificial with a splash. The young angler raised his rod tip calmly. He showed such control for someone so young. The fish was soon on shore wriggling. The boy quickly dispatched the trout and added it to his wicker creel. Then he was false casting above his head to dry off the fly.

Tock watched from his perch on the hill above the child. The sun felt marvelous on his skin. He soaked it up like a capacitor. The boy fished with an easy intensity. The rod was an extension of his body the line was an extension of his will. The natural world hummed along in harmony and he blended in. He was doing what he was supposed to be doing. Here was the 'oneness' that philosophers barked about and monks tried so hard to cling to. Here in this farm boy.

Tock slid his coils over and around each other. Testing his temperature. His purple-black tongue bungeed out of his closed mouth tasting the air. There was time enough. This kid wasn't going to leave. It would be pleasant to watch him play for a little while. Tock admired his skill and his total participation in the event. There wasn't a single scattered thought in that kid's head. Just watch the fly and set the hook. Simple perfection. Tock wondered now if this young man's brother had also shared in this sort of gift. He would never know, maybe it was better not to think on it. He had killed him last night in his sleep. There was no reason to dramatize his act. He slid into the sleeping child's bed and watched him for a moment and then struck his fangs into its neck. A little mercy. The little guy probably didn't even wake up entirely before he was a little corpse.

And now here was the brother, gone fishing before the sunrise. He would never know that the little guy that followed him around wherever he went was as cold as a stone. Another little mercy.

Tock hated this form. His eye's barely functioned. He was forced to constantly adapt to this shape. It was not like the days before Bander had taken him prisoner. Then he walked as a man. He could read books, enjoy a pipe, and eat soup. Little things that made him happy. Bander stole all of that from him. Well not that he wouldn't have done the same thing to his mortal enemy but he had lost. And to the victor go the spoils. Well, in this case to the victor goes the loser forever.

In life, before Bander changed his existence, killed his body, trapped his soul, Tock was an assassin. He studied martial arts, weapons. It was ironic and painful to him now that he no longer had his body. The body that he spent a lifetime tuning. Each muscle had been trained to react in perfect coordination with the rest. He could make a sword come to life in his hands. How he missed the sword fights! That was the way men were made to do battle. Face to face and no question of the conclusion or how to choose a winner. To the death. Hacked apart by inanimate steel. The better man would win.

Now there was a job to do. Bander's magic left no choice. He could only fight it for moments at a time. But he didn't know if he was really fighting it or if the magic allowed this tiny leeway to allow for planning. There was just enough free will afforded him to keep him from running fangs first into each encounter. It allowed him to survey a situation and to plan. But the magic was always there like a hunger. He loathed this form, a serpent, the vilest creatures. When he was a man he killed animals indiscriminately. They were there for humans to eat. Hell, he killed humans; animals or beasts were nothing to him. And now he slithered on his belly as one of them. If he ever broke this spell or got the chance he would kill Bander for doing this to him. The thought of Bander making the run for the ultimate power drove him crazy. His mouth slightly opened involuntarily as the anger raged through him. His reptile eyes were perfect spokesmen for his mood. Intense killing rage. Tock slithered down the ledge towards the child. Maybe this was the last of the freaks. Maybe with this kill he would be able to return to his sleep.

The little fisherman bent down to the stream to unhook a medium sized silver trout. He carefully wet his hands before handling the delicate fish and then with the care of a surgeon he gently released the fish back into the sun-speckled waters. He felt the sting in his leg. The venom burned in his veins like acid. He fell face first into the water.

Tock recoiled. He watched the creek carry the boy away. Now let's see if the Thumpers come or if I am done. Tock thought. There was a scratching in the bushes. And a disgusting little troll of thing crawled tentatively towards the giant snake. Why can't I kill something significant? Tock thought while the nasty Thumper told him where to find the next on his seemingly never-ending list.

Chapter Five

Grento picked up the pace. Larry and Bob were not used to hiking but they kept up. The terrain became rockier. Every once in a while Grento would hesitate and then change directions. The party weaved its way toward the rock outcropping. Grento made it clear that he was not to be bothered with common banter while they hiked today. He needed to think. Larry kept catching himself staring at the ground as he walked. It was an old habit. He liked to look at the various rocks and plants he stepped over but he knew that he must stay alert to his surroundings.

The sun was settling down for the night when they made the rock formation. As Grento said, a quiet little lake stood at its foot. The three travel weary companions set their packs down and rested.

"What a day," said Bob.

"Really. That was enough walking to last the rest of my life," said Larry.

"Hey Larry," said Bob. "I wonder what everyone in Agea Hills would have thought of that Dungeen today. Or that field of, of whatever that was. Not a one of them would have made it through that experience like we did."

"No, I don't suppose they w,w, would have" agreed Larry. "Grento," Larry said. He still didn't feel completely comfortable talking to the Gelk. He was too much of a stranger and they depended upon him too much to not trust him. The combination made him uneasy. "Where are we going? How are we going to find out why Tock is after us?"

"Tock has no choice. We are going to find someone who can tell us why Tock's master wants you dead. We cannot go see him until we get some water from this lake. We will get the water in the morning," said Grento.

Everyone settled in as the sun went down. After a long day of walking even the uneven ground felt good to lie upon. The steeper the walk, the better any bed feels. The camp was pleasant. They stored their gear between the rock, which jutted up out of the ground like a bone through the skin, and the lake. The smallest of breezes rippled the water of the lake just enough to create the shimmer of moonlight on each tiny wave. The silence of the woods settled like a blanket. The nice weather and quiet surroundings were balm on the brother's spirits. Here they were; away from familiar things with unknown things ahead of them and they casually joked back and forth.

"So Grento, where are we going tomorrow? Perhaps we can do battle with more hideous beasts?" asked Bob.

"The things that you will see tomorrow will make you long for the things that you saw today my fine comedian," replied Grento.

Bob swallowed hard.

"Wh...where, where are we g..going?" asked Larry.

"To solve the mystery of Tock. Why would someone want you dead or any of the other folks? We will travel to a series of small caves on the sandy dunes. Hopefully we can solve the riddle of the dunes and we will be able to talk to the thing that lives in the caves. It will know where we can look for our answer," said Grento.

"How will it know?" asked Bob.

"It is ancient and knows more about the world than all others," said Grento.

"Are you sure it will help us?" asked Bob.

"It will if we bring it some water from this lake," said Grento.

"What is special about this particular lake?" asked Bob.

"This is the only water for miles. There is no rain between here and the dunes and even beyond that," said Grento.

"What? No rain, but that's impossible. There are trees and grass."

"This lake supplies all the water for the regions immediately around it. It is fed by an underground spring. The fiend that lives in the lake controls the rain. By preventing the skies from raining in this valley he forces the animals to attempt to drink from the lake. And then he eats them."

"Are you kidding me?" asked Larry. "You expect us to ferry water from one monster to another in the hopes of finding out why another monster is chasing us?"

"Sounds like a full day doesn't it?" chortled Grento. Grento turned onto his side succumbing to his weariness. "Get some sleep."

Larry and Bob lay there in the darkness and went over their options. They could leave. Grento didn't act like they were forced to stay with him. As a matter of fact he made it seem like he was doing them a favor. Some favor. Of course, as they followed their thinking through the twists and turns of what would occur if they left, they realized that the first thing they probably would have done would have been to stock up on some water out of the lake which apparently holds some lurking terror. Grento would have woken to a fresh day only to discover that they had both walked down to the water where they had been promptly eaten.

So they knew that they would be better off with Grento than without. Their minds were carnivals of whirling thought as they drifted into sleep.

The morning broke gently as it does in the wild. It snuck up on the travelers like a tide. Grento still lay in his cloak enjoying the stretches and slumbers of a Sunday. Larry and Bob followed suit, as they weren't sticklers for getting an early start on visiting monsters. The sun rose into the morning sky and finally Grento got up. He looked to the sun and then to the rock and then to the lake and said, "You guys should start getting up. It's almost time now."

Bob and Larry, grateful for the extended sleep time, got up without complaint. "It's almost time for what?" asked Bob.

"To get the water," replied Grento.

"Yeah, I was meaning to ask you about that. How do we get the water if there is something in the lake that waits for people to go get the water?" asked Larry.

"As usual, Larry, that is a very good question but I can assure you that, in this case, you do not have to fear for I know the secret of the lake. We will have no problems getting our water," said Grento.

Bob looked at Larry and rolled his eyes. He was obviously a little apprehensive. Grento saw this and simply said, "You men get your stuff together and I will handle getting the water."

Larry looked at Bob and then shrugged his shoulders as if to say I will take that deal any day. Grento tightened his cloak around his frame and grabbed all the available water casks they had brought along for the trip.

"Oh no!" Grento's words sounded like the bell of doom. "Bob, Larry, quiet, and don't move!"

Larry and Bob turned to see Grento with water casks in hand staring at the edge of the lake. They stood perfectly still per the Gelk's warning. For a moment you could almost hear the brother's brains racing for information. The morning's sounds continued. Nothing exceptional. Moths and other small insects danced near the water's surface. Larry caught sight of something moving. It was hard to see clearly at this distance. Whatever it was it was about the size of a large pig and covered in tan fur with big white spots. It scurried on four short legs and its large butt waddled back and forth. It wasn't close enough to get them but after what Larry had seen so far in the waste he would trust Grento's judgment on this one.

Bob's eyes had ferreted out the object of interest as well. He stood still but the coffee mug he held was getting heavy in the position he had frozen in. If he could just shift his fingers a little then he could hold it comfortably for a long time. Grento's beard and cloak billowed in a sudden breeze. He did not move. Bob decided to bear the uncomfortable position a little longer.

The animal seemed not to have noticed them. It waddled around smelling the ground.

An impossibly bright flash filled the morning accompanied by a simultaneous crack of thunder. The sound was so startling and powerful that none of the three men could keep from flinching. But each went still again. The animal lay dead, struck by a bolt of lightning.

Bob couldn't believe it. Surely this was a coincidence. He looked up at the sky, searching for the guilty cloud. And he found it. A dark gray island in the sky. A silent stalker. All around it the sky birthed brethren thunderclouds. It looked like a churning pot of water about to boil, with each new cloud a bubble rising to the surface to escape. The breeze turned into a wind and within minutes the sky was completely dark. Huge droplets of rain splattered into the dry ground around the men's boots. They left little dirty mud circles marking where they hit. Then as if the water had finally reached the boiling point. The clouds let loose. Gigantic sheets of rain lashed the men and their campsite. The whole lake was a boil with rain splats. They got completely soaked and the wind chilled their skin and hair. Still Grento didn't move so neither did the brothers. Turrets of rainwater formed gullies and poured into the lake. Bob watched his pillow as the water dragged it down the slope and into the rising waters of the lake.

A storm like this never hit Agea Hills. Larry shivered in his drenched cloak. The water had run down his legs and into the opening of his boots soaking his feet in a disgusting clammy way.

He wanted to go home.

Then the storm slowed and stopped completely. There were still the dripping of water off of rocks and plants but the deluge was over.

"You can move now," said Grento.

Larry and Bob came back to life. Their water soaked clothes clung to them like remoras.

"Where did that storm come from?" asked Larry

"I've never seen anything like it," added Bob taking off his cloak to wring it out and hang it over a tree.

"That was the thing in the lake," said Grento.

"What, the storm?" asked Larry.

"Of course. Look at the carcass of that animal," said Grento gathering his water logged pack. The men looked over to the muddy bank. The dead animal was gone.

"Where is it?" asked Larry.

"It's in the lake," said Grento. "The rainwater washed it in."

Bob noticed the wet rivets, tiny tributaries that looked like arteries leading back into the now still waters of the lake. "Did the thing make it rain?" asked Bob.

"Yes," said Grento. "That is how it feeds. It controls the weather, the lightning, the rain, everything around here ends up getting washed into the lake."

"Well for crying in the night!" said Larry exasperated. "How are we going to get the water now? Maybe there is enough water in puddles and dripping off of the leaves. We won't even have to mess with the lake."

"No, that is too much of a hassle. I can get the water. You guys dry out the gear and I'll handle this one. You can get the next one," said Grento smirking.

"Very funny!" said Larry.

"Grento," said Bob. "I don't want to impose but I did loose a rather valuable item. If the opportunity presents itself, do you think you could perhaps retrieve it for me?"

"What are you," started Grento.

"He is talking about his precious pillow," interrupted Larry.

Grento raised an eyebrow at Bob. With the containers in hand, he turned and walked down to the edge of the lake.

Larry and Bob stopped their busy work and turned to watch the old Gelk. As he got near the water's edge, they half expected something to lunge out of the depths and drag him below the gentle waves. But nothing happened. Grento bent down and slowly, deliberately filled the containers. When he finished he calmly walked back to their campsite. The entire episode was as gentle and without incident as cotton falling off of a tree. Which didn't explain why Grento was sweating.

"Wow, that was easy," said Bob.

"Yeah, after yesterday I fully expected today to be fraught with demons as well," added Larry.

"Do not be fooled," Grento whispered until he gained control of his voice. "I was risking my life gathering that water. Even though I know the secret of the lake it isn't any easier to walk into the mouth of the beast."

"What is the secret? You know, in case we are ever back here and need some water," asked Bob.

"It's simple. See how as the sun rises, the rock we slept beside casts a shadow on part of the lake? In order to avoid the monster's attention you must stay entirely within that shadow. If I approached from any other spot, casting my shadow on the lake, I would have been... well you don't even want to know what lives in the depths. That is often true in life: don't cast your shadow on the depths. Now, let us get on our way. I will need both of your help to solve the riddle of the dunes." Grento led the way out of camp.

Chapter Six

The assassin watched the hooded figure stride boldly through the woods. From his perch on the hill he could observe without fear of being seen. He crouched in the shadow of a indent in the rock. He steadied himself with one hand on the hard stone. He felt his heart beating firmly underneath the camouflaged cloak he wore. Concentrating on his breathing, he calmed his amplified nerves. Years of cutthroat employment had taught him to be conscience of all the details when on an assignment. The sun was behind him; the wind in his face masked his scent from his prey. This would be his greatest accomplishment. Not since his first kill had he felt the trepidation that accompanied him now. This one was tough. But this one would be worth it. The noble faction that employed him offered more gold for this than he had made in his lifetime.

He watched his victim with eyes that searched for weakness. There was no weakness. The man walked unconcerned, focused on his destination. Yet a palpable revulsion emanated from the dark figure. This man was dangerous, a killer. He would strike hard and fast. He would use the environment to his advantage. His weapon was invincible when used correctly. He slid his gloved hand into the pocket of his cloak and pulled out the bag of Stonethorn. The weight of the small weapons felt alive. Each little seed weighed as much as a coin and each was covered in stony spikes. The poison that waited inside the seeds would explode out of the thorns on contact. Each Stonethorn tree produced only one seed per year but nature had insured that that would be enough. Whatever animal stepped on a Stonethorn seed fell dead on the spot and nourished a new sapling. He spent painstaking hours gathering the seeds for weeks. Now he would throw his handful into the face of the figure below. Death would be instant with no chance for a counter attack. It was not as romantic as his youthful days of knives and swords but he was older and much wiser now. The Stonethorns had kept oil in his lamps for many years.

Last moon the nobles approached him. He made himself easy to find. He had no need to hide his profession or his where-abouts. His crimes left no witnesses and no direct link to him. But rumors surrounded him and most people afforded him a wide path. The men that slipped him the note in the tavern were more secretive than most. He had to dance to their rhythm for days before he sat in the dark of the room at the inn to hear the deal.

He was to kill the one man who everyone feared. The one that no one dared to confront. They were dripping with sweat as they forced themselves to lay out the plan. As if even talking about the proposed deed would alert the Lord Bander.

He didn't blame the nobles. His own heart jumped momentarily when they named their target. It took him time to embrace the idea. Why not kill Bander? He was a man, although he was painted as an immortal by the stories told to children on dark nights. He had killed and conquered; of that there was no doubt, but he always hid behind his soldiers. The stories of his youth and his rise to power were too fantastic to be credible. If they were to be believed than Bander was hundreds of years old. He would also be the greatest sorcerer the world had ever known. He would also be more evil than was possible for a human. He would have to be some sort of monster. The nobles offered no altruistic reason for ridding the realm of its ruler. They were being forced to live substandard lives by their standards. Bander stood in the way of a new era of prosperity. He was an old general of a war since forgotten. The new blood was hot.

The assassin was to rendezvous with the men back at the storeroom at the inn three days from now. To prove the deed was done he was to bring them the necklace with the severed lizard head on it. He would have to act now. He had tracked Bander for three days on this mysterious journey. It would take him three days to return. Maybe less, as he felt that the lure of the gold would pull him quickly home. Still, it unnerved him that Bander walked through the wasteland as if he owned it. No one should walk with that kind of confidence through the wasteland. Unless he were a fool. Or perhaps desperate. Where are you going? He wondered to himself while he watched Bander's unswerving walk.

Bander felt weary. His joints creaked with each step. This body was all but too old to be useful anymore. He wouldn't need it much longer he told himself. He was so close. He'd known the location of the key for more than 65 years but until now he wasn't ready. It was safe and waiting as it had waited for each great man before him. The histories of the key were well documented in the library of the Keep. Only a man willing to pay with his own flesh could retrieve it from the nest and such men were rare indeed. What a brilliant first trap to stepping into the circle. To step into the circle you needed the key. To get the key you must pay the price and, once paid, would a man be strong enough to face what waited inside the circle? First blood drawn by the ancient architects. They were beating you before you even could open the circle. Bander thought about the rulers that had come before him through the distant ages. The men that had taken their chance at the circle and now guarded the treasure they had hoped to secure. Brave, strong men but each lacking something. Something the circles creators had planned for. Bander knew he would succeed. He was almost to the nest. Just one small thing to take care of first.

The assassin saw the figure stop. What was he doing? The assassin followed Bander's gaze to a square stone structure. Smaller than a building the structure looked like a mausoleum. A eternal house for the dead. Dead, brown dried vines covered the quiet tomb. Who could be buried there? thought the assassin. Perhaps a noble family from ages past. Was this Bander's destination? Three days walk to visit a dead relative? Maybe Bander was more human than he thought. Carrying around grief for the departed. Bander stood staring at the mausoleum but not approaching it. What was he waiting for? This must be what he came here for. Well opportunity was presenting itself and it seemed fitting that Bander would die here with his loved ones. The assassin dumped a handful of Stonethorns into his gloved hand carefully. The weight of the death contained in each thorn was exhilarating like the cutting power contained in the weight of a sword. He could probably hit him from here. But it would be a long throw. That would be foolish. Jump down and throw them in his face.

"I will need to concentrate on my task," said Bander to the woods.

The assassin's breath caught in is throat.

"So I suppose I shall deal with you first," Bander continued.

The assassin listened.

Bander turned and raised his black gloved hand and gestured for the assassin to approach.

The assassin felt terror. How did he know I was there? He stood his ground. Should he attack now, should he run? He was confused for a moment and just stood there.

Bander's voice changed to a hiss, "Approach!"

The assassin felt cold terror slide into his body at the sound of that voice. That was the voice of the dead. His mind was shutting down. All the options that he had a few seconds ago were gone. He stared wide eyed in panic as he began to walk trembling, knees barely holding him up towards Lord Bander.

"You thought to kill me?" Bander hissed at him. "You? You thought I didn't know you followed?" Bander's voice was getting louder as anger crept into his tone.

The assassin walked within three feet of Bander.

"Stand still!" Bander hissed through clenching teeth.

The assassin obeyed. His body so completely afraid that Bander's commands were the only orders registering in the man's brain. The assassin looked into the face of Bander. Bander's eyes were angry and his face was contorted into a moving snarl that swept over his face like the oceans surface. Bander's eyes moved to the Stonethorns in the assassin's hand.

"And this is how you would do it?" his voice rose still louder.

"You would strike down Lord Bander with a seed? You not only tried to murder me you tried to humiliate my death."

The assassin was so close. If he could gather his wits he would be able to throw a whole handful of Stonethorns into Bander's face. He couldn't move. Some instinct more powerful than his will had kicked in and he was petrified. A quivering mass of life.

"You do not deserve my attentions," Bander's face was more evil than human, hate was oozing out of his skin and glowing off of his face.

Behind Bander the assassin saw something move. A tiny flicker of hope came to him. There was movement to the left. Bander paid no attention to whatever was approaching. The movement materialized into a creature covered in black fur. It was so furry that its features were hard to distinguish. It looked bigger than a dog. Its eyes were black and he could barely make them out accept for a gleam of light when it reflected the light. Then there was another one. It came running through the woods and stood next to its kin. They stood behind Bander waiting — watching — about 20 feet away. Another appeared and then more then the woods filled with the things. They formed a circle around the two men. The assassin saw one of them open his fur covered mouth. The mouth was much larger than he would have thought and full of teeth. The whiteness was striking compared to the black obscurity of the animal itself. It was stretching its jaws then it closed its mouth and the teeth were hidden once again.

"You deserve nothing. You should die in your sleep while dreaming of sleeping!" Bander's voice was loud now his words filling up the surrounding woods. " This would be a good spot for a grove of Stonethorn trees so I give you your grand undeserved death!" Bander turned and walked towards the surrounding beasts. The things jumped into each other and tripped to get away. Bander paid them no attention and walked towards the mausoleum.

The assassin watch the circle of things shrink around him. They were keeping their distance while they sized him up. There must have been fifty of them. The assassin found that now, out of Bander's immediate presence he could move, though he trembled. Several of the creatures darted in from behind him to swat at him with their paws before jumping back to a safer distance. The assassin shifted the thorns in is glove. He threw a thorn at the nearest one and it fell dead. He turned and threw at another and again found his mark. Again and again he killed them, their furry bodies littering the forest floor. There were too many. He fought and fought; they lunged at him and he would turn them to fertilizer. One clipped the back of his ankle and knocked him down. There was a surge and the things ripped him apart.

Chapter Seven

The hiking was gentle for the first two hours and then the ground became sandy and they needed to rest often. Larry was flabbergasted with the immensity of the world. They were within two days hike from his town and he had already seen new forests, fields, and now the sand. His brother Bob seemed to have taken to this change better than he had. He watched his brother plod along kicking up tiny sand storms as he walked. To Larry, each step felt like the world was clinging to his foot.

"How far is it to the dunes?" asked Bob.

"It's not far now, probably another hour. We must begin to figure out what we are going to do once we get there," said Grento.

"I thought that if we gave the water from the lake to this person they would give us an idea as to what is going on?" said Larry.

"True," said Grento. "However just as the lake kept a secret so does this 'person' as you put it."

"I don't like the way you say 'person,'" said Larry.

"Let me first tell you the riddle of the dunes as I remember it:

Where nothing that enters exits again,

everyone sucks in the sand,

silence alone allows you to win,

never to regain the land.

"I have puzzled over it many times but I have never come to a definitive conclusion of what it means. You see we seek a 'person' that lives in a cave in one of the sand dunes we are nearing. I don't know which cave this 'person' is in. Well, that isn't entirely true, the 'person' resides in each of the caves we will see."

"What do you mean?" asked Larry slowly with a look of concern creeping across his face like a spider.

"This 'person' is in fact a horrible, gigantic, old-as-the-ages, villainous thing plucked as if from the depths of Hell. It lives in a sand dune. At the bottom of the dune, there are a series of caves, one on each side. They all look the same. Inside each cave is an arm of the creature."

"Whoa, hold on, just how big is this thing?" asked Bob.

"It fills the dune," said Grento. "It lies waiting for someone to wander in looking for shelter from the nightly sand storms. Once a traveler is inside the cave, the thing lunges out and grabs the help-less man. That tunnel then collapses and the victim is eaten. I saw it happen from a distance. It was eerie, a shifting of sand and the tunnel entrance disappeared along with the explorer."

"Well that sounds just lovely," said Bob. "Why did I even think that it might be different? I guess I got spoiled by how un-eventful the gathering of the water was. Oh yeah, how are we sup-posed to give this thing the water if it will drop a tunnel of sand on our heads?"

"Because, Bob," said Grento raising an eyebrow. "One of the tunnels does not contain an arm of the beast but the fiend's head."

"Oh, well there you go," said Larry pleasantly. "You see Bob, we will just walk into that cave. I am feeling better all ready."

"You would be wise not to joke about this Larry. I need your help to figure out which cave has the head in it. You see the creature cannot collapse the tunnel above it's own head, it would suffocate. If we can get into that cave we can bargain with the water."

"Why do you think that the thing will want the water?" asked Larry.

"Like all creatures, this one has a weakness. The thing that lives in the lake doesn't let it rain, so there is little water in this area. Because of the dune-creature's immense size it cannot stand the heat of the sun. It would quickly lose what little water it stores in its system if tried to move across the dunes. It only uncovers itself at night and that is only to reconstruct its caves, its "traps." I think it might go to the lake and fight the thing that lives in there if it weren't so afraid of getting caught out of the sand when the sun comes up. It cannot hurt us if we choose the right cave and it will be grateful for the water. Why wouldn't it help us?"

"Well, Grento, that certainly sounds like a well thought through plan," said Larry sincerely. "I want no part of it. I don't believe I can convey strongly enough how little I want to do with that plan. I wish you and Bob all the luck in the world. Have fun."

"Yeah, I think I'm going to have to vote with Larry on this one Grento," said Bob. "You see, I'm not even that good at 'find the pea' a little game we play at the bar where you have to figure out which cup the pea is under. I don't think I would be much good at find the nefarious-creature's-head. Sorry."

"Enough! You have no choice. You will die if you leave me. If we don't figure out how to deal with Tock he will find and kill you. There is no escaping him." Grento felt frustrated at their farm-boy way of dealing with problems. "Life doesn't always grow slowly like a crop," he thought to himself.

Grento started walking again. "Now try to figure out how we can tell which cave conceals the head," he said as he walked.

Larry looked at Bob. Bob looked at Larry. Their decision was made as Grento kept walking and they had to follow or risk losing him.

As they walked their imaginations soared with visions of what a thing that lived under a mountain of sand would look like. Eventually they began to try to reason out the riddle of the dunes.

"How many tunnels are there?" asked Larry.

"Four or five Larry, I think, I didn't circle the dune to find out," said Grento.

"And they all look the same?" asked Bob.

"As far as I could tell they looked the same. Maybe there was some subtle difference that I missed," said Grento.

"Could we send Bob just a little ways into the tunnels and then see which one tried to grab him?"

"Very funny, you would have a better chance of getting me to swim across that lake we just left," said Bob.

"No variations in the caves appearances?" asked Larry.

"Not that I could tell, but when we get there I will need you and Bob to look them over. Perhaps, from your unique perspectives, you will notice something that I didn't," said Grento.

As noon approached, the party tired from carrying the water bags, which had grown hot from the sun. They decided to rest and take their lunch. Although the terrain was still a mixture of sand with scattered scrub brush, it was starting to feel like a desert. The ground was hot. They had to sit on their bags to be comfortable. On the horizon they could see the outline of the dunes. They loomed innocently like a possible future not an inevitable destiny.

A small lizard darted between shrubs. Every once in a while the wind gusted but it was no longer the refreshing breeze, it was now hot like the gust of heat from opening an oven. They ate some of the provisions that Bob had taken the time to pack and imagined what it would be like to confront the thing inside the dune.

"Maybe since the creature wants to protect its head it would have made the cave it's in smaller or higher on the dune to discourage chance animals wandering in," Larry thought out loud.

"I'm afraid that all the caves are the same," said Grento.

"Is there any difference to the slope of the caves, I mean do some point more up than others?"

"No, the caves are perfectly uniform. At least the entrances are. One would have to go exploring to see how they meander once inside," said Grento.

"No thanks," said Bob.

"That lizard gives me an idea: could we send some sort of animal into each of the caves to see which ones collapse? I mean how would the monster know what we were up to?" asked Larry.

"I thought of that," said Grento. "But where would we find the animals? The creature builds the cave to draw animals to it. Living things of any size are rare in this desert. This journey would have been nearly impossible had we brought four or five large animals with us. I don't think that small creatures like the lizard we saw could trigger the monster's attention."

"Maybe we could throw rocks into the caves to test them," said Bob.

"That doesn't work. I heard from a friend of mine." They looked at him with renewed interest. "A Gelk," Grento added. "He said that the caves have curves inside them, apparently one must walk in past a certain point before the creature drops the roof on you. I get the feeling that the monster can tell the difference between rocks and live food. It's probably the way a spider can tell the difference between the wind on its web and a fly."

"You sure paint a vivid picture," said Larry

"We are the flies? Is that the picture he's painting?" exclaimed Bob.

"Bob, we are going to solve this problem. Remember that if we pick the right cave we will be safe. The monster cannot collapse the sand on its own head. It would die of suffocation. Remember also that even though it could completely uncover itself if it wanted, the sun would bake it. So it will be trapped in its hole with us. We will have the advantage," said Grento.

Larry looked concerned. "Ah Grento, what is to stop the creature from uncovering itself once the sun has gone down tonight?"

"Yes Larry, that is good reasoning," said Grento.

"What's going on?" asked Bob.

"Oh, Bob, Larry here just realized that the creature will uncover itself at night. Just to be clear, it hunts on top of the dunes at night. If we do not get the information we seek and get off of the sand by night the beast will eat us."

"Oh, well of course," said Bob. "I figured it couldn't be as easy as all of this. Just find the cave and get the info. I'm surprised you told us before dusk. It would have made more of an impact, as far as stories go, if we would have had to make a nice run for it."

"Maybe we should talk while we walk. I don't want to cut this any closer than it has to be," said Larry.

"Fine," said Grento getting to his feet.

The party started walking towards the beautiful dunes in the distance.

"There must be a way to tell which cave it is," said Bob, "it can't be this hard."

"We know that the thing doesn't like the sun so maybe we can figure it out from that," said Larry.

"Yeah," said Grento, "I tried that angle in my own reasoning but since the caves meander light cannot get in from any cave."

"Could we try collapsing some of the caves to see if the monster would give itself away somehow?" asked Bob.

"The caves are big. I don't know that you could collapse them if you tried plus you would probably have to climb all over the dune to try and that does not appeal to me," said Grento.

The breeze was hot and the sand clung to their feet like weights. It kept them moving at a good clip though, as hot sand will do.

"Why does this thing know what we need to know?" asked Larry.

"Well Larry, I am not sure that it does. But this creature is old. According to history, this thing was not always confined to the dunes and it hunted wherever it wanted. You can imagine a thing of this size running rampant. Whole villages could be destroyed at a time. It also has the ability to speak and there are even books that were supposedly dictated by the creature. It's a thing of the past that is wise to the patterns of the future. It will know if there is something about your eyes that demands your death," said Grento.

Early afternoon was upon them and so was the dune. Although each brother had an image of the dune in his respective imagination during their walk, it was bigger than both images put together. Larry scanned the horizon to try and get an idea of how far they would have to travel to get off of the sand. He had the feeling that they were painting themselves into a corner. But he trusted Grento's judgment. Well, he sort of trusted Grento's judgment; it was more a trust of necessity. Grento seemed as lost on this new problem as they were.

"Grento what was the riddle of the dunes again?" asked Larry.

"It was:

Where nothing that enters exits again,
Everyone sucks in the sand,
Silence alone allows you to win,
Never to regain the land,"

said Grento.

"Is that supposed to tell us which cave to pick?" asked Larry flabbergasted.

"I'm not sure anymore. It's called the riddle of the dunes with the implication that it will allow you to determine the right cave. It seems to me that it merely warns travelers to stay away from the dune."

"Well let's see..." Larry furrowed his brow and began to think.

The party continued to approach the dune until they were no more than a hundred feet from the entrance to one of the caves. It was a maw. It lay there quietly beckoning to them. There was an almost palpable draw towards its throat. Perhaps years of evolution left an instinctual yearning for the cave's protection. Or perhaps the romanticism of hidden treasures and curiosities pulled at the subconscious mind. And true, they walked over a desert with the gaping hole serving as a fixed star. They walked directly to it. The creature's gimmick would fit in any carnival.

Bob seemed fascinated by the tunnels structure.

"Man, this creature is good. What keeps the sand from collapsing in upon itself? And it's such a good circle. Water couldn't have worn a better tunnel through rock. I'm going to hike around the dune and look at the other tunnels. Maybe there is some physical difference that I can spot," said Bob.

"That is a good idea," said Grento. "We'll wait right here."

"Bob has a good eye for construction. If there's something to notice about the structure he will see it," said Larry.

"I hope so," said Grento.

Larry watched Bob walk away around the perimeter of the dune. He then turned his attention back to the cave. The sun baked the land and the shade called to him. He was glad to have Grento's company yet again. He knew that on his own he would never have thought not to go into the cave.

Bob felt confident that he could find some difference in the other caves. No matter how clever this monster was, he figured that it had to think like a practical handyman. Just as he had planned how to fix the leak on his roof, he felt sure that the monster had its own idiosyncrasies about its own house.

The sun beat on Bob's shoulders and face but he felt it less now that he had a project to work on. Something about solving a problem was so fun to him; he disregarded nature's unpleasantness. It didn't take him long to find the next cave. It came into sight just as the last cave disappeared behind the bulk of the dune.

His first impression was positive. The cave felt quite a bit different from the last one. It was roughly the same size. It had the same general look as the last one. Of course, the terrain leading to the cave was slightly different. The wind swept the sand into unique patterns. Bob relaxed a moment and allowed the problem to present itself to him. He allowed his handyman muse to survey the scene. All of the things critical to the cave as a dwelling seemed the same as the last; there was no difference in the slope of the entrance, no size difference, no elevation from the desert floor. Then Bob's muse spoke to him and he turned around. Perhaps the difference is in the view from the cave he thought to himself. From this vantage point he scanned the sand to the horizon where he could make out the silhouette of hills. There was nothing special right off but maybe compared to the view from all of the other tunnels he could put this puzzle together. Not wanting to get too wrapped up in a single cave he moved on around the dune.

The next cave appeared again as soon as the former slipped out of sight. He estimated that he was about half way around the dune. It appeared that the Gelk was right about there being four or five caves total. That was something anyway; at least they weren't dealing with bigger numbers. It wouldn't be any fun to have the percentages working against them too. Of course, two caves was one too many for him.

This one seemed just like the other two. It looked like a good place to get out of the sun. Bob wondered if he could sneak just inside to where the shade started without the thing collapsing on him. Maybe the creature would treat the trespass with a sort of professional courtesy. He chuckled to himself at his indulgent thoughts and turned to survey the view from this cave. More sand and hills stretched away. The distant trees looked slightly taller but it was hard to tell.

He turned his attention back to the hole in the side of the dune. The simplicity of the cave made clues elusive. The tunnel entered the sand in a straight line like the other caves. It got dark past the first forty feet. Bob's schedule forced him to move on to the next cave. Perhaps the repetition of seeing one after another would jar something loose in his brain.

The next cave looked just like the last one. Almost perfectly like the last one. This one offered a different view. The sand didn't extend as far and the terrain appeared covered with large boulders. It looked bizarre compared to the smooth rolling quality of the waves of sand. Bob didn't see how this was relevant but it was, at least, a difference.

He took some time to look over the entrance but found no abnormality. He needed to get to the last cave and then back to his companions. Perhaps they were making out better than him. Bob walked to the point where this last cave disappeared from sight and then sure enough, within a few steps, the next cave appeared. The sweat poured down his temples and the sand stuck to his feet and calves. As he approached the cave he found Larry and Grento seated against a small hill of sand near the mouth of the cave.

"Hello," said Bob. "Well I appear to have come full circle. That didn't take as long as I thought it might have."

"So, what of the other caves? Are there differences?" asked Grento.

"Not that I could tell. They all look like this baby here," answered Bob pointing to the cave. "I noticed the even spacing."

"What do you mean?" asked Grento.

"Well, every cave is spaced so that you can never see two caves at the same time. Every time one cave just went out of view, the next appeared."

"Interesting," agreed Grento. "I imagine that's so that any man or animal or whatever walking in the desert can spot at least one cave."

"It made me think," continued Bob. "Maybe there is something special about the view from the caves."

"Hmm, I hadn't considered that," said Grento.

"The next cave has a view of some hills on the horizon, you know, where the sand recedes. And the cave after that shares a similar view, but the last cave, the view changed dramatically. The sand doesn't extend as far and the terrain changes to a field of boulders," said Bob.

"Oh yes, I know where you are talking about," said Grento.

"So what conclusions have you drawn from this?" asked Larry confused.

"Well Larry, nothing really, I was hoping you guys had thought of something."

"You walked all the way around and you hoped that we had thought of something?" said Larry.

"Did you?" asked Bob.

"Nope," answered Larry.

The three sat there in the hot sand for a minute in silence. There didn't seem to be anything to say. The problem was patient; it wasn't going anywhere. They each thought about it some more taking turns to glance at the cave looking for something they missed.

"What are we going to do?" asked Larry.

"We are running out of time, by my calculations we would need to enter the cave right about now to have time to make our way back across the sand before nightfall," said Grento. "We definitely don't want to be out here come nightfall."

"Maybe we should go? We can get away from the sand and we can talk our way through this at camp," said Bob.

"Finally a decision," said Larry obviously a little frustrated from the heat and futility of the days hike.

"There is nothing else we can do. Let's go," added Grento.

The party gathered up their packs and the increasingly heavy water bags and began their walk back. The leather on the water bags collected heat while they sat and were now painful to touch. Larry shifted his bag between his hands.

"Bob," asked Larry suddenly. "How many tunnels did you say that there were total?"

"There were four caves. One on each side of the dune," said Bob.

Larry thought for a moment, looked like he was going to say something, and then started to think again.

Grento noticed the two stopped and said, "Come on you two, we need to keep up a good pace to get off of the sand in time."

"Grento," said Larry. "I know which cave we must choose!"

Bob and Grento stared at Larry with astonishment. "Are you sure?" asked Grento.

"Yes, I think so," said Larry.

"Then let us make for the cave, we still have time to get this done," said Grento.

The men turned and headed back toward the dune. Larry took the lead.

"How do you know which one it is?" asked Bob.

"Yes, I'm rather curious myself," added Grento.

"I simply thought about that riddle Grento. It had a sort of singsong phrasing to it. I pictured it in my head, written out like a poem. Each line seems negative except for the line, 'Silence alone allows you to win'. At first obviously one would read that as a clue about how to enter a cave. Even if it seems like common sense to keep quiet. But that isn't what we were trying to figure out. We wanted to know which cave to enter. So it couldn't have been that the words were meant literally, the clue must be hidden within the words. When Bob said that there are only 4 tunnels it made sense. There were four stanzas to the riddle one for each tunnel. A tunnel for each direction on a compass. The frame of reference was what I needed. In the riddle, each line began with the first letter of one of the compass points. Since only one of the lines was positive, that must be the answer. South, we must enter the south cave.

Where nothing that enters, exits again,
Everyone sucks in the sand,
Silence alone allows you to win,
Never to regain the land."

"That makes sense," said Grento. "Wow, I never would have thought of that but now it seems so obvious."

"What if it's just a coincidence?" asked Bob.

"What if the monster usually makes seven caves or five and he simply felt lazy last night? We could have caught him on a bad day. Couldn't it be a coincidence that the riddle's lines start with the letters W, E, S and N? Are we going to risk it?" asked Bob.

The dune now loomed before them once more. They stood at the entrance to the south cave. It looked nice and quiet, ominous.

"Let's get this done. We haven't much time," said Grento.

"Should we all go in?" asked Bob.

The other two stared at him as if to plead for him not to cast any doubt on their already fragile confidence.

"We need your share of the water. Two cannot carry all of the water and I have a feeling we will need all of it to bargain with," said Grento.

Bob understood his functionality. The job required three sets of hands. He started forward. Side by side the tiny party entered the cave. Larry felt a chill shoot through his body as he stepped into the shade of the cave. It felt like being swallowed. The suns heat no longer beat upon the tops of their heads. The sand under foot changed to pleasantly cool. Sand really holds the cool. It felt like a heavy cool.

Once inside the cave they paused to gather themselves. They had no idea how far they needed to walk. Reflected light guided their first tentative steps but up ahead they could see the complete darkness lurking.

Grento produced a small candle from his cloak and lit it. The tiny flame cast a huge amount of light in the dark of the cave. Slowly so as not to disturb the candle they walked into the depths.

Larry and Bob let Grento walk a few steps in front of them. He had the candle, so of course they shouldn't block its light. Although the few paces were practically insignificant, that small distance created an imagined buffer zone against whatever nightmare lay ahead.

Bob refrained from touching the sand-walls. They looked sturdy but he wasn't sure.

Larry was sure something was going to jump out at them. He had a vision of trap-door spiders that build tiny caves and then lunge out at unsuspecting prey. Man, he wished he hadn't thought of that.

Grento didn't like this cave either. He held his little candle gently although he also carried a water skin in that hand. He was getting tired and they had walked far enough that he began to feel confined by the mountain. They were way in there, underneath tons of sand. He had expected to find the monster by now. The cool air of the cave made their sweat-soaked clothes feel cold and clammy, very unpleasant.

The tunnel curved towards the right and they followed. The candlelight cast upon a fork in the tunnel. The party stopped, completely dumbfounded. For a moment they all just stood there looking at the two possible routes they could choose from.

Larry felt cheated. He had figured out the riddle, he should win. There shouldn't be another life or death choice.

"Well now what?" asked Bob.

"Larry, any ideas?" asked Grento.

"I say we take this water back..." said Larry.

"Water?" the sound came whooshing through the caves knocking sand from the ceiling and walls. Whatever made the noise was huge.

The party froze where they were. The candle in Grento's hand trembled. Larry managed to move his eyes to look at Bob. Bob looked back and widened his eyes as if to say "what now? Did you hear that? I don't know." Larry's eyes answered back, "You got me."

"We have water," Grento whispered.

"Ahhhhhhhhhhhhhhhh, bring it to meeeeeeeeeeeeeeee," the voice said. They couldn't tell from which cave the noise emanated.

"We wish to talk to you," said Grento. "We will give you the water in exchange for truthful advice."

"Yesssssssss," the voice intoned. The voice sounded like it had an accent but it didn't. It was overemphasizing its enunciation as if it was concentrating on making the sounds precisely. Perhaps the creature did not talk often enough to have a casual speaking voice.

"I will tell you. Bring the water to me."

"Which cave are we to take? The one on my left or on my right?" asked Grento.

"It is right," said the voice.

Now the group needed to decide quickly whether to trust the creature or not. Grento looked at Larry as if he might know what to do having solved the first riddle. Larry didn't know. Suddenly Bob said, "We will leave the water here. After we have seen the monster and gotten the information we need we will fetch the water to the monster."

"Ah, I didn't realize you had a business man in your midst," the voice said. "You may come to me down the left tunnel."

Now they were confused. Apparently the creature had lied originally.

Bob said, "You two go down the left tunnel, he can't be far. Once you see him call to me. If he is trying to lead us astray I will dump the water into the thirsty sand."

Grento and Larry took their water skins and laid them on the sand next to Bob. They entered the cave on the left guided by the candle.

Bob stood, watching the light from the candle fade into the tunnel. The darkness swept over him like the bugs that ate the creature in the field. His ears strained. Without the candle's light Bob found himself very alone. He felt as if he were teetering on a high wire. Any movement would send him into danger. Boy, would it suck to have to try and get out of the cave without light. What if the creature called their bluff? Was he prepared to dump the water and flail for the exit? Damn straight he would, he thought to himself.

"That is far enough," hissed the voice.

"Augghhh!" Larry and Grento screamed.

"Are you guys all right? What is going on?" shouted Bob.

"Wwwwwe, we're alright," Larry said. "Just startled."

"Get the water," said the voice.

Bob could hear Grento stammer, "Yes, ok, let's go get the water Larry."

Bob saw the candlelight as the two men emerged from the pitch.

"Are you guys all right?" asked Bob.

Larry just shook his head quickly back and forth. Grento looked at him and then said, "It's okay, let's do what we came to do."

Grento and Larry bent down and picked up their water skins.

"Remember that we're short of time. We must find out what we can and get out of here. If we dawdle, the monster will have the water and us when the sun goes down," whispered Grento.

They quietly walked back towards the thing with Bob following. And then the thing's head appeared.

"Augggh!" Bob shrieked.

"Augggh!" Larry and Grento shrieked in reflex to Bob's scream. They stopped so that the edge of the candlelight just barely illuminated the thing's head.

It was horrible. Its skin was practically transparent. They could see the blood pumping through its giant veins, purple. The veins looked like ropes. Bits of sand clung to it. The cave had ended and here, at its end, was the start of something vile. The creature's head filled the entire cave. Wrinkled skin hung down from its neck. There were smooth patches on the sides of its neck and head where the sand had worn the skin. It looked like something from the bottom of the ocean. It had huge spiky teeth two feet long; sand clung to them where saliva had dripped down them one time. Its eyes shone like pools of evil. They were the only things in the room that reflected the candlelight with a shine. The blood pumping under the thing's skin kept a regular, intense beat. To Larry it looked like the kind of thing that appears rooted to the ground only to be surprised when it lunges at you with lightning fast speed.

Sand slid off of it as it furrowed its brow and winced its eyes to get a good look at them. One of its pointed ears was cut halfway off, an old injury. A jagged scar ran from its forehead all the way to its cheek right through the spot where the eye was. Evidently the eye had escaped permanent damage. Larry wondered what could possibly have done such big damage to such a big thing. Whatever it was he didn't want to run into one of those.

"Give me the water," it said with lips that moved against each other like sand paper.

"We will be glad to give you the water. We would like some information from you first however," said Grento.

"Of course," said the creature.

Grento began to quickly tell of how the brother's discolored eyes had made them candidates for assassination.

"And you, of course, are a Gelk," said the thing with confidence.

Grento affirmed his ancestry.

"What town are the brothers from?" asked the beast.

"We haven't much time," said Bob.

Grento quickly saw through the creature's plan to drag out the talk to sunset. It still had visions of getting the water and eating them.

"Creature," began Grento. "We must have our answers quickly, we can still dump this water and get away from you."

"Don't threaten me you pathetic child. I didn't expect your water and I can survive without it. Can you survive without your information?" said the creature.

"Yeah, b, b, but aren't you thirsty?" asked Larry coyly.

"My thirst is endless my hunger never fulfilled, but my knowledge is great. You have no idea what thirst is. I could flay the skin off of your body and as you screamed and begged for death, that yearning wouldn't approach my chasm, my void. How can an ant imagine the depth of feeling of a complex being? There is no point, I can anguish in my knowledge when you are gone and I have the water." It paused.

"Very well," said the creature and it moved its head towards them. The tiny fraction of forward movement surprised everyone and drew startled gasps from the men. The creature liked to mess with people and obviously wasn't intimidated in the least.

"What you seek lives in the Swarm Caves."

Larry and Bob (and Grento for that matter) didn't like the sound of that one bit. Caves of any kind were to be avoided. That much had been burned into their subconscious minds. They already would look forward to many nightmares. That is, if they could make it out of this particular one.

The face contorted itself and then it blew a gust of air at them causing the candle to go out. Complete darkness enfolded them. Trapped with the thing.

Grento worked quickly to relight the candle though his hands trembled in the dark. Bob and Larry remained still, not wanting to loose their perspective of where they stood in relation to the creature. Their thoughts focused on detecting any sensation, breath, sound, and touch.

Grento lit the candle.

"I have never heard of the Swarm Caves," said Grento cautiously.

"Gelks all think they know the world. But you don't. You surely call them something else now, or perhaps a fire burned them. It has been so long since I hunted outside the sand.

"How could caves burn?" asked Bob.

"They aren't really caves," the creature answered. "Swarm Caves names the twisted thicket of the Tanglewood forest.

Grento nodded. "I understand what you mean. Why should we go there?"

"Because, Gelk, inside the Swarm Caves lives a group of creatures that will know the answer to your riddle. Would you like me to go into the details of their existence? I will happily discuss whatever you want. I don't have visitors often."

"Grento, the time," said Bob.

"Could you specifically answer our question?" said Grento.

"I have already succinctly answered your question. Do you have another? You will find your answer from the witches that live in the Swarm Caves, now give me the water."

Grento looked at Larry and Larry looked at Bob. "Let's go," said Grento.

He started to back away from the head.

"You must pour the water into my mouth!" said the creature.

"That was not the deal," said Grento. "We said we would trade you the water for the information. Well we are leaving you the water."

Grento and the guys began to walk as quickly as they could without causing the candle to go out. "Come back to me!" shouted the creature with murderous tone.

The group made excellent time during this escape. At one point the cave shook a little as the creature shifted trying to prevent their escape without collapsing its air tunnel. The cave started to brighten well before the entrance to their sensitive eyes. When they came within sight of the opening they had to shield their eyes.

The three of them burst from the mouth of the cave like bats. The sun hovered about two fingers above the horizon. There was still time but not much. The guys could have won a smiling contest as they slid down the face of the dune. Grento set the path and the party headed for the safety of the hills.

They walked quickly. The adrenaline in their blood kept them going. It desert held a lingering heat with the sun low on the horizon.

"I can't believe how you talked to the thing back there," Larry said to Bob.

"I'm surprised myself," admitted Bob.

"You were both great," said Grento grinning.

"Do you think that the creature will try to come after us once the sun goes down?" asked Larry.

"Or maybe it will spend its time trying to open those water skins."

"I bet it will come after us first," said Grento. "That's what I would do if I were in its place, it can always work on the water skins during the day."

"How far to those hills? They seem close but they've looked that way for a while," said Larry.

"If we keep up this pace I think that we will make it. But who knows how fast that thing can move on top of the sand. I sure don't want to find out."

"Even once we get off the sand I don't think that we will be safe from it," said Bob.

"What?" said Larry exasperated?

"Well, Larry, why would it stop? If we're still within its reach it will chase us."

Larry didn't like the sound of this at all. For some reason he had been comfortably entertaining the idea that the hills, like in a childhood game, were base. That they could stand a few feet from the sand and taunt the infuriated creature, "Can't get us, we are on base, ha, ha, ha." Of course, as Bob pointed out, this was delusional. A new urgency gripped Larry. "Well, what, what are we going to do?"

"Larry," said Grento. "We are making good time plus maybe the creature wont be able to track us."

Larry and Bob turned around to look at the three nice and neat sets of footprints they had left in the sand. Grento turned and admitted "Well sure, if he looks at those..."

The party increased its pace. Without the water it was much easier to move quickly. Plus the thought of that demon catching them in the twilight spurred them on.

They made the edge of the hills right as the sun began to set. They could still see, which was nice since Grento made them abruptly change directions as he sensed another creature's trap. They decided to try and circle the ring of danger thus putting some dangerous thing in between themselves and the sand monster. Maybe the two things would fight each other and they could find safety.

They heard a low grumbling, or perhaps they only felt it. Grento looked back over the horizon of the sand and, in the twilight, saw a cloud of dust rising. The dune had collapsed. The monster was free.

They moved through the grass that covered this terrain as quickly as they could. Grento led the way. His cloak flapped against his legs as he hurried along. They crested a hill. Bob looked back and saw something that resembled a giant spider on the sand. It was too far away to get more than a sense of what it looked like. A sense of it was more than enough for Bob. The group hurried down the hill. The sun's light was now a faint memory in an old man's mind. They would have to find a spot to rest for the night that would provide some shelter and hopefully disguise their whereabouts. They climbed another hill, this one bigger than the last. Small bushes grew scattered around. They were surprised to see the light from a small campfire close ahead. They stopped and conferred.

"Who would camp out here?" asked Larry.

"It must be another Gelk," said Grento.

"What if it's a trap? Perhaps it's another beast that lures travelers to its light," said Bob.

"No, there's nothing waiting here. I would sense it," said Grento.

"Maybe we can hike just past the light. Then we can make a cold camp. If the monster tracks us all the way here, it will think we are at the fire and will attack whoever is down there," said Bob.

"I would hate to be responsible for whoever is in that camp. It must be a Gelk. We could use his help if the creature does attack," said Grento.

Bob could sense the prairie world coming to life around him. All the nocturnal creepies were stretching their legs or wings or whatever and getting ready to hunt. He looked up at the faint glow of the sky and caught glimpses of the choppy flight of bats, each of them swooping into various bugs and ripping them out of flight. An aerial battle that took place each night. The absence of the sun's rays felt like putting on a cold shirt. Something about the campfire unnerved Bob. He didn't think that they should intrude on anyone. The wasteland was such a secluded place. Whatever happened out here would most likely never be heard of. Bob didn't want to disappear. He wanted to tell his friends about his adventures. He wanted to fix his roof.

"Ok, there are three of us," said Larry.

"Maybe we could just get a closer look?" said Bob.

"Okay," said Grento. "Are you ready?"

Bob nodded in agreement. Slowly, quietly the group descended, like moths to a flame.

Chapter Eight

Quid fiddled with his collar. The damn laundress had starched it and it itched. He was on important business, business from Bander. He had little time for such annoyances. Here in the field, he was in charge. He held all of Bander's power without the burden of being the ruler. He wielded the knife and, at the end of the day, could set the knife down. He liked his position.

He stood at the rear of a group of twenty men, including five prisoners. The countryside was hushed and ominous as the group looked into a narrow gulch. The slave's agitation was palpable and their eyes darted back and forth from the gulch to each other in silent communal terror.

"Gelk!" snapped Quid to no one in particular. "Where is that damned Gelk?"

A man whose body was covered in bruises and broken skin marked by dried blood stepped over to Quid. "I'm here, sir," he said softly, careful not to make eye contact.

"Oh, good," said Quid still scratching at his collar. "Are you sure this is a cell? Remember that lying does you no good and it doesn't help the slaves. We will simply beat you again and then you will tell us again and we will keep doing this. I know that your breed is supposed to be stubborn but have some sense. You have no choice, so why make it difficult on yourself?"

"The feeling is very strong here, sir, more than usual. Please can you not take my word for it this time? There is no need for suffering. I assure you that some foul thing lives in this gulch."

"Good. I am glad that you found a way to absolve yourself of some of the guilt you are about to feel by imploring to my pity. You may use that tactic every time in the future as long as it is not too winded. Did anyone bring any food? I swear that between the itching and my stomach I can hardly do my duty."

A soldier brought Quid some bread. The big man dwarfed Quid's little, anemic, wormlike body. Quid took the bread and began gnawing on it while continuing to give orders.

"Send in one slave," he said in between bites. The soldiers untied a prisoner. His body seemed to beg them not to do this. He looked like the wax run down the sides of a candle. He wanted to drop to the ground but kept his feet.

"Slave," said Quid. "Cross through that gulch. No one will follow. You'll be free. Maybe the Gelk has lied to us again. It wouldn't be the first time and he has cost us a couple of slaves. But to tell you the truth, I think that he was punished sufficiently to dissuade any further nobility. We don't know what we are going to find here so it is with keen interest that I will monitor your progress. Use whatever guiles you posses to make it across. If you are fleet of foot, then run. If you are quiet, then sneak. As for the rest of you slaves, I would suggest that you watch your comrade's progress and think on what method you will employ to make it across. You will all get a turn, no exceptions."

Every eye was intent on the trembling little slave as he took the first few steps towards the gulch. He moved cautiously. He turned back to look at his captors and his friends in the slave line. Fifteen big soldiers stood blocking his return path. His choice was certain death from the hands of the soldiers, or probable death from whatever lived in the gulch. Freedom beckoned him. He turned back to the terrain in front of him and began to walk.

The soldiers and slaves watched the lone figure. The slaves knees trembled as they watched their friend and wondered which of them the soldiers would pick for next. Only the Gelk averted his eyes.

The slave stopped. He looked around. For several minutes he stood completely still.

"What the hell is he doing?" Quid asked nobody in particular. "We don't have time for this!" Quid stooped to the ground and picked up a rock. He threw it at the petrified slave and although it missed, it had the desired effect. The slave turned at the sound and then almost too fast to see there was movement from behind some rocks. Something like a singular black leech flew through the air. It whipped at the slave and struck him across the throat. This thirty-foot long tendril sounded and looked like a whip snapping. The slave fell to the ground without a single struggling movement. The thing struck him in a flash and then was hidden completely behind the rocks.

Shock at the severity of the weapon resonated with these fighting men. The rest of the slaves were hysterical, each of them dripping urine.

"Whoa, what the hell was that? He didn't have a chance. I think that the odds on the slaves just went down," said Quid. "Soldier, is there anymore of that bread?" The soldier handed him another biscuit. "Tell me when you are ready to send in another slave," Quid was loosing his collar and his attentions were there.

"Hey slaves," he called loudly while eating, "If I was you I might try running across the cell. Slow and steady doesn't seem to be working."

Chapter Nine

They got within about forty yards of the fire. They could see a man sitting hunched over, perhaps cooking something. Grento didn't like this situation. He'd encountered lots of things in the wasteland but a solitary figure had no place here. As he figured it there were only three possibilities, the man was a gelk, this was a mirage, this was a trap. He felt bolder than he perhaps should have. The darkness concealed their approach. This allowed a leisurely appraisal of the situation. Still something told him this was trouble. His Gelk-sense remained silent, like the imprint of a long-dead wife on her side of the bed. It should be there but it wasn't.

He felt responsible for these two men. He still owed for his gift and, like all those who came before him, he would make good on his bargain. He would take these men to where their paths directed.

The man went about his business, calmly staring into the flames. Occasionally he would poke at the fire with a stick. He seemed right at home. He didn't look dangerous.

In order not to spook him, Grento spoke quietly. "Hello, may we share your fire?"

The man calmly answered, "Of course, the nights can be cold."

The stranger did not get up as Bob, Larry, and Grento entered the light of the fire. He was an average sized man with long black hair that reached his shoulders. It was messy and wind combed. His eyebrows were high arched and distinctive. He was wrapped in a burgundy hunter's cloak.

"Please, share the fire. Although I enjoy the solitude of the wild, it's nice to have company occasionally," said the stranger.

"Thank you," said Bob.

"Thank you," said Larry.

"Thank you," said Grento.

Grento made the introductions, "This is Bob and Larry Masefield from Agea Hills; I am Grento."

"It's a pleasure to make your acquaintances. I am Sargasso." And then he smiled. It was the biggest smile any of them had ever seen. The edges of his mouth curled in little wrinkles that made the smile more spectacular.

"Have you been traveling long?" asked Sargasso. As he spoke his eyes flashed open wider on the accent in each word. This coupled with the huge smile made for a unique face.

"We've been out for several nights," said Grento. "We're being chased by a giant creature that lives in the sand dunes."

"Yeah," said Bob, "Huge and nasty."

"Oh, not to worry, my lads, that thing won't venture off of the sand at night no matter how mad it is at you," said Sargasso.

"How can you be sure? Have you seen the creature?" asked Grento.

"I've done more than that. I've had conversations with him," said Sargasso.

"So you figured out the riddle of the dunes as well? Marvelous. How long did it take you?" asked Grento.

"The riddle of the dunes? I don't know what you mean. I just walked up to him one night and talked to him."

"On the sand?" asked Larry with some amount of confusion in his voice.

"Yes, on the sand," said Sargasso.

"Why didn't he eat you?" asked Larry nervously.

"Because my lads, I'm poisonous," said Sargasso.

The way he talked was almost hypnotic. He had the most animated face Larry had ever seen. It was a strange quality. Larry couldn't pinpoint the reason but he decided that he would never introduce a girl he liked to this man. It was the aura of confidence of an animal that is completely unaware of itself.

"I'm sorry," said Grento. "I assumed because you were traveling the wasteland by yourself that you were a Gelk."

"I can see how you could make that assumption; no harm done. Would you gentlemen care to share in my bounty?" He pointed at what appeared to be a rabbit lying in the fire-pit's edge.

"Thank you," said Bob who produced a loaf of bread from his pack. He handed Sargasso the bread.

"If you're not a Gelk," said Grento, "then how do you survive in the waste? And what do you mean that you're poisonous?"

"It's simple," said Sargasso with a smile and a flash of the eyes. "If some stupid thing eats me, it will die. I'm poisonous. The thing that hunts on the dunes is old enough to remember my people, he knows he will find no water in me."

"Interesting," said Grento.

"And as for getting around in the waste ..." continued Sargasso, "I take my time, keep my eyes open, and face whatever challenges slink my way."

"Unbelievable. I have heard of men who walk the waste moving from fight to fight but I thought those were nothing more than the romantic dreams of poets and drunks," said Grento.

"There's nothing romantic about me," said Sargasso. "But I do enjoy feeling life's lighting coursing through me. I imagine that you men have felt it many times in the past few days."

"Oh, we, we've, felt it," stammered Larry.

"Is that the feeling where you want to throw up and hide but you can't because some horrible beast out of the devil's imagination will eat you if you do?" asked Bob.

"I think that's it," said Larry.

"Then oh yeah, I've felt it," said Bob.

"Ha!" Sargasso's eyes opened even wider and he laughed heartily and unabashed. "I think I like you men already."

Larry hadn't decided if that was a good thing but he smiled anyway.

The firelight danced the tango with Sargasso's face. His wide-eyed expressions and his easy smile/snarl were deepened by the ambiance.

"It's amazing to watch the sand creature cover itself," said Sargasso. "Too bad the moon isn't full or you could watch it tonight. He looks like something Satan coughed up. I think it's for the best that he's under the sand by day. Now, tell me of your travels. Where are you going? Believe me, I am more surprised to see you out in the waste than you are to see me."

Larry and Bob began to tell Sargasso their story, each one interrupting the other at the good parts. Grento listened uncomfortably as he wasn't sure how much of the story should be told. He didn't have any reason to be suspicious of Sargasso but it was in his nature to be cautious.

Larry and Bob on the other hand were as genuine as a baby's smile. For all the years living good lives in Agea Hills, the past two days spilled out of the Masefield Brothers like champagne over the edge of a glass. They teased each other about their bravado in the face of danger. Sargasso drank in the story with satisfaction.

Cool gusts of wind attacked the men briefly and then the warmth of the campfire fought it back. They each sat on various rocks and they had to adjust often to keep from getting too stiff and once their fronts got hot, their backs were cold, so they would have to shift positions.

The winds howled through the night but the guys managed to sleep soundly. Larry felt rested when he got up. All the hiking over the sand had tired him out. He looked over at his brother who was still sleeping. Bob's head was gently cradled in the folds of his travel bag. From the smile on his face Larry could tell that he was dreaming. Larry was going to nudge him but then decided to let him sleep. Larry turned to the fire where Sargasso was already cooking something that smelled like wood smoke and bacon. The scent reminded him of the fall festival in Agea Hills. There was a cooking contest each year and Sam usually won. His stew had a smell just like this one. No one could ferret out his secret ingredient. Larry smiled out loud at the thought of secretive Sam protecting his special recipe. He hoped that Sam was all right and that the Thumpers hadn't bothered anyone in the town since they left. Sargasso looked over at him and tilted his head to the side indicating for Larry to join him at the fire. Larry stood up and felt his joints creak 'top of the morning' to him.

"Morning, Larry. How's it going?" said Sargasso.

"C, c, can't complain," said Larry. The conversation died away. Larry sat on his haunches staring at the fire. In most of his life he was surrounded by people that he was familiar with. Folks that knew him and his brother. Friends that had known his parents. In the past couple of days he was adjusting to dealing with complete strangers. He wished Sargasso would ask him a question or something to break the awkwardness.

"That s, s, smells g, great," said Larry.

"It should be done soon," said Sargasso.

"What is it?" asked Larry. "You see it smells just like stew my friend makes at home."

"It's just a common Fuzztail," said Sargasso.

"No way," said Larry. "You mean one of those little skunk things?"

"Yeah, they might smell bad when they are frightened but if you skin them and cook them over a fire they taste like sunshine," said Sargasso stirring his pot.

Larry looked over at Grento and his brother still sleeping. He saw his brother's eye open for a moment and then snap closed again as he tried to squeeze the last drops of slumber from the morning.

"Sargasso," began Larry.

"Yes," said Sargasso.

"Are there really lots of towns? I mean besides Agea Hills," asked Larry.

"Hasn't Grento told you all about the world? You would think a Gelk would know more than just about anybody," said Sargasso.

"Yeah, he told us about some of it," said Larry.

"Oh, I see... you are not sure how much faith to put into your new friend. You're looking for a second opinion. Is that it?"

"Naw, I'm just wondering."

"Well, I don't know what to tell you exactly. There are many towns; there are even some cities. I have never been to Agea Hills but if it is within a couple of days of here I imagine I will get around to it someday. I don't care for towns though. Too confining. I like the wasteland. It's more honest."

"How far is the nearest town?" asked Larry.

"Well, let's see. I guess if you were to walk in that direction," he said pointing straight in front of him. "You would get to a little hamlet called Yorg's Walk. And that way," he said pointing behind Larry, "leads to the Sister Cities. They are much larger than Agea

Hills. They have markets and unions and soldiers. You won't catch my shadow in those places, too many man-made rules. I like the rules that apply to everything equally. Tooth and fang, hunger and thirst. There are towns all over. I imagine you could walk for your entire life and never see them all. Of course walking around in the wasteland isn't a good idea for townsfolk like you and your brother. It is best to keep to your cell. Leave the wondering to the Gelks."

"Do you have a family?" asked Larry.

"No," said Sargasso curtly.

The beam of sunlight that had found its way to shine on Bob's closed eyes had finally driven him from his slumber and he joined them at the campfire.

"Bob, doesn't this smell remind you of something?" asked Larry excited to share his discovery.

Bob was not quite awake yet and stood there rubbing his eyes.

"No, not really," he said in a disinterested, sleepy kind of way.

"It's Sam's stew, from the cook off."

"Oh, yeah, I guess maybe," Bob said not interested.

Larry let the matter drop. It was no fun to share exciting news with a grumpy baby.

Grento joined them. Sargasso offered him some of the fuzzytail hash. Grento took some eagerly.

"I thought you only ate Mako root," said Bob.

"No, I eat Mako root for lack of anything better. This is a rare treat. I don't have the patience to catch a fuzzytail. The Mako root appreciates it too, I'm sure. The more varied my diet the more nutrients I provide to the root."

"It looks like you are about fifty years old, judging from your Mako," said Sargasso.

"It's a little fresh in the morning to be talking about age isn't it?" said Grento.

"Sorry," said Sargasso.

"How can you tell how old Grento is by the root?" asked Bob.

"When Gelk's come of age, I think it's about fifteen?" said Sargasso.

"Yes," replied Grento. "Fifteen."

"When they reach fifteen their fathers break off a bit of their own Mako root and give it to the sons. The kids then nurture the root. It grows very slowly with a new host. It can take years for it to fully accept the boy as its new symbiotic partner. Once the root has grown around their neck in three loops the boy is a man and leaves the village to wander the wasteland."

"So how can you tell how old he is?" asked Bob.

"Oh yeah, by the thickness of the root," said Sargasso.

"But if you got it from your dad, wouldn't it be as thick as the root on his neck which would be very old?" said Bob.

"No," said Grento. "Once the root has grown around your neck three times, you make a slit in it and feed the end into itself. See." Grento showed him on he root he wore around his neck were it grew back into itself. "The Mako then sends out shoots that I eat. But the main stalk gradually gets thicker over time. My dad gave me a shoot off of his. It's a easy way to tell how old a Gelk is."

"Cool," said Bob.

Sargasso had never heard of the Tanglewoods or the Swarm Caves. Since Grento knew where to find them, Sargasso decided to accompany the group. He made quick decisions. The hike would take nearly two weeks.

But since the weather was fine and they had so much to learn from each other the time passed quickly. Bob and Larry got on Grento's nerves as they constantly teased each other and acted like children. Sargasso seemed to enjoy their company but at night he took to sleeping a ways off from the group. He was wild and needed his space. Everyone accepted this about him. Grento led them in a serpentine path that wound around unseen dangers. A couple of times the rest of the group had to talk Sargasso out of marching into a danger area. He wanted some action and was quickly growing restless. He wouldn't have to wait long as they soon reached the edge of the Swarm Caves.

Chapter Ten

Bander stroked the stone face of the tomb. The sounds of the assassin being eaten — a growl over a choice bite, a bone snapping between firm jaws — faded from Bander's awareness as he focused on the task ahead. The sepulcher was home to the remains of the holy woman of a king long dead. He probably consulted with her on spiritual matters. She offered redemption for the sins of governing. Everyone looks for relief from who they are, Bander thought.

The mausoleum had once been painted and probably was a beautiful monument to a beloved woman whose children had shed their tears here on these stones. Now Bander clawed at and removed the misshapen lichen-covered rocks stacked in front of the entrance to the abandoned tomb. The commotion would surely wake the thing that lived inside the tomb but that was inevitable.

Bander had spent much of his life preparing for what must be done. These same stones had been removed many times. Every man that grabbed the key yet failed to reach the magic was trapped forever to stand guard against the next challenger. The thing would retrieve the key and return to this nest replacing the stones waiting for the next challenger.

There was a noise inside the tomb. Bander stood still, listening. The hairs on the back of his neck stood up. It sounded like a soft laugh, like that of a child's. Then it was gone. Bander shook off the chill and began breaking into the tomb. He wrestled a dead dry brown creeper vine off of a rock. It clung with long-dead tendrils. The clouds rolled in overhead and Bander felt the cool of the sun being obscured. He turned to look at the sky and noted that the dark clouds would bring rain. The wind gusted, blowing the vines around. A storm was coming; Bander redoubled his efforts at the doorway. An hour later he had cleared a way into the tomb. Piles of

113

stones lay scattered behind him. In front, the doorway was mostly still obscured except for the top three feet. Bander could climb in but he continued to dig. He wasn't sure what sort of guardian nested inside but he wanted to be sure that he could leave quickly if he wanted to. He heard the child's laughter once more but also other strange sounds. There was an impossibly loud clanging followed by the sound of running water. Then, after enough quiet time that Bander started to wonder if he had really heard those sounds, he heard the sound of panting, like a big dog. Then that too went away.

Aside from the noises, was the smell. It was a smell Bander knew too well. It was the smell of disease. The smell of imminent death. He smelled it on the battlefield many times in the days following a conquest. He had smelled in the Leper's Unity outside of his realm. And now, he smelled it radiating like heat out of the tomb he was about to climb into. His stomach clenched and he fought back a gag reflex each time the breeze shifted and he got a full lungful of the stench.

When the rocks were completely cleared from the entrance, Bander sat down on the ground and stared at the doorway. The rain started and he sat ignoring it while it washed away the sweat from his hair and face. He looked at the doorway and felt his breathing. He tilted his head to one side and redirected the rain to wash down his cheek. He had waited for so long for this moment. It didn't feel like he imagined it. This felt more real. More wet and tired and smelly than his musings. Once his heart rate slowed to normal he stood up and strode without hesitation into the tomb.

Chapter Eleven

The stink of the dark tomb assaulted Bander's nostrils like a warning shot over the bow. Whatever waited for him did not show itself. Bander mumbled something under his breath and the eyes of the severed lizard head he wore around his neck glowed bright red. The form of a raised coffin dominated the small room. Bander studied it for a moment looking for danger. Nothing moved and Bander walked into the noticeably cold chamber and over to the dust covered coffin.

The histories spoke nothing of what he was to do now. The location of the tomb was clearly noted in many of the journals. Each of these writings, done by the scribe of the man who dared to take the key, intoned a warning. There was never anything specific. Perhaps the danger was deleted from the texts. Maybe the vanity of the champions censored the scribes.

"The master went in while I huddled frightened from the bushes and he walked out holding the key shaped like a tuning fork."

"Mr. Lete walked with a strength I think few generals could match. The room held its secret and Mr. Lete looked prepared to beat the key out of the immortal guardian beast. He returned triumphant, the fork firmly in hand but the price…"

"History will record this as the act of a madman. To dig into a crypt to challenge the dead to give up their treasures and to pay for it with a curse no man can conquer."

Bander studied the stone coffin. It stood off the floor supported by four stone carved male legs. The legs were muscular and strained against its weight. On the top of it there was a bas-relief carving of a group of people with their hands joined forming a circle. The circle of people faced outward. A path led to the circle and on it walked a procession of people. They looked determined and angry. Some carried curved swords and torches.

These scenes were familiar to Bander. The red light cast by his necklace seemed to intrude upon the marble people. He pried at the lid to the coffin. It was much too heavy for him to move. His arthritic fingers begged him not to try again.

Bander didn't want to use his magic too soon. He didn't know what would alert whatever nested in this room. Plus it was never a good idea to give away too much to an adversary. He liked to save his magic for a surprise for his opponents.

Bander pulled out a knife and slid it into the crack around the lid to the coffin. If he could use leverage he might be able to lean his weight onto the knife to pry open the casket.

Something grabbed his leg. Bander jumped and wheeled around startled. Only the dusty floor illuminated by his glowing red pendant met his agitated gaze. He calmed himself. He realized that he held the knife above him in a threatening pose. Whatever had touched him had elicited an ancient instinctual fear response in him. That rarely happened. Bander thought that he had trained his body long ago to observe only the orders from him and to ignore instinct. This gave him advantage over most. He decided what to do. He assumed the control of his actions and chose wisely. This response unnerved him. He cast aside his personal reflections and searched the chamber. Other men would have allowed their fear to tell their minds that this didn't happen. There is nothing in the room. I imagined it. But Bander didn't make mistakes. Something had brushed against his leg and then disappeared.

"So, you are a sneaky little bastard eh?" Bander said aloud his words absorbed quickly by the stone enclosure.

This acts just like a Thumper, Bander realized. He said, "Amoonde," quietly, under his breath. Bander's call was answered nearly immediately as three Thumpers clawed their way out of the ground at his feet. They served him well and came when called like a domesticated dog. The Thumpers eyes darted to each corner and every shadow of the room discovering where they had been summoned.

"There is something hiding in the stone of this place," Bander spoke curtly. "Seek it out for me."

The Thumpers climbed back inside the solid floor. They would scour every inch of the walls floor and ceiling to find their masters want. They would fight over which would bring it to lay at the masters feet. If they were made of a more corporeal substance they might even hurt each other. The minutes dragged by, heavy like sacks,, while Bander listened to the sound of the rain starting up outside. It would be a sloppy trek back to his Keep. He figured that the key must be inside the coffin. That was really the only place that made sense in this empty room. Perhaps the guardian held it. If whatever he was confronting was a Thumper or similar to a Thumper then the key could be actually hidden inside the solid stone of the walls. This was annoying. Bander would have the key. It was only a matter of how much effort he would have to expend. The rain outside intensified and the thunder echoed while the sky cleared its throat.

Then a Thumper began to emerge from the ceiling. It climbed out of the rock feet first. Bander wondered if it might be dragging something out with it. Another Thumper appeared by it and climbed out feet first as well. Bander's armpits sprang to life secreting sweat as his anticipation welled. What would it be? What would a guardian of the ages look like? Bander's face was lit up with excitement and the red light made him look like a grinning devil. His slightly parted lips clamped back together and his eyebrows dropped while he watched the struggling forms of the Thumpers suspend in the air. They each were grasped by a huge black clawed hand. The hand and arm extended into the ceiling and there disappeared into the stone. The Thumpers kicked and thrashed at the grip around their necks but the black arm and hands held firm. Whatever it was that had them was big. And it could hold onto Thumpers, quite a trick.

Bander watched with fascination as the black appendages squeezed the life out of the struggling Thumpers and then cast them to the floor. They landed with heavy sounding thuds. The arms slid back into the stone. And then they were gone. The ceiling looked like nothing had happened. The floor was a bloody mess of crushed Thumpers.

Bander stood in the red glow of the tomb considering his options. Whatever this creature was, he would kill it; but how would he retrieve the key first?

"Amoonde," Bander whispered.

The third thumper was still somewhere in the walls. If Bander could find him perhaps the Thumper could retrieve the key from the casket for him.

The Thumper, as if reading his mind, popped its grotesque little head up from the center of the lid of the coffin. Bander smiled. The key would be his. But then the Thumpers head rolled down the side of the coffin. The creature was playing with him. Fury surged through his old frame. Bander extended his old knarled arm from out of his cloak and focused on the coffin. He snarled and the heavy stone lid was ripped off landing against the wall. He strode over to the coffin and peered inside. The rotted corpse of the old spiritual advisor to the king lay staring through empty eye sockets at the living world. The smell of the decay and rot was disgusting. It should have decomposed years ago. Why was this corpse so relatively fresh? Some of the Thumper's blood and gore decorated part of the box.

Most of the corpse's muscle and skin fed bacteria years ago but the strings of red hair remained on one side of the skull down to the shoulder. Some of the deceased dress remained as well. Faint blue and white pinstripes decorated the macabre figure. Bander's eyes scanned over the body without consideration. The partially mummified hand with the long fingernails didn't catch his eye. Around the neck was a small silver chain on the end of the chain was attached a plain key shaped like a tuning fork. It was just like the histories described. It was the key to the chamber.

Bander reached out a greedy hand but pulled it back as some movement on the corpse stopped him momentarily. Then Bander watched a huge black clawed hand materialize up through the corpse's torso and close around the key. It pulled the key down inside as it disappeared from where it came with the key. Bander stared at the keyless corpse in anger. So close!

The guardian now had the key and the guardian lived in the walls. The key was encased in solid stone now. It could be anywhere and there would be no way to retrieve it.

"No!" Bander screamed furiously at the silent corpse.

Lightning flashed outside the tomb momentarily illuminating it in white light. Something slapped against Bander's back. He spun to see a tail sliding back into the stone floor. A clawed hand grasped at his ankle. Bander struck at it with his hand and his hand went right through it. It had no solid mass except for where it was grabbing him. Another arm ascended from the floor and caught Bander's other leg.

Bander felt the creature's strength. He was no match for it. In moments he would be dead. He summoned Thumpers. Dozens of the little trolls crawled up through the floor. It looked like the judgment day as they clawed up from the floor.

"Kill it!" Bander commanded them urgently. The pain in his legs grew more intense with no feeling of letting up. The Thumpers dove into the walls and back into the floor. They made screechy animal noises while they furiously attacked. The floor looked like the a bubbling pot of stew, with arms and legs kicking and moving all around. The black hands that held Bander slid back into the floor. Bander rubbed at his ankles and breathed a blast of relief as the blood returned to his feet. The screams and flailings of the thumpers surrounded him. Somewhere in the walls a battle was going on that Bander would have liked to have seen.

Parts of torn-up Thumpers fell from the ceiling, an arm here, a clawed little foot there. Bander watched the remnants of his minions soak the floor with blood. A black back rose momentarily from the wall in front of him and then sank back into the wall like a fish breaking the surface of the water. Bander calculated the number of dead Thumpers surrounding him and realized that he was losing. The thumpers were no match for the guardian. Soon their numbers would wane and then the creature would turn its attention back to him. Bander reached into the coffin and lifted the corpse partially up by the remnants of its hair.

"Put her down!" said a anguished voice.

"Ah, your lady, I presume?" replied Bander thrilled that his guess was right.

"I will rip you to pieces!" said the guardian as its head emerged from the wall.

"Give me the key," said Bander.

A pair of Thumpers clawed at the guardians eyes and it ripped them away and cast them to the floor. The guardian was busy fighting off dozens of swarming Thumper's but managed to continue to face Bander.

"Anyone may take the key that wants it," said the Guardian. "Put her down!"

Bander lowered the corpse roughly back into the coffin.

"The key," Bander stated.

"Take the key. And take its curse." The guardian extended its black hand towards Bander the key dangling from the chain it clutched. Bander reached out and grabbed the key.

The creature sank back into the wall and renewed its battle with the Thumpers. Body parts fell like autumn apples. Bander turned towards the door. Fury swept through him. He turned back towards the coffin.

"Damn you!" he snarled at the walls. "Guardian. You are a common thief. You do not fight man to man. You coward! You protect nothing."

"Fool, I was protecting you," the guardian answered.

"You?" snarled Bander. "Protect me? You can't even protect your... love."

Bander leaned over the open coffin and spit. The spittle covered the rotting woman's body and then caught fire. Bander turned and strode out of the room with the key in his hand.

"No!" Shrieked the guardian. Arms erupted out of the walls and urgently tried to put out the burgeoning flames. The spell was not stoppable. Bander stepped into the rain of the outside world. He could smell the burning flesh of the long dead girl. Her clothes and hair crackled while his fire consumed them. He felt a angry satisfaction at the guardians pain. He had the key. But the price was high indeed. The architects had leveled the playing field. He was blind.

Chapter Twelve

The woods opened up in front of them like a devil's yawn. The twisted trees branch's intertwined to form a virtually impenetrable thicket. The morning fog had not burned off entirely and the remaining wisps of white rested heavily near the ground like mold. The party surveyed the gloom.

"Well, this certainly looks like fun!" said Bob.

"I can't say I expected anything less after what we have been through," added Larry.

"Adventure!" said Sargasso with a gleam in his eyes.

"I'm afraid that there's some explaining to do now," said Grento. Larry and Bob looked at each other knowingly as if to say, "Here we go again."

"What do you m, m, mean?" prodded Larry.

"Inside this labyrinth of living walls is a courtyard in which we will find the sisters."

"Is that all?" interrupted Bob suspiciously.

"After all we have been through we can handle a few scrapes. It'll be a nice change to avoid little dangers instead of big ones," said Larry.

"You didn't let me finish," Grento said calmly. "We must navigate the tangle of trees to find the witches hideout. Getting through will be tricky. The Tanglewood trees grow so close together and their branches intertwine so we will have to climb through them. However, if we choose the wrong route we could stumble across something less than pleasant." Grento let the last line hang in the air like a smoke ring.

Larry looked from Bob to Sargasso back to Bob and then they all turned to Grento.

Grento picked up where he left off, "The witches selected their hiding place well. It's as safe from organized attack as any castle on a hill. There are guardians that live within the twists of the Tanglewood branches.

"What kind of guardians?" asked Larry.

"They are called Spiderworms. They live on the underside of the branches. They are nasty things. They look like yellow worms with hundreds of tiny legs. Their circular mouth's sharp mandibles spit a stinging brown acid. They can be as small as a few inches long but the big ones are ten inches across their backs.

"They prevent large numbers of men from entering the woods. Any attack made in haste will quickly become a swarming mass of yellow worm food. We must choose our path wisely and then move carefully. The worms are waiting. The bite from a small one irritates like a wasp sting. But the big ones we must spot and be careful not to disturb. They hunt by vibration. Since the trees are all twisted together the vibration on one branch is translated to the others and the worms know right where to find you. Once one worm has you the vibration of the struggle sounds like a dinner chime to all the other worms. It doesn't take long to be completely covered in biting worms. The trick is to sneak through.

The rest of the gang, Larry, Bob, and Sargasso, looked less than pleased. Even the adventurous Sargasso didn't like the idea of twisting his body into the confines of the trees where he would not be able to fight.

Larry didn't want to go into the woods. He knew that he would see a worm. He knew that a worm would probably touch him with its cold-segmented shell, its horrible little legs probably equipped with tiny grasping claws on the tips. Every bit of Larry said, "No, this isn't a good idea. Do not do this!"

Unfortunately it wasn't his choice. At least it didn't feel like his choice. Tock was after him and his brother. They were in this together. The inevitability of the situation pressed him onward.

Bob's thoughts were quite different. He had already, to some extent, conceded the fact that he would have to persevere. There was a yucky job to do but it had to be done. It was better to find the elegant solution and then roll up your sleeves and do it.

Bob surveyed the thicket and tried to figure out the best way to proceed. He thought about lighting the woods on fire to burn out the witches. He dismissed this plan as it might kill them and also they might not be keen on giving up information if their hiding place was destroyed. Bob concluded that he should concentrate on not being the first person into the woods.

"Can you sense where the worms are?" asked Larry. "Does the same sense that allows you to avoid monsters in the Waste allow you to avoid the worms?"

"I'm afraid not," said Grento. "My sense tells me to avoid these woods entirely."

"Great," said Larry.

As the party approached the tangle of trees the mood was somber. Sargasso cracked his neck from side to side. Larry tried to take deep relaxing breaths. Grento strode with eyes narrowed examining the possible entrance holes.

The tree's branches reminded Larry of a giants interlaced old fingers. He felt like a fly trying to sneak into a place that could suddenly spring to life and crush him.

One by one they stepped into the Swarm Caves. There was no possible way to navigate the branches without climbing on them and touching them. The rough bark was cool and lifeless. The air smelled of decomposing leaves.

Larry thought it was lucky that they hadn't seen a worm yet. This ambiguity allowed him to enter the thicket. It was like fishing: you're excited to go and you know that there are fish in the lake but your heart really doesn't start thumping until you see one jump, or get a bite. In the case of the thicket, they would be glad to avoid the latter.

Grento suggested a single procession. They would need to play the percentages. They chose small openings. Bob reasoned the big worms would probably prefer to eat big things and that meant, to Bob, avoid the places big animals would go.

Grento, who had volunteered to go first, slowly pushed his head into the hole. He craned his neck and could see the backside of many of the branches. There were no worms. He backed his head out and informed the group that they had chosen wisely. You would think that this would be good news but it simply meant to Larry that now there was no reason not to enter this hole and so there was no tuning back and worse, no delay.

Grento's form wiggled its way into the hole. Sargasso was right behind him. Each man carefully avoided disturbing the branches unnecessarily to avoid alerting worms. Inside the natural cavern there was enough room for all of them to stand comfortably. Bob and Larry crawled in only to see Grento halfway into another cave of branches. Sargasso looked back at the men and winked. He was obviously warming up to the challenge. He followed Grento and motioned for the brothers to follow. The next twist in the undergrowth took the party through a series of open areas where the trees parted and they could move about freely.

The group huddled and made nervous conversation. Grento chose a cavity in the trees to press through. One by one they followed. The tough bark felt like dried leather. It wore at their skin patiently. It was hard for Larry and Sargasso to keep their tempers. Each man more than once caught himself punching a branch that snagged him or obscured his way annoyingly. This worm-pit was a trap for the hot-headed.

Bob and Grento seemed right at home in the briar patch. Grento would slide his head into a hole to survey the backs of the logs and Bob would calmly follow. There was a growing uneasiness. They hadn't seen any worms, but the forest began to look all the same. They used the sun as a guide whenever they could but wriggling under branches made navigating difficult.

"Grento," Larry whispered. "How far is it to the witch's hideout?"

"I'm afraid I don't know Larry. One doesn't stumble around this living trap long enough or often enough to remember landmarks. We'll find it but it may take some time. If we can find a suitable spot we will make camp for the night," said Grento.

Larry felt his stomach tense. He hadn't planned on camping inside the Tanglewoods.

Grento's hand rested on a branch while he spoke and a tiny worm darted out of a hole in the wood onto it. Larry saw Grento's eyes bulge wide with pain. His lips curled up to show his clenched teeth and he stifled a scream as he yanked his hand away. The little worm crawled back into its hole nonchalantly.

"Are you alright!?" asked Larry. Bob and Sargasso turned to see what was going on.

"I will be fine," said Grento wincing. His hand was swollen and red. Grento was as mad at his own carelessness as he was at the pain. "Enough time is wasted on me now, let's go," said Grento. The party moved on. Everyone was careful where they put their hands as they squirmed through the trees.

Bob wondered if the little worm's appearance meant that there would be more big worms around or less. He knew that often little animals meant that there would be few large animals around as little animals often avoided big animals. Of course he knew that just the opposite was often true as well. He wondered which way this one would go.

It was hard to determine the time of day as the trees in the area blocked out the sky. The guys felt a coolness to the air which signified to them that the sun was setting. Grento increased the speed they were traveling slightly. He was anxious to find an open area to make camp.

Everyone was worn out. The navigation through the trees was physically demanding but the constant threat of worm bites and the maintaining of their composure, being quiet all day, had drained their strength.

Grento passed on two spots that looked like good places to camp because roots were exposed on the ground and could offer the worms tell-tale vibrations. The trees finally opened up a bit and they stopped for the night. The campsite was actually quite nice. The ground was level and they could see the sky. The group felt a little better here because the trees were a comfortable distance away. They wouldn't accidentally put their hand on a worm.

Sargasso walked up behind Larry and Bob and slapped them both on the back. "Well lads, we've made it this far into those witches' hideout." Larry and Bob turned to him and smiled knowingly.

"At least only one of us has been bit so far," said Bob.

Grento turned to him at this with a scowl.

"I mean, well not that I'm glad you got bit, I just mean as far as the percentages go, one out of four in a day isn't bad."

Grento continued to stare at him.

"I mean it would've been better if no one got bitten. How's your hand anyway?" Bob said.

"It's fine," said Grento returning to looking through his cloak.

Larry and Sargasso looked at Bob and then at each other and started laughing. It felt good to Larry to let out some of his built up tension.

"Shut up, Larry," said Bob defensively.

"Or what?" said Larry between chuckles.

"Actually," Sargasso broke in "only having two of us laughing is pretty good when you think about the percentages with the four of us." At this Larry's laughter got much more intense and Grento joined in the revelry. Pretty soon even Bob started to laugh at himself and the group shared a moment of joy.

They decided to run a cold camp, as they didn't know what attracted the worms and what repulsed them. There was no reason to call attention to themselves. They shared the different food items each had stowed away in their respective packs and cloaks. Well, no one wanted any of Grento's root-necklace. But that didn't seem to bother Grento at all and he chewed away at the foul plant.

The group arranged to sleep with their heads all near the center of the clearing with each man's feet aimed out. This way, they figured, if anything tried to crawl onto them in the night it would crawl on their feet and wake them up before it had any possibility of crawling into their mouths or ears.

Laying there in their little formation they all stared up at a beautiful starry night. Although tired, they enjoyed the comradery. It felt like a boys-sleep-out in the woods more than a cold camp in the heart of worm country.

"Grento, do you think that we will find their hideout by tomorrow?" asked Sargasso.

"That's hard to say, these woods play tricks on the mind and navigating is tough," said Grento.

"How's your hand?" asked Bob.

Sargasso and Larry chuckled together at the question.

"It's fine now," said Grento. "Apparently the bite of the little worms is but a painful irritation. Still, I wouldn't like to be stung again."

Bob spoke up, "Hey Sargasso, where were you going when we found you? That night when you were camping."

"I was camping," said Sargasso flippantly.

"Yeah, I know that, I mean why were you camping? Was it just for fun? Are you going somewhere, what?"

Sargasso took his time answering. "Well my friends, as a matter of fact, I am hunting for a lost treasure."

"What kind of treasure?" asked Larry enthused.

"Oh I am afraid that, my new-found friends, we do not know each other well enough for me to elaborate on the specifics of my most magnificent treasure. I hope that you're not offended if I keep a secret to myself for the time being."

"That's fine with me," said Grento. "Fools often die in search of treasure."

"True," said Sargasso, "but that's my choice and I don't put it on you."

"Wow," said Larry as he stared at the stars that were just coming out. "The world is so much bigger than it was a couple of days ago."

Larry didn't even want to begin to imagine what Sargasso's treasure was like. Usually he would be able to spend hours daydreaming about it but now his thoughts were pregnant with visions of witches and worms.

No one pushed Sargasso for more information about his treasure and he seemed disappointed. The talk continued for a while as everyone relaxed and stared at the vastness of the universe overhead. Larry tried to keep his eyes open as he searched for shooting stars, a tradition with him on his childhood campouts.

Sleep came gently to them all.

"Aughhhhh!" A shrill scream woke the party up. Larry lay listening to the noise. His eyes were not adjusted to the dark and he could not see anything. "Aughhh," the scream came again. This time Larry recognized it as Sargasso.

"Larry are you alright?" came the concerned cry from Bob. In the pitch black everyone fumbled to get up while the sound of thrashing and Sargasso's screams filled the night.

Larry felt his heart pounding. His eyes were wide open trying to identify anything in the darkness.

"Sargasso!" Grento shouted from where he had been sleeping.

"The pain!, aughhh, I can't...augghh!" Sargasso shouted.

Bob and Grento crawled on the ground feeling their way quickly to the sound of the commotion. Bob's hand jerked back as he felt the wiggling legs of a big worm.

From the sound of Sargasso's yelps and the thrashing noise it was clear to Bob that the worm had Sargasso. He had no time to plan. He overcame his natural instincts and forced himself to pound at the worm. His fists hit the ground as often as they landed on the worm. Each time he missed his target the bones in his hand let him feel it. Several times he hit the worm. He couldn't tell if he was hurting it. But he flailed away with reckless abandon.

Larry found his way to a section of the worm as well and pulled out his small knife. He stabbed at the worm; mostly he only hit air but there was nothing else to do. Each man simply struck out. Sheer fear and immediate necessity drove them. They were like animals running from a fire. And then in a flash of light the worm was illuminated before them. Sargasso lay writhing on the ground a dozen feet away from where he had gone to bed. His body contorting in pain and his screams were awful. The worm lay still on the ground, dead.

Larry and Bob looked around surveying the scene as quickly as possible. A small campfire blazed in front of Grento. Grento quickly moved to attend to Sargasso. Larry looked back to the worm in front of him. It lay relatively still except for the occasional twitch of one of its horrible little legs. The worm was huge. It was thicker around than a man's body and its length was longer than their camp area. The worm's body stretched all the way from Sargasso to the edge of the trees and then into the trees. Larry saw the tiny puncture wounds his knife had made in the exoskeleton of the beast. They looked trivial. Bob joined Larry to make sure that he was all right. Larry could see that Bob's hands were bleeding and bruised. They both ran over to Sargasso and Grento.

"How is he?" asked Larry.

"I don't know," came Grento's reply.

Bob found himself staring at the head of the worm where it lay near Sargasso. The disgusting thing had no eyes. Bob shuddered as he moved around it. Each step brought his attention to more miniscule teeth each covered in Sargasso's blood. Dirt interrupted the bright red where it caked onto the creature's maw.

Sargasso was bleeding from his hip. The worm had bitten through his clothes and broken the skin. The bite didn't look as bad as they would have thought. It looked like the worm only bit him once. He pulled away before those little teeth could grind away at his flesh.

Sargasso became a little calmer as the sting of the worms bite began to subside. Grento, Larry noted, had a nice bedside manner. He wiped the sweat from Sargasso's face and spoke softly to him. It was strange to see someone who appears so hard on the outside acting this way. In a way, Grento was being just as tough and exacting as ever. He applied to the situation the necessary balm. Sargasso needed to be calmed down and Grento spoke quietly of relaxing things.

Larry and Bob watched the worm's poison fade in Sargasso. Although more intense, Sargasso's pain subsided in about the same amount of time as Grento's had. Bob's eyes scanned the dim light for any signs of worms but everything was still.

The morning broke. As the light finally crept through the trees they tended to their personal injuries while Grento stayed with Sargasso.

Bob and Larry uneasily looked at the worm. It was huge. Both men's lips wrinkled in disgust at the filthy thing. Bob found a stick and poked at the worm. The worm's legs had become stiff.

Larry noticed the areas where Bob had beaten at the thing with his bare hands. Several of the legs were broken at this point. Larry's knife had done more damage as he had punctured the worm several times but there was no way that those infinitesimal stabs killed this worm.

Sargasso got to his feet with Grento's help as Larry and Bob joined him.

"Are you alright?" asked Larry.

"Aye," said Sargasso as he walked over to the worm's dead body and kicked it. "How are you guys?"

"Well, Bob might have broken his hand trying to beat that thing to death," said Larry.

Sargasso looked over to Bob with a hurt look on his face. "I'm sorry to hear that," said Sargasso. Sargasso was not used to being responsible for the pain of others. Well not anymore anyway. Since his family's death and the circumstances involved, Sargasso had been careful to stay free of any and all attachments. Maybe he was getting older now and no longer held the same convictions he did for years after the incident. Maybe he was getting a little rounded at the edges.

"Well it's damn lucky the worm chose me for its dinner," said Sargasso.

"I was thinking the same thing," said Bob. "But why do you say that?"

"Cute, Bob," said Sargasso. "I say that because it was my blood that killed him. If it would have gotten a hold of anyone else we wouldn't be able to play pinochle tonight."

"Oh yeah," said Larry. "You're poisonous."

"Quite poisonous actually. That worm started to die the second he punctured my pretty hide," said Sargasso.

Larry's stomach felt bad. He realized that Sargasso was right. It was extremely lucky that the worm had bit him. If the worm had come out of trees on the side where he slept he would have awoken to the gnawing of those horrible teeth. They needed to get out of these woods.

The group was anxious to get moving. It was light enough to see their way clearly.

"Grento," said Bob. "I think that we should follow the worm's body to where it came from."

Grento looked at Bob without saying anything then shook his head in confusion.

"I'm not sure why I think that this way would be better," said Bob. "Just a hunch I guess. Maybe the witches sent the worm."

"Or maybe," interrupted Larry. "The worm came from a nest of the suckers!"

"Actually, Larry," said Bob. "Usually in nature where there is a particularly large individual of a species there will not be others around. It's because animals are often cannibalistic."

"Well, what about spawning season? Isn't it true that the biggest animals attract the most mates?" said Larry with buggy eyes and a hint of sarcasm on his tongue.

"We could argue this all day," said Grento. "But we must make up our minds. I agree with Bob. It will give us a direction anyway, and we can see how big this worm is and what type of holes it chose to go through. It might not hurt to learn a little about the habits of these things."

"Fine," said Larry. He really didn't care which way they went. He was just letting off steam with his brother.

They gathered their gear and started backtracking the worm's path. Everyone felt glad to be moving. Glad it was daylight.

Sargasso moved with effort as the bite, although not terribly deep, bothered him quite a bit. Larry couldn't help wondering at what sort of fellow Sargasso was that his blood could kill something as large as the worm almost instantly.

The worm's body wound through the brush, a constant reminder of what could be awaiting them at every turn. They proceeded cautiously following the curvature of the dead worm. It didn't show any sign of getting smaller or ending. They must have seen thirty meters of worm. Luckily they didn't run into any other worms. Maybe the smaller worms were afraid of whatever killed their big brother and kept to themselves, thought Larry.

Just then the dead worm moved. Larry thought that his eyes must be playing tricks on him and he stared at the corpse. He called to Bob. "Hey Bob, I thought I saw the worm move. I think that I'm losing it."

Bob turned to Larry and was about to say something derogatory when the worm moved again. This time everyone in the party froze in place staring at the worm.

The worm's body shook again but the legs were as dead as ever. Then the worm's body was violently yanked and the whole worm started moving towards where they had come from. Something was pulling it. The party stared in confused horror as the worm's tail finally came into view and then followed the body back into the bushes from the direction of their previous camp. "What's going on?" asked Larry.

"Something has gotten a hold of the worm and is pulling it away," said Bob.

"What in the world could pull something that big?" asked Larry.

"Perhaps an even bigger worm," said Grento.

"Let's get out of here," said Bob.

"I agree," said Sargasso.

"Follow me," said Grento disappearing into the underbrush.

The party moved with urgency. Grento still stuck his head into hidden nooks to be sure they were worm-free before proceeding but the others did not linger. Sargasso no longer messed with his wound. Everyone focused on staying out of the way of whatever was strong enough to move a giant worm. Grento turned back towards the men after sticking his head into yet another opening with what looked like a nervous smile. "We're here."

Chapter Thirteen

In Bander's castle Quid made his report.

"Lord, this creature is amazing. It killed all the slaves without risking any danger to itself. We can only guess its bulk. It hid behind the rocks. One would have to get within its striking distance in order to get a look at it. I sent the last three slaves in at the same time to see if the creature had any problem with numbers but it struck them down one after the other with such precision they died within heartbeats of each other."

"So it is an efficient hunter; can we use it?" asked Bander.

"I do not think so my lord. The soldiers and I waited until after dark in the hopes of getting a look at the beast. I figured that it had to come out to eat the men it killed at some point."

"Perhaps it leaves the bodies on the ground in plain site to attract other scavengers," noted Bander.

"Yes, that makes sense. After dark our torches were hardly sufficient to see how it retrieved its meat, but the morning found that all the bodies were gone. We think that, judging from the drag marks in the dust, the thing whipped out it stinger and secured the prey pulling them to it. It is my recommendation that because of the way in which this creature relies on its surroundings and the difficulty we would have in procuring it that we take another batch of slaves out and try another cell."

"Do it."

"It will be done. Lord, there is another matter troubling me, the attack on your life during your secret journey…"

"Watch your tongue," snapped Bander. "Everything I do is secret." Bander mentally flogged himself for telling Quid about the attack. But Quid's contacts throughout the kingdom heard everything. If anyone could find out who initiated the assassination attempt it would be Quid. He kept Quid around for this reason.

"The attack was paid for by a handful of nobles. They mistakenly thought they could surprise you."

"Do you have their names?"

"Yes my lord. Two of them were surely involved. The rest were probably connected. The details become sketchy when passed from bedchamber to the stinking breath of a drunk to one of my spies for a price. But I believe that we have sorted out the general heart of the group responsible. Certainly enough to make a statement to any further foolish thoughts."

"I can't be bothered with these political parries now," said Bander growing frustrated with the minutia of ruling. "I have important matters at hand."

The little man that ran along Quid's stream of consciousness stumbled at the idea that Bander had things more important than assassination attempts on him.

"Might I have the pleasure of handling this for your lordship?" Quid asked as meekly as he could.

"You already have a plan I assume," said Bander.

"The state will throw your lordship a party. As it will be obligatory for all nobles to attend, your betrayers will be here together. I will kill them in my personal chamber. The other guests will get the message and further attempts on your life will be avoided and more importantly, the idea that now is a time for change will be firmly put down."

Bander nodded his approval to a triumphant Quid. Bander, having heard the report, turned and left his visiting chamber. His mind was already on other thoughts. His eyesight was gone. Although he used his powers to navigate the Keep he was not the man that had ventured into the Guardians Tomb. Quid might have noticed his masters new affliction but he might not have. No one looked into Bander's face. Everyone stared at the ground or in his general direction when in his company. No one wanted him to look into their eyes. His gaze would feel too penetrating.

Bander returned to his private chambers. It was here alone that he could relax. It seemed like lifetimes ago when he had made his moves. When he took power and no one noticed. That is the real trick he thought to himself; they couldn't see it coming. People rarely do; still, he had been clever. Give them something to worry about; someone to worry about and they turn their backs on you. Fear is key as well. Keep them afraid of you but more afraid of the alternative and then give them something to occupy their time, something to twist any passion they might have harbored, some-thing that they want right now. Work them hard so that the light is burned out of them and all they desire is sleep. Then let them sleep.

Bander wondered why he even thought in political schemes anymore. He had laid the groundwork years ago and once in place there was very little that needed his attention now. He poured some water from a pitcher and drank.

There was something new to think about now. The witches had warned him of the two brothers. Tock was hunting them. And Tock wouldn't stop until they were dead. Still he found it so unlikely, so utterly impossible that anyone could cut through the fabric of the web he wove so many years ago as to harm the realm or his person. He felt the icy tickle of adrenaline at the prospect of another battle. He was old and most of his fights behind him but just the thought of another was romantic. He would deal with them through the pragmatic channels. That was only smart. But part of him, an old part of him, hoped that the fates had read their cards right and that he would get the chance to face down these champi-ons.

Ah, to eat their livers.

Chapter Fourteen

The trees parted, revealing an opening large enough for a party ten times as big as theirs to camp comfortably. In the center of the clearing smoke wisped out of a large hole in the ground.

"Where are they?" asked Larry.

Grento pointed across the opening to the trees on the other side. "There," he said.

Sargasso and the brothers followed Grento's finger to three small houses ringing the open space. The dwellings were built into the trees. The trees grew perfectly to provide shelter. The dark doorways snarled at them like little dogs.

"Well I sure am glad we decided to brave the worm infested forest now that we're here," said Bob sarcastically.

A woman appeared in the doorway. She was pleasant looking. Her tall thin frame wrapped in a gray cloak looked like a lone tree on a mountain that the wind has already picked clean and only the narrow lines remain, the parts impervious. She was middle aged. Or maybe she was a little younger. Larry felt his temperature rise at the sight of an unexpectedly attractive woman.

Her dark hair was thick, like a horse's mane, and the wind teased a lock in front of her haunted eyes. She took a step towards the men and Bob felt his breath catch.

"Sisters," she spoke.

Two women walked out of their huts and flanked the first. They both looked pleasant and unassuming like the first. One of them walked with a cane and the other's face was nearly covered with a purple birthmark. The three witches stood confidently side-by-side facing the men.

Bob didn't know what to do. It felt like two big predatory animals had stumbled onto each other and were momentarily surprised into inactivity. Each assessing the other before charging.

Grento was the first to gather his wits about himself. "Hello."

Then Sargasso, "Yes, hello. I am Sargasso and this is Larry and Bob," he said with a flourish pointing to the brothers.

"Well, aren't you gallant," said the woman to their left though her face devoid of emotion.

"And what is your name?" the middle woman asked Grento.

"My name is Grento."

"A traveler?"

"Yes, I am a Gelk."

The women walked closer to the men and introduced themselves.

"I am Syta and this is Ponta," she said pointing to the woman with the cane. "This is Dubla," she said indicating the woman with the birthmark.

"May we camp in your clearing?" asked Grento.

"You may," said Syta. "We would invite you to share our dwellings but unfortunately there is barely room for each of us inside," she said without any animation to her face like she was thinking of something else entirely while her eyes jumped from one man to the next.

"That's quite alright," said Grento. "We are becoming accustomed to the peculiarities of these woods."

A shiver ran up Larry's back and the recollection of the past night's peculiarity.

"As it's already getting late, why don't you fellows set up your camp allow me and my sisters to prepare a meal to ease your weariness."

"That is very kind of you," said Sargasso.

The women turned and without as much as looking at each other scuffled back into their homes.

Larry and Bob stepped closer to Sargasso and Grento. "Well, what do you think?" asked Bob.

"What do you mean?" answered Larry.

"I mean, this is it? These don't look like witches. Am I missing something?"

"They seem nice," said Sargasso.

"Yeah, I know. So what, we risk our lives climbing through giant biting worm forest just to set up camp and have dinner with some woodsy ladies?"

"Bob," said Grento, "These are the witches. Don't let yourself be fooled by a beautiful face."

"Beautiful? Eh?" said Bob smiling.

"But also, maybe more importantly," Grento continued over Bob's comment. "Don't assume the worst. Sure, we came here looking for witches, hags, crones, but why assume that they want to harm us? All we want is a little information. We mean them no harm. As long as we keep our wits about us perhaps we can figure out what we came to figure out over a pleasant meal."

"That s,s, sounds good to me," said Larry feeling a little more relaxed. "But be careful, witches are sensitive," said Grento. "They're sensitive to the world around them, the weather, the animals, and to the subtle inner workings of men's minds. If you distrust them they will sense it."

"Well this is a fine time to clue us onto this Grento," said Larry.

"Sorry," said Grento.

"What, do you think? They're going to cook us?" asked Sargasso.

"Who knows," said Grento. "Let's get our camp set up."

The ground was already nice and clear with no rocks or roots. The distance from the nearest branch was a welcomed comfort. As he fumbled through his pack, Larry kept a watchful eye on the doorways. It wasn't long before he caught sight of them returning.

The men made their camp area around the fire hole in the center of the clearing. And it was to this hole that the woman approached. Dubla carried a bundle of twisted branches and when she got to the pit she placed them inside. As she did Larry took a long look at her face. The birthmark was the most severe and striking he had ever seen. Her face was so pretty that the mark looked almost good. Larry studied the outline of the color where it started at her neck and worked its way up her jaw line and then cut across her face just inside of her right eye. It disappeared into the hair on her left side. Larry looked quickly away when her eyes darted to meet his. Larry swallowed hard and tried to look nonchalant.

Ponta returned bearing cookware and silverware. She placed them near Larry with a warm smile. Her wooden cane was carved with naked women. Where it touched the ground it was two pronged legs of a woman. The figure had another woman standing on her shoulders and then another standing on her shoulders all the way up the cane. At the top, the final woman held a sphere above her head. This was what Ponta gripped as she steadied herself. She didn't look injured. What Larry could see of her legs, where they vanished into her robes, looked healthy and good. Maybe she had an old injury that no longer showed.

Syta carried a large bulging burlap bag. She slung it down next to Bob and Grento with a grunt and then straightened herself and smiled warmly. Syta carried herself with confidence. Bob thought she was a little too much woman for his taste. He couldn't picture her cleaning a fish. He could picture her in negotiations or in a fight.

144

The women turned and walked back into the homes leaving the men to make conversation amongst themselves. It was funny how just the presence of a woman makes a group of men slightly uncomfortable, thought Larry. Perhaps mothers instill this in children to ensure obedience. The women came back, this time burdened with blankets and spices and two jugs of wine.

"Please do not go to much trouble at our expense," said Sargasso.

"It's no trouble, it's probably hard for you to imagine how few visitors we receive and how we treasure their company. My sisters and I know each other's perspectives so well we need the stimulation," said Dubla as she spread the blankets on the ground to make a comfortable dining area. Ponta hunched over the pit and in a few seconds a fire flamed to life.

Syta opened the burlap bag and pulled out a dead worm. Larry's stomach lurched at the sight of the thing. He had been expecting something more resembling an acceptable food item. The worm's head was cut off and a brown-ooze marked the spot. Syta noticed the unpleasant expressions worn by all the travelers. "Perhaps we better make this into a stew. Ponta, get some roots for stew and a pot." Larry doubted that a few roots would disguise a worm but anything would be better than biting into one of those little legs.

The day cooled as twilight approached. The men relaxed around the fire. The witches kept themselves busy preparing the stew and adding fuel to the pit. When the stew was finally passed around, it smelled good. Sargasso tasted his soup first. He did so with a violent abandon. Apparently he enjoyed the irony of eating one of the things that had tried to eat him the day before. When he didn't drop over dead, the rest of the men sampled their dinner.

"Wow," said Bob. "This tastes just like the beef stew back in Agea Hills."

"What?" said Larry. "You're crazy. This tastes sweet like pudding"

145

"Strange," said Grento. "My stew tastes spicy. How can one food taste so different to each of us?"

"You're not used to eating food prepared with the Cullah root."

"The what root?" asked Sargasso.

"The Cullah root. It's a spice that's influenced by the eater's taste buds. Every person tastes the Cullah root differently but pleasantly. Grento, you like spicy so you taste spicy. And Larry likes sweets so he tastes sweet. There's no magic, just varying perceptions. You need nutrition and Spiderworm is nutritious but also unpalatable. The only way to eat this is with lots of Cullah root."

"Amazing," said Bob. "The world is simply amazing."

The men ate their food tentatively. With their bowls empty and their stomachs satisfied, Grento spoke for the group. "Thank you for this meal."

While Grento talked, the witches busied themselves with cleaning up the dishes. "You know we found you on purpose. Well, of course you do. Who would ever cross these woods accidentally?"

"We know that you have sought us out Grento," said Dubla. "However, the Cullah root will make us tired. We will discuss these matters in the morning." And with this statement the witches concluded their clean up and walked into their cabins.

Larry was already sleeping, Bob noted as he looked at the others.

"That's strange," he said with a yawn. Sleep soon took them all.

In the morning Larry and Bob awoke to a gentle shake from Grento. Sargasso was at his side and the two men looked intensely upset. Their demeanor and stern looks commanded quiet reverence and the brothers woke silently.

Bob shook his head from side to side to ask "What is it?" Sargasso merely deliberately turned his head to the side. Bob and Larry followed his gaze to the edge of the trees. There they saw every branch was covered with worms. The trees wriggled and bustled with a million legs. The yellow, segmented bodies pulsed around them like a cluster of veins around a cancer. The brother's eyes bulged wide at the revelation. They were surrounded. They lay still like crickets within the eyesight of a gecko. Afraid that movement would incite the lighting quick attack they could not survive. The worms writhed around their little pocket of safety.

As the men realized that the Spiderworms weren't going to attack, the witches appeared from the doorways to their shelters. The worms recoiled from the emerging witches. Ponta reached out her hand and plucked a medium sized worm from a branch above her head. The worm squirmed to get away but went limp when she grabbed it. It was dead.

She carried the worm's body towards the men. Three or four feet of it dragged on the ground behind her. The three witches said, "Good morning," and began to work on the fire and preparation of breakfast. Dumbfounded, the men stared at them.

"I trust you all slept well?" asked Syta.

"No complaints," said Sargasso meekly.

"Sometimes we get a gentle rain in the evening but not last night. You boys have the devil's luck," said Dubla with a pretty grin.

"What the hell is going on?" exclaimed Grento.

"Oh," said Dubla, "Are you referring to the worms?"

"Of course! I'm referring to the worms what do you think?" said Grento exasperated.

"Well, pay them no attention. They will not enter our camp, and besides...we called them here."

A cold realization settled over the men like a chill from an open window. They were trapped and the witches had trapped them.

"Could you send them away?" asked Bob.

"Of course, don't worry. We get so few guests that we thought it would be nice for you to stay for a while," said Syta.

"This is outrageous," said Sargasso incredulously. "We are men, not worms!"

"That's clear," said Dubla and then aside to her sisters, "Isn't it strange how men need to remind themselves and others of their gender. Women never do that."

The other witch's faces registered understanding as they continued with the preparation of food.

"Are we prisoners then?" asked Grento calmly.

"That's a matter of perspective gentlemen. Perhaps you will see yourselves as guests. I will explain your situation so you don't make mistakes as desperate creatures sometimes do. The worms will not leave unless we command them to. If you try to get through them they will surely kill and eat you. If you harm or kill any of us, the worms will swarm into the camp's circle of protection. If you think to kill us so quickly as to prevent us from calling the worms upon you, the worms will still encircle you blocking any escape. We will now leave you alone to argue amongst yourselves as to how to proceed. Once reason is restored to your thought processes we will eat breakfast."

The witches got up and calmly walked into their huts leaving the men.

"Well, well, well," said Larry quietly to himself.

"Any chance that they're bluffing?" asked Bob of the group.

"Perhaps," replied Grento. "But that's a bluff we cannot call."

148

"Maybe they just want to talk for a while and then they will let us go?" said Larry.

"That would be nice," intoned Bob.

"We must keep cool heads about us," said Sargasso uncharacteristically. "I've been in messes like this. We need more information. For the moment we don't seem to be in any immediate danger, let's not act like we are."

"What else do we know about these witches?" asked Bob.

"Good, we need to look at our options," said Grento.

"They said they are lonely," said Larry. "They also seem to control the worms and did you see the way Syta killed that worm with nothing more than her touch?"

"These women are so pretty yet the worm tried desperately to get away from her. Things aren't as they seem."

"I wonder how she killed that worm..." Larry trailed off as the three women emerged from their dwellings.

"Now that you have surely reasoned yourselves calm we can eat," said Dubla.

"Actually," said Grento. "We're not ready for another nap just yet. Who can say what surprise we might wake to this time?"

"Oh my," said Dubla, "Do I detect displeasure in your voice?"

"How would you feel?" hissed Sargasso.

"Enough silliness," said Dubla. "Why don't we talk about why you're here? Congratulations on your patience in navigating our briar."

"Well, it appears we have some time on our hands so I might as well begin," said Grento. And so he related the tale of Tock, how the imprisoned soul had been forced to chase down and

149

destroy the two brothers because of their varying eye color. Of how the 'thing in the dunes' told them to seek out the witch's advice and of their meeting with Sargasso. He left out a few things. How they outsmarted the sand creature and how Sargasso's blood had killed one of the worms. Now it was the witch's turn to squirm. They flashed glances at each other and for a moment they looked shaken.

"That is quite an adventure," said Syta. "I wish we could help you but we rarely leave these woods and we don't know why someone would want to harm these brothers."

Larry felt a pang of dread wash over him. They risked the dangers of the worm-infested wood and now the witches held them trapped for nothing? This was unbearable.

"You don't have any idea who is after us?" asked Bob incredulously.

"No," said Ponta, Dubla and Syta.

"Why would the sand creature think you would know?" Bob continued.

"I don't know," said Ponta. "How did you get the creature to tell you about us? I have heard that the creature is fearsome."

"Maybe," said Grento. "He took pity on us."

At this comment Dubla frowned.

"You men play games with us," said Syta acidly. And the three women got up and returned to their dwellings.

"Well this is a fine cup of tea we've brewed," said Larry sarcastically.

"They are lying," said Sargasso.

"I agree," said Grento.

"What are we going to do?" asked Bob.

"Let's look at our options," replied Grento.

"Options! What options?"

"There are always options my friend, no matter what the circumstances, one always has options. We could run into the worm-infested forest for example."

"We would be eaten to death!"

"I, for one, am not willing to exercise that option," said Larry.

"Well, perhaps we should consider the opponents motivation," suggested Bob.

"Excellent," said Sargasso venomously.

Larry looked at Bob nervously, then back to Sargasso.

"We know that the witches are lonely. We offer the outside stimulus they crave. They want to keep us around to entertain them since they are bored with each other."

"The sand creature said that they would know who sent Tock and why. I believe they know something. They offered too curt a reply not to be hiding something and besides why would the sand creature lie? He really wanted that water. No, I'm sure that these witches know something. Of course that could be wishful thinking, I would hate to think Sargasso took that worm bite for nothing."

"So we know that the witches can kill worms, control worms, that we are trapped,"

"That they want us for entertainment," added Larry.

"They know more than they are letting on."

"They really seem to be able to read us. Do you know what I mean? How did they know that we would need time to get used to the worms and that we would not outright attack them. I feel like they are anticipating our thoughts. Perhaps they are eaves-dropping on us right now."

"Talk without moving your lips," said Bob through still lips.

"What!" said Grento and Sargasso and Larry at the same time.

"Talk without moving your lips," repeated Bob still keeping his mouth still. "Perhaps they are reading our lips."

"They aren't deaf, they're witches Bob," said Sargasso.

"Well it seems that we have two goals... find out why Tock is after the Masefields and to get the hell out of here."

"Bob, why don't you focus getting us out of here and Larry, you figure out why Tock is after you."

"What? What are you and Sargasso going to do?"

"We are going to work on a plan B. Something to do if you guys can't solve our problems."

"I think that we should stay away from that Cullah root as well," said Sargasso.

The men opened their packs and cloaks and divided up some of their various rations. Bits of drying bread and hard cheese were welcome nourishment compared to the risk of the Cullah root. Each man absconded with their allotment and ate it quietly in thought. Grento and Sargasso wore solemn expressions as men planning violent acts often do.

Bob had been given the task of finding a way out of their trap. He was perfectly suited to this sort of reasoning and normally would welcome this challenge with quiet pleasure. But this time, too much depended on him.

Larry felt as though he had drawn a shorter straw than anyone. He approached his problem with complete bewilderment. He sat on the ground staring into space like a child hearing a foreign sound for the first time. Completely transfixed and completely confused, he spent several quiet minutes in denial figuring that the task should be allocated to one of his friends. He tried to calm himself and focus, to look at the facts and solve the problem but the facts were a cloudy soup that he could not hold in his brain. And then, like the opening of sleepy eyes, everything became clear.

Larry stood up, grabbing the attention of the rest of the group, and walked over to Dubla's hut. Then without any hesitation, he walked inside.

Bob, Grento, and Sargasso watched this scene like one watches a feeder mouse walk in front of a snake, "Don't do it," you want to say, but you say nothing, stymied by your astonishment.

Inside the hut, Larry's eyes tried to adjust to the dim light. The smell of wildflowers and cinnamon gave the dwelling an earthly, homey quality. Dubla sat in the corner amid numerous shelves. She stared hard-eyed at Larry. Not knowing whether he was friend or foe, she watched.

"Hello Dubla," began Larry.

Silence; Dubla seemed as if in a trance. The light from a candle danced shadows across her face. Then, as if Larry said a magic password, she smiled, and said, "Hello Larry. You men surprise me from time to time. How refreshing. What do you want to talk about?"

Larry stepped deeper into the room like a bug into a carnivorous plant.

"I need to know why you and your sisters want to keep me and my friends here." The words suspended. The thought conveyed, causal patterns arranged, the chess piece placed.

"Oh," said Dubla quietly. "Yes, I guess you would want to know that... I suppose you must have suffered miserably with the possible reasons three witches would trap you. Did you think we would eat you?"

Larry swallowed and shook his head as if to say "of course not" but his demeanor wasn't very convincing.

"We don't want the marrow in your bones. All we need is the stimulation of your perspectives. We will only keep you until we have assimilated your personalities and individual experiences into our own. We will get to know you."

"But we told you that Tock is after us. We need to stay ahead of him. Is there any room for negotiations? Perhaps we have something else you want instead?"

"No Larry, you don't. Your individuality is the thing we most covet."

"But it's not us specifically that you want, anyone would do?"

"Well sure, we didn't choose you specifically. Why do you ask that? Do you think you would be of interest to us? Is there something," she paused searching for a word, "special, about you?"

"No," said Larry taken aback.

"Larry, why did you choose my hut to enter? Didn't you get the impression that Syta makes the decisions around here?"

"I don't n,n,n know," stammered Larry. "I didn't really think it through."

"Are you sure there wasn't some ulterior reason for choosing mine? Perhaps it is my birthmark? Your eyes mark you. My stain marks me. Maybe you felt a kindred spirit...?"

"I don't think so," said Larry.

"Well that is no matter. Both of my sisters also carry the scars of birth. There marks are not as visible as mine though. You could say that my looks are the most honest."

"I don't know why I chose your hut, you," said Larry. "If it doesn't matter who you keep then let us go, we'll find someone to take our place."

"No, we would have no guarantee of you keeping up your end of the bargain."

"What if I stay here and talk with you and your sisters while my brother and my friends go and find someone to fill our place? I will be friendly and open, you will get to learn from me, and you know that they will return because of a brother's bond. Then you'll have a new person to talk to and we can go on our way."

Dubla's eyes rolled in her skull and then snapped sharply into focus on Larry's.

"Agreed."

Larry turned and walked out of the hut, both happy and worried about what he had done. He also felt slightly unsure of himself and confused as to why Dubla agreed so readily to his bargain.

He emerged from the hut like Jesus from the cave. Even Sargasso wore an expression of admiration. Larry had never been held in this light and for a second he let himself notice it, and then he hurried to his friends and relayed what happened and the deal he struck.

"Where are we going to find someone to take your place?" asked Sargasso to himself.

Grento scratched at his patchy beard and concluded, "Well done Larry, it's a fine deal. Where four of us were trapped, now only one, and that one has a hope of freedom that none of us had before. Plus you will have time to figure out what they know about Tock. Well done indeed. This is much preferable to the plan Sargasso and I were working on."

Syta, Dubla, and Ponta appeared from their homes.

"You may go now Grento, Bob, Sargasso," said Dubla while the worms to their left began crawling, their little feet making a horrible insect clicking noise as they moved. The worms rearranged themselves and left a small opening into the forest for the men to enter. "When you find the proxy you may return. Knock a stick on one of the outer trees to signal the worms. We will let you enter unharmed. You must go now. Know that we will not harm Larry. He is our company and our guest."

Bob did not like this deal one bit and began to protest but the others ganged up on him and convinced him that it was for the best. With their packs gathered, Grento led the way through the trees followed by Sargasso and then Bob slowly with an unsure look back, stepped into the trees and the worms filled in the gap. They were gone and all that was left was the witches and the worms.

Chapter Fifteen

Grento, Bob, and Sargasso made their way through the forest with ease. The worms parted at a point that got them started in the right direction to quickly reach the edge of the woods. The three men had not spoken a word as they made their escape. Now that they were clear of the woods they felt relaxed enough to talk.

Sargasso and Grento debated back and forth as to where they might find the proxy. Both men had traveled extensively and were eager to feel useful. Bob busied himself by marking the spot that they exited the woods for when they returned. Bob listened to Sargasso's argument while he scratched an x on a rock. Sargasso was quite a character, he thought to himself. Here stood a man who by his own account was a loner. Now, free from the witches, he was still committed to saving Larry and putting himself into possible danger. Some men feel obligated by their word. Or maybe Sargasso actually cared about his brother. Whatever the reason, Sargasso was a good man and Bob felt buoyed by his allegiance.

"So where are we to find someone who will take my brothers place?

"Well, after much debate," said Grento "I have bowed to Sargasso's experience. "We will go to a town about three days travel from here. The town, called Ule is relatively big and we should find our man there."

And so they crossed a great open area of swaying grass. The expanse of the terrain did their spirits good. It felt nice not being surrounded by trees. The three days passed without incident. As the sun set on the third day the group entered Ule.

The town consisted of a series of buildings made out of wood. Lights appeared in some of the windows. Bob, completely amazed by the sight of this town, stared at it with the wonder of a child first experiencing fireflies. The architecture differed from Agea Hills. The one story wooden shacks were painted in dull greens and browns. The air smelled of pungent mushroom. The people were shorter than most people he knew and moved in quick jerky motions.

Sargasso grunted, "Ule, boys," leading the way. Bob got the impression that Sargasso didn't like towns. He looked uncomfortable. Still, he led on to a building that was larger than the rest. The people that saw them looked startled but tried their best not to react strongly. After an initial flash of recognition they continued on their ways.

"This is a inn where we can set up a base," said Sargasso walking towards the building.

The building was made out of weather warped wood, aged gray. The light from inside peaked out through cracks in the boards. Smoke rose from the chimney in little gusts that brought the smell of cooking meat.

Bob felt uneasy walking in this town. Although the people he saw quickly looked away, he felt self-conscious. He noticed all the little details that only a stranger to a place sees. Grento and Sargasso walked through it like they owned it. Sargasso threw open the doors with authority. And in they went. Every single person inside got quiet with eyes glued to the strangers. After the moment became too awkward to bear, a short man behind some sort of decorative plant, walked over towards them.

"Sargasso?" he tried.

"Ko!" said Sargasso with vigor.

"Well as I live and breathe I never thought that I would smell your stinky breath again," said Ko.

"I couldn't deny you that pleasure!" Sargasso and Ko shook hands and Sargasso introduced everyone. "Ko here owns this inn and is one of the better gamblers around, just ask him he'll tell you."

Ko stood a foot shorter than any of the other guys with Sargasso. He was bald on top with long stringy hair hanging over his ears like moss over a tree branch. "Sargasso is too kind, and if memory serves, he owes me money."

"What an imagination, memory, sense of humor..." said Sargasso.

So with introductions made, the men sat down at a table to order some food and to rest.

The locals tried to go on with their business but remained desperately interested in the strangers. Bob remembered Agea Hills folk's reactions when Grento showed up.

The food placed before them, sizzled on platters. Its aroma made their mouths water in anticipation. Crispy pork with wonderful spices was a welcome change. Everyone ate voraciously. Ko and Sargasso shared stories back and forth. Grento and Bob attended to their stomachs. Eventually everyone felt satisfied.

A crash at the doorway gathered everyone's attention as a group of men entered the room like new years day. The patrons tried to sink into their beers. The men's boisterous calls for beer made Bob dislike them from the start.

Sargasso looked up and then returned to his conversation with Ko. Grento didn't even look up. Only Bob felt his temperature rise and his muscles flex at the intrusion. Bob didn't like confrontation. He never had.

Bob was in good shape. He worked with his hands all the time and was fairly strong. So he didn't particularly fear physical challenges. Getting into a fight didn't bother him but he didn't like the scene that led up to fights. Everyone in the room would look at him and he often couldn't think of the right retort to a snide comment. He worried more about throwing a punch that looked goofy than about getting hit in the teeth.

The five men in the group soon turned their attention to Bob and company. At first they were surprised and nervous to have discovered intruders in their haunts. But like a dog, who gathers his courage with grunts and then yips and then barks, the group's rise in bravado was palpable.

Bob noticed the group whispering amongst themselves and then pointing. Eventually they raised their voices for the benefit of the room, like buskers entertaining a crowd.

"Well, my friends the night brings us a treat."

And another intoned, "We are humbled by visitors gracing our lowly community."

Grento, Ko, and Sargasso were oblivious to this display. Bob was quite tuned in however. He could feel sweat drip down his sides, an unwelcome reminder of his trepidation in the face of conflict. Grento got up and walked over to the bar to get some beer from the bartender and the men engaged him.

"Hello, stranger, what brings you into Ule?" one of the thugs asked pleasantly.

Grento waited for his beer while the group filled in around him. Sargasso and Ko continued their conversation not so much a glancing over to where Grento stood with the five men. Bob tried to act like nothing was going on but his senses stood at attention. He wished desperately that Sargasso would notice this scene and do something. He had to do something. Bob started to get up but Sargasso caught his attention and shook his head no. Bob sat confused while Ko and Sargasso dove deeper into their conversation.

"Hello, friend I don't believe that you are from around here."

"No," said Grento. "I'm not."

"Well," said one of the men putting his hand on Grento's shoulder. "We would like to welcome you to Ule."

The man left his hand on Grento's shoulder and as Grento gently tried to move away the grip tightened. Grento dropped to a crouch and punched the man in the groin. He then exploded up and punched another one of the group with an uppercut. The man's teeth snapped together making a loud chilling click noise with the impact. The three other men reacted slowly and clumsily. Grento turned on them in a second. As one went to grab him Grento shifted his weight and deflected the man's attack into his friend in the same movement he punched the third man in the throat. The man backed away holding his neck and collapsed backward onto a table. The remaining men came after Grento with a fury now. Grento faked a lunge to punch one in the stomach. As the man's hands came down protectively, Grento boxed his ears. The man fell to the ground writhing in pain. Grento and the last man squared off. The man made a feeble lunge for Grento, which he easily deflected, and Grento dropped the man with a solid knuckle to his temple.

The bar was quiet, like the kind of quiet after a bomb goes off and the debris is settling to the ground. Grento looked at the men on the floor in various stages of disrepair and satisfied that they no longer posed a threat, turned to the bartender to buy his beer.

"This round is on the house," the bartender stammered. Grento returned to the table with the beers.

"Are you ok?" asked Bob.

"I'm fine."

"That was amazing! You beat up five guys."

Some of the town's people helped escort the hooligans out the door and the locals around bar looked at Grento with checked admiration.

"Took you long enough," said Ko.

"This isn't the kind of beer I ordered," teased Sargasso.

161

"I don't understand," said Bob. "How did everyone know that Grento would win? You guys didn't even pay attention to what was going on."

"Sure we did. Five town bullies fell down while Grento was getting the beer," said Sargasso.

"He could have been really hurt," said Bob with sad squinty eyes.

"Nah, they were just acting tough. You need to watch out for the ones that don't have to act tough. The quiet ones. Stay away from the quiet ones."

"You could have told me," said Bob trying to relax.

"Bob, you couldn't have been that scared. You were about to throw yourself into the fray," said Sargasso with pride.

"It sure felt like scared," said Bob. "I don't know how you guys got so brave."

'The only people that have shown any real courage on this quest is you and your brother," said Sargasso.

"What?" said Bob incredulously. "Me and Larry jump at the slightest sound. Grento led us into a worm-infested forest. You got bitten by a worm and killed it."

"True, but me and Grento went into that worm-nest knowing our capabilities, you and your brother went into that squirming hell with nothing more than your boots." Sargasso drained his beer and went to get another round.

"After we have drunk our fill," said Grento. "We will sleep in beds tonight. Tomorrow we will find a person to sit in for your brother. And, if we can't, then we will plan his escape."

The night was pleasant. Drinks flowed freely. Everyone got good and drunk and slept well.

In the morning the men regrouped in the bar/dining room

where Ko waited with three glasses of his homemade hangover cure. Everyone was sick with headaches and glad to have a cure. The concoction smelled like molasses coffee but it tasted like crap. Each man forced it down and after fifteen minutes they still felt the same. Ko shrugged his shoulders and said, "Yet another version that doesn't work. I will figure it out one of these days."

After some breakfast everyone felt moderately better. At least the taste of that horrible drink Ko gave them was out of their mouths.

"Where will we find someone who is going to go for this?" asked Bob.

"Ko will ask around. He'll find us a lead."

"So do we just wait here?"

"No, let's explore the town a little, perhaps we can find someone ourselves."

Chapter Sixteen

Larry sat down to dinner with the witches. He felt more than a little uncomfortable with the probing stare of three women. They had been nice to him, even leaving him alone for several hours to get used to his isolation and his surroundings. But now here they were... Larry didn't feel so good. "Please don't be scared Larry," said Dubla.

"Oh, let him be scared," said Syta. "It's interesting."

"I'm doing ok, ok," stammered Larry. "Don't let me scare you," he tried at humor and forced a smile that quickly faded. There was a rustling from the trees as a big worm shifted its weight. The branches groaned and creaked in protest. "So," said Larry trying to lighten the mood. "Tell me something about yourselves. I, I mean if you want to... that is."

"Yes," said Ponta. "I will start." The two other witches rolled their eyes at each other. "What would you like to know?"

"I don't know eh...have you always lived here?"

"No," said Ponta. "We were born in a little town by a big river. We are triplets but you probably already guessed that."

"No, I hadn't guessed that, you all look so different."

Ponta's eyes flashed white around the edges at Larry's comment.

The fire's flame went out leaving glowing embers. Dubla waved her hand over it and it sprang back to life as if she were fanning it.

"Wow that's a cool trick," said Larry. The witch's faces responded to his pleasure like the fire to Dubla's caress.

"It's a simple trick Larry. I merely invited the air to the fire and it accepted. The fire needs the air and the air rushes to the fire's call. Sometimes it needs a little shove to get there."

"Is that how you killed that worm this morning?" asked Larry hesitantly.

"No that is a bit different. Witchcraft is understanding the living wild world. Often people see themselves as separate from everything else. Once you accept and realize that we are all varying perspectives of the same energy you can control things that you thought were outside of your reach. With the worm, all I did was focus on that aspect of myself that was the worm and then I let that part of me go and the worm died. A part of me died. Do you understand?"

"Well I understand what you are saying but I don't think that I could ever imagine a worm being a part of me."

"Larry, that sort of enlightenment generally takes a long time to develop. Luckily we've had a long time to work on this."

Larry reflected for a moment and looking across the fire into the faces and eyes of the women, he caught, for a second, a flash of something eternal something that he felt a part of for an instant he understood and then it was gone.

"It's late and you should get some sleep. We will talk more tomorrow," said Syta. The witches got up and faded into the darkness at the fires edge.

Larry lay back on the ground with his jacket under his head and stared at the stars. As he drifted off to sleep he felt another flash of the eternal staring at him from the heavens.

In the morning Larry awoke to the smell of breakfast and the sounds of the women bustling around the fire.

"How did you sleep?" asked Ponta.

"Fine," said Larry. "Thank you."

"Today we will teach you some magic."

"Can anybody learn?

"Most people can, it is a matter of approaching the spell with the right perspective."

"What should we teach him girls?"

"How about how to control worms?" said Larry smiling.

"No, I don't think that would be a good idea. You might run away," said Dubla.

"Let's teach him something simple that he can use. Let's teach him 'concentration'."

"Is this a joke? Why did you get me excited if the only spell I get to learn is how to concentrate?"

"Do you already know this one?"

"Well I don't know the spell but I know how to concentrate."

"Isn't that useful?"

"I guess."

"Larry, do you see that medium sized worm that is walking along that dead branch?" asked Ponta pointing towards the trees.

"Where? Oh yes I see it."

"Which of its thousand legs is injured?"

"What do you mean?"

"I mean that one of its legs is hurt and it is walking with a slight limp, do you see which one?"

"Of course not. For one, it is too far away and two, it has a million legs and three, how could I ever see a Spiderworm limping?"

"Well watch me walk across this spot." Syta got up and walked in front of Larry and she pretended to have a bad limp.

"Can you tell that I am limping?"

"Of course."

"Then why can't you see the worm's hurt leg? We are both right in front of your face? I will help you out Larry. It's a matter of concentration, nothing more. Do you still think that it's a stupid spell?"

"Are you saying that if I learn this spell I will be able to spot the hurt leg?"

"You will be aware of whatever you direct your focus towards."

"Cool."

"Let's begin."

The witches stood in a circle around Larry. Larry stood and watched as the witches joined hands and started rotating their circle around Larry.

"Larry, turn in a circle in the opposite direction as us," said Syta.

Larry did as he was told and his world became a dizzy view of witches arms and faces. Each woman started speaking to Larry as they turned. Larry could only hear snippets of what each one said as they spun past his field of vision and hearing. Their voices blended together into an unintelligible babbling. After a couple of minutes of this sickening activity Larry collapsed and his world continued to spin. Larry felt like he was going to be sick.

"Larry, sometimes to learn something, it's important to see what it's not. You have just experienced the opposite of focus. Remember it."

"Thanks for the lesson ladies, I think I've had enough of magic." After a few minutes Larry's world started to slow down and eventually it stopped spinning altogether and he felt better.

"Larry, did you notice how as you lay on the ground your vision began to slow down and finally you returned to normal? This is an analogy of you focusing. When you look at something in this world you must realize that the world is spinning and you must slow it down until it stops. This is the perspective you will use to master concentration."

Larry wondered what he had gotten himself into.

Chapter Seventeen

Bob and the guys weren't having any better time of it in Ule. They spoke with everyone they could and no one was keen on going to live with the witches. Sargasso had managed to get slapped by two different women. Something he was whispering into their ears apparently didn't agree with them. Everyone in the town wanted to make friends with Grento. He ignored their envious stares. Bob mistakenly thought there would be adventure-seekers who would lunge at the chance to encounter witches and spiderworms but everyone in the town was scared to venture out of the boundaries of their home. It was understandable, Larry and him would never have left Agea Hills without the threat of painful death chasing them out. Bob hoped there was an elegant solution to this problem. He certainly wasn't prepared to threaten anyone to get them to leave their comfortable homes. They wandered from building to building visiting with the locals. Word of their arrival had spread like warm butter. On the fourth day the group met, as was their pattern, at Ko's Ale House for lunch. They sat around a circular table and exchanged thoughts. No one had gotten any closer to finding the proxy.

Sargasso's mood had soured as he didn't like city life. He was a man built to sail. Bob and Grento remained hopefully optimistic.

"Perhaps we should look at this problem from a different side," suggested Bob.

"We have been over that..." began Sargasso.

Something big dropped onto the middle of their table.

At first everyone thought a part of the roof had fallen in but in the split second it takes for life to come into focus, the serving boy screamed. A huge black snake recoiled from its deadly strike.

Grento and Sargasso threw back their chairs and Grento grabbed the back of Bob's coat and yanked him backward onto the floor. The snake snapped at the air where Bob's arms had rested on the table a moment before.

Ko's reflexes were much slower and he was last to move from the round table. But the reptile paid him no attention.

Grento dragged Bob backwards and up to his feet in seconds but the snake was after them. It was incredibly fast and it struck out over and over again each bite landing just shy of Bob as he stumbled away. Bob got himself turned around and now he ran full speed away from the snake. He ran past three townsmen who were digging a trench in the street. They saw the snake and formed a wall in front of it, each brandishing his shovel. The snake recoiled in front of them and then one man stepped forward to hit the snake with his shovel. The snake launched itself through the air sinking its fangs into the man's neck. The man began to fall immediately and the snake used his body like a springboard and bit the second and the third man in one motion. The three men fell dead. Tock slithered like quick silver into the bushes and was gone.

Sargasso caught up with Bob and Grento a quarter of a mile down the town's main road. Bob couldn't remember running so fast in his life. The three men caught their breath while they looked in all directions for any sign of the snake.

"So that was Tock eh?" panted Bob.

"Yes," said Grento. "He's gone for the moment. He uses surprise in his attacks."

"Well," said Sargasso. "That was a good one. Surprise. That snake killed four men in seconds. I've never seen anything so deadly."

"Let's get back to Ko and assess the damage. Keep to the middle of the road and keep your eyes open," said Grento.

Chapter Eighteen

Larry and Syta practiced his concentration spell for the next couple of days. On the fourth day of his captivity, the women who were usually so attentive towards him, ignored him.

"Tonight is the full moon. We have much to do in order to prepare," Ponta confided in him when asked. This was fine with Larry. He enjoyed a little time to himself.

He wondered how Bob was doing and what adventures he was having. The witches mostly stayed inside their homes. They talked very little and seemed intense in their anticipation. The day passed quickly as Larry took a couple of naps. No dinner was prepared and Larry made do with the meager supplies left in his pack. He watched as the full moon rose over the tops of the trees. Dubla, Ponta, and Syta rearranged their dresses and each wore many various colored scarves

"They are merely ceremonial but very important," said Ponta. "Ceremony and ritual helps create the right perspective." Dubla extinguished the fire Larry was enjoying and the night's darkness was revealed. Larry sat still, not wanting to intrude on whatever was going to happen. He heard the panting of the women who were obviously working on something. As his eyes adjusted to the moonlight he became aware of the silhouetted shapes of the women. They were dancing around the camp. They thrust their arms up towards the moon one second and then crouched to the ground the next. The scarves tied around their bodies flickered and fluttered with the movements of the dance. They looked like wraiths in the night.

In the distance some animal howled and in turn was answered by others. The women also made animal noises sort of grunts and moans. The air was filled with vitality. Everywhere in the night, life surged around them. Larry thought that perhaps this ritual brought the eternal nearer to him. The witches all joined each other in the center of the wood and bent to the ground. When they rose, they communally lifted a goblet. Larry hadn't noticed that before in the darkness. They held the cup above their heads in some symbolic gesture. Dubla put some sort of stick into the cup and waved it at Syta, Syta then took the stick and did the same thing towards Ponta. Ponta repeated the gesture towards Dubla and then they came after Larry.

It was one thing to be an observer but the sight of the three dark wraiths advancing on him was something from a nightmare. No longer were these the women he had grown to trust, but the devil's concubines, with veiled intent. They were on him like the wind and together they grabbed his arm and held it out and then they flicked the stick at his arm. Larry felt something wet splatter all over his forearm. The women let him go and went back to their dancing. Larry tried to wipe off whatever they had splashed on him but there was nothing there. More rituals he thought to himself.

The next morning Larry woke up on his own. Usually the witches woke him. As he stretched and left his dream world for the real one he noticed that Syta was lying next to him. Looking around he saw Dubla and Ponta also sleeping on the ground.

"They must have danced themselves to sleep," thought Larry. Not wanting to wake them, Larry crept quietly over to Dubla's hut. He thought it might be good to practice his concentration spell a little in the peace and quiet of the morning. Then, before he sat down on the rock in front of Dubla's hut, a compulsion to go inside came over him. The doorway beckoned him like a child towards a well. Larry looked back toward the sleeping witches and seeing them still safely asleep, turned and snuck into Dubla's lair.

He had been inside once before when he boldly and un-characteristically stormed in to find out the witch's intentions. That time Dubla's presence had dominated the room. Larry had no idea what would happen to him if he got caught but he didn't want to be a captive forever. Any action, no matter how dangerous was bet-ter than sitting idle. He popped his head out and checked on the witches. They were still sleeping where he had left them. He knew he would have to act fast so he ducked back inside and began to look around.

The dim room revealed a mound of dirt in one corner, Dubla's bed. In the other corner was an old desk covered with trinkets. It looked completely jumbled but Larry was sure that Dubla had her own system for keeping track of things. Time was ticking away and he knew that he couldn't dawdle. He wanted to root through the drawers but perhaps Dubla could tell. Who knew what sort of methods witches had to protect their stuff.

On the back of the desk stood a cage that at first glance appeared to be empty but on closer inspection housed a large praying mantis. It used its large front legs to hold small instruments. It looked like it was knitting something. Two threads entered the cage and fed down to the bug and whatever it was making cascaded into a pile at the bottom of the cage. Larry hoped that it wasn't some sort of record of the goings on inside Dubla's house. The praying mantis cocked its head and looked at Larry looking at it, and continued its work. There was something mechanically scary about the insects stare. Larry forced his attention away from the cage.

In the other corner of the desk was a sandbox. A tiny tornado swept serpentine across its surface picking up sand and redepositing it rearranging the surface. It was very cool to watch and slightly hypnotic. But again Larry forced himself away.

There must be some clue in here or at least something I can understand, thought Larry to himself. How long had he been in here? It seemed like only moments but he didn't know. There was a scuffling sound behind him. Larry turned. Near the bed there was a small coffee table made out of glass. The table contained a maze and inside there were two horrible little creatures. They looked like scorpions except that they were hairy like spiders. A third creature, a tiny man, caught his eye. He seemed to be trying to get away from the two hunters. A breeze blew through the hut and Larry turned to the door. There was no one there. Larry's nerves were fried and he quickly snuck back out of the house. The three sisters were still fast asleep where he had left them. He sat down a ways from the houses and tried to relax. That was a dumb move he thought to himself. He felt bad for the little guy in the maze.

Chapter Nineteen

Bob, Grento and Sargasso left the comfort of Ule. Tock's surprise attack had shaken them. It made sense to leave before Tock could surprise them again. They picked a random direction and walked quickly, spurred on by a now more real threat. Their conversation had been mainly about the attack. How had Tock found them? Where was he now? What could they do, etc. Grento reasoned that they should be fine. They would be hard to track in the woods and they moved much more efficiently than their pursuer. Sargasso was still amazed by the sheer violence and deadliness of the snake. He admitted that initially he hadn't thought too much of their foe. But now he had a new appreciation for what kept them moving.

The distance they were putting between themselves and Larry worried Bob. He wondered how his brother was getting along with the ladies. Probably a lot better than he was doing. Everyone felt horrible for the deaths in Ule. If they had never shown up things would be different. Grento led the way and, although they had no specific destination, they had to move.

The fields of grass gradually gave way to softer ground. Each step landed on light green moss. As Bob stepped over a lumpy bit of moss a slithering shape made his heart stop momentarily. He froze in mid-stride and a large green snake darted away from him.

"Snake," he said feebly.

"What?" said Grento and Sargasso.

"Snake," he said pointing and they both jumped backwards. The snake glided away while the three men quivered.

"A little jumpy Bob?" said Sargasso grinning.

"I just thought you guys might like to see..."

Grento and Sargasso were already moving.

"...the snake," said Bob to himself. He shook a chill off and then ran to catch up to them. From the conversation between Grento and Sargasso, Bob got the impression that neither man had been this way before. Grento's Gelk-sense or whatever it was allowed them to navigate without fear of stumbling into some monster's trap but offered no destination.

The spongy moss clung to their boots with each step. The further they went the harder it became to keep their balance as the moss became slicker and less rooted. Then with a yelp Grento fell and disappeared. Bob and Sargasso froze in their tracks. They looked at each other.

"Grento?" said Sargasso quietly. "Grento!" he shouted when no reply came. Neither man had moved yet.

"I'm okay!" called a disgruntled Grento.

"Where?" answered Sargasso.

"Over here. I fell into a damned hole!"

A wave of relief washed over Bob and Sargasso and both men relaxed their stances. Bob tentatively moved towards where Grento had been leading. The ground was very slippery and he didn't want to join Grento. Grento kept cursing from his hole until Sargasso and Bob ever so carefully peered in over a ledge of mushed moss. Grento was about ten feet down. His hand was bleeding where he had tried to catch himself.

"Are you ok?"

"I'm fine, just get me out of here!" Grento said angrily. He was embarrassed.

Without trees or vines to lower in it might be tough. Luckily the hole wasn't that deep. Bob and Sargasso held onto each other and Bob offered his hand to Grento. Unfortunately they were just short of reaching him.

"Sometimes it's like problems have a mind of their own," muttered Bob. "I mean really, if this job needed a wrench, my wrench would be one size too big or small."

"Patience Bob," said Sargasso. "Sometimes you have to make your own luck...aug!" The moss under Sargasso gave way and he slid, dragging Bob with him, into the hole. After all the cursing died down and they brushed all the mud and moss off, they surveyed their surroundings.

"Nice of you fellows to join me," teased Grento. "That was the plan, was it? Jump down here to get a view from my perspective and then figure out how to get me out? Well, done!"

"Shut up," said Sargasso. The hole was just deep enough to hold them. Bob tried to get a grip on the moss that grew on the sides of the pit. It offered little grip. Sargasso started swinging his arms back and forth apparently preparing to jump as high as he could on the moss hoping to get a foothold. Bob turned to watch this attempt with comic anticipation. Sargasso leapt with the heart of a salmon but as soon as he grabbed at the wall he fell right through. There was no wall just a cavern entrance obscured by hanging moss. Sargasso disappeared through the moss with a squeal followed by a thud and then cursing. Grento called into the mossy darkness, "Are you alright?"

"Yeah I'm fine," came the embarrassed reply.

"That was some jump," said Bob grinning.

"I thought you were going to make it," laughed Grento. Sargasso's head poked out through the moss.

"Laugh it up girls, but I think I might have found us a way out of here!"

The others cautiously felt their way through the moss towards Sargasso. A deep cavern stretched before them.

"Let's see where it goes," said Sargasso with a glint of excitement in his eyes. The cave was large enough for them all to walk side by side. Standing side by side, with the outside man touching the cave wall they inched their way into the darkness. Bob realized that by using this formation they would avoid taking any turns or becoming lost as long as both men on the ends maintained contact with the wall. This was a short-term plan as they all expected the cave to end or a telltale light to reveal the exit. The ground was soft. Years of cave dust blanketed the floor. As they felt their way in the darkness the men joked back and forth to ease the tension. Five minutes in and they were still in perfect dark. The temperature dropped noticeably. It wasn't cold like they were used to. It was cold like all the heat was missing, like emptiness. Bob's mind raced with images of horrible cave monsters. He remembered the sand creature and shivered. Well, he had gotten through that and he couldn't think of anything worse...so he should be ok. But his mind would not stop thinking of possible monsters.

"Don't worry guys," said Sargasso "I don't think that any animals would want to live in this nice dry cave."

"That is not helping," said Bob.

The cave walls slid easily under Sargasso's hand, he was on the left and Grento on the right. The smooth texture of the walls was pleasant though cold. Bob had thought himself lucky to be in the middle when they started out, but now, in the dark he walked forward in constant anticipation of hitting his face on a rock or the ceiling or a bat or a spider web or anything his mind could race to come up with. Deeper they moved into the cave. Bob wondered what could have made this cavern when they saw a light.

The pinpoint of light was unusually bright, as their eyes had become accustomed to the dark. The light came from so far away it looked like a star.

"Never a doubt," said Sargasso.

"Yep," said Bob.

"We are not out yet," said Grento quietly. The men walked towards the opening. The light became slightly less painful as their eyes adapted. It looked to be a great distance off but they soon found themselves within twenty feet of it. Grento and Sargasso's grip on Bob's shoulders tightened sharply

"Stop," they said in unison. Bob froze where he was standing.

"There is a change here," said Sargasso.

"My side too," said Grento. "Back up one step."

The men took a step back. Bob stood still while Sargasso and Grento felt the edges of the walls trying to determine where the cave was going.

"The cave veers left" Sargasso concluded.

"No, it turns to the right," said Grento.

"Nope, although those were both good guesses," said Bob "it drops straight off."

The men felt around the cave floor where Bob knelt and there was no doubt, the cave ended in a drop off. They looked longingly at the shaft of light. Although the hole was but a pinhole, they felt confident that they could make it larger. Three men digging would make quick work of the cave wall. But now they would have to turn back. The thought of the excruciatingly slow walk back through the dark didn't appeal to them.

"Do you think there's anyway to get over there?" Grento asked. Bob pulled out his matches. "Let's see." He struck the match and the bright flame hurt their eyes. Quickly he dropped it hoping to send it over the edge. Of course it stuck to his fingers slightly and dropped to the ground at his feet illuminating his boots. He kicked at it trying to knock it over but succeeded only in kicking cave dirt onto it extinguishing it.

"I'm not going to say anything," said Sargasso holding back a chuckle.

"We already know where your boots are Bob, maybe we should drop a match over the side to see how far down it is?" said Grento.

"What a good idea!" said Bob sarcastically. He lit another and managed to drop it over the edge. He watched it fall like a little shooting star streaking into the unknown. It only fell a short ways and then landed on the floor. They watched the fire and the circle of illumination it provided. It cast light revealing a smooth floor approximately eleven feet below them. Quietly the flame finished its dinner and they were left in the dark again.

"Well what do you guys think?" asked Bob.

"Well, I'm a forward kind of man," answered Sargasso.

"Down is easier than up," added Grento.

"What if we can't enlarge the hole? We might be trapped," said Bob.

"I think we have just as much chance of climbing our way back up to here as climbing out of the hole Grento fell in," said Sargasso.

Grento snorted at the label, "hole Grento fell in."

"It should be easy to climb this rock. Much easier than that stupid wet moss," said Sargasso.

They agreed and Sargasso went first. He felt his way to the edge and slowly lowered himself over as far as he could and then in the darkness he let go. He called out while he fell, probably to ease his nerves. It was a short fall. He landed with a thud and a grunt and then shouted up to the others, "Wow! What a rush! I wish I were up there with you men so I could do that again. What a feeling!"

"Just go see if we will be able to dig our way out of this hole," said Grento.

"You had better crawl towards the light Sargasso," warned Bob. "For all we know, there could be another drop off."

"That I will," said Sargasso. Sargasso scuttled to the light without any problems. He talked his way there, letting Bob and Grento know all about how lucky they were to still have the blind fall ahead of them. Once at the wall, Sargasso dug at the small hole and succeeded in making it slightly bigger.

"It looks like we will be able to get out," shouted Sargasso. "As a matter of fact this feels like it is a door!" Sargasso continued working on the hole and the light was coming through a crack where a door was built into the rock face. "I am going to need your help," he finally concluded. "This door is made out of rock and is too heavy for me to open."

So Grento and Bob took their turns jumping into the darkness to join Sargasso. Bob insisted that they crawl and Grento agreed. Soon they were assisting Sargasso in trying to open the door.

There was no handle so they tried pushing but it wouldn't budge. After a lot of heaving and cussing they went back to work cleaning the crack around the door to let in more light. All the work didn't help them to budge the door at all. Bob found a torch stuck into the wall on the left side of the door and then Sargasso confirmed that there was another on the right side.

"Well someone built a door to this room, it makes sense that they would have a way to see," said Bob.

They struck a match and lit the torch. The flame took slowly. The room they had come to know through touch and imagination was revealed. It wasn't big. They could now see the maw of the cave that had brought them here. Grento and Sargasso glanced up at it casually joking about how short the drop was from the cave to the ground. Sargasso quipped that he had seen babies fall out of taller trees without so much as a complaint. Bob stared at the way the cave that had led them here jutted out over this room with a concave curve beneath it. He started to say something and then swallowed wrong and had to cough to right himself.

"What's that you are trying to say?" asked Grento still grinning from Sargasso's comments.

Bob cleared his throat. "It's a trap," he said.

"What do you mean it's a trap?" asked Sargasso.

"Look at it," said Bob exasperated. "It is a classic trap. Almost every trap I've ever made is based upon this principle. Lure something into an opening that they can climb down into but not out of again. Look at how the room is carved out from under the cave's mouth. We can't climb that."

"But we weren't lured in Bob. You make it sound so desperate and sinister," said Grento.

"What was the light then? It pulled us like a beacon in the night, like a guiding star. Hell, I even pretended it was a guiding star."

"Well if it's some sort of giant trap, whoever made it is long since dead," said Grento.

"*The undisturbed cave dust attests to the fact that no one has been here for a very long time," said Sargasso. The light from the torch would not light the room entirely. The darkness closed in around the halos of torchlight. The torches wouldn't burn forever so they explored the room. They started with the floor. If there were any drop-offs or hazards it would be nice to know about them. They stayed together under the umbrella of light. They circled the perimeter of the room looking for additional passages and when they were about a quarter of the way around the room, they found one.

This tributary of a cave was only large enough to allow one man through at a time. With limited options and time running out Sargasso took the torch and headed into the cave. Grento and Bob watched the flickering torchlight reflect off of the ancient walls until it softened to black.

Bob stood there in the cold futility of a trap and thought about his brother. He knew that because of his idiocy he might not be able to return to save him. Of course Larry was condemned to live out his days in the company of three women while he was going to die in a hole with two men. He knew he was being overly dramatic in his morbid fantasy but he felt entitled to a few moments of self-pity.

"Whoa!" came a shout from Sargasso. "You guys have got to see this!'

"What is it?" shouted Bob.

The torchlight grew brighter on the cave walls. In another moment Sargasso joined the group.

"Is it a way out?" asked Grento eagerly.

"No it is something..." Sargasso let the thought hang in dank air, and then dissolve into the silence. "Well I've never seen anything like it. It sure took me by surprise. Come on you will need to see this yourselves."

Sargasso led them in single file towards whatever. The cave opened into a little room. They all fell in besides Sargasso and in the center of the room was a table made of rock and beside it sat an empty chair, also made out of rock, the other side, in another chair, sat a man.

He was covered in cave dust and carved out of stone. Although he was part of the chair in which he sat he had a spooky realism to him. The men brought the torch closer to the man's face. Erie shadows danced across his frozen countenance.

"Look at the detail on him!" said Sargasso.

"It's amazing," said Bob. "It even has eye lashes."

"It looks like he sat down to dinner and froze in place."

Bob wiped his hand over the surface of the table, brushing up dust. Under the dust was some sort of design and even some writing. 185

"What's this?" he said using both hands to clean off the table.

"It's a design. Whoever built this statue and table set probably signed it there or made a tribute to whoever was rich enough to have commissioned the work," said Grento.

They lowered the torch to the table but could make no guess as to the designs meaning. Along the side of the table there was some writing that they could read. As Bob brushed dirt off of the side, Sargasso held the torch near.

"Whoa," a startled Grento exclaimed. "Its hand moved."

"What?" asked Bob.

"Your friend is right." The statue opened its eyes. All three men jumped back and the light dimmed on the statue. "There is no reason to be afraid," continued the statue in a calm relaxed and comforting voice.

"You can talk?" stammered Bob.

"Obviously sir," came the reply.

"What the hell is going on?" asked Sargasso.

"Are you a machine of some kind?" asked Bob.

"No sir, although I guess I must look quite strange to you, but I assure you that I'm a living man."

"But that's impossible. You were a stone-cold, dust-covered statue a minute ago," said Grento. The statue/man was becoming more alive and animated by the second.

"I am a man."

"What are you doing down here?" asked Bob.

"I was trying to get out of this trap."

"What do you mean?"

"Whether you know it or not, you are in a trap and the only way out is to sit in the chair and play 'Trench.'"

"I've never heard of that game," said Bob.

"Well it's rather simple unless one is foolish."

"Why are you sitting there still? Why didn't you play the game and get out of here?"

"Oh, yes, well one has to win the game to open the door and I'm afraid I made a couple of dumb moves."

"Whom do you play against? Where are they?"

"Oh you see... you play against the table."

"Against the table? That's preposterous!"

"No sir, it's simple and it's true. There is a drawback, if you lose the game then you can't get up out of the chair and the door doesn't open."

"How long have you been sitting here?" asked Grento.

"Oh, I have no idea but judging by your outlandish garb I would guess at least twenty years."

"That is impossible! How did you live? What did you eat? It's not possible."

"The table took care of that. You see when I lost my game, I froze solid like a stone, but my brain continued to function. What an agony I have endured! I have been alone in the dark with only memory and fantasy to keep me sane. But now you have come as I knew you would. Soon we'll all be free of the trap."

"What do you mean? You want one of us to sit in the other chair and play the game? That's crazy we don't even know how to play."

"Oh but you don't have to know. I know how to play and I can help you win. There is no doubt we will be victorious as I've had nothing but time to go over every aspect of the game, every nuance, every move I could have made, and the repercussions of that move. I will help you win. It's in my best interest. When you win, the table will release both of us and the door will open and I will finally walk free."

"This all sounds too incredible to believe," said Sargasso.

"Why would somebody build a table with a game that would open the door?" asked Bob.

"Gentle sirs, I assure you that I don't know why this was built but I am sure it will work. Everything is spelled out along the side of the table. Read for yourselves."

Bob looked at the side where the figure pointed and there was writing along the edge but it was in a language that he had never seen before.

"Do either of you speak whatever language this is?" asked Bob pointing at the carving.

"Nope."

"I'm afraid not."

"Well you can take my word for it," said the man. "Remember, we share a common interest."

Sargasso motioned the others over to him. "Let's go survey the big room again, and get some privacy."

The other men nodded and started towards the exit.

"You can't just leave me here. Please reconsider."

"We will be right back," said Sargasso gruffly. "We want to use the light of the torch to see if this really is a trap like you say."

They left him there mumbling to himself in the dark. Sargasso wanted to see how tough it was going to be to climb out and he wasted little time handing Grento the torch and trying.

Bob assisted him and try as they might, the shape of the room simply wouldn't let them out. If they had used a rope to lower themselves down it would be no problem. They tried the door again. They pooled what tools they had at their disposal and even with the help of knives they couldn't make significant headway against the door.

"Well," said Grento. "We know that there's some truth to what he is saying because he is stuck to that chair and he was a damn statue when we got there. If he has really been down here for twenty years without food or water there must be magic involved."

"I agree," said Sargasso, "but this is very strange. I certainly don't want to end up like him, stuck in a chair forever. Whatever curse is on this place I want nothing to do with it. We will dig our way out. Even if it takes a long time. With three of us, I think we can do it.

The mumbling continued from the side cave. Bob strained to make out the words while Sargasso dug at the edge of the door with his knife.

"There is no other way," came the faint voice to Bob's ears. "Give in to your reason. I can assure you safe passage. Please don't let fear of the unknown seal all of our fates. I have waited so long for someone to come along and beat this wicked game. One wrong move has cost me my freedom. Oh we are so close... so close," and then the voice stopped.

Bob continued to listen but that was it. The end of the soliloquy. "Bob, could you give me a hand? Let's try this door again," said Sargasso.

Bob and Grento helped Sargasso. Their efforts produced a lot of sweat but little results.

"Well, that door isn't going anywhere," joked Grento

"Yeah I am glad we finally got it shut," said Bob.

Sargasso gave them an unamused stare.

"Oh, you wanted me to pull?" continued Bob grinning.

"Let's face the facts," said Grento. "There's a possibility that we will not be able to dig out of this hole. It stands to reason that whoever designed this pit planned for the contingency that we might try to get out."

"So what are you saying? That you want to take a seat in that crazy chair?" asked Sargasso.

"No, of course not," said Grento. "I think we should have Bob sit in the crazy chair."

"Now you are talking," said Sargasso.

"Very funny," said Bob. The other two men continued to stare at him without smiling. The weight of the inevitable pulled down Bob's mood. Bob began to feel a little uncomfortable but as he had already decided that one of them should try the table he said, "Sit in a chair...play a game... it seems that I get all the cushy jobs."

Sargasso and Grento smiled.

As they returned to the little room they had to light the other torch. Now there was a timer of sorts on their cave adventure. The men knew that they needed to get out of the cave before the torch was out or they would be once again in darkness.

The man in the chair had returned to his statue state and the men took the moment to stare candidly at him and his table. As if his countenance might reveal some truth about their situation. Nothing revealed itself. There was just a stone in the shape of a man seated at a table with firelight playing on its stoic features. Bob brushed dust off of the top of the table as he had done before and once again this breathed life into the sleeping figure.

"Oh, joy! My friends you have not abandoned me and gone to your graves in futile endeavor. So you have decided to play the game?" he asked with eyes that gleamed with frenzied anticipation.

"Not quite," said Bob. "Why didn't you simply play the game again after you lost? You say you know how to beat it."

"Oh, didn't I tell you? The stakes change if you play twice. It's all spelled out in the rules written on the side of the table."

"We can't read the rules...remember?" said Sargasso crossly.

"Oh that's right...well if I played a second time and won I would die. I have been saving that option for when the boredom becomes unbearable. The hope of you showing up has sustained me."

The men let this new knowledge sink in. Grento and Sargasso were quiet. How could they ask their friend to risk his life? Bob was the best choice. His aptitude for puzzles had already been proven. Even the best chance might be the wrong one. How could they tell Larry that they had stood by and watched as his brother turned into stone. This decision was Bob's alone.

"Well," said Bob slapping his hands together. "How do I play?"

The statue explained the rules of 'Trench'. It seemed relatively straightforward. Bob played a game in Agea Hills that was somewhat similar. The game consisted of the table covered with concentric circles. Within the circles there were spaces. Along the outer ring were the player's main pieces. The object of the game was to get one's main piece into the center of the board and occupy the center circle. After the three men were sure that they understood the rules, they went through the various strategies. The statue told them what sort of moves to expect from the table and how they would counter them.

"The torch is starting to get low," said Grento. Bob looked at the other men's faces and saw that they were grim.

"Sit, sit, there is nothing to fear the sooner we start the sooner we will all be out of here. Oh I am going to eat all the sweets I can get my hands on! Oh how I have missed the taste of pies," said the statue.

191

Bob spun his arms in circles, did a couple of deep knee bends, and cracked his neck from side to side and with deliberate movement sat down in the chair.

As soon as he was in the chair the table came to life. Lights glowed from the circles on the board creating a hologram effect. Pieces that before had only been described, appeared on the board and lined themselves up in front of him like little soldiers.

The statue man tossed his head back so that Bob could only see the underside of his chin and then he brought his head forward again and fixed his eyes on Bob's. They no longer looked like the benign eyes of a friendly fool. They were confident and glaring and crazed. The eyes of a madman. Cruel laughter trickled out of him and he coughed up cave dust. Each cackle looked like he was breathing fire. Grento and Sargasso instinctively jumped back. Although the statue man was physically unchanged the character difference in him was palpable.

"What's this," Bob started to say but the statue cut him off.

"Fool, fool, fool! All these years of waiting...like a damned spider in a dark corner. Oh yes! It feels so good." He continued to rant and cough up dust and cackle like a madman. Bob and company stared in amazement and wonder as he raved.

"Don't you see?" he continued. "You don't..."

Bob noticed that there were game pieces in front of the statue as well. "Play against the table...you play against me! All these years I have practiced how I would trick someone into sitting down with me. Just as I was tricked so long ago. All those years of playing the game over and over in my head. Ensuring myself victory when my day would come."

Bob tried to get out of the chair instinctively but he was stuck to it. He didn't struggle because it was apparent that he couldn't even use his leg muscles to strain against the bond.

"What if I refuse to play you?" asked Bob.

"That is your choice. But if you don't play we will sit here forever. I am used to that by now. But you, you will surely go mad from the boredom and hopelessness. You do not have my willpower to stave off insanity. The longer you wait to play me the duller your wits will be. Your best chance is to play now while you can think clearly. I have been sporting with you. I have told you the rules of the game or have I...you fools will not know until it is too late." He went on laughing maniacally. "And the longer you wait the worse your odds. I relish this, oh, a perfect plan. As I was duped I have tricked you. Sweet revenge."

"Can I talk this over with my friends or better yet can they help me with my strategy?"

"Of course. Three empty glasses quench a thirst no better than one. You bastards."

Bob looked at Grento and Sargasso. They both looked a little lost. For a moment he'd felt a little hopeless himself but that feeling was quickly shrugged off. The one thing that Bob was good at, really good at, was looking at a problem, no matter how hopeless and coming up with a good solution. The current problem had the feel of a challenge to him. "Well, don't just stand there, get over here and let's discuss my strategy. I'm ready to play."

Bob twisted his torso as much as he could, to allow himself to face away from his opponent and confer in private with his team-mates.

"Yes, please, by all means use all your resources."

Bob and the guys continued to whisper amongst them-selves. After a couple of minutes Bob turned back to his opponent. "Who goes first?" asked Bob calmly.

"Ah, Bob, I am afraid that the challenger goes second. Shall I begin?"

"Good luck," said Bob.

This brought on a snort of laughter, "Indeed! It is you who should pray for luck." Then the laughter turned to hatred. "You insolent little worm! You will grow to rue that comment. You will go over this conversation a thousand times in your head while you sit here frozen and trapped."

Bob stared calmly into the man's eyes. This infuriated him even more and then he calmed down and returned Bob's placid stare. The statue smiled and in the same motion selected one of the game pieces placing it in the outermost ring of the game board.

The circles changed colors with the addition of the piece. Bob studied the move. The piece was one of the insignificant pieces of the collection. It served usually to hold a location and that was it. Not defensive and without attack capabilities. Bob took his time. The pieces in front of him represented nearly limitless possible moves. He knew that there was the chance the statue had lied to him about the rules.

His confident opponent appeared anxious to get the match over with. Bob figured that the rules of the game were very similar to what he had been told. The statue wanted him to be able to play and certainly lose. From the description of the game and the capabilities of the pieces, Bob calculated how many moves it would take the statue to win if everything went the statue's way. Bob liked to know the parameters of the game. In this case, Bob figured if he advanced one piece undeterred towards the center of the board at each crossing vector it would take a minimum of twelve moves. Of course any one piece wouldn't be allowed to reach the center without much finagling.

The pieces were problematic. The first piece played seemed straightforward but some of the others would take some practice. One of the pieces, called the 'time traveler', was shaped like a little man wearing a funny hat. This piece fascinated Bob because according to the rules as presented, it could travel in time. Once put into play the piece could revert backwards to whatever space it had occupied three turns ago or the piece could vanish from the game entirely traveling backwards to the point before it was put into play. Bob chose this piece to start his game.

"Interesting choice," oozed the statue. He grabbed a piece that looked like a woman with her hands raised above her head, and placed it on the board. Bob took his time selecting his next move. Sargasso and Grento stood on either side of the table helplessly watching their fate be decided by a rigged game.

Sargasso shifted from foot to foot while Grento kept clearing his throat and occasionally said, "Take your time."

The speed of the game picked up as both players got all of their pieces into play. The statue moved with precision. It appeared that he had spent his time anticipating every possible move and the counter move to follow it. Twice the statue pointed out possible moves that he had failed to mention as he played these new rules to his advantage. Sargasso voiced his objections to these blatant strategic omissions. Bob just trudged along doing the best that he could and trying to understand the game better. Grento tried to follow the back and forth of the strategies but found himself having trouble. Bob began to talk strategy with the statue, commenting on his moves. At first these comments elicited little response but as Bob persistently talked about the game the statue responded.

"Do you see how your game is doomed yet?" snickered the statue.

"No, I still have hope."

"Well you have been doomed since your seventh move. It's obvious to anyone who sees this board."

They continued to play. Bob took his time and the statue was ready with the correct corresponding move before Bob had moved his arm back from placing the piece.

"Oh," said Bob after the statue moved, "I think I'm beginning to see what you mean, I'm running out of options."

"That you are. You only have two moves left before I win."

"That can't be true," said Bob. "I see how you have me here. That I give you, but don't you see how I've got this woman piece to within one of the final circle?"

"One away! Ha! Yes, fools look at the board and see that it is one away and think that means something. You have to be able to move it that one space and I will never give you the free move required to move it. You might as well need to move 20 squares, it is the same."

"Well of course that isn't my only strategy," said Bob "I'm still developing other pieces and in a little while they will come into play."

"Developing other pieces?" spat the statue. "As I said, you only have two moves left."

"Uh, oh fellows, I believe he might be right I better do something fast." Sargasso and Grento quickly moved to the table and each of them grabbed one of the statues arms.

"Ugh! What is this?" The statue fought trying to free his arms. But Grento and Sargasso were able to use their weight and securely held the arms. Bob meanwhile placed his next move and then stretched his arms across the board and made the statues move for him. Bob then returned his hand to his piece and moved it into the center circle. The winning piece glowed purple in recognition of the victory and then the table's lights turned off and the pieces disappeared and, quick as a crawdad, Bob got out of his seat. Sargasso and Grento released the thrashing arms and jumped back a step.

"Traitorous, bastard, horrible, evil cheaters!" it screamed and shrieked and made noises that weren't much more than expressions of utter agony.

"No time to waste," Sargasso said pointing at the cave's tunnel. There was a dim light emanating from it. They ran through the twisting shaft aided by the light. When they reached the main part of the trap, there, right where they had left it, stood the door to the outside. But this time, it was open.

Chapter Twenty

Dubla shook the dried-up leathery bag. The drawstring that sealed its opening couldn't contain the blood and the red liquid oozed and spurted out with each violent shake. Her stomach clenched and she told herself she was being stupid. There was no way that this young man could be one of the lost. They had been exterminated. Bander's great triumph that put him in power all those years ago. If one survived, who knew what the repercussions could be? The bag in her hands was a shifting sack. She used it to store her comb and other practical trinkets. Neither of her sisters knew of its secret powers. She kept a few guarded truths to herself and she was sure that they did the same. Her sisters had eaten lots of Cullah root tonight, of that she had been sure. Their sleep afforded her the time to dash her foolish fears. The blood that sloshed between her fingers and ran down her forearms was her own. She felt lightheaded from the loss. She had to use enough to fill the sack. The little magic left in the shifting sack slept deeply and only a witch's blood could rouse it.

She rotated the bag in front of her. The contents swirled against the sack and with bated breath she set the bag down on the dirt and backed away. She watched the ripples in the outside of the bag while the contents continued to swirl. Now they circled on their own. The drawstring began to slip open. It was as if invisible hands continued to swing the bag in circles faster and faster. Blood started to spatter up out of the sack as the centrifugal force got too great for the container. Dubla felt her heart beating in time with the rhythm of the bag. Then the drawstring gave out and the contents splattered all over the dirt in a bloody circle with the bag at the center. Dubla crawled over to the edge of the mess and looked down at the pattern of the little bones she used in the sack.

Dubla shook her head, "No, this is impossible," she muttered to herself. She rushed to collect each blood-covered bone and kicked dirt over the scene. When she was sure that no one could tell what she had done here, she absconded with the shifting-sack back into her hut.

*　*　*

Larry enjoyed his time with the witches. He liked talking to them. They each wanted private conversations with him. Each wanted to glean special individual secrets that the other two weren't privy to. They cooked for him and the Cullah root was heaven. A few words before he sampled any meal had it tasting like the best of whatever they mentioned. Of course he slept a lot. The root had that effect on him, but life was easy so he indulged himself. After all, he was doing his part, waiting for his brother and friends to return. He practiced his "magic" from time to time but he had lost most of his interest in that. He wondered what was going on with Bob and Grento and Sargasso.

After a delicious bowl of spiderworm soup, which tasted just like sirloin stew, he stared at the night sky while he felt the Cullah root drug his mind. Waves of dizziness washed through his brain. He let his eyes partially close, smearing the starlight into fuzzy halos. His thoughts began circling around and around a whirlpool of consciousness each time he spun around one side the centrifugal force would open his eyes a little bit and then they would close until he went down the hole and slept.

Two hours before dawn the drug released its grip on Larry but still he slept. That is, until he felt the small hand slip over his mouth. As far as ways to wake up go, this ranks near the bottom of the list. The hand was sweating and smelled bad. Larry thrashed around flailing his arms and futilely kicking out with his legs. The hand clamped firm on his mouth and another grabbed the back of his head. It felt as if someone was trying crush his skull between their little monkey arms. Larry made violent snorting sounds as he struggled.

"Easy," said the voice of his assailant.

200

Larry couldn't see who held him.

"Larry, be quiet," said the voice brusquely.

Larry jolted at the sound of his name. This wasn't the voice of any of the witches nor was it Bob. Could it be Sargasso? Larry stopped struggling but remained keenly on edge. The grip didn't slacken.

"Listen to me very carefully," said the scratchy voice in his ear. "You're in grave danger. The witches are almost done with you. They are not to be trusted. Do you understand?" Larry nodded his head. "Good." The hands still held his head firm and his mouth shut. But as Larry wasn't struggling, it wasn't too firm. "Know this Larry, before I let you go, I could have left you. I could have let them have you. You were out of my way." Larry nodded again. This wasn't Sargasso.

"If you scream, I will break your neck." Larry wasn't a fighter by any means, mostly because he had the strength of a spring rain. He didn't scream and he didn't fight. The grip relaxed around his head and then tentatively the hands let go.

"Who are you?" whispered Larry.

"My name is Torth. I am the man from the maze."

Larry heard the words but they didn't make sense to him. He wasn't about to question someone who was obviously in charge of the situation. "We do not have time for a lot of questions right now," Torth said as if reading Larry's mind. "I'll answer your questions later. Right now we need to get out of here!"

The words struck a chord of nostalgia with Larry. He had sort of forgotten about leaving his home with the girls.

"Leave?" he whispered.

"That's right. We are going to escape, follow me." Torth grabbed Larry's arm and pulled him through the darkness. Larry thought that Torth's strength was increasing, his hand felt bigger too. Was some other person leading him on now? Torth pulled Larry away from the witch's huts and towards the edge of the forest.

"The worms," Larry began.

Torth cut him off. "Don't worry about the worms."

Larry was dragged through the dark towards the edge of the trees. The arm that pulled him seemed like it was hooked up to a horse. When they got to the edge they stopped. Larry heard the rustling of hundreds of Spiderworm feet crawling around the dense trees.

"We will wait here until the sun comes out enough that we can see," Torth said, and then as an afterthought, "Do not talk and do not move." Although the voice was but a deep whisper there was all the conviction in it of a father towards his kids in church.

Larry sat down and was quiet. He looked at the fading stars. How close he was to the edge of the trees he couldn't be sure but from the sound of the spiderworms he was right next to them. Who was this Torth? It sounded like he was busy digging.

Larry felt very uncomfortable. It was one thing to let himself be whisked away. That all happened so fast, he was groggy and scared. Now as he sat in the dark listening to scary noises he wasn't so sure whatever was happening was for his benefit. He could call out to the witches surely they could save him from Torth. What was the plan anyway? There was no way out. No way past the worms. Whoever this fellow was he was going to be killed and eaten by giant worms. That didn't sound like something Larry wanted anything to do with. What had Torth said about the witches being bad? That was surely a lie. Larry's mind was almost made up when the sun broke over the horizon. In the dim light that filtered through the Tanglewood trees Larry saw the writhing mass of worms. And out of the corner of his eye he saw Torth for the first time. The man was huge.

"Ready," Torth's whisper carried through the still morning air. Larry was about to say no when Torth bent down and picked up a big rock. With a grunt he threw the rock all the way across the clearing to the other side of the witches homes and into the trees. Torth bent down and picked up another rock and threw it to the same place and then a third in rapid succession. The big worms near them obviously felt the vibrations of the rocks banking off of the distant trees for they immediately went after the disturbance. Torth threw one more rock, this one he threw even farther. Then he turned to Larry and with eyes big and serious he grabbed him and threw him over his shoulder and ran into the trees.

There were still worms on the branches just not the big giant ones. The little ones bit at Torth as he crashed through the forest. Larry was scared as hell. He bounced while Torth carried him like a sack of potatoes. Worms dropped onto Larry's back and crawled under his shirt biting him over and over. The pain was excruciating and Larry bucked and kicked trying to get away from them. Torth wouldn't let him go and forced his way through the openings in the trees.

Every time a cluster of trees seemed too congested to run through, he tore at the branches with his free hand and ripped the trees apart like weeds. The big worms realized their mistake and pursued the pair of escapees. Torth ran like a man possessed. Larry was delirious with pain. The hand that secured him felt like a steel vise and blood ran down from it. Larry's head was jostled all around and his view of the world was as well. He could see the big worms coming though. Giant ferocious monsters with fever-ish intent swarmed over the trees and the broken remains of trees that marked Torth's path through their home. The home that they protected. And then there was grass. Larry watched the trees slip into the distance and the frightening shape of worms cover them like ants over a hill.

Torth set Larry down on the ground and then sat down himself and although he was covered nearly completely in cuts and his own blood, he began to laugh. As the sun rose over the grassy field Torth's deep laughter filled the air and in spite of the pain from bites, Larry laughed too.

Chapter Twenty One

Larry looked towards the edge of the trees, to the frenzied worms. He couldn't believe that he had been inside the Tangle-woods and back again.

Torth rolled on the ground in sheer delight like a dog on a summer day. He was huge, Larry guessed that he must be nine or ten feet tall. The dirt and grass stuck to his blood but he didn't seem to care. Larry didn't know if he should feel grateful or scared or what.

"Freedom," said Torth to himself and he rolled some more.

"I can't believe you made it through the trees and the worms," said Larry. "That we made it. I thought it was impossible."

Larry stared at the big man. Although he was lying on the grass and dirt, he could tell how incredibly large he was. He almost looked like a different animal, not human because he was four or five sizes bigger than a man. His neck was as broad across as Larry's entire forearm from elbow to hand.

"Well, Larry," Torth said smiling. His full voice sounded like a bass singer's early in the morning. "We had better put some distance between us and those hags. I doubt they would leave the protection of the trees, but who knows and they seemed to be growing rather attached to you."

Larry was scared and still in a bunch of pain.

"Ok," he said, afraid of this behemoth of a man.

Torth stood up, like a grizzly bear. Larry stood up as well. It seemed like the thing to do. The worm bites throbbed like burns from splattered bacon grease. He could only imagine how bad all the worm bites on Torth hurt. Being a big man has its disadvantages too, more surface for the worms to bite.

"Let's go see if we can find Sargasso and that brother of yours."

"How do you know my brother and Sargasso," asked Larry wincing in pain from the bites.

"I heard the witches talking about you guys," said Torth.

Larry looked confused. "What?" he said.

"Let's talk while we walk. I will explain some things to you. There's a bit that you should know."

Larry and the big man walked away from the trees.

"Where too?" asked Larry.

"Do you see that tall mountain over there?"

"Yes."

"And do you see that growth of trees off to the left?"

"Yes."

"Let's aim for right between them,"

"But there is nothing there."

"Exactly," said Torth. "People always aim for a landmark. If I was a creepy crawly I would wait for my food right between land marks and seeing as our starting point is the edge of a forest we should aim at the open areas."

"That's a good idea," said Larry. Wow this guy is smart too. Larry thought to himself. Why do people think that size and brains don't go together.

They walked towards the space between the landmarks. The flat prairie grass made it easy hiking. They walked in silence for a while. Larry's thoughts were pretty much absorbed into thoughts like 'Ouch, this hurts.' Or 'make it stop'. 'Stupid worms.' The walking did them good as it pumped the worm's poison through their systems. After a while the pain began to subside.

"So how do you know my name and my friends?" Larry asked meekly. The size and strength of Torth was as intimidating as a crazy fighting dog.

"I told you that I'm the man you saw in the maze. I overheard the witch's conversations when they were in Dubla's room and they talked plenty about you and your friends. I would listen to them with keen interest as I'm sick of their usual mumblings."

"How did you get out of the maze, or rather, how did you get in it?"

"Once the witches caught me. I wouldn't give them the pleasure of my conversation. Their stupid mind games wouldn't work on me, no offense."

"Oh, n, n, n, none taken," said Larry thinking that over.

"So the witches resorted to torture. They tried everything they could think of; worms in the ears, pins up my nose, they pulled out my toenails with a pliers, but I wouldn't talk to them."

"How in the world did you endure that kind of torture?" asked Larry grimacing at the thought.

"Well as you can see, I'm not exactly the same as you, no offense, for one I am about twice as big as you or," he looked Larry up and down, "maybe I am three times as big, anyway I also have a high endurance to pain. That was easy to explain. I'm bigger, much bigger and I can handle my pain much better."

"You don't say," said Larry. "So all those worm bites didn't hurt?"

"Sure they stung a little but I hardly noticed them."

"So how did you end up in the maze-box?"

"Well, those diabolical witches figured out that I wouldn't dance through their hoops no matter how much they tortured me. So they took away my size. Somehow they shrunk me while

I slept. They put me in the cage with those demon-things. While they closed the lid they taunted me and told me that no matter how much pain I could endure that one sting from either of the creatures was sure death. They had figured out how to get though my hide, those witches! Without my strength I could not escape and because I couldn't rely on my toughness against the stingers on those things I had to run and hide. It makes me sick to even admit to it now but those critters chased me around like a cat after a fly.

"The witches would spend hours gazing into my personal hell and commenting on the choices I made in maneuvering the maze. They would talk to me, pretending to be helping me only to steer me into the path of the monsters. They would watch with delight as I fought for my life and ran away through blind alleys and turns that could lead back to the monsters. They always told me that there was a way out if I could only find it. I knew there was no way out"

"What did you do?"

"I waited." The witches get bored easily and I knew that I would become yesterday's soup soon enough. One night after Dubla fed and watered me and my roommates, she left the lid slightly askew. I could have climbed out if it weren't for the beasties chasing me. That night I ran myself almost to death trying to lure them away from the opening so that I could sneak by, but one of them always cut me off. After that night I vowed the next time there was a gap in the casing I'd make my escape or die trying. Once the witches got you and your friends, Dubla became more careless with my cage. Some days she would forget to feed me altogether but I was happy because I knew that she would slip up with the lid and sure enough, last night, she did.

She came in late. She looked really pale and her arm was bleeding. She must have needed sleep terribly because she dumped a whole pile of Cullah root shavings into her tea and drank it down in one gulp. The drug hit her so hard she stumbled to her bed and fell into my cage on her way. She knocked the lid askew as she fell onto her bed. I took my chance."

"That is an amazing story," said Larry.

As they walked, Larry gradually began to feel sort of comfortable in Torth's company. Torth seemed to be on his side and having a giant for a friend... well, maybe Torth wasn't a giant but he was the biggest guy Larry had ever seen. They continued to walk and talk. A gentle breeze waved the prairie grass back and forth.

"So that explains the little hand that clamped over my mouth when I was sleeping."

"That was me, I was in the process of returning to my usual size at that point. I waited until I thought I was big enough to handle you before I woke you, no offense."

Larry shook his head to indicate none taken. "So a, are, are, are you going to g, g, get bigger?" asked Larry.

"Nope I'm back to normal," said Torth.

"Your normal is pretty b, is pretty big," said Larry. "You said that the witches were evil or something and I, well, after what you have been through, well, I understand why you would feel that way but they sure acted nice to me," said Larry "No offense."

Torth looked questioningly at Larry, sizing him up, then he made some decision about Larry's comment and burst into bellowing laughter. "None taken!" he howled.

Larry smiled at Torth's amusement at his joke but his smile lost some of the acuteness at its edges while he watched the thickness of the muscles jiggling on Torth's body. Torth's laughter faded to a distant thunder.

"I'm starving," Torth said. "Larry do you mind if we rest for a minute? Maintaining this frame takes a lot of nourishment."

"Not at all, I could use the rest. My nerves are still a little jumpy from the, er, our morning jog. Torth didn't laugh at this forced attempt at humor. Perhaps to him, plunging through the dim light of a worm-infested wood was a morning jog. "I only have a couple of small things to eat in my pack, some dried meat and well let's see..."

"No need my friend, keep your food. I'll fend for myself." Torth stepped to the side and pulled up some of the prairie grass and began shoving it into his mouth.

"What? You're eating grass?" asked Larry incredulously.

"Sure, grass is my main food. Man I would never get full if I had to chase rabbits for meals. How did you think a big thing like myself could maintain my energy?"

"I guess, but yuck, doesn't that taste bad?"

"No, on the contrary, it's very good."

Torth kept shoveling grass into his mouth and the conversation died down. Larry picked at his meager rations, mostly bits of dried food that he'd carried since Agea Hills. He was going to need to find food quickly if he was going to survive. Life in the circle had been simple. His thoughts drifted to how he was going to find his brother. Bob would have headed for whatever place had the best chance of finding people to bring back to the witches. Torth continued to graze. He reminded Larry of a cow or maybe a horse back home, a happy content animal chewing on some grass.

"Those ladies weren't so kind to you as you think Larry," said Torth between bites.

"What do you mean?" asked Larry.

"Well, about two weeks ago I was in my cage and Dubla and Syta were tormenting me. There was a strange sound out in the circle. They went out to investigate. Apparently it was someone they knew and someone nefarious. He walked calmly right through the protective forest and the worms let him pass. They parted for him like pigeons around your feet. The worms didn't attack him and they acted as though they didn't want to get stepped on. Everything I'm telling you is based upon hearsay. The witches talked about this encounter on and on and when they were in Dubla's house,

I listened. At some parts of what I overheard I thought perhaps they were speaking in my presence for my benefit, you know some sort of cruel mental game, but I heard something from outside of Dubla's hut that was not fake, and corroborated their story."

"What did you hear?"

"I'll get to that."

"Sorry."

"I just need to tell my story in my way to maximize dramatic effect."

"Oh."

"Any who, this stranger is someone the witches know and someone they are scared of."

"Wow, I can't imagine them being afraid of anyone, not with their powers and stuff."

"Well they were terrified once they realized who it was. Syta fainted and Ponta began babbling like a mad woman. It turns out this guy is named Bander and he is big trouble. The girls are doing whatever he says. They are openly crying while they are running this way and that obeying his orders."

"What did he look like?"

"I don't know, he never stepped into Dubla's hut. But from the things they said about him, I am guessing not too pretty. Anyway, he wasn't there long. Those girls were trying to placate him with food and drink but he wasn't about to eat or drink anything made by three witches. Then the screaming started.

It was horrible, first Ponta, then Dubla then Syta and all of them at once. They were screaming in sheer agony. Whatever he was doing to them, it didn't sound good. I actually felt sorry for them at that instant. Even after enduring their torturous ways. Anyone would have felt bad for the pain that they were obviously in.

After a while the shrieks turned to sobs and then quiet. The witches didn't return that night. I think that Bander had left them and that they slept out in the dirt of the circle. I remember feeling happy to be in my cage, out of sight, irrelevant. Most of what I know about that encounter I learned over the next week while the witches talked incessantly about their experience." Torth ripped some fresh grass and chomped on it while he let his story gather some suspense. "It turns out that this Bander fellow is a real bad guy who already knows all the same witch tricks that the girls do plus a lot more. He lives in the west, somewhere called Bander's Keep and the reason he was here, is that he was looking for you!"

"Me?"

"Well, you and your brother."

"He said that?"

"Well, no not exactly. I mean he is looking for you now."

"What?"

"This is what happens when I can't tell the story without interruptions."

"But I didn't interrupt you."

"Well...ok I just said he came here looking for you for shock value."

"Well, what's the real story?"

"Alright, apparently he wanted some information from the witches."

"But they don't know anything," interrupted Larry. "They never leave the safety of the circle."

"What did I just say about interrupting? But yeah, you're right. Oh and Larry, that story they told you about how they became witches well I think that was mostly false. The witches are part of a lineage of witches. There used to be more of them, even maybe hundreds, I don't know. But I do know that these witches use to know a lot more spells than they do now. They used to pass down their teachings through stories and prophecies, even legends that were metaphorical truths of the world and magic. This is why Bander came to see them. He wanted information, information that would only be remembered in the old stories.

"Bander's legions of followers (apparently he is a king or something) informed him that an old truth-teller had prophesied that he would be cast out of power. But that was apparently the bulk of the message. No details and the old man died so he couldn't be further interrogated. Bander knew that the witches would know of the prophecy so he came here to get it. The only problem is that the sisterhood of witches has let most of their knowledge slip away. I don't think the sisters ever recited the old stories. When Bander told them what he wanted to know, they told him that they hadn't heard of that prophesy. So he tortured them. That was the scream-ing I heard. They told him they had lost the old stories and that they never sang the old songs. But he didn't believe that either. So rather than be tortured to death they made up a prophecy."

"Wow, and he believed them?" Larry asked enthralled in the story.

"Luckily for them, he did," Torth's expression became one of pity as he looked at his new friend. "Unfortunately for you the story they fabricated led Bander to believe that a pair of brothers who bore the mark of blue and black eyes would be the ones to undo him."

"What?!"

"I don't think that the witches knew that there was such a pair. I think that they figured Bander would send his people to search for the brothers to no avail."

"What did the witches say exactly?" asked a flustered Larry.

"They said, and remember I am piecing this together based upon their later discussions of the day, that unless Bander killed you his plans would fail and he would come to ruin. Sorry."

"So that is why Bander is after us."

"It would appear so."

"Oh you don't think that Bander would go after my brother himself?"

"No, the witches were sure that Tock would be plenty to kill the likes of you, no offense."

"So they were lying to me the whole time. They knew they had sent Bander after us and I told them about Tock. I wonder if they had planned on handing me over to Bander."

"I don't think so, I think that they wanted as little to do with Bander as possible. They probably thought that you would be relatively safe in their circle and they could learn from you. But who knows what's boiling in a witch's pot?"

They both got quiet for a moment and without comment they picked up the stuff they had set down while they rested and began walking again. Torth took his time chewing the last patch of grass he had put into his mouth. Larry was lost in thought. It was midmorning. The fields of grass became patchy, with clumps of brush here and there. Every once in a while Torth would pick up a good sized rock and heave it across the arid plains. Sometimes this startled a bird or two into flight. After a while Larry broke the silence, "Well, this sucks!"

Torth did not respond.

"So me and Bob have some super bad guy, more powerful than the witches after us and he wants to kill us all because the witches made up some fairy tale about the prophesy of the brothers with the different eyes. It is not even true!" Larry said exasperated.

"Yeah, I feel for you," said Torth. Larry rolled his eyes at the giant.

"We have got to find Bob and tell him what is going on."

"Well, after that deal I heard you make with Dubla I bet they went to either of the nearest towns."

Larry weighed his options. On the one hand it might make sense to wait near the Tanglewood forest because that is where Bob knew to look for him. But waiting had its disadvantages.

"Tell me about the towns."

Chapter Twenty Two

"Quiet, Larry!" Torth motioned them towards a growth of trees. Larry followed obediently, wondering what was going on. From the small trees Larry surveyed the ground they had just covered. He saw nothing interesting. The savanna had given way to patches of trees and bushes. Larry figured there was an underground water source these trees roots drank. Torth put his hand to his ear signaling Larry to listen. Larry heard the buzz of insects but nothing uncommon. He took this opportunity to practice the focus magic the witches had tried to teach him. The soft myriad of sounds, bugs, gentle rustling of leaves in the wind, fell away while he focused and then he found it. Something underneath the other noise, something gentle. He focused upon it. It seemed a rumbling, more constant buzz or vibration. Larry enjoyed the noise. He was proud of himself for finding it amongst the background sounds. Torth must have good ears he thought. And then he noticed that the sound was getting louder. Suddenly it wasn't fun, something was coming.

He scanned the horizon and still he saw nothing and then he saw the source of the sound and he pressed up against the trees. What appeared to be millions of tiny goats flooded the landscape. They ran and jumped with abandon and then they were flowing past. The animals were no more than two feet tall so Larry didn't feel scared. It was quite a sight to see. They seemed never ending. Larry thought they were cute, these little running, jumping creatures. And after a couple of minutes the last of them were past and running into the horizon.

"Wow, that was amazing!" said Larry, exhilarated from nature's spectacle. "What were they?"

"Those were common Stripes," said Torth. "I thought they might be a larger breed that would be harder to avoid. I'm surprised that you've never seen them."

"No, my town is surrounded by trees. They must avoid it. They were so cute."

"Yeah, they are cute," agreed Torth "and they must be good to eat because most of the creepy crawlies lie waiting for a herd to run through their traps. Those things get eaten almost as fast as they can run. Luckily for the breed, they reproduce very quickly."

Larry licked his lips and could taste the dust that the stripes had kicked up. "Life is so wonderful and so tragic"

"That it is," agreed Torth.

The two men headed towards a town Torth knew in hopes of finding the missing companions. Larry was optimistic, as it felt good to be away from the witches and on the move. He couldn't wait to find Bob and tell him about his adventure. They had never had to look for each other before in Agea Hills. They had no signals or secret places or anything to guide him. He tried to think like his brother, pragmatic, slow. But it wasn't easy for Larry. Torth was similar to Sargasso in boldness of personality so Larry thought that there might be a chance he could lead them to his friends

The walk took two days. The town bustled with activity as they entered it. As they walked through the throngs of people no one gawked at Torth as Larry had worried they would. Perhaps the townspeople were used to seeing a ten-foot-tall man. The sheer size of the town filled Larry with awe. This was the first town he had ever been in outside of Agea Hills and it was huge. It looked like the dwellings went on forever. The people they passed looked like anyone that might have lived in Larry's village, but their dress was different. The clothes used fabric and color not found in Agea hills. Various domesticated dogs ran around carefree sniffing and playing. This city felt like an autumn festival, busy but rural. Larry could hardly take in all the sights and sounds around him and he snapped his head this way and that at the spectacle. Torth seemed right at home, walking casually and still smiling. His mood had not deteriorated since his freedom found him.

Four men dressed in matching clothes approached. Larry felt his stomach tighten at the imminent confrontation. Torth just kept on smiling. Easy for him to do thought Larry.

"Welcome travelers," spoke the largest man of the four. "We are the Keepers. We are here to register your presence." Larry looked to Torth for explanation.

"Visitors to Delis must register upon arrival," the man continued.

"What do you mean?" asked Larry nervously.

"We need to record your matter of business," replied the man.

"Well, we are looking for some friends of ours."

"And how long will you be staying?"

"I'm not sure."

"I will put down one week then. If you decide to stay longer than that you will need to inform us so we may update the register."

"Do you know if someone named Bob with a couple of other men registered in town within the past two weeks?"

"I'm sorry, we didn't register them but this is a big city and they could have signed in with any of a number of Keepers."

"Well how could we find out?"

"You will have to make an appointment with the Keeper's office. They will be able to pull the records and tell you the goings on in Delis for the past two weeks. Now there are a couple of more questions to be answered. Do you have any weapons on you?"

"I have a knife," said Larry.

"May we see it?"

Larry pulled out his knife. The Keepers stared at it and then made some notes on their parchment

"You may put it away." The Keeper's eyes rolled over Torth and Larry like waves on a sea, obviously looking for concealed weapons.

"Do you have any alignments, associations?"

"No, I don't have any alignments," said Torth.

"I wouldn't think so," said the head Keeper "Most giants don't."

"So you have seen people like me often?" inquired Torth.

"Oh, I wouldn't say often but we see your folk pass through this city enough to know that you are a good lot. On the other hand you," he said pointing to Larry. "I've never seen your kind here before. Interesting eyes. You can bet that the Keeper's office will assign a watcher to you."

"What is a, a, watcher?' asked Larry trying to sound casual.

"Someone hired by the township to report any peculiar behavior you might engage in. This is a peaceful town."

The Keepers finished scribbling on their notepads and checking off various categories on their lists. "Enjoy your stay," said the Keeper and then the bureaucrats left them.

"That was weird," said Larry.

"Yep," agreed Torth. The town continued to bustle around them. Larry's gaze flickered from pretty girl to pretty girl and found that many of them were gazing at Torth. That didn't surprise Larry at all. Torth was quite a sight and Larry had always considered his own looks to be less than extraordinary.

Well, at least they had a destination, thought Larry. The Keeper's office. Surely they would have made a note about Bob, Sargasso and Grento.

One side of the street was lined with vendors selling food and supplies. It was a treat to smell the variety of wares. One moment the smell of fresh fish dominated and the next, cinnamon, and then some smells that were completely foreign to Larry. It was wonderful to be in such a metropolis. Torth's eyes grew wide and a big grin spread across his face when they came to a restaurant with a sign advertising dandelion wine.

"Look Larry, they sell dandelion wine! I haven't tasted that for a long time. Do you want to go in for a while?"

Larry thought about it. He had never tried dandelion wine and it sounded exotic but he needed to find out if they were in the right town.

"You go ahead Torth. I'm going to go find the Keeper's office and see if Bob is here."

Torth looked torn. He looked at the restaurant like a dog at a treat his master had warned him not to eat until the signal.

"Do you want me to come with you?" asked Torth.

"No, it shouldn't be too hard to find the office, no sense in both of us looking for it. You stay here and I'll go talk to them. When I'm done I'll come back here and try some of that wine. There probably is a line at the office.

"Ok," agreed Torth "but you'd better hurry. I might drink it all before you return."

"I'll hurry."

So Larry left Torth to the restaurant and turned back to the street to find the Keeper's office.

As he walked through the throngs of people in no particular direction, Larry felt oddly alone. This was the first time he had ever been really alone in his entire life. It was an exhilarating feeling. Somehow it gave him his own agenda, no social obligations, no duty. As he put distance from Torth he felt alive and like he was experiencing his own company for the first time. Larry enjoyed the independence he was feeling. He walked casually stopping here or there to look at a merchant's wares. He asked a man selling plants how to get to the Keeper's office and was politely directed toward a group of large similar buildings.

Larry found the Keeper's office easy enough. It was nestled amongst other government buildings. Sure enough, there was a line of about twenty people waiting. From the expressions on their faces Larry could tell that they had been there for a while and their collective mood was souring. Larry quietly waited and made some small talk with the elderly woman in front of him. When it was his turn he walked into a small office and sat across from a squirrelly little man with piles of papers on his desk.

"Please state your name and your agenda," intoned the worker.

"My name is Larry and I'm here to inquire about my brother, Bob. He possibly arrived in town within the past two..."

"Name and agenda sir. That is all," the man interrupted Larry in a bored condescending tone.

Larry paused to think and then said, "My name is Larry," pause and then, "and I'm looking to review the Keeper's records."

The man was barely listening while he filled out information on a form. "A record check should tell us if your brother is in town. When did he arrive?"

"Well, I'm not sure, that's why I'm checking."

"So when do you think your brother arrived?"

"Within the past two weeks."

"And what is the name?"

"Bob. Bob has the same kind of eyes as me," Larry continued. For the first time the man looked at Larry and noticed his eyes.

"Well, that is unusual, surely that will be in the record." The man swiveled his chair to the left with a jerky twist of his hips towards a large ledger on the edge of his credenza. He looked down his nose through his glasses as he scanned page after page of entries. Larry sat quietly hopeful that the man would find Bob's name. After a moment the man stopped and appeared to have found something. He took his time reading a large entry on the page and then reached into his desk and pulled out some paper.

"Did you find him?" asked Larry optimistically.

"No, I am afraid not. He is not in this ledger but there is one more place you could look."

"Where?" asked Larry. The man began writing on the paper. He signed it with a flourish and then folded it.

"Take this authorization to the government building that is due west when you leave this building. It is the big one set off by itself." The man poured hot wax onto the folded letter and mashed an official seal into the wax. "Give this letter," he handed it to Larry, "to the secretary at the front office and she will direct you to our office of foreign affairs director who will let you look at their registration directory. If your brother's name isn't on that one either then he has not entered this town within the past two weeks."

"The one just west of here?"

"Yes, good day." The man's attention went back to his ledgers and Larry got up and left the way he came. Once outside, Larry had to figure out which direction west was. He felt stupid, as it seemed implied by the man's directions that it should be obvious to anyone. Larry solved this problem through process of elimination. There was only one large building in one direction so Larry headed toward it. Luckily there was no line at this office so Larry was able to walk right up to the secretary and give the letter of authorization to her.

"I'm trying to find my brother," Larry explained.

"Did you go to the Keeper's office?" she asked while she broke the seal on the authorization.

"Yes and they directed me to you. I'm supposed to check the ledger"

"Could you wait a moment?" she interrupted him. The secretary walked to the back room. After some shuffling of papers she returned. She didn't have a new ledger as Larry expected but two muscled men with her. The men walked right up to Larry with practiced uniform precision and grabbed him by each of his arms.

"What is going on?" shrieked Larry.

"Sir, could you please step this way," one of the men said leading Larry forcibly towards a door. Larry shrieked and pulled at them but they both had a good grip and apparently they had done this before. The secretary opened a door and the men carried/ dragged Larry through it and down a hall. At the end of the hall sat an even larger man in front of a door. When he saw the men approaching with Larry in tow he got up and unlocked and opened the door. The men dragged Larry to this ominous end of the hallway and pushed him through the door and onto the ground. They let go of him and turned and walked out the door. Larry stared in utter astonishment as they closed and locked the door.

Chapter Twenty Three

Sargasso yawned and stretched in the cool morning air. Grento and Bob were still clinging to their slumber with stubborn hands. The small animals of this valley woke up and shook off the night.

This was the life Sargasso loved. Although he wasn't used to traveling companions, he found that it was nice to have the company. And although he would never have thought it possible two weeks ago, he found himself having grander adventures with this group.

There is something anticipatory about a brisk morning. He liked the way his coat kept him warm yet he could feel the chill on his eyes and face. It's nice to win a battle of nature versus ingenuity. Nature could easily conjure a storm to shred his defense of warm clothes.

Sometime it's important to appreciate when you have enough to eat, he thought while shaking the dew off of the kindling for the fire.

Bob stretched the kinks out of his back and joined Sargasso at the small fire he brought to life.

"How did you sleep?" asked Sargasso.

"Oh, I imagine about as well as anyone would on the ground," answered Bob.

"I don't know about that," said Sargasso pointing over at Grento. Grento was still sound asleep and by the sound of his snoring he wasn't having any difficulty.

"Well that means that he will miss out on the coffee."

"Ah, one of the best things about waking up chilled, is coffee," agreed Sargasso.

The two men busied themselves with the fire, coffee, and small talk about the morning and the surrounding terrain. This river of conversation had an undercurrent that remained unspoken. Two weeks ago they left Larry. Each passing day had seen them move further from him. A sense of urgency was ripening on the vine.

"I've been thinking," said Bob. "If we're going to help Larry our number one concern must be avoiding Tock. We can't do Larry any good if we are dead or if we lead Tock straight to him."

"We should be alright as long as we keep moving. Tock might be vicious and smart but he can't cover ground like we can. I think we should head to the big town. There are so many people there that it will be hard for Tock to stay out of sight if he follows us, plus more people improves our chances to find a proxy."

Grento sat up. He stared straight ahead letting sleep radiate off his body while he adjusted to the waking world. His hair was matted on one side and sticking up on the other. He looked like a Halloween mask that had been put through the washing machine.

"I don't know if I should offer him some coffee or drive a stake through his heart," joked Sargasso smiling.

"Ah, there's nothing as welcome as levity first thing in the morning you jackass," returned Grento.

The men stood around the little fire drinking the morning coffee and quietly staring into the flames. The little fire fighting off the night chill was more than enough to entertain the imaginations of the adventurers.

Bob thought how cyclical life was watching the fire consume and turn organic matter into heat and light that they might be warm today and in the future their bodies would perhaps warm some other travelers. The pleasure of the warmth of the fire wouldn't die it was merely passed along.

Sargasso watched the flames and thought of moths. He wondered if they were aware of the death that the fire would bring and if they couldn't help themselves. If the yearning for the light was so primal they could only watch in horror as their valiant wings strained against gravity and pushed on. Or if they knew of the danger and didn't truly believe that they would burn. Perhaps they thought themselves invincible, kings of flight. Maybe they knew that flying into the fire meant death yet they chose this destiny. Some part of the romantic in Sargasso wished that the little insects somehow were cognizant of their condition and made some choice, but he figured that they were probably just brainless bugs that fly instinctively towards the light.

Grento's thoughts remained where he left them, in a dream of a pretty girl. The movement of the fire was the rippling of her dress in the wind. The red coals that glistened were her lips. The wood smoke was her perfume, one that would take him back into her arms at any time.

They drained their cups and stowed their gear. Then they marched on towards a new town.

Chapter Twenty Four

Larry was in a large room filled with beds. Everywhere people engaged in various activities. Some sat on the beds others lay asleep. Some ran around some jumped from bed to bed. The scene looked like some sort of macabre carnival.

Larry, so as not to draw the attention of anyone in the room, quietly got to his feet and then tried the door. It was locked and solid. He tentatively tapped on it trying to get the man's attention on the other side.

He felt something clutch at his sleeve. He jumped at the sudden contact and turned to see a disheveled woman. She was plain looking with a large forehead and sad eyes. She looked like Hemmingway's sails.

"They won't let you out," she said in a voice that scraped at the bottom of hopelessness. She stared at him. Those eyes looking through him to places she'd already been. Larry felt afraid of her. She was a small woman, not threatening, but there was something about her that wasn't right. Maybe she stared too intently, or perhaps she stared at him without trying to see anything. She reflected nothing; the humanity she emanated was dim. Larry pulled at his sleeve and she let it go. Larry moved away from her and she watched him walk away.

The room was horrible. Larry's breath caught in his lungs as the overwhelming stench of urine attacked him at various spots along his walk. Some people took notice of him. But most either ignored him or didn't see him. He came near one bed where the inhabitant had climbed underneath his mattress and looked out like an eel from its hole.

Further along he saw a man with no hands and no feet rolling around on the ground like a worm. The man ignored him.

229

Larry maneuvered across the room towards a hallway. He tried to shut out the images around him and to shut out the sounds. He moved quickly now, his anxiety growing. He needed to get out. Finally he made it to the hall. He felt like reaching the hall, would be better, anything would be better than this room of tortured souls. Hallways lead to places he thought to himself. He stared down the dark hall. Anywhere is better than here so nothing to worry about, he thought to himself. That was an easy decision. But as he crept away from the noise of the crazies, he felt cold. It was nearly completely dark now and Larry heard water dripping from somewhere ahead.

"Hold," stated a voice in the dark. Larry froze in place, his ears full of blood. There was a movement off to Larry's right side. His eyes madly searched the dark for movement trying to give shape to shadow. There was nothing to see.

"Where are you going?" Now the voice was behind him.

"Nowhere really, j, jus, just exploring," stammered Larry.

"Well, you are about to meet George. I hope you are friends with him for your sake," said the voice.

"I,I,I have well, actually I have n,n,not met George y,y,ye,yet."

"George lives up there and he won't let anybody go in there, if you try he will get you. Nobody ever visits George and George never comes out of his hiding spot."

"I d,d,don't want to bother him," said Larry." "Who are you?"

"My name isn't done yet."

"Where are we?" Larry was less afraid now "What is this place?"

"This is the asylum, this is the hospital."

"What?" Everything started to make sense to Larry. The Keeper must have written something on that paper telling the guards to lock him away in here, but why? He wasn't crazy or dangerous. "If this is the hospital, where are the doctors?"

"They are here amongst us. Ever since the doors were locked for good the doctors couldn't leave either. Now we all live together."

"You mean that they locked the doctors in with all of the patients?

"Yes. I can take you to one of the doctors if you want but not George, he doesn't let anybody visit with him."

"Let's leave George alone then." Larry turned back the way he had come and could just make out the small form of his new guide. As they walked into the light Larry was able to see clearly that he had been talking to a small boy, probably eleven years old.

"How long have you been here?" asked Larry.

"I've been here for a long time," came the answer. They were back in the main room and the little boy weaved his way through the human zoo. He stopped at a pile of boxes and began knocking on them with his dirty little fist. "Doctor, there is someone here who wants to talk."

There was a scuffing from within the boxes and a middle aged balding man emerged. The hair above his ears was white and his bald scalp was covered with age spots.

"Yes?" he answered in a meek voice.

Larry stepped up and began, "Hello, I understand that you're a doctor?"

The poor old fellow stared off into a personal abyss.

"Doctor," the boy spoke snapping the silence.

"Er, eh,... yes I was or well I guess I still am a Doctor"

"What happened? How come they locked you in?'

"Well there is the question of the hour. Why indeed. Damn politicians!"

"Do you mean the Keepers?" asked Larry.

"No they are low level bureaucrats dancing for their dinner. I'm sure that the order came down from the Senate, probably from Bander himself." The man spit on the ground at the mention of Bander. The punctuation of the spittle on the ground was like a board being ripped off of a boarded window and light streamed in illuminating the room.

Bander, of course. If Bander were a ruler then surely he would send out orders to detain anyone fitting their description. The Keeper must have read the orders in his book and then calmly sent Larry to be imprisoned until Bander's troops could arrive to finish the job or maybe they would send Tock. He must escape!

Yet even through this personal revelation Larry felt sad for the doctor and the other people living here. What agony it must be to be trapped here. Someone ran from the side and into Larry pushing him over. "What the hell was that?" asked Larry looking up from the floor.

"That was one of my former colleagues," replied the doctor. "He spends all day watching for people who aren't paying attention and then he runs into them, then hides. I don't know why. Adjusting to our new surroundings has been very difficult for all of us. From a clinical perspective it would be fascinating if it weren't so terrible. You see there is much to bridging the gap between patient and doctor. We're always on one side of the river trying to bring our patients to us through various clinical psychological constructs. But the river shrinks noticeably when the Doctor is forced to become more like the patient. I now understand that they aren't really that crazy. That person over there, for example, wouldn't seem so strange if he didn't have to put everything he comes into contact with into his mouth. Take away that one idiosyncrasy and all of a sudden he's not so bizarre. We all have ways of dealing with life. Some are culturally acceptable, others aren't."

"Well I need to get out of here, any suggestions?"

"There's no way out of here, this asylum was built to confine people. The builders knew how hard it is to contain humans. There are no vents to climb through, no way to force the doors. I'm afraid you will have to try to adapt to this new life."

"Well, as pleasant as that sounds, I don't think I'm going to abandon all hope yet."

"Here, I will show you where I sleep," said the little boy pointing towards the other side of the room.

Larry would have preferred to stay and talk with the Doctor but he slid back into his boxes. Apparently their session was over. Each sight that assaulted Larry's eyes was more disturbing than the last as he followed the boy.

Here a middle-aged man crouched on the floor and stalked an unfortunate bug which he managed to catch and eat. On a cot lay a woman ripe with bedsores, quietly moaning in agony. And from everywhere he felt the eyes of these damned souls reaching out to him. Some of the resident's eyes pushed at him, they wanted him gone.

The boy stopped at a radiator near a wall. This, apparently, was their destination but the boy offered no explanation he just sat down on the floor and seemed to forget that Larry was there. Larry looked around the room and a feeling of revulsion overtook him. He felt that it would be utterly impossible for him to acclimate to this environment. He had to get out. There was no choice in the matter. One night among these people — they didn't seem like people — would be unbearable. He would surely go mad as well. The boy hadn't moved since sitting down and even when Larry spoke to him, no response. Larry decided to explore a little, avoiding the hallway. The room's construction was basic. It was rock without frills.

Chapter Twenty Five

The path that twisted up the mountain to the entrance to Bander's Keep was lined with Nobles from the town. The people were dressed in their best clothes. The normal townsfolk colors of brown and gray were replaced with burgundies and emerald green. The wash of color looked like a giant snake winding its way up to the scary gothic Keep. The sun set directly behind the towers of the keep and the would-be revelers had to shield their eyes with a hand or look down at their feet. Bander watched the approach of the throngs with casual interest. Quid's party was an annoyance to him but a necessary one. Each year the inhabitants of the town were forced to walk through Bander's trophy room. It served to remind everyone who was in charge. It also sparked the rumors that would permeate the nightmares of the community.

He did not inquire as to Quid's plan to punish the insurrectionists. He focused his attention on the details of presenting himself to the masses. His body withering and his sight gone— he didn't make a strong impression sans costume.

His powers were never greater. But his image was diminishing. The common man only understood what he could see. Bander selected a tall staff from a closet. It was made of bones with a cheap chunk of quartz set at the handle. It was nothing more than a piece of art, if that. But the people would bow to it, cringe from it and dream about it. Within days everyone in town would be talking about Bander's invincible staff of death. His enemies would devise plans to steal the staff. And all the while the staff would be sitting back in the closet its one use fulfilled.

Bander picked up the staff. He lifted it too hard and it rose in the air slightly. He managed to maneuver well without his eyesight but although he could sense objects spatial locations, he could not see them to estimate how much they would weigh. He was constantly applying too much force to light things and not enough to heavy ones. This could be a problem when he used the key. There would be all sorts of adversaries on the other side. He would need to start his journey completely intact if he was to finish it. He needed to steal some new eyes.

*   *   *

Quid watched the townspeople fill the trophy room. The women steeled themselves against the sight of all the horrible stuffed monsters decorating the chamber. Many entered the room with their heads bowed and their faces pressed to the chests of their male escorts. The men hid their fear better but Quid still watched with amusement the shaky knees and the trembling hands.

In a balcony, a band played some traditional hill music with a festive rhythm. Quid scanned the crowd for the nobles he would personally entertain this evening. He spotted one of his appointments quickly. The man moved with confidence. He was obviously shaken by the room but he was made of stronger stuff than most people. He would have to be, thought Quid, to try and murder Lord Bander. And now to walk through his masters Keep with swagger. Did he think that he was going to get away with the attempt? Did he dare to think that he could keep his traitorous machinations secret from Quid's spies?

Quid pulled his eyes off of the crowd. He fumbled through a stack of envelopes and debated to himself which ones to use. Each note was sealed with the stamp of the order, black wax covered the seal. On the front each had the name of a noble written on its face. Quid knew from his spies that their were probably only three or maybe four people involved in the failed assassination plot. Yet he held twelve letters. Each an invitation to a private chamber during tonight's festivities. Each an honor that couldn't possibly be refused and each a death sentence.

Quid considered the person that each note represented. He momentarily thought about the persons standing in the community their family relations, their government connections and then he shuffled all of the letters together and handed them to the soldier standing at attention at his side.

"Deliver these to the person they are addressed to," Quid said allowing himself to feel the power he was wielding.

"Yes sir," the soldier intoned and moved to do his duty.

The music stopped suddenly and all eyes went to the center balcony. Standing like a gunslinger Bander addressed the crowd.

"Good people of the town and country welcome. Tonight we cast aside government formality and bridge the chasm between the Keep and the city. Dance and drink, catch the ear of a politician and offer your suggestions. We are stronger united and working together," Bander's voice was both commanding and casual. He was a leader among his friends. And so radiating confidence that it hurt the eyes.

Quid watched the multitudes force smiles at the words and find comfort in Bander's presence as if he would protect them from the blob-like fear that permeated their frames. All the while, mounted ghouls leered over their shoulders and glared with accusing hateful eyes. Bristling hair and shiny scales and teeth and claws were all frozen in attack mode as if patiently listening to the man that had slain them.

Quid noticed that there was something different about Bander. Ever since the attack on Bander's life, a fact that he had kept secret from everyone, Bander moved differently and seemed somehow different. It was harder to notice now, while he spoke. Bander seemed to get younger and more intimidating with each public event.

Quid tore himself away and into the shadows. He was the one person who could be excused from the address. Tonight was but a formality to the Lord. He despised the details of rule but acknowledged them nonetheless. Quid kept his mind open to learning from the wizened master. He had to ready himself for his own performance tonight. Bander gave him total leeway on handling the guests and he was not going to miss this chance to have some fun and test his private chambers.

*   *   *

Charlie looked down at the letter in his hand. It bore Bander's official seal and invited him to attend a private viewing of a new prize catch. He didn't like the thought of being singled out by the leader for any reason. The rest of the trophies scared him and seeing a new one close up didn't sound so good. He walked to the buffet table and poked at a piece of smoked chicken with a tooth pick. His friend Harold approached holding a similar letter. He slapped it with his other hand, making a snapping sound.

"The night is full of mystery, friend. I see you got an invite as well."

"Yeah, to be honest, I'd rather just stay in the main room with everyone else," said Charlie.

"What, don't be modest or whatever it is you're being. We have been selected to view the latest addition to this great hall," said Harold.

"Why us?"

"Well, to tell the truth, there are several noble men selected. It seems that it isn't that exclusive of a party."

"Oh, well it will be interesting I am sure. How are things with your family?"

"Can't complain, can't complain. My oldest son is started school."

"Wow, already?"

The men continued to poke at the chicken and experimented with dipping it in the various colored sauces provided. The yellow sauce was so spicy it made Charlie's nose run.

"Yeah, that yellow sauce is pretty strong stuff," agreed Harold sympathetically.

When Bander finished speaking the crowd burst into enthusiastic applause. Bander disappeared back into the shadows of the curtains behind the balcony.

"I guess we better head on over to the alcove," Harold said filling his mouth with one last gob of food.

"I wonder if they will have more food inside?" wondered Charley. He didn't like being singled out and he sure didn't like leaving his wife there alone in the trophy room. He would hear about that for weeks but there was nothing that he could do. You just didn't offend Bander in any way.

The nobles followed the soldier escort down the stairs to the next floor down. From this level they could still hear the muted sounds of the celebration overhead. On this level gone were the decorations and pleasantries. Simple torches stood in the rock of the hallway. Usually the torches wouldn't be lit. The person would light them as they walked if they needed continuous light, which was rare. Usually a man would carry his lantern with him. No sense in wasting fuel. But tonight the stone hallway was lit up with torches. As soon as one faded into the darkness further on another shone hot. There was little question as to where they were going. Someone was obviously expecting them.

"Off you go," said the soldier flapping an arm in the direction of the torches.

The group of men looked to each other for a moment. Each wanting conformation that they were doing the right thing. No one wanted to appear indecisive, so quickly the entire group was marching nearly in file down the illuminated hallway.

Quid sat at his ornately carved wooden desk. Angels and devils battled up the legs of the desk and, as each of them strove to reach the heavens, it appeared that they were stretching and worshiping Quid where he sat.

"Welcome, friends. Welcome," said Quid earnestly.

"Master Quid," the group returned from various mouths.

"Congratulations on your selection! Lord Bander has very special feelings for each of you," Quid continued.

The room surrounding Quid looked like a cloak and dagger museum. There were knives mounted on the walls. One shelf was covered with bottles of poison each bearing the universal sign a skull and crossbones. Of course they also had a spider picture or a snake picture or whatever the particular poison was. There was a human skull at each corner of the desk. On a podium to the left of Quid was a stuffed monster. It stood like a guardian over Quid. The shelves along the east wall held all sort of torture devices from clamps to razors to mallets to ice picks. Each thing was nasty.

"I hope that everyone has been enjoying the party," Quid addressed the assembled men. "However there is a trite matter that needs to be dealt with. As you know, Lord Bander is a patient magnanimous patriarch who lives to serve the people of the city and surrounding hamlets, but he is also our commander and as such he must enforce the law as he sees fit."

The nobles looked from one another wondering what was going on.

"If I may," began a noble.

"No!" Quid shouted momentarily loosing his temper. He quickly regained it. "You may not. I am the bearer of unfortunate news but I humbly hope that I can cast a positive spin on the situation.

The men stared silently ahead not wanting to anger Quid who was known for flashes of uncontrollable anger.

"There has been an attempt upon our leader's life," Quid let the weight of the words sink them into the hearts of the listening assembly. When his moment of silence had burned its effect into the quiet of the air he continued. "It is known that the party responsible is in this room right now. It is also known that this was not a simple act of one delusional soul but a conspiracy amongst several men. There is some ambiguity as to the perpetrators identities. Not much but enough that it could cause me to lose some rest over the matter if I did not do every possible thing in my power to relieve the innocent of the shadow of guilt cast by their murderous peers."

Charlie didn't like the turn this invitation had taken. He knew that Quid would hardly lose sleep over the death of innocent men. Charlie wanted to get back upstairs to his wife, back to the party, away from this lunatic, and away from the other nobles.

"And so in the interest of fairness, for the sake of justice, and to insure that the guilty are punished, I have devised a little test."

Charlie looked back casually at the hallway. How many of them were there? A dozen. Quid was all alone, which was unusual for him. Maybe he didn't want soldiers trampling all through his personal office. It didn't seem likely that he could harm them, not by himself. He was a sickly little possum of a man.

"Each of you will select a box," Quid said waving his arm to indicated a pile of boxes bricked on top of each other.

"And if we don't?" said Hunter with a royals indignation.

"Then you confirm your guilt and you will be put to death as a traitor of the realm." Quid answered with his head slightly down and venomous glee radiating from his eyeballs.

"Let the sin in your hearts guide your choice." Quid indicated that they were to choose now.

The small wooden boxes looked nearly identical. There were differences in color, age, condition, etc. but they were the same type of boxes. The kind used for storing dried salt meat. Some were stained and some looked new. How to choose?

Someone grabbed a box and moved to open the lid.

"Not yet," Quid snapped. "Everyone must choose before you open your box."

Charlie and his friends didn't know where this was going and didn't want to be the only one who refused to pick a box so one by one they made their selections.

"There," said Quid. "Now, look inside."

Charlie felt the weight of his box. There was something heavy inside. He looked around at the other men and waited for one of them to look into theirs.

"What are we afraid of?" said a big noble opening his box.

He peered into the wooden mystery and then looked quizzically at the contents. He shrugged his shoulders and then stuck his hand inside. He retrieved a pair of velvet gloves. He held the gloves up to show everyone. He dumped the box upside down to be sure that there was nothing more inside and nothing was.

Spurred on by the mildness of the first contents the rest of the men gingerly open the lids to their own boxes. Charlie watched them pull out similarly benign items. A belt from one. A pipe from another. He nonchalantly let the lid to his own box slip open for a moment and when nothing evil emerged he opened it. There was nothing more than a book. He set his box down and turned the book over to peruse it. Quid watched all the activity from his desk. If the test was in progress, Charlie couldn't figure out what was being tested. Everyone knew that the leader of the soldiers had strange ways and perhaps wasn't completely sane. Perhaps the item that you picked said something about your character like tarot cards did. Maybe which ever box one chose was not pure luck but a matter of fate. Either way Charlie felt relieved to find something non threatening inside his box. They all did. The pressure of the moment oozed away from the bursting point and everyone began to think about getting back to the party.

"The choices have been made," said Quid.

"I don't get it," said Harold. "Who is the guilty person? How can you tell anything from who got which box?"

"It isn't up to me," said Quid leaning back in his chair.

As he spoke a tiny movement caught Charlie's eye. A thin clear string of spittle hung from the mouth of the stuffed monster on the pedestal next to the desk. Charlie blinked and focused his eyes to be sure of what he was seeing. There was no mistake; it looked like the thing was salivating from its frozen-open mouth. Charlie tried to process the information and do something with it. But there was no time left.

"You see, my distinguished guests, you cretins, you lying, conniving, plotting fools. There is no good and bad. You will be examples to the realm. Your death is your gift to the realm. To attack the Lord Bander was to commit suicide."

"But I didn't do anything!" exclaimed Charlie.

"I don't care, and now you all are holding something of mine. And as you're about to learn my pet can be a bit protective. In the eyes of the Spitt you are threatening me."

Charlie looked into the eyes of the stuffed monster and all doubt disappeared. This was the Spitt.

"Kill them," Quid shouted slamming his hand down on the desk.

The Creature closed its mouth. Its beady eyes darted back and forth way too quickly. It looked crazy. Its body was red skin draped over tendons. It looked like an emaciated elephant's skin, but red. The creature leapt from its perch with shocking speed toward the wall. It landed on the sheer surface and stuck like a fly. It twisted its head around quickly and spasmodically surveyed the men. Then it launched itself again, this time to the ceiling. Everyone backed away from it but each jump corralled the men in different directions. Quid leaned back in his chair and clasped his hands behind his head. A nefarious smile oozed up his face.

The creature kept bouncing around the walls and ceiling like a monkey until unexpectedly one of its jumps took it onto Harold's chest. It quickly rebounded back to a wall and then to its perch. But Harold's throat gushed with blood. The Spitt claws had ripped his neck apart. Harold held his neck while the blood pumped out between his fingers. Everyone felt their stomach's tighten and their puke impulse kick in while Harold dropped to the ground. The creature continued to jump all around them, darting closer. Its buggy eyes stretched open and white.

Some of the men tried to open the door back to the hallway but it was locked and immovable. Quid taunted them.

"This is what traitors bring onto themselves and their peers. If any of you is feeling victimized then let me assure you that you are as guilty as the assassin. Every man here is associated with every other. You are all nobles. Don't cry foul when your team gets treated like a team. I know that you all maintain some vestige of hope. Let me assuage you of that notion. The Spitt will kill each of you, no exceptions. It has the strength of all of you put together and it has been bred to protect to a level bordering on madness."

The creature slammed into another man and ripped the side of his face and neck to shreds. His screams would not be heard in the celebration above. He thrashed around into the other men who were forced to shove him aside so they could try to maintain their focus on the animal.

Charlie watched his friend die. He held Harold in his arms while Harold's fear turned quiet. Charlie felt a similar calm settle over himself while the other men dashed back and forth waving their arms at the creature. Some tried to catch it out of the air.

There was no way out of this room, Charlie understood now. Quid was too relaxed. He would die here with his wife upstairs and his children sleeping in their beds.

Charlie gently laid his friend down on the stone floor and charged at Quid. It took only a moment for him to reach the desk and Quid's smile was just fading when Charlie's fist hit Quid's mouth. The force of the attack knocked both Charlie and Quid back over the chair and onto the ground. Charlie hauled back to hit him again when the creature was upon him. Charlie felt his hair pulled back the same moment he felt the sharp pain of his throat being ripped out. His blood spurted out onto the horrified face of Quid. In moments, Charlie was dead.

The men in the room watched confused while Charlie used what was left of his life on his own terms. The creature bounded to its perch and then to the ceiling while Quid climbed out from under Charlie's body.

Quid screamed commands at the creature causing it to attack the men with every jump. Blood covered the walls as jugular veins released the hot fluid. The slaughter took only a few moments and then the creature panting out of breath landed on its perch next to Quid.

The moment Quid had anticipated and planned for, his grand entrance back to the celebration upstairs with the news of the death of the traitors was finally here, and Quid sat at his blood covered desk holding a cloth up to his mouth where three of his teeth had been knocked out.

Chapter Twenty Six

Larry looked around the asylum at the tortured animals. He marveled at the resiliency of humanity and he felt inadequate. He knew that he was not up to the task of assuming the role he was called to play. He would not make friends here. He refused to fight for a spot of urine-stained-floor to call his own for the night. Here he was like a plant without sunlight. Here he would die.

His survey of the room revealed no means of escape. His only hope would be for someone to rescue him. But that seemed unlikely. Perhaps his brother would find his way to this town but then he could only hope that they would throw him here as well and that was not something that he could wish for.

Suddenly a thought startled him, Where does George get his food?

Why hadn't he thought of that before? A glimmer of hope percolated in Larry's chest. Perhaps he hadn't run into a wall, maybe he had a spoon to dig with. He returned to the boy he had met upon first arriving in the hospital.

"Does anyone take George any food?" he asked quietly afraid of the answer.

"No, mister in here you have to get what you get yourself unless you have a friend to help you and George sure doesn't have any friends here."

Larry felt a moment of hope.

"Does anyone here have any matches, or anything we can light to make a torch?" asked Larry.

"No, there's no fire and I'm glad. Who knows what would happen if some of these guys could start a fire?"

"Tell me more about George. Why doesn't he get along with everyone else? Is, is he a b, big fellow?" asked Larry, his stutter returning.

"George was the janitor in the hospital when all the doctors could leave," the boy began. "He never talked to anybody then, I don't think that he can talk."

"You mean he is a mute?"

"I don't know where he was born, but he has never been able to talk. He just emptied the trash and sometimes he would chase the patients around. I saw him hurt a couple of patients one time and once when Vick tried to sneak up on him and knock him over, George threw him against a wall and broke his arm. He is mean. I don't think that even the guards of the door would mess with George. He can't hear so you can't talk him down, you can't surprise him because he's always on edge he always thinks that you are trying to fight him or making fun of him. He always did his work though."

"Interesting. Not good, but interesting. Let's go get some advice from the doctor."

Doctor was tending to his boxes when they approached. For a moment the doctor was unaware of their presence and Larry got a chance to see him acting natural. The doctor's tongue kept slipping out of his mouth while he worked to separate two pieces of wood nailed together. He looked crazier than Larry had first noticed.

"Doctor?" said Larry

"Yes?" he answered turning around and collecting himself.

"Could you give me your expert opinion on the mental health of George, the janitor?" asked Larry.

The doctor switched into doctor mode and began to swim in jargon. Larry stopped him before his inertia could get going.

"Well George is a classic case of we don't know," he continued. "He wasn't a patient and due to his muteness, I gathered little from him through the course of our daily interactions."

"Is he dangerous?"

"As dangerous as anyone I suppose, living here isn't the same as civilized society. There are no rules no rulers and no guarantees. Of course, as with any group, one would expect there to be several really aggressive people and several gentle. Of course, those gentle folks died in here. So, since George is still alive, it's obvious that he has what it takes to compete with the species. And yes, I think that definitely makes him dangerous."

One of the doctor's boxes fell down and he turned to replace it. His attention was back on his four by six area. Larry turned and left him to his repairs.

"Let's go meet George," said Larry quietly.

Larry and the boy snaked through the beds and the abandoned patients towards the George's dark hallway. At the entrance, Larry felt his fear grow from unpleasant anxiety to primordial fear.

Larry sat staring into the dark hallway and waited for his eyes to adjust. The boy watched him with curiosity. He listened to the dripping of water somewhere in the abandoned hall. The smell of mold and decay indicated disuse. How could he do this? George sounded like a real bad man. And Larry was thinking about sneaking right into his domain unannounced. This felt like when he stormed into Dubla's hut. Why he did that and where he found the courage was beyond his comprehension. Yet here was another pathway he faced. His knees trembled. He pulled out his knife but it felt diminutive in his hand like a child's toy weapon.

Larry had the luxury of knowing that there really was no choice in this, he was going to go into the hallway. The alternative of spending his life with the crazies was simply unacceptable. So now, given that, he was allowed to ladle out of the soup of courage spoonful upon spoonful onto his resolve. Unfortunately the soup cooled quickly.

His fingers trembled, and he stared at them like instinctive signals of danger. His heart betrayed his measured courage and his head felt slightly dizzy and heavy. Of course this pissed him off because you would think that when you have time to anticipate danger your body would be in top form. Ready for any challenge but no, his was shaky and dizzy. He would be lucky not to faint at any unusual noise.

Once his eyes adjusted to the dim light of the hallways entrance, he tentatively moved about 20 feet into the darkness.

"I'm not going in there," said the boy.

Larry would meet George alone. He stopped and let his eyes adjust to this new level of dark. That was his plan. It wasn't much of a plan but he could take his time. He made no noise. No sense in drawing any attention to himself.

He wondered what George looked like. Was he the sort of madman that would snarl and bark like an animal or, worse, was he the silent killer type? The kind of madman that has no dilemma upon seeing an intruder, no moral struggle waged in his heart. The kind of guy that hits you on the head with a hammer upon first sight and then forgets about you the next minute like swatting a fly. Death without consideration, action unchecked.

Larry started forward. He could see, barely, but being able to see a little sure beats stumbling forward blindly. He kept to one wall and slid his hand like a feeler along its surface. The wall was covered with an oily film. He proceeded very slowly and his shuffling steps were almost silent. With any luck he would be able to see George before George saw him.

"Do you see George?" yelled the boy down the hallway.

"Eh?" Larry muffled his reactionary reply to the loud attention gathering noise. Larry's eyes were as wide as they had ever been. Blood was gushing through his brain.

"Well? Larry? What do you see?" shouted the boy again.

Larry did not answer. There was nowhere to hide in the hallway. He crouched down a little to be smaller and listened as hard as he could.

The boy didn't call again. Perhaps he'd figured out that that wasn't such a good idea. Silence. He fully expected to have awakened the bear of the cave but nothing happened. Larry continued on. The moments clicked by like months. At the end of the hallway hung a partially ajar door.

Larry swallowed to stiffen his resolve before entering but of course he swallowed wrong and started coughing. He couldn't help it. The spittle had gone down the wrong pipe. Larry tried to muffle the coughs by covering his mouth with his hand and fighting to keep his mouth closed but all that he succeeded in doing was changing the tone of the coughs to a strange sneezing sound. Larry was horrified but there was nothing to do. Instead of running back to safety, he ran straight into the doorway. He threw it open in full fighting readiness. His fists clenched, his muscles poised to strike, and still coughing, he challenged anything to take him on.

What a spectacle he would have looked to George, while he had his little fit and swung his uncoordinated fists in the air. He had all of the ferociousness of a drop of water on a hot skillet dancing itself into vapor. But the room was empty.

The door swung back silently and touched him on the shoulder. Larry shrieked like a little girl and whirled around. Realizing his mistake, he turned his attention back to the empty room. Larry saw a hole on the far wall leading to the outside of the compound. George must have tunneled out. Imagine all this time he had been deathly afraid of a danger that was long gone. Perhaps George left a long time ago. The boy had said that anyone that went down this hall never came back. They must have each found George's escape tunnel and gotten out themselves. If he left now, and didn't return to the room every one would assume that George had gotten him as well. For a moment he considered his options and then decided that inside the hospital was not the place to do this and he wormed his way out through the hole and into the cool night air. The sky was awash with stars.

Larry wasted no time finding Torth. The big man was still drinking dandelion wine at the bar where the two had parted ways. Larry's adventures had taken all day but Torth seemed glad to drink the time away with no worry about anything. The sheer amount of wine consumed in this binge was already becoming something for the legends. He had a harem of town girls hanging on his arms and a bunch of townsmen trying to be the big man's friend. Everyone was glad to buy him his drinks and he seemed to be having the time of his life. Larry felt bad about asking him to leave.

Torth took the timing in stride and was glad that the universe had sent this sign that it was time to stop drinking and move on. Giants often needed reasons to stop drinking since their tolerance was so high.

The men headed for the edge of town. They hid in the pockets of dark between the candlelight in store shop windows. By now the Keepers might have noticed Larry's disappearance and they didn't want to take any chances. Soon they were out of the busy, dense part of town. The sparkling lake of candlelight was behind them.

Larry knew that they needed a direction. They also knew that they were leaving civilization and heading back towards the waste, back towards the monsters that patiently waited for them. Sargasso had said, "Always pick one star and follow it; at least you'll wander in a straight direction. Most folks would probably choose the "Traveler's Star" because it is so bright above the horizon, but Sargasso being Sargasso, said he always followed the star just to the left of the Traveler's Star; something about making fresh tracks. Larry found the bright star and then the one just to its left. He felt a little nostalgic for his adventurer friend but pushed those thoughts from his mind. Larry and Torth began walking towards the star.

Chapter Twenty Seven

Quid looked into the hole. The burly guards stood around him nervously. Everyone stared into the little tunnel that had allowed their prey to escape.

"This is utterly inexcusable!" said Quid shaking his head.

The assembled Keeper's representatives shifted nervously on their feet.

"Three days? You couldn't keep the prisoner for three days? I've eaten fish that keeps better than you Keepers. What kind of system of imprisonment is this? Throw them into a jar and leave the lid off?"

The Keepers were not used to such reprimands but they understood the hierarchy of the world. Quid, though he was hard to take seriously, represented Bander's sovereignty and that, they took very seriously.

The hole stared up at them like an animal's morning trail. It was evidence of something that happened while they were all sleeping.

"Is there anyway to determine when he left?" said Quid shaking his head in disgust.

"It's hard to say," responded one of the Keepers. "Sometime after we threw him in here, I imagine," said another.

"Are you trying to be funny?" anger flashed across Quid's face.

"No sir, just trying to help."

"Then get down and crawl through the hole and see where it goes!"

The guards made a move towards the Keeper and that was all the encouragement he needed. He dropped down to the floor and began wriggling his way through the escape tunnel. Quid shook his head in frustrated disgust at the fools he had to put up with. Then turning to the remaining Keepers, "Take us to the other side of this wall."

The men turned and walked back down the hallway to the jumbled confusion of the main housing area. The lunatics bounced on their beds and ran around shrieking.

"Perhaps we should question these freaks. Maybe the criminal told somebody where he planned on going," said Quid to the guard on his left. Just then the crazy old fellow that liked to run into people streaked through the ranks and knocked Quid right out of mid sentence. He then ran away through the confusion to some unseen hiding place.

"What in the hell was that?" said Quid picking himself up off of the ground. "Am I bleeding? Well it feels like I'm bleeding. It's probably internal. This is going to bruise at least."

The guards and the Keepers looked back and forth to see if anyone else thought this as funny as they did but they dared not to laugh.

Quid and his entourage passed through the door where the guard sat on his stool keeping watch. Quid shook his head and glared at the guard as he passed. Behind the hospital, the grounds were overrun with scrub brush. Litter that had escaped on the wind found its way into the clutching craws of the spiny plants.

A soldier's shout brought everyone to the tail end of the hole. It was hidden from view by the weeds and looked like the home of some small animal.

"Any suggestions?" asked Quid with a sneer.

"Well, we could track down the giant this Larry arrived with, his whereabouts should be easily attained from my ledger back at Keeper's headquarters."

Quid turned his head slowly towards the Keeper who offered this suggestion his eyes getting wider with the turn. "He had a friend?"

"Well, eh, yeah," the Keeper responded.

"And nobody thought that we should check that out until right now?"

"Do you think he might have gone after his friend?"

"Guard," said Quid to a soldier. "Punch this man in the stomach."

The guard slugged the Keeper doubling him over and dropping him to his knees.

"Next time..." started Quid reprimanding but his voice was drowned out by the town's bell chiming the noon hour. Quid led the group out of the weeds and towards the Keepers Center.

Chapter Twenty-Eight

The men circled the campsite. Through the bushes and the trees they could clearly see the smoldering coals of a fading campfire. Whoever these travelers were, they were stupid. Out in the wild of this wood, campfire smoke and light attracted attention. It had brought them here. But they knew that others would be lured to this juncture now as well. It would be good to deal with these two quickly and then leave before the forest scavengers arrived.

The group of men circled the two campers. One of the sleeping men was huge. The other was ordinary, maybe a little less. The camp was poorly constructed, hastily made. Perhaps these two were on the run. Or maybe they were lost, they were relatively near the town. One thing was certain; they wouldn't last long out in the wild no matter how big the one man was. There were plenty of things out here that would love a more mouthful-sized bite.

The men worked silently, flashing hand signals towards each other in the dim starlight. With a silent rush the men charged.

There was a moment of confusion while the sleeping men struggled somewhere between dreams and consciousness. The giant hurled one of the attackers away and into the trees before turning onto the next.

"What the...Larry? It's... hey it's Larry," said one of the attackers.

"Grento?" Larry couldn't believe his eyes. It took him a moment to recognize his friend.

"Everyone stop!" Grento shouted to the other men, "It's Larry!"

His command, although heartfelt and full of authority fell moot as the only one still standing behind him was Torth. Bob and

Sargasso could be heard moaning from the bushes where the big man had thrown them.

"Hey Bob, it's Larry!" Grento shouted.

Torth looked menacingly down at the Gelk, unsure of this situation. Larry seeing the giant's muscles begin to tense quickly said, "It's okay Torth, this is my friend."

Slowly and tentatively Bob and Sargasso limped into the campsite. Larry and Bob's faces both exploded into overjoyed grins.

"Larry, I can't believe it! You're ok. How did you get away from the witches? They aren't here, are they?" his eyes darted back and forth across the campsite.

"No, I escaped. With the help of my friend Torth."

Everyone seemed to realize that everything was going to be okay and they started to relax. As Larry made introductions, Torth went right back to being his friendly old self. Sargasso and Bob both liked Torth right away. It was easier to like him than not and they both had new bruises to freshen their opinions.

The reunited group packed up the camp. They couldn't stay here because by now the light and smoke from the fire would have gathered unwanted attentions. Grento led them in search of a new spot to bed down. They had to stifle their casual laughter as they were trying to be quiet. There was a good feeling in the air. Everything was as it should be. It was one of the moments that all other moments in life try to emulate. It was contagious as Torth, who was a stranger to all but Larry, felt energetically at home.

When the group reached an area suitable for Grento, they stopped to rest, and talk. The night was evaporating around them. The new light showed Sargasso's new bruises clearly. Bob didn't look much better. Torth's powerful throw had landed Bob against a tree and his chin bled from a nasty scrape.

Bob and Larry squared off against each other like a couple of farmers who both knew when it was going to rain and wanted to be the first to tell. Bob relayed the story of his adventures. Larry got so absorbed that he forgot how bad he wanted to tell his news. Bob liked to tell a story slowly while his eyes bulged wide open for effect. When he got to the part about Tock almost killing them, Larry's heart was beating as if he was experiencing it.

When the tale was told including how desperately everyone wanted to get him back from the witches and how they were attacking the sleeping campers in hopes of using one of them as a proxy, Bob let his bugging eyes close halfway, in what could be considered a farmer's challenge to try and top that story.

Larry quickly summarized what had befallen him. How the witches treated him well. He told about sneaking into Dubla's hut and seeing Torth in his cage. Torth interrupted him a couple of times to add his deep feelings about the witches. Larry described his meeting with the giant and their flight through the worms. Grento and Sargasso's ears perked up when he told the story of Bander and his torturing the witches. Larry spent the most time telling about the insane asylum and his long walk down that dark hallway to confront 'George'. When the narrative was over Bob nodded his head and raised his eyebrows as if to say 'not bad'.

"So where does all this leave us?" asked Larry.

"Well, on the one hand," said Bob. "We're being chased across monster filled lands by another monster that wants to kill us. We're low on supplies and we have no direction other than away from everything..."

"And, a, and, on the other h, hand?" Larry prompted.

"On the other hand," continued Bob. "We're better off now than we were a day ago. We're all together now."

A warm feeling filled Larry as his brother made this point. He felt good. Bring on the monsters.

Sargasso engaged Torth in adventure-storytelling to which Grento listened, but did not participate. Bob and Larry rested against a fallen tree and continued going over the details of the past couple of weeks apart. The sun slowly rose, bringing warmth.

After resting for a while and getting further acquainted and caught up Grento led them to the south. The trees were spread out and the ground was uneven. There was a river running to their left as evidenced by the green snake-line of trees following its path. The men stuck to the path set by the Gelk knowing that most predators knew to hunt near watering holes. As the day progressed the river stayed to their left and the terrain became more mountainous.

The light blue sky carried quickly-drifting islands of clouds. The clouds looked like they were on their way somewhere, important things to do. Torth took to his new friends like a kid to a good book. He managed to find plenty of grass to munch on even though the hills were giving way to mountains.

"Guys, I've been thinking," said Bob as they walked.

In the shrub bushes to their right a small lizard darted at the sound of their footsteps drawing everyone's attention momentarily.

"If Tock is never going to give up looking for us, I mean he can't stop can he? Then we're going to have to keep moving forever. Are we supposed to become Nomads? Well I don't know about all of you but I'm about the exact opposite of a Nomad as you can get."

"I don't want to be a Nomad eith...either," added Larry.

"Ah, now you men are talking! So we hold our ground and fight."

"No, I'm the opposite of fighting too," said Bob.

"It seems that Tock is but the flower on the weed," said Grento.

"Do you think that we should try to find Bander? He sounds even worse than Tock!" said Bob.

"Maybe we could reason with him," said Larry. "Maybe he sent Tock because he didn't understand that we don't want to hurt him. Maybe if he got to know us he would call off Tock."

"I have to say I don't think so," said Torth. "He tortured Syta just to get information. He didn't waste any time getting to know what they knew. He seemed to be a man with an agenda."

"Well, even if we wanted to, we don't know where Bander lives. I'm sure the Keepers in the town know, but I don't want to go back there and ask them," said Larry.

"I don't mean to change the subject, but have any of you noticed that we seem to be following a path?" asked Sargasso looking at the ground.

"You're right," said Torth. "Its common in these hills to find that you have assumed a path. I admit it is a little unsettling to notice that ones direction had been guided by outside forces but that's a matter for the philosophers. In the hills the path of least resistance is taken by all the wandering animals and these paths are common."

Everyone besides Torth looked to Grento for confirmation if the way was safe. Grento sensing this said, "We're headed the right direction. I'd feel if there was danger lurking ahead."

Torth looked at Grento oddly as if that was a strange thing to say.

"So if we're ever going to be able to go back to Agea Hills, and be with our friends to tell our stories of grand adventure, we're going to have to confront Bander," said Bob.

"There must be other options," said Larry getting agitated. "I mean, there are always other options. One of the great things about being alive is the choices. We need to keep our various choices in mind."

"Sure," said Sargasso. "There are always options."

"Yes," agreed Grento gruffly. "We could throw ourselves off of a cliff. That would certainly prevent Tock from catching up to us. Or we could separate and each run in a different direction to be killed one by one. Or we could sit here and wait for Tock and then try to reason with his twisted reptilian brain. Sure there are always options. Bosh!"

"You paint a pretty picture, Grento," said Larry. Grento turned his attention back to the path they were now following. Torth didn't say anything as he was still getting used to his new friends but took a position beside Larry while the group climbed the hills. They walked in silence for a while as the weight of a decision hung from their backs.

Bob imagined each possible scenario to its probable conclusion. Bob enjoyed untangling knots; the tighter wound, the more satisfying. To an observer, Bob was walking along the path like a turtle. But his mind was a whirl of booms and lightning strikes.

Larry's struggle was more apparent. His eyes were squinted. His hands were sweating. His breathing was not normal. But on Larry's behalf his struggle was much more difficult than anyone else's. Larry fought his fears. He was a man wading out into a violent sea during the night. The waves of dread hammering into him from the darkness. He persevered. The sweat that ran down his face attested to the strength of the sea he was fighting. The worst part for Larry is that if he can make it through the waves he will find himself in the deep water where he really doesn't want to be.

Sargasso was fascinated with Torth and the two continued to trade stories about the countryside. Grento was a stoic as ever. Irritated, but doing what needed to be done. Grento seemed like a father and somehow had assumed this role towards these very different men.

The path led the men like a suspense novel. Ruts in the dirt from past spring runoffs made for tricky footing. Grento didn't slow and showed no concern for what might lay ahead so on they went. Finally, Grento stopped in front of a small cave.

Well, it looked like a cave from a distance; up close it was merely an indentation in the side of the mountain. There was just enough room for the men to take shelter from the sun in its cool shade. Larry hadn't realized how high they were getting until he turned his attention to the view.

Distance creates a surreal nature that draws distinct boundaries between the sharp edge of the near and the soft colors of the distant, the world through old-man eyes. Looking out on the vista of canyons with their various green patches of life and the rust red patches of iron rich clay was like standing on an artist's etching and looking down into the grooves the acid had eaten away. The group's dreams and imagination were but a smudge of dark on this vista.

Small sharp rocks covered the ground. Their uniform tannish/pink color, marked them as shards broken from some familial rock.

Two larger rocks, from different families, rested on the edge of the drop-off. They were completely immobile — perfectly still — yet their precarious location near the edge gave them a potential nature. How many years could those rocks sit looking over that edge waiting to fall, Larry thought? What eternal patience. Do they cling or is their nature to seek the lowest ground and find their satisfaction in falling? Larry was tempted to liberate them, but didn't.

Twisted dry brush jutted out from the cave face, living a solitary existence here where so few walking things have tread. There was nothing to feed on them, nothing to step on them. Here they were welcome to live. What fortunate gossamer thread cast these creatures here? Larry knew he was just allowing himself a chance to be romantic. It was silly and he stopped.

Sargasso stepped up beside Larry to take in the view. Larry smiled at the company, sharing a moment of eternity with him. Sargasso snorted and kicked one of the rocks off the edge.

The group got up and continued along the path leaving the shade behind.

"There's a man down on that ledge!" shouted Bob, pointing.

The man was barely breathing when they got to him. He lay whimpering below the trail. His body was covered with cuts and scratches. His hands and feet were the worst. Apparently he had been running along the trail when he lost his balance and fell over the side. Now he lay with a broken back, his moans surely triggering the saliva glands in all carrion eaters within earshot.

Grento approached him guardedly. With his hand he signaled everyone else to stay back. The group of men watched in silence while Grento climbed down to the man. The approach of death demands a quiet respect, the way a judge in his chambers does. The man, although badly injured and unable to move, was acutely aware of Grento's presence. Wide eyes betrayed his fear. Grento's caution was well founded for the wounded man bore a resemblance to bait.

After a careful study of the situation Grento decided things were okay and he bent down to offer comfort to the dying man. He called for Larry to throw down the small water pouch he carried. Larry complied and Grento helped the man to take a sip of water. There was no room on the little precipice for anyone else to descend so the group stayed up top while Grento talked to the man.

The quiet was shaken by a loud whimper and then a thud and silence. Everyone rushed to the edge to peer down to Grento. Larry's stomach lurched. Grento stood over the man's body and a medium sized rock lay where the man's head use to be. Grento looked up with older eyes. "He was suffering."

Bob turned and emptied his stomach. Sargasso put his hand on Bob's back. Torth bent down and offered his hand to help Grento up. Without any more discussion everyone got moving.

"It's strange how death is a private matter," said Sargasso. "As much as we try to share it through various rituals and services it's our individual burden. Even brothers cannot divide the pain between them."

Bob looked at Sargasso and saw kind sympathetic eyes. Sargasso clamped his strong hand onto Bob's shoulder. "Dealing with death is when we are most alone and the most ourselves."

No one spoke for a while then Torth called everyone to stop and pointed to a thin line of smoke where the trail bent between two mountains.

"Who could that be?" asked Larry quietly.

"That is a group of men led by a bastard named Quid," answered Grento through his teeth.

"What?" asked Bob.

"The man we found dying was running from them when he fell over the edge. It seems he was enslaved by Bander and this Quid fellow works for Bander."

"We have got to get out of here!" Larry said. "If Bander catches us he will kill us for sure!"

"Easy Larry, they are still some distance off. Quid is searching for animals to subvert for Bander's army. He sends slaves into areas that a Gelk has indicated holds something horrible. I can't believe a Gelk is helping them in this way," Grento said spitting on the ground. "The slaves draw the fiends into the open where Quid watches the thing rip them to shreds while he takes notes. He calculates which demons will work for Bander's evil intentions. If he desires the creatures, his group of soldiers sends slave after slave into the lair while they look for weakness and ways to capture the thing. The man we found was one of the slaves. He said that he was the first to ever get away from the monsters."

"How did he get away?" asked Sargasso.

"He said that he knew there was no hope for him so while the creature was engaged with a group of slaves that were ahead of him in line he ran directly at the beast ahead of his turn. The creature was either not used to things running at it or it couldn't eat all of them so quickly. He ran right past it and up this trail until his fear ran him right off of this edge."

"Vile," said Bob. "Well, we can't stay on the trail or we will run right into these lunatics."

"There are more slaves," said Grento quietly.

Everyone let these words sink into the quiet waters of their souls. They were not going to leave the trail. They couldn't.

"How many soldiers are there?" asked Sargasso.

"It sounds like about one hundred," replied Grento.

"I feel sorry for them," said Torth.

Sargasso began to laugh. Bob and Larry didn't know how to feel and Grento began walking down the trail. Larry and Bob walked side-by-side discussing the predicament they were putting themselves into.

"What are we doing?" asked Larry

"Isn't it obvious?" replied Bob. "We're marching into the camp of our enemy, a guy that wants to kill us, at odds of five to a hundred in order to try and free some men we've never met."

"That's what I thought," said Larry. "And we are doing this because..."

"Because we have a moral obligation to, that's why."

"I know," said Larry. "But if we are heading into a situation that we cannot possibly win, where all we will accomplish is to get ourselves killed too, are we still morally obliged?"

"Yes, I'm afraid so," said Bob.

"How do you know?" asked Larry.

"The same way we know all ethical dilemmas; we feel it."

"Well, that's just great!"

"What are you two girls arguing about now?" asked Sargasso grinning.

"Larry was just telling me how he wanted to be the one to scout out the enemy camp," said Bob.

"Of course," said Sargasso catching onto the joke. "I think that sounds like a fine idea."

"Well, as much as I want to be the first to rush into the line of fire I'm sure that Bob is more qualified," said Larry.

"Well be that as it may, you called it. I think that fair play dictates that we allow you your due," said Sargasso.

"This day just keeps get, g, getting better," said Larry, resigned to the fact that they weren't going to let him out of this one.

Grento, sensing that Larry's resolve and confidence were beginning to wear thin, broke in with, "We will all handle this together. They don't know we are coming so we'll use that to our advantage."

The plume of smoke that marked the enemy's camp got closer and closer. The slope of the trail became sharper and gravity pulled them towards their destiny. There was no plan, only objective.

"Sometimes an objective is all you need, Larry. The universe will provide the means. The trick is not to stop until something stops you," said Torth.

Grento wheeled on them. "Let's leave the trail here. Even an unsuspecting army will have its eyes on the trail." Quietly the party melted into the rocks and the trees.

Soon they heard the army. They were loud and obnoxious and it sounded like there were more than a hundred of them. The sun was on the verge of setting.

Sargasso had them walk in a single file line, each man watching the man in front and noticing which stones were loose and which to step on. Torth led the way.

They reached a spot from which they got their first glimpse of the enemy. It looked big. The army camped at the base of the mountain where the trail ended. It was easy to spot the slaves. The camp looked as if it was built around them. The 15 prisoners were tied together. Even if they could escape the rope, they would have to run through the entire camp. Of course this was also true of anyone trying to get close enough to free them.

Larry and company peered from behind rocks and bushes at the bustling circle of warriors.

"What are we going to do?" asked Bob. "We can't sneak up through all those men."

"If we each attacked from different spots in the night perhaps we could cause enough confusion, a couple of us could reach the captives," said Torth.

"That isn't exactly an elegant solution," said Bob.

Grento turned and with narrowed eyes said, "We don't have to get to them, we can get to the Gelk." He motioned for Sargasso to follow him and for the rest to stay put. Torth, Larry, and Bob watched Grento and Sargasso sneak from shadow to shadow towards one hundred armed soldiers.

Sargasso didn't know why Grento wanted to capture or free the Gelk but he didn't have to. Grento had demonstrated that he was a man of character, a man to be trusted and so he waited behind the rock.

Grento spotted the Gelk right off and the sight of him turned his stomach. How one of his own people could lead men to their deaths was beyond him. Even if he were a captive himself it would be better to die than cause the deaths of others. He would make this Gelk pay.

The Gelk appeared to be a prisoner as well although he wasn't kept with the slaves. Quid probably didn't want him to become friends with the sacrificial lambs. It could be harder to point to their graves. Instead the Gelk wandered about the camp, but with escort. The guard was medium-sized and armed with a sword. That's all the guard needed for a coward like this. Grento knew that when he got close enough to the other Gelk they would be able to sense each other's presence. It was just the way Gelks were. It would be interesting to see if the man walked towards him or away from him once he realized that he had company. Grento anticipated the man' path and chose a spot in the shadows to wait for him. He was not close to the perimeter of the camp but close enough to sense another Gelk. The Gelk and his escort continued on their walk and it was obvious to Grento when the man sensed his presence. He nearly fell over. His guard looked at him stupidly thinking he tripped on a rock.

The Gelk quickly regained some of his composure. He looked around in the direction of Grento but all he saw were shadows. Then he turned around and headed away.

"Run you bastard," Grento whispered to himself. Grento slipped out of one shadow and into the next until he was in position to intercept the Gelk again. This time the man did not fall over when he sensed Grento's presence but he again turned to avoid walking towards Grento. Grento intercepted him again and again he countered. This time his path led him away from most of the camp.

Sargasso watched with glee as the traitorous Gelk and his guard zigzagged through camp and headed right for him. He held a good-sized branch in one hand and a small rock in the other. He was perched slightly above the ground on a rock outcropping that hid him from the approaching men.

Sargasso was lit up with anticipation of the tactical move he was about to try. He had to decapacitate the soldier and get control of the Gelk without any alarm being raised. Not easy. He couldn't wait to try. And then his chance was upon him. The soldier and Gelk came around the corner and he leaped. While in the air with the impromptu club outstretched in one hand he threw the rock with the other. The rock landed about eight feet away from the man but its sound drew both men's attention away from himself and in that moment the club struck the soldier's head and he dropped unconscious. The Gelk turned to the sound of the tree on skull and there stood Sargasso with his belt knife out and a finger to his lips. He led the Gelk back towards the others.

Grento was waiting with the others when Sargasso and his prisoner joined them. Sargasso was still flushed with the excitement of the capture and prodded his trophy on with unmasked pride.

"You got him!?" exclaimed Torth with a new sense of respect.

"Right from under their noses," added Bob.

"Of course I did," said Sargasso. He was torn between acting nonchalant about the incident and bragging in detail about how it was accomplished. He decided to be casual at first and later to allow himself to be persuaded to give a recount of the terrific feat of skill.

"Perhaps we should retrace our steps a ways and make a camp, we're unnecessarily close to them," whispered Torth.

"No," Grento's voice was lifeless. "I have plans for this...traitor."

The Gelk did not flinch at Grento's threat. He looked like he was going to faint. There was no color to his face. He stood quietly.

Larry didn't like the energy in the air. The hate his friends wore now was a suit tailored for someone else.

"Why do you do this?" asked Larry. The Gelk tried to answer but his throat was dry. He choked on the first words and then having swallowed replied, "I have no choice."

"Every man has a choice," said Grento.

"Like hell!" said Sargasso at the same time.

"If it were only me, I would die. But I don't have that luxury. Bander has my family. If I don't follow orders they die and suffer, not me. My will is gone as is my choice. I am already dead."

"Why didn't you cry out when you were taken then?" asked Bob with furrowed brow.

"I thought he might kill me," he said pointing to Sargasso.

"You were right Gelk," said Sargasso.

"But wouldn't you prefer death?" asked Bob searching for the truth.

"I can't die or else one of my family will be forced to take my place. If these murders will be done, let them be but my responsibility. My dignity is in eating all the poison myself; more will taint my soul no farther. It's for this reason that you must release me."

"What? Are you crazy?" said Sargasso.

"My death, though deserved, helps nothing. You cannot free the remaining slaves. I will be replaced and the soldiers will hunt you as well. Let me go." The Gelk's speech was almost devoid of emotion.

Bob knew that he spoke the truth. Tendrils of sympathy skirted his emotions but it was hard to feel sorry for the executioner. Intentions, free will, and determinism all mixed in a miasma. What he did was wrong and no rational or emotional argument could cleanse its stink.

"There is no time for this talk," Grento spat. "Sargasso, lead them to that bunch of scrub-bushes we passed and wait for me there." Grento slid his belt knife out of its sheath. "You," he motioned to the Gelk with the point of the blade, let's go!"

"Grento?" asked Larry confused.

"Follow Sargasso, I'll join you in a little while."

Sargasso hesitated for a moment sizing up Grento's intent and then sheathed his own knife and putting his arm on Larry's shoulder turned him and said, "Come on guys."

Grento and the Gelk walked into the darkness.

Larry, Bob, Torth, and Sargasso left the lingering sounds of the army behind them.

"You don't think," Larry began.

"I don't know," interrupted Bob.

"No," said Sargasso. "Grento's a good man."

"Well, after what happened with the slave we found..." said Larry.

"That was different," said Sargasso. "He was suffering. This Gelk is healthy."

"I feel sick," said Bob.

"Maybe we should go back," said Larry.

"It's too dark now," offered Sargasso. "We would never find them without running into the soldiers."

They found the bushes and each man sat on the ground quietly. There was nothing else to say.

Grento shuffled his feet as he approached the meeting spot so not to startle his companions. He was alone.

"We can all get some sleep," he said. "But we will need to be up at dawn if we are to free those men."

"Grento," said Larry coyly. "You didn't happen to k, k kill him... did you?"

"What?!" a wave of comprehension washed down Grento's face. "Oh, Larry, of course not. That man is the key to freeing the slaves. Sleep easy, we've a trying day ahead of us."

*   *   *

The morning found Quid in a foul mood.

"Well, is the Gelk injured?" he barked at any of the three soldiers that stood before him.

"No, sir he is shaken up and claims to have a headache, but he will live."

"That's good for you, for all of you. I want the three of you to fill in for the bumbling fool you had guarding him last night. How the hell did a tree fall on him anyway? Wouldn't he have heard it? We are lucky the Gelk wasn't crushed."

"It was just a large branch sir."

"If the Gelk was killed we would be marching back to Lord Bander without our Gelk and without any information on a new beast. The last two creatures we've found couldn't be used. Bander would know they couldn't be used. We are but extensions of the beasts, if they cannot be used, we cannot be used. The pitiful slaves are more useful to our lord: they serve a purpose.

"Listen to me; explaining the essence of power to fools. I might as well pick up a rock and talk to it! Go guard the Gelk!"

The soldiers were used to Quid's soliloquies and jumped at their cue to exit. One never knew when Quid would talk himself to a conclusion that involved killing someone, maybe a soldier.

The rest of the soldiers in camp were going about their morning routines. To any trained eye, this group was slovenly. They only snapped to attention and tried to look busy when Quid was nearby. Otherwise they tried to snooze as long as possible; they didn't maintain their hygiene and they goofed off. Stale jokes were recycled from one end of camp to the other. Soldiers without enemies were undefined. A soldier bent down and picked up a handful of gravel and dirt. He threw it at the sleeping slaves. There was no reason to rouse them this early but the sight of them sleeping while he was forced awake made him mad.

"Get up you dogs! Don't expect food today, what's the point? Ha!"

The slaves sat up and gently woke up the rest of their companions. They treated each other with a gentleness that was in sharp contrast to the soldiers. Their humanity endured like a glowing ember on the underside of a log almost hidden from sight.

After the soldiers were full from their breakfast, Quid was ready for the day. The soldiers brought the Gelk to Quid.

"Well Gelk, you know the routine by now, and we didn't make camp here for no reason. Where is the beast?" The Gelk strode towards the perimeter of camp flanked by his guards and Quid. They followed him unquestionably to the edge of camp.

"Between that slope of the mountain and that dried up river bed lies the beast," he said pointing to the landmarks while he spoke.

The area looked completely benign, covered with dried, waist-high grass, undulating in the breeze.

"This is a vile monster," said the Gelk letting his voice trail off. This was what Quid wanted to hear. Like a fisherman or a hunter, he tensed with excitement.

"I haven't felt a creature this big in my life. Once provoked, it could leave the confines of its lair..." The Gelk shivered and took a step back. The guards quickly grabbed both of his arms and held him fast. All the while, they looked apprehensively at the field of grass.

"Show some backbone you coward!"

"Sir," said the Gelk. "We should climb over the rocks to the east of the riverbed. That way is safe and we will surely find a different creature to test. This one is too big!"

"Silence!" snapped Quid. One of the soldiers slapped the Gelk in the in the face and he dropped to the ground whimpering.

Quid's eyes sparkled like the fuse on a bomb. The guards, although on their best behavior in front of Quid, shared nervous glances and then scanned the soft-looking field for hidden danger.

The slaves were quickly brought to the edge of the field. Getting the men organized to watch was easier than usual. This group had seen many horrible, bloody shows and they welcomed the chance to see the next. Word quickly spread through the ranks of the Gelk's warning and, although this promised to be the best show yet, no one tried to edge himself closer to the swaying grass.

The Gelk whimpered and tried to position himself towards the east. A couple of the men followed his example and glanced at where they would run if there was trouble. Quid motioned to a slave and then to the field. Two guards dragged the man to the edge.

"You know the routine. Have some pride, give yourself a chance, pig." There was no color in the man's face and he was shaking terribly. Then he ran. The slaves knew they had to run. That was their hope. He tore into the grass like it was on fire. It was a pitiful sight like feeding day at the zoo. Twenty-five hurried paces into the grass he was yanked violently down out of sight, a horrible scream followed and then silence. It was as if the field had swallowed him and now it rocked quietly back and forth as if nothing had happened.

There was perfect silence for a few moments and then the soldiers began to cheer. Blood lust raged through them. They raised their swords and shouted. The slaves were agitated and huddled together talking excitedly. It was hard to say what relationship the dead slave had to the remaining ones. They often fainted and had to be revived at the sight of their relatives being fed to monsters.

Quid was not pleased. He wasn't paid to feed the beasts. He was paid to determine their usefulness to the order of Bander.

"Send in two this time and get one of the big ones!" he said to the guards. The two slaves met the same fate as their friends. Their screams carried through the air.

275

"What manner of devil is this?" Quid asked no one in particular kicking the ground with his boot. "We've got to get a look at this thing! Send in the rest of the slaves!"

"At the same time?"

"Do it."

Quid's decision brought a hungry cheer from the ranks of men. The slaves were lined up at intervals along the edge to the field in order to force the creature to show itself if it wanted all of them. With a shout of the guards the slaves all bolted into the grass. Once into the reeds they all converged on the center point where their forerunners had met their fate.

"What are they doing?" asked Quid. As the question escaped his lips, the slaves began to be yanked out of sight two and three at a time. The valley was full of their shrieks. As the first slave was yanked out of sight, the Gelk broke from his guards and sprinted into the field. The shocked guards took an instinctive step after him but then caught themselves and halted watching the Gelk commit suicide. And within seconds the soldiers stared at the gently swaying empty field.

Quid stared in amazement at the field.

"There is something moving in the grass!" shouted a soldier.

Quid's eyes came to focus on the movement first in one spot and then in another. At first the movement seemed benign, a curiosity, but in an instant the grass began to teem with movement and whatever it was, was coming directly at them.

Every man froze while registering what was happening. Something snaked its way through the grass towards them. A shriek crawled out of the field and nested in the ears of the soldiers. A sound of the damned. The sound of something horrible sent Quid and his men scrambling back, tripping over themselves.

To the east of the riverbed they ran, twisting their ankles as they lurched over rocks and crevices. The movement in the swaying grass swept towards them like a wave. Something primal was at work in their brains as they stumbled over each other dropping their belongings as they ran. The dried riverbed just over the rocks beckoned them like an island at sea. They ran headlong into the beast.

The apparent safety of the rocks was a camouflaged nightmare. Dusty arms lifted themselves from the ground and whipped into the men. These arms were fifty feet long and covered with two-foot long spikes. Every man's footfall seemed to have unleashed a spring and these spike cords sprang through them impaling men and lifting them off of their feet as it did.

The men tried to stop running but most were too far into the lair. Screams and gurgles and thuds filled the air as groups of men were lifted off their feet impaled on a tendril. Then rising up was the body of the beast. It could have been a rock for its coloration but when it shifted its enormous body one could see the glistening red wetness of its mouth.

It moved and its mouth was hidden from view but as bad a sight as that was, it was nothing compared to the sight of those huge spiked arms wiggling in the air covered with the broken bodies of the impaled and bleeding men. One man slid off of the spike and he no sooner landed on the ground than a different arm whipped into him puncturing his arm and side and lifting him up to let his blood drain down out of him. Not all of the soldiers met this fate, some of them stopped in the nick of time and they watched their friends gored to pieces. Quid rubbed his knee where he had hit it when he fell. This was the sweetest injury of his life.

Chapter Twenty-Nine

Grento led the slaves quickly up the riverbed. They used the tall grass to hide their passage at first and then once around a bend in the mountain they stood. Torth brought up the rear in case any of the soldiers made it past the beast or figured out the deception early. No one followed.

"Good job, Grento!" said Sargasso enthusiastically. "That was one hell of a great plan."

"It seems that we have the devil's luck with us," replied Grento with an uncharacteristic smile. "Sometimes the universe provides. The grass that hid our escape, having a man on the inside."

Everyone turned towards the traitorous Gelk. "His name is Stip," said Grento. "That took great courage to do what he did. Granted, he didn't display his courage earlier but perhaps we all need a little direction to release our potential."

Stip walked on, crying. His body was racked with emotion, the joy of freedom, the guilt of his past actions, the tension of his deception and his worry for his family.

The slave's feelings towards this reformed executioner needed a centrifuge.

Larry thought about Stip. Do glorious actions cleanse one's soul of their past actions? We do not blame men for the mistakes they made as children. Does it not follow that we not hold them accountable for their past? Or was Stip's soul already turned off, like a switch or like a match doused in water — gone. And no matter what change of heart or action those sins had left him forever tattooed in blood.

He watched Stip where he stood crying.

"What do we do now?" said Bob.

"Well really there is no choice... we must stick together. I mean without Grento's help the slaves would stumble into trouble," said Sargasso."

"The slaves are in danger with us and they want to get back to their families. Perhaps Stip could lead them where ever they need to go."

"I will lead these people back to their village," said Grento.

"But Grento, we need you here with us," said Larry shaken.

"Stip must get back to his family. He risked everything he cares about to free these people. He must attempt to free his family before they are killed or forced into Bander's service. I admit, I feel empathy for them, they are Gelk."

"So where does that leave us?" asked Larry.

"You may either accompany me and the slaves back to their village or travel with Stip."

"Stip? He's no leader. We'll stay with you, of course."

"Think on it. Sargasso and Torth will stay with you as well. I wish I could stay but there is no way. The slaves would be in danger from Tock if you traveled with us. Sargasso and Torth accept that risk. The Gelk is going right back to Bander's land. Back to your destiny."

"Destiny?" said Larry. "Isn't that a little strong? I mean all I want to do is have a little talk with Bander and clear some stuff up."

"Larry you are fooling yourself," said Grento. "Look at these people. They didn't get emaciated and scared themselves. Bander did this to them. He sent a Tock to kill you. I don't think he will be open to conversation."

Grento shook his head in frustration. He seemed sorry that he had been so cross but determined to say what he had to say. "Come on," he said to the slaves.

Larry watched them walk away.

*　　*　　*

Stip led them through a field back around the mountain. It felt odd to follow Stip, like putting a shirt on backwards.

"Won't we run into what's left of the soldiers?" Bob asked.

"We might see them but there's little to worry about. Without me to guide them, those fools will have to retrace their steps back to Bander's Keep. We will move between the cells and easily get in front of them. We must hurry. I must rescue my family before news of my treachery reaches the soldiers in Bander's Army. From what Grento told me, you fellows won't mind the haste and putting some ground between you and that snake."

"That's true," said Bob.

Bob had already adjusted to the new situation. That was one of his gifts. He was able to differentiate the things in his life that he could change and the things in his life he couldn't. Whatever the situation, he found a density in which he floated.

Larry on the other hand, could be in the same circumstance and floating but he couldn't help but thrash about.

Torth and Larry passed the time talking about the witches and the tales riveted everyone else. Everyone got especially interested in Larry's discussion of magic. Except Sargasso.

His experience with magic usually involved pain. "What those witches do, and what spells they cast, is not for us Larry!" His eyes danced wild. Magic was something he didn't understand and his world had no use for the knowledge.

Magic fascinated Bob. To him this was a new tool, a new science. The little snippets of magical knowledge he could gleam from Larry were like a stolen bite of turkey from a protective cook.

Larry enjoyed being the cynosure of their group. Sargasso offered careful warnings while Bob dug for information, Torth interjected stories about the witches and their evil ways. There was always a hint of nostalgia when he spoke though, the same with Larry. Somehow those three women, who could be so cruel, had planted some warm feelings. Women have their ways and even the most foul, especially the most foul, can stir an emotional attachment. Like a bad taste that still makes you salivate.

Stip led without comment, his thoughts were elsewhere and he wasn't friends with these men. They had saved him, but his debt was with Grento. Plus these men scared him, especially Torth. These guys walked the high path, something that he hadn't been able to do. This represented a sort of power to him. It showed him where he was weak. Like a flashlight illuminating a crack in a basement foundation, obscured by cobwebs and darkness.

"That is the stupidest magic trick I have ever heard!" Sargasso intercepted a comment from Larry to Bob. "What do you mean you concentrate? What good does that do?"

"I'm not sure," replied Larry "I think that the lesson was maybe more of an exercise in thinking than conventional magic."

"I think it was a distraction," interrupted Torth "A bit of cleavage to disguise the knife at the belt. If you know what I mean."

"I don't think that was it," said Larry with a smile. "I really think that there's something to it. It's hard to describe but it's like a state of mind, but not a state of mind, more like a state of receiving sense data. It's noticing all the crap you are experiencing at any one time and letting it blur together and then being able to let one thing in, something that you choose to let in."

"What good does that do you?" asked Sargasso.

"I don't, know. It might be that once you have acquired this alternate frame of mind where your reality is different, different things are possible."

"You mean like the way emotions can affect a person's reality?" asked Bob.

"Kind of. Look at good old Torth here. He is always happy therefore things are possible to him that aren't possible to others or, rather, things that are possible to anyone are not shut away to him because of some limiting belief or emotion."

"Anything is possible in your dreams?" said Sargasso scoffingly. "That is the tallest steaming pile of crap I have ever heard! Why don't you two philosophers talk yourselves out of existence?"

Stip led them back past the valley where he'd escaped. They kept far enough away to avoid stumbling across any soldiers that might have survived the monster.

Stip was Gelk and Grento had trusted him to lead the men through the wasteland safely, but the men didn't trust him immediately. They worried about his intentions and his skill in choosing the safe path. Grento had made it sound like Gelks could just tell which path was right. But were all Gelks equally adept in this capacity? Bob followed without trepidation. Worry wouldn't make it any safer so he decided to trust him and that was that.

"We'll be to the town by nightfall," said Stip trying to be friendly and make a little conversation with everyone.

"Who was the guy in charge of the soldiers?" asked Sargasso.

Stip's voice turned to acid while he described Quid to them, "You think Bander is bad? Quid is every bit his equal in evil. Bander may give the orders and his appetites light the fires, but Quid carries out the orders. His hand animates the blade. If the beast I pointed Quid and his men towards got him and still sucks the

283

living flesh from his bones, then good. His crimes cannot be paid back. There, justice falls short," spittle flew from his mouth.

Larry looked over to Torth and saw a look like he felt. Something akin to, 'This guy is way too angry and maybe a little crazy.' It was nice to have friends that thought like he did. It made him less lonely and validated his feelings giving him confidence. It was as if through friendship he could tap into another's strengths and use them like his own. He wondered what possible strengths he might have that others would think were admirable.

"How are we going to rescue your family?" asked Larry.

Stip turned on him as if an invisible ghost had whispered into his ear, "You are under no obligation to help me. I'm in your debt."

"Of course we'll help," said Sargasso slapping Torth on the shoulder. "This gang thrives on adventure!"

"It defines us," Bob joined in playfully. Torth let out a bark of a laugh. Tears pooled in Stip's eyes and he took an inward step back towards humanity.

"They'll be living in the compound at the base of the mountain where Bander's fortress stands. The compound is enclosed within the walls of the city. They will not be well guarded because the walls of the city are patrolled. That is, unless news of my treachery reaches Bander before we do. That is not an option."

"This doesn't sound like a challenge worthy of our daring," joked Sargasso.

"Sargasso," said Stip. "The stakes make this the most extreme challenge of all for me. If one guard calls out an alarm because a mouse spooks him, my family will be worse than dead."

Chapter Thirty

That night they saw the city. An impressionist's abstraction, a dark canvas bespectacled with dots of firelight. The wall was easily seen as a straight line of equally placed torches.

"So it's walled-in?" said Bob "I kind of figured it would be."

"The walls will be guarded by patrols," said Stip. "Although the guards are more for show and keeping folks inside, they still can signal an alarm."

"The darkness is our companion tonight," said Sargasso "If we keep our distance from the torches, and mind where we focus our eyes, we should be able to stay out of the guard's sight."

The men stared down on the twinkling city. It looked so peaceful and so pleasant. In the dark they could hardly see each other, so establishing the attack plan was slow going with phrases like "You see the third light down from the left side?"

Although Stip had to describe the layout of the city, as he was the only one who had ever been there, Sargasso's love of tactics had him stealing the show and laying down plans.

Once an entry point was established, in single file they slid into the city like a crocodile into the water, each man holding onto the man in front's coat tails for direction.

The wall offered little resistance as Torth easily boosted each man in turn up and onto the wall. The walls were about six feet thick and built so that troops could fire through the shelter of the edges. Interestingly they allowed firing both away from and towards the town.

In the distance, guards could be heard engaged in casual conversations. Torth had to get a bit of a running start to bound up and pull himself up the wall. He made a little bit of a grunt and whooshing sound as he dragged his body over the edge, just enough to make everyone freeze in the darkness with eyes like owls and ears like space, but not enough for the guards to notice. They held their poses for a minute while they caught their breath and blended in with the normal night sounds. They grouped up and, without talking, formed a line and began following the edge of the wall. Larry noticed that he was thrilled. He had smeared adventure all over his skin and now he itched with it. He inhaled in the living night air and concentrated on staying quietly in line.

The murmur of guard's voices grew louder as they proceeded. Bob had one hand on the Larry's cloak and Torth's big hand, pawed at the hood of his cloak.

Bob's mind wandered. Here they were, being led by a man two thirds crazed with panic, through the dark. Still, they didn't stop. Interestingly, Bob knew that no matter the upcoming danger, the line would not stop unless the front of the line called halt. Humanity wants to follow. It almost feels instinctive yet even while he reflected on this Bob knew that he wouldn't stop unless the one he clung to, stopped. What type of man could stop? Would it be an admirable, noble quality to be able to act individually when the herd says "mush?

The voices grew louder and Larry felt his "thrill meter" click from the 'Green adventure' zone into the 'red, alert,' danger zone. Not good. They silently eased around the guards and down some stairs into the city. Stip stopped moving after they were out of earshot of the wall guards. "This is going better than I hoped," he said in a whisper.

"Where to now?" asked Bob.

"My family is kept in a housing complex on the west side of town. I would like to proceed alone. It'll be quicker, with less chance of discovery."

"Are you sure? We're in this for the long haul," said Sargasso.

"What if you need our help?" asked Bob.

"If you wait right here I can go check and come get you for help. But I must at least give my family the chance. I must warn them to flee and hide even if I can't free them myself. I will let them know it's not safe. Once they are warned I can return to get your help.

"If you think it's the smart thing to do than I have no objection," said Sargasso.

"Agreed," said Torth.

Stip stood for but a second in quiet acknowledgement of their help and then turned and padded off into the darkness. Torth and Sargasso made snorting sounds that Larry took to mean "Oh well, good riddance."

And then they stood near a wall. Somehow it gives a purpose to standing. As if standing in the open isn't justified but if there is a wall there then it is ok. That probably dates back to a survival instinct where the open is exposed and a wall is cover.

Here these rapscallions were, in an enemy camp on a mission, wanted by the authorities and, because they were together, they stood around telling jokes. Their gentle voices would be taken for guards if any one heard them. "Gees, Larry," said Torth "You were pretty heavy to lift up on the wall. Maybe you have been eating too much sugar bread."

"Maybe someone could stand to do some pushups," replied Larry.

"Now, now girls," said Sargasso. "I'm sure that you are both right."

Torth and Larry turned with furrowed brows towards Sargasso and he reflected back sunshine. After a while the conversation slowed down and everyone began wondering when Stip would return and if at some point they should go looking for him.

Stip did not return. As the sun began to rise the men knew that they would have to find a place to hide before morning. They all felt a little strange about abandoning their post in case Stip needed help but they had little choice and they would be no good to anybody if the soldiers captured them.

They found a run-down inn, the kind of place where folks would rather not know what was going on inside. Sargasso went in alone to see if he could secure a large room that they could sneak Torth and Larry and Bob into without them being seen. He found and rented the room and from the back of the establishment the three secret guests climbed through a large window opening.

Once inside the men all felt a whole lot better. Here they could rest, regroup, and make plans. Sargasso was the scout of the group as he was the only person that would not draw the immediate attention of the soldiers. Torth stood out, well, like a damn giant and Bob and Larry's eyes marked them for whom they were.

"Well at least we have a base," said Bob.

"Yeah, but we can't stay too long or we run the risk of being found by Tock," replied Larry.

"We need a plan," said Sargasso with his animated smile.

"We can't just sit around and hope that Stip finds us. We have no way of finding out where his family lives or if he was successful in freeing them," said Bob.

"What about Grento?" asked Torth.

"Yeah, how is he going to find us here?" asked Larry.

"We can't worry about Grento," added Sargasso. "He can take care of himself. He'll find us. Of that you can be sure."

"We all know what we have to do," said Bob. The men looked at Bob expectantly... "We have to go to Bander's Keep and see what we can do to get Tock off of our trail."

No one said anything for a moment while each man came to grips with what that would entail.

"He's r...r... right," stammered Larry. "There's no other way, if we stay here we are basically prisoners until the guards eventual find and arrest us. If we go back into the wasteland we will eventually make a mistake and Tock will have us. The dishes in this sink have soaked long enough."

"Larry, my friend, you never cease to amaze me," said Sargasso slapping Larry on the back. "What do you say Torth? Shall you and me add a chapter to our adventure with the Masefield brothers?"

"Well I was planning on finding some dandelion wine in this town and drinking myself silly for a week or two but I suppose I could storm into the muskie's lair with you guys. Why not?" said Torth.

Chapter Thirty One

Bander's Keep perched above the town, built into a mountain. Looking up at the Keep from the town was like looking up to a ceiling and unexpectedly seeing a spider. Not good. Scary, really scary.

Inside the main entrance room of the Keep, Quid paced. He waited for an audience with Lord Bander. The pacing released nervous energy and he kept his eyes on the ground.

This was Bander's Trophy room. The place was full of stuffed creatures. Every beast that Quid and his men had brought to Bander over the years was stuffed and on display in this room. There was every imaginable shape and size of creature in here. Most of these foul things had killed many human slaves and it had taken numerous attempts by many soldiers to rip these nightmares from the cells in which they lived in the wasteland. Yet Bander had killed them all.

Quid brought the things to be inspected and if they were not brutal enough for Bander's liking —and they never were — he killed them and had them stuffed and then put into this room. This was the only room of the keep that the townspeople were ever allowed to enter. And in fact, Bander made it a law that every person in the town was required to visit the keep and walk through this room. It was a testament to his power and drove the point home about who was in charge.

Quid got his audience and walked down a hallway to talk with Bander.

"Lord, we have found a new beast for you," said Quid.

"Of course you have," Bander said in monotone.

"This one looks like what you have been looking for, my lord, they call it a Goar. I think it might be..." said Quid.

"It is about time," said Bander at Quid's presumption.

"This beast surpasses all others, my lord, if you went to a monster store and asked for them to put something together with all teeth and claws, this is what you would get," said Quid.

"Good," said Bander.

Quid took this as his sign to leave and did so quickly. Bander did not have any patience and would not tolerate anything. It was best to stay clear of the man.

As Quid left, Bander felt a tickle of anticipation at the prospect of the new creature. He always looked forward to testing the things but this time he was especially excited. Quid might be a fool but he had been bringing him all sorts of creatures for years and he would know when one was special.

Bander turned towards his personal chambers. Past his hot springs he walked. The chamber smelled of sulfur. The walls were wet rock; mold grew everywhere. Bander wound his way past the stalagmites that jutted up from the floor and slid into a small opening in the rock. He felt the chill of the ghosts of time as he walked down this sloping tunnel. The only men to have walked this path before him were all still in the chamber ahead. Not dead, but not alive either. They were trapped forever, lost, great men, the champions of each of their days. But they had come up short in their quest for power and paid the price of the ante. Now it was Bander's turn to try.

He would not fail as they had. He had taken his time, done his research, and planned for all possibilities. He would claim the magic as his own. And this beast, if it were as good as Quid said it was, would be the secret to his victory.

Bander paused just outside the room to acknowledge the power contained inside and in silent reverence for all the great men of power whose souls guarded the magic. He held the key in his hand and though he could not see he would have no trouble opening this door. The key looked like a tuning fork because that is what it was. A bit of metal made so that when struck it would vibrate at a specific pitch. This pitch and only this exact frequency of sound waves would release the locking mechanism in the door. Bander felt the stone of the wall with one hand and hit the key against the wall. The quiet ringing sound this created dominated the cavern. Bander held his breath. After a moment there was a click and the door opened. Then he tightened his black robes around himself and went inside.

In the center of the circular room stood two carved vases. They sat side by side each carved in the shape of a wolf howling at an unseen moon. The life-sized vases had openings in their mouths big enough to swallow a man's fist. Stone teeth protruded beneath their rippling snarls.

Around the perimeter of the room a surreal mosaic casts an eerie glow. This shimmering mural told a story of battle and struggle. At the beginning of the story there was a golden sphere that seemed to radiate light and warmth. Reaching towards the orb was a man with tormented eyes. His right arm stretched towards the sphere and his left held a sword aimed behind him. Stretching towards this man was another man who is in the same position; one hand longingly reaching ahead and one hand defensively protecting his back. There was another man behind him and another behind that and so on. The basic pattern was the same all the way around the room. Each man was different. Some of the characters weren't even men but things that looked like they belonged in Bander's display room. But they all were trapped the same, striving for the sphere and fighting off and protecting it from everyone to come after them.

These were the men of legends, the men that defined their age. All of them had come to this room, each had made his plan and then each had thrust his arms into the guardian vases to begin the combat and to try and make it through the ranks of defenders.

Every man had failed and was therefore bound to stay and protect the magic.

Bander stood facing the walls but seeing nothing. He knew what images would be in front of him if he could see. The histories and all of his research filled his mind with what the room must look like. It smelled empty.

Bander admired the genius of the vault. Now that his time had come the magic was more protected than it ever had been before. But that was no matter for him. He would triumph, of that he was certain. Now that he had found his vessel.

Chapter Thirty Two

Sargasso slipped out of the room and went down to the common area of the inn. He had to maintain appearances to the other patrons and the owner of the establishment. This meant drinking with the locals. A man's got to do... he thought to himself. One of the girls that served the drinks had caught his eye when he rented his room and now he scanned the bar for her while he enjoyed his ale.

No one paid him much attention. He fit in, just another tired traveler seeking a few moments of relaxation and revelry. He finished his drink. He wanted another but it didn't seem fair for him to kick up his heels too much with his friends all stuck hiding in a cramped room. He needed to use this time to scout out the town and learn as much as he could about Bander's Keep, its location and its security system and anything that might help them to break into it. And he wasn't going to do that sitting here. Besides if he chanced across another drinking hole during his reconnaissance well, it couldn't hurt to stick his head inside.

Sargasso left the inn and began walking down the city's streets. He stayed in the open and walked with urgency. He knew that a man who walked with confidence was seldom looked at suspiciously.

The town was big. He crossed several neighborhoods and the buildings were getting nicer and there was less trash. He didn't feel as comfortable in the new part of town. His clothes looked rustic compared to the people milling about. He had gone far enough, he slipped into a new bar. The bartender looked him up and down and then took his order. They must not get too many non-locals in this place, Sargasso thought to himself. He didn't care. He enjoyed the attention. He held up his glass of ale and savored the golden color before taking a swig and returning his glass to the bar. He almost fell backwards out of his chair when the glass almost set upon the top of a three inch long Spiderworm.

The small worm scurried across the wooden bar and over the far edge out of sight. Sargasso gathered himself and looked at the bar where the worm had been. For a moment he relaxed and took another sip of drink and laughed at how squeamish he had acted. Then a wave of uneasiness swept over him. How could a Spiderworm get here, even a small one? He didn't think that they were very common except back at...

"Hello Sargasso," said a familiar voice behind him. Sargasso felt his blood cool and he turned around. There, standing right behind him like a specter from a dream stood Dubla wrapped in a burgundy cloak. She looked serious, like a mother who has secretly spied on a child committing a crime.

"Dubla?" exclaimed Sargasso. "How did you, what are you?"

"It's a pleasure to see you as well," smiled Dubla menacingly. "Why don't you buy me a drink?" She sat down next to him.

"Why don't you buy your own drink?"

"Be civil, Sargasso. You wouldn't want to alarm the worms on the underside of your bar stool would you?"

"Why it's," said Sargasso surprised. He looked down at his legs and his feet resting on the ring around the bar stool. Just then a mass of wiggling, disgusting Spiderworms scurried over the tops of his legs and then stopped —as if on command — not biting, but waiting for instructions. It was very hard for Sargasso to remain still but Dubla broke the mood.

"There now, nothing to fear. Let's talk."

"Well you certainly know how to make an entrance," said Sargasso, finishing his entire beer in two big gulps. He motioned the bartender to bring them a couple of fresh ones. "So," said Sargasso. "are you and your sisters still enjoying Larry's company?"

"You know perfectly well that Larry has escaped us," came Dubla's acidic reply.

"Really? Good for Larry and good for my conscience. I was beginning to feel a little guilty for abandoning Bob and Grento."

Dubla's eyes narrowed while she studied Sargasso who was busy pounding another beer.

"So you don't know where Larry went? Or his brother?"

Sargasso took a moment to belch loudly, which brought him dirty looks from the more civilized patrons in the bar.

"No I don't," he said while ordering another drink.

"I don't believe you," said Dubla and the worms shifted positions. Some of them climbed inside the bottom of Sargasso's pants and up his legs.

"Whoa," said Sargasso in reaction. "Isn't this getting a bit personal?" Sargasso's words were slightly slurred and his eyes were glazed. Dubla turned and quickly walked away. Sargasso slammed another beer and then turned and she was gone. A slow deliberate glance down at his legs and feet revealed that she had taken the spiderworms with her.

The bartender noting Sargasso's glass was empty asked

"Another one?"

"Nope," said Sargasso, exhaling. "I'm good."

*　　*　　*

There was a scraping at the door and a jiggling of the lock. Bob and Larry stared at the handle. Their muscles tensed and they waited to see what would emerge. After a couple of intense seconds the door opened and Sargasso stuck his head inside.

"Shh, it's me," he said, closing the door behind him.

"How did it go?" asked Bob quietly.

"Lads, it never stops with you guys," answered Sargasso.

"What do you mean?" asked Larry crinkling his nose, as he smelled all the alcohol reeking off of Sargasso. "What, did you fall into a keg?"

"I had a few, and a good thing I did or we would all be back in the Tanglewoods with the sisters!"

"What?" exclaimed Torth.

"That's right," replied Sargasso. "Who should I run into, complete with Spiderworms and all, but your old friend Dubla the witch!"

"What happened?" everyone said over each other. And so Sargasso told them of his meeting.

"But the witches can tell when you are lying Sargasso," said Larry.

"I've found that it's much harder to read a person when they're drunk," said Sargasso. "It's a secret of a couple of card players I've known. So you see I had to get sloshed."

"Well, bravo, indeed," said Bob. " You really took one for the team."

"But how do you know you weren't followed?" asked Torth.

"That's where I really fooled her," said Sargasso grinning. "I went outside and passed out for a couple of hours. I doubt she would have waited that whole time to follow me."

"Well there's nothing to be done about it now," said Bob. "If she followed you she knows where we are, if not, it's only a matter of time. We need to hurry up and find a way into Bander's Keep. We have too many enemies looking for us."

"I, I, I ag agree," said Larry.

Over the next couple of days Sargasso continued on his scouting and on the third morning the men made their plans. Since Bander was trying to have them killed, they obviously couldn't go through the normal channels to talk with him. They couldn't attack Bander because one, that wouldn't necessarily stop Tock and secondly, since Bander was the most dangerous man in the world, they didn't stand much of a chance. Even if they made it into Bander's Keep and got to talk with him there was really no reason for him not to just kill them. So they needed leverage, something to stay Bander's hand while they pled their case. The only leverage they had was Larry and Bob, and Bander wanted them. Basically they had no plan.

Chapter Thirty Three

Quid smiled like a lizard that had just stumbled upon a defenseless nest of eggs. He had finally found the particular beast that pleased Lord Bander and now he had found those elusive brothers. Right here, in his town! He would enjoy hearing their screams echo through his dungeon while Bander dealt with them. Quid and five of his guards stood in the kitchen of the inn where the guys were hiding. The innkeeper was doing his best to be cooperative.

"I heard a bunch of guys talking up in that room," said the innkeeper. "Of course, I've only seen the one who rented the room come and go, but I know they're in there. I can hear them talking even when the one goes out."

Quid handed the innkeeper a bottle. "Whatever that man orders for dinner you put this in his food." Quid snapped his fingers at one of his guards, annoyed, until the guard handed him a big bottle of wine. "Give him this bottle of dandelion wine also, tell him it's your birthday or some reason why you are passing out free wine."

Quid turned to one of his guards, "If that giant is still hanging out with him I want him sedated. We know from the Keepers in Ule that he loves dandelion wine." Then Quid turned back to the innkeeper, "You did right by the Lord by informing us of these strangers. If you can manage to pull this off without them suspecting anything, we will be able to remove them quietly from your inn. We might not even knock too many holes in the walls."

*   *   *

Larry dreamt he was on a tall sailing ship. The sea was high and violent. A captain kept barking orders at him, most of which he did not understand.

"Hard to port! Mind the Boom!"

Larry dashed all over the ship setting sails and trying desperately to do the right thing. With each change he made, the huge ship responded turning with the wind. All around the ocean there were thousands of ships all trying to survive the storm. Some were sinking and some were on fire. They were all in his way and threatened to sink his own ship. Then he woke up.

Larry looked around. He was no longer in the inn. He was in a dungeon cell. Bob lay sprawled on the floor nearby and Larry gently shook him to wake him up. Bob was slow to wake but came around like a lizard after a cold night. The others were in the cell too, and began to wake up. Except for Torth. He was in the cell to the left of theirs, chained to the wall.

"What is going on?" asked Larry.

"I don't know," said Bob.

"Where are we?" asked Larry.

"Looks like a dungeon," answered Bob earnestly.

"Thanks, I can see that. How did we get here?"

"The last thing I remember was watching Torth drink all that wine. The food, it must have been poisoned!"

"That rat-bastard innkeeper!" said Sargasso.

"He must have turned us in!"

Torth still slept in the adjacent cell.

"I bet they drugged us just so they wouldn't have to fight Torth."

"Maybe they wanted us alive for some reason," said Bob. "I mean, why not kill us, why stick us down here?"

"I feel like when we had eaten the witches Cullah root," said Larry. "I wonder how long we've been out of it?"

"It's hard to say," said Bob.

"We don't even know if it is day or night."

The dungeon was pretty standard. The walls were lined with holding cells. Torchlight illuminated the stone stairs leading up to a single door. The walls across from the cells contained a workbench, which was a cluttered disarray of hammers and other tools. Items, which wouldn't be so ominous if they were hanging off of a carpenter's belt.

Sargasso was up and examining the iron bars of the cage. With every movement he discovered a new twinge of pain. "I feel like they dragged me all the way here," said Sargasso."

"So do I," said Larry.

"So do I," said Bob.

"How are we going to get out?" asked Larry.

"I have a feeling, that if there is a weak spot, Bob will find it," said Sargasso. Bob smiled at the praise and silently agreed.

"Maybe once the big fellow wakes up he can break out of those chains?" said Sargasso. The men gradually gathered their senses and shook off the effects of the drug. Bob began inspecting each bar that held them. Sargasso quickly paced, he was not good at being confined. Larry tried to wake up Torth. "Torth...time to get up...come on there is lots of nice grass to eat," Larry cooed. Torth didn't respond.

"Is he still breathing?" asked Sargasso.

"Yes, I can see it," answered Larry.

"Grento," said Bob. "When Grento comes to look for us, he can let us out."

"How is he going to find us?" asked Larry.

"He's a Gelk isn't he? He'll figure it out. We'll use him as our plan B," finished Bob.

"What is plan A?"

"I'm still working on it," said Bob. Something scurried across the far side of the room and disappeared into a small hole in the wall. The men settled into the quiet of the room. Larry got a puzzled look on his face which Sargasso noticed while he paced.

Sargasso held up his hands in a shrug and then blurted, "What is it?"

"Shh," said Larry. Bob and Sargasso stared at him with curiosity. Larry looked like he was trying to think of something. "Guys, I can hear Torth breathing,"

"Yeah? So can we. He's a damn giant they are big and loud," said Sargasso.

"Let m...m... me finish. I hear Torth, I can hear you, and I hear Bob breathing but I can hear someone else breathing too. I don't think that we are alone down here."

Sargasso and Bob held their breaths and listened. After a moment they shook their heads. "Your hearing things Larry. We are the only ones down here."

"You really know how to take a dismal situation and throw a glass of water on it," said Bob.

Sargasso resumed his pacing when a voice said, "Larry, I see you have been practicing your concentration exercises."

"Dubla?" said Larry. Just then a figure removed itself from the dark shadows of the corner of the cell just to the right of theirs. It was Dubla. "You've been there the whole time?" asked Bob stunned.

"Yes."

"Why didn't you say anything," asked Sargasso.

"I've found that I can learn more by listening."

Larry walked over to the edge of the bars that separated him from her.

"Larry! Stay back," shouted Bob.

"She's fine," said Larry calmly. "Besides she can't get to us from inside that cell." Larry felt strangely happy to see Dubla. He felt comfortable, at home. "Why are you here?"

"I came looking for you. My sisters and I wanted you back."

These words were strangely comforting to Larry and his brother sensed this and didn't like it.

"Bander tracked me down and threw me in here," said Dubla.

"Why don't you escape?" asked Larry. "You're a witch."

Dubla stepped closer to the bars so that she was completely illuminated. There was a small tether trailing after her with one end growing out of the middle of her cell and the other sticking into her chest. She held up the slack part of the tether. "Bander has tied me to this spot with magic. The rope is tied to my heart I cannot leave or I will die."

"Why don't you cut it?" asked Bob curiously.

"This is made of Bander's magic, nothing can cut it. Bander is the only one that can release the spell."

"I'm sorry, Dubla," said Larry sincerely.

"Don't worry about me, Bander isn't the only one with magic. I'll figure something out. In the meantime you all need to listen to me."

"Why should we do that?" said Sargasso boldly.

305

"Because," and Dubla's eyes flashed with insane intensity "your lives depend upon it!" Larry and Bob looked at each other uncomfortably. "You all," she paused pointing her finger at Torth, "need to listen." And as if on command Torth woke up.

"What's this?" the giant murmured as sleep fell off of him like rainwater. As he rolled over the chains made that distinctive steel-on-stone scraping sound.

"It's okay Torth," said Larry quickly, "We're all here. The food and wine was drugged. We're in Bander's dungeon."

Torth took in his surroundings and his eyes narrowed menacingly when he saw Dubla.

"Don't worry Torth," continued Larry. "She is tied to the ground. She can't hurt you."

"Well, maybe I can hurt her!" Torth tried to move around in his cell but the chains held him fast.

"Behave yourself Torth," said Dubla. "Or maybe you'll find yourself back in my maze." Torth didn't like this threat at all but didn't respond.

"Bander is going to try and take an ancient magic. He must be stopped!! You must stop him!" said Dubla loosing control of her voice.

"Look lady, in case you didn't notice we're prisoners here just like you," said Sargasso patronizingly.

"We couldn't stop Bander from doing anything!" said Bob exasperated.

"You must. There is no other choice," said Dubla. "While you were unconscious, Bander stood down here in this dungeon and looked you over. He tormented me with his plans. He is half insane."

"Why didn't he kill us? I mean if he was down here and we were defenseless?" asked Bob.

"You still are defenseless. To Bander, you are nothing. He dispatched Tock before he realized that you offer no real threat. He holds you here to bring Tock to him. Once Tock has killed you he will be ready for Bander to use once again. But this cannot be. Bander must be stopped. If he gains the old magic he will be all-powerful."

Dubla went on to explain about the chamber and the circle of guardians that protect the magic. "It sounds like a lot of powerful guys have tried to get the magic and all of them have failed. Why do you think that Bander will succeed?" asked Sargasso.

"Because Bander is not only powerful, he's smart. And he's old. None of the men who have taken the Hero quest waited like Bander has. Bander has scoured the wasteland looking for a creature so vicious that it would have no match. Last week they got it. I think that Bander is going to use the creature as his champion to destroy all the defenders of the magic. But most of all, because Bander told me he was going to succeed. Bander doesn't brag and when he says that he will succeed, I believe him!"

"Well then, that's that," said Torth. "You can't stop the sun from setting."

"But he must be stopped!"

"But he can't," said Bob.

"The chamber is deep in the keep, past his private area. Lie in wait for him; destroy the vases that allow him into the battle. Drop rocks in front of the chamber...Stop him! The universe will provide the means. Now go!"

As she spoke these words, Spiderworms scurried out of her cloak and across the dungeon floor. They climbed up the iron bars and into the keyholes and there was a click and the cell was unlocked.

The men watched in disbelief but Sargasso quickly scurried out of the cell and retrieved keys to unlock Torth's cell and chains. Soon all the men were free and climbing the stairs to the lone door. Larry looked back at the witch and felt pity. The men snuck out the door. Soon they were out of the dungeon and into the keep.

Chapter Thirty-Four

Bander wasted no time. The creature that Quid had finally secured for him was free of the drugs that had been necessary to capture it. Even drugged to a fraction of its healthy capabilities, it had killed eight soldiers and many slaves. Now it sat hunched in the furthest corner of its cage eyeing Bander with sheer hate.

Edgar Allen Poe couldn't have dreamed up a thing so foul. It would kill all those in his way. Bander had closed the door to his private chambers and left Quid and some of his soldiers guarding from the outside. What he intended could have no interruptions.

The Gour watched Bander make a fire. Shadows danced to silent evil rhythms. Bander pulled an ancient knife from the mantle and the shadows danced to a crescendo as Bander viciously thrust the blade into his stomach. Pain welled up in him. The blood vessels in his neck throbbed with his straining heartbeat. Tears poured from his eyes. He slid the knife out of the wound in his stomach releasing a torrent of blood. He dropped the knife casually and then gathering his strength he thrust his hand into the wound. Blood poured over his fingers and pain surged through his spine and then his fingers found what they were probing for and out he pulled a twisted black root.

He held the root, which was sprung from a seed he had planted in himself all those years ago, up and stared wide eyed at the little black thing that now shared part of his soul.

With the blood trickling down his forearm and the lights going out in his body he cast the foul bit of himself into the fire. For a moment he watched the fire take it and then his body collapsed. The putrid black smoke weaved like a serpent through the air and into the nostrils of the Gour. The beast had a moment of realization that something was wrong then its eyes rolled bloodshot up into its skull. Its body spasmed and when the eyes rolled back, Bander looked out into the room.

Chapter Thirty Five

Tock slid like the plague along the corridors of Bander's Keep. His reptilian body patiently hunted for smells or quick movements. The brothers were close, he had just missed them in the dungeon but he would not let them out of the keep. The agony he had felt the first times Bander cast his soul in mortal pursuit of some unsuspecting person had dulled with time. Like the annoyance of the first few drops of rain passes as you get soaked through. Tock was soaked through and the guilt and moral dilemmas were dull. The floor felt cold on his scales. He kept hunting.

*   *   *

"Keep your eyes on that room, soldier!" snapped Quid. "The only way any one can approach is through that damn trophy room."

"Sir, with all due respect, no one is going to try and come through a trophy room full of demons to battle fifteen armed men to get into Bander's chambers where Bander would kill them instantly. Not going to happen."

"You still ask the ladies in town to go out with you and we all know that's not going to happen, so guard your post soldier!" Quid said loudly trying to get a laugh out of the other guards. They didn't laugh and Quid was left standing there in the silence, exposed and embarrassed.

"Watch these passageway with your lives. I will return shortly." Quid's men stood at attention while he walked away.

"Where do you think he is going?" said one of the soldiers once Quid was out of earshot.

"I don't care. Anywhere but right here is fine with me."

"He is probably going to go get his pet Spitt. He has been on edge all night. I hope he doesn't bring that thing down here."

"It killed all of those men you know. The ones at Bander's celebration."

"Yeah," the man shuddered.

* * *

Larry followed Sargasso through the halls of the keep. The passageways smelled like moldy wood. The walls of veneer probably covered sweating stone. The halls turned and several times the group was forced to decide on a door or fork in the way. The sound of soldiers voices made most of their choices for them. They turned away from the sound and meandered through the rooms and halls of the keep. Twice they were startled by rats hugging the floorboards going about their dirty little rat lives in the dank.

Bob's imagination interrupted him several times as the architecture switched from wood to exposed brick to smooth natural stone. Many of the rooms looked to have been constructed by different people from different times. He looked up to his brother or Torth to make some comment on the interesting things he noticed but didn't say anything when he saw the tense sneaking pose each struck.

* * *

Quid heard the voices as they passed by the room he occupied. He felt his heart leap in his chest. He never took these back passageways. What luck! This night's excitement didn't disappoint. Bander miscalculated. The old man was too focused on his magic and his conjurations. He left the men for Tock to kill and now they had escaped. Quid wanted this kill intensely. This was unexpected, and immediate. There was no time to waste. Bander would not want them to interfere. And Bander wouldn't be around for hardly any time now. Quid knew that Bander had lost most of his sight the night he was attacked. He hadn't let on and Bander hadn't offered any information. Of course he wouldn't. He never trusted Quid — not that he should have — but Quid resented it nonetheless. Bander was starting to make mistakes and Quid was starting to clean up the messes. Scales began to tip.

Quid scurried along the floorboards and behind a wall. The Keep was full of partial walls and hidden doorways. He felt alive. He could call for the guards or double back and bring reinforcements. But the giant would be hard to fight in closed quarters. There was only one sure way to kill the four men, he must get them to his chambers, to the Spitt.

*   *   *

Torth kept his steps as quiet as he could in the deserted passageways. His chest tightened as this reminded him of Dubla's maze. He walked at the rear of the group, a living wall of protection from attack to the others. He would protect these men that had befriended him. Larry shared the experience of the witches with him. That was no small thing. In Dubla's hut Torth had been made small. He had become vulnerable and he had schemed of escaping and helping Larry to escape the torture that he had endured. Torth was not unaware of his giant's nature. Once his instinctive protective emotions kicked in he would forever feel bound to protect his master. This was the result of years of selective evolution back in the days when giants were bred to serve men. They were somewhere between pets and slaves. Although that was a thousand years ago the instincts remained.

Torth felt the pang of protection kick in and hit him in the temple when he heard Larry catch his breath.

"Hello," Sargasso said tentatively.

"Don't hurt me," whispered ragged figure crouching in the shadows in front of the group.

"What is it?" Torth demanded.

"There is someone up ahead," whispered Larry.

The group gathered together and surrounded the little figure. He looked like a soldier but smaller. He cowered in front of them with his hands up in a defensive gesture.

"Please don't hurt me. Don't turn me in," said the little man.

"What is this?" asked Bob.

"Who are you?" demanded Sargasso briskly under his breath. He motioned to Torth to keep an eye behind. Torth understood and turned to face the hall they had just traveled.

"I am just a servant to the realm. Nothing more. I must have wandered down the wrong passageway it is easy to get lost," said the man.

"Don't worry," said Larry. "We aren't going to hurt you. We will be on our way."

"Thank you," said the man.

"Hey do you know your way around this keep?"

"Of course sir. I have worked in humble service for most of my life," said the man.

"Do you know where Bander's room is?" asked Bob.

"Yes, but why would you want to go there? Bander is best avoided," said the man.

"Never mind that," said Sargasso looking around to see if anyone was coming.

"Can you show us the way?" asked Bob.

"If you don't turn me in, I will take you there," said the man.

"Okay, it's a deal," said Bob. "Lead on."

Larry watched the man with the bent over shoulders scurry ahead of them. "I guess the universe provides again, eh Bob?" he said.

"Yep," answered Bob.

The man stopped and opened a door. He paused for a minute to check if it was empty inside and then motioned them in.

One by one they crowded into the room.

"What w, w, was th,th, that?" asked Larry.

"I heard it too," said Bob.

"It was just a rat, running from the sound of our approach," said the man as he walked over to a large ornate desk that dominated the room. Bob and Larry felt the pang of fright when their eyes focused on the stuffed creature perched to the left of the chair behind the desk. It took a moment to realize that the thing wasn't moving that it was locked in a pose similar to the things in the trophy room. The goose bumps remained on Larry's arms while his brain argued with his instincts that everything was alright nothing to fear from the dead.

"This must be Bander's room," said Sargasso.

"I thought it would be more grand," admitted Torth wiping at a big cobweb that his hair had mopped off of the ceiling.

"The master keeps a small chamber," said the man walking to the far side of the desk.

Sargasso picked up a book off of the shelf and bored with it tossed it down.

"Be careful with that!" spat the man.

"It is just a book. Where is Bander?" asked Sargasso.

"He will be here," said the man.

Larry looked around the room. It was cluttered with old books and potions and tools. He figured Bob was loving it. The piles of yellowing parchment. The bowl where something had been burned. It all smelled familiar. Something was, he couldn't figure it out but he was sure that he was noticing something. It reminded him a little of Dubla's hut. The clutter and the items that he had no idea what they did and something else. He felt nervous and not just nervous because he was about to confront Bander but nervous like something was hidden from sight. It felt like something was going to jump out of the dark reaches of the piles of junk.

"How do you know?" asked Bob.

The man looked up from the desk into Bob's face.

"How do you know that Bander will be along soon?" Bob repeated.

"Well I should think that serving the Lord Bander for the past 16 years I would know his habits," said the man.

"Serving?" said Bob.

"With pleasure," said the man perfervidly.

Sargasso looked to Torth. The big man nodded in agreement that he was ready to fight.

"Allow me to introduce myself," said the man. "I am Quid, leader of the soldiers, Bander's eyes and sword, and the man responsible for your deaths."

Bob surveyed the scene quickly. Larry stood right next to the desk the closest to Quid. Bob stood in front of Sargasso and Torth was hunched over near the door.

"That is mighty impressive," said Bob. "But unless Bander is on his way, it looks like the four of us will have something to say about that."

The men stood still eyeballing each other. No one wanted to make the move that would send events quickly to their conclusion. Quid sat behind the desk and a evil curling smile played across his face. He seemed to be savoring the moment. This confidence kept Sargasso and Torth from leaping at the scrawny man.

"You see, you never had a chance. From the moment you were born with the mark on you," Quid raved. "There have been others you know, with the dead eye. Tock has murdered each of them in turn. It is strange how drifting trash gathers more trash to it." Quid said turning his glance to Sargasso and then to Torth. "Like attracts like. Oooh, a giant and and, well, I guess you would be an adventurer. You must be the scum of the world. The dead eye marks the most base of all creatures." said Quid turning back to Larry and then Bob. "The mark is the mutation. You are like a bird born without feathers or a three legged dog. Usually the marked are quickly killed and eaten. That is the way it is supposed to work. Mankind has screwed it up. There is no kindness in perpetuating a mistake. Your kind must struggle just to survive. The very dregs of humanity. Well, here you can finally rest. Quit your thrashing against the inevitable. I will be your angel."

Larry's arm lashed out. His hunting knife was in hand and without any motion towards Quid he sank the knife into the Spitt. The thing instantly animated and screeched. Its hands clawed at the knife that had sunk to the hilt in its furry chest. Blood gushed over its hands and it thrashed on its pedestal until, weakened from blood loss, it fell onto the floor with a whimper.

Quid sat petrified, his eyes were wide open. The flush of color from his impassioned speech was gone. His mind raced to comprehend the impact of the past moments actions.

Sargasso and Torth and Bob all stood tense looking from Quid to Larry wondering what to do. And then Quid grabbed at a rope that ran up the wall behind him and pulled vigorously.

"Guards! Guards!" he yelled while the rope clanged a loud bell somewhere overhead.

"Run!" shouted Sargasso.

Everyone darted out of the chamber. Sargasso passed Torth and assumed the lead. Larry and Bob ran as fast as they could following the men around corners and down dark passageways. They found themselves racing through strange halls. The sound of the alarm bell rang all around them. Quid's voice could still be heard shouting orders and spurring on troops.

Chapter Thirty Six

Torth, Bob, and Larry waited in a dark room off of a hall-way. The sound of the alarm rang through the Keep. Sargasso was out scouting for a way out as one man was able to move more quietly than four.

"This is crazy," said Torth. "Now everyone knows we are here."

"I think they knew that while we were in the dungeon," said Larry smiling at his friend.

"Well, now they really know," said the big guy.

Sargasso slipped into the room.

"Sargasso, did you find a way out?" asked Bob.

"Better, I found where Bander is," he said with a gleam.

"T, th, th,that doesn't sound b,b,better," stammered Larry.

"No, it doesn't," agreed Bob.

"It is what we have to do. Remember, we were convinced that Quid was some tough guy too and he turned out to be a squealing pig," said Sargasso spitting on the ground.

The men stood quietly for a moment each of them thinking back on some pleasant memory that they held as their own. Each of them aware of the moment and what it meant. Their lives were cemented to each others. There purpose unified and personalized.

"Let's go," said Torth voicing the groups resolve. And they moved after Sargasso into the hallway.

Larry followed Sargasso. The Keep was even bigger than it looked from the outside. Larry knew that Bob was probably completely caught up in the idea of underground tunneling architecture. All Larry could think about was the sound of the alarm bells and the dozens of soldiers searching for them.

Torth was not doing too good however. Many of the hallways were tight with low ceilings. This keep reminded him of the maze and the witches. He wanted out. Ahead Sargasso led them on. He stopped to check around corners and then signal them forward. He looked like he was having fun, like a kid playing a war game. Above them the sounds of creaking boards betrayed the presence of soldiers.

Bob wasn't thinking about the architecture. He was thinking about how his brother knew to kill that Spitt in Quid's room. Ever since this adventure began Bob started to notice that there was something different about Larry. He couldn't tell what it was; it felt more like a feeling or mood. Larry was the nicest guy he knew and in spite of his stutter and his uncomfortable personality Larry was getting along just fine. But since the interlude with the witches, Larry seemed to be getting stronger or more confident. It was the kind of thing that only a brother would ever notice but there was something changing in Larry. Of that he was sure. Well, they probably all were changing. That is what happens when you are chased across the wasteland. Bob figured that he would find it weirder if they hadn't changed at all.

Sargasso signaled for them to be alert and then he led them into Bander's trophy room. The huge disgusting beasts leered at them from all sides while they quietly crept to a hallway in the corner. The sounds of men's voices belched out of the hall. Guards. They would be the ones in the way. As they got right next to the hallway,, Larry looked to his friends for answers. This plan had run its course. There had to be a least eight soldiers down that hall. Each of them surely armed with swords or knives or something heavy and metal. It didn't look like there was any back way in. No lucky break at the last minute. If they wanted past the guards they were going to have to charge into what would almost surely be a lot of pain and possibly they would get stabbed or their arms cut off or maybe even killed. Or have to watch their friends get killed.

"What do we do?" Bob whispered so quietly Larry almost had to read his lips to understand him.

Larry shrugged and looked to Sargasso. Sargasso's eyes darted from side to side. He seemed to be teetering on the edge of a decision. Torth tilted his head from side to side cracking his enormous neck. The sight of his big friend was pretty scary. Larry was glad they were in this together.

"I'll take the ten in the middle," Torth said seriously.

A grin spread across Sargasso's face like a dam bursting into a dried riverbed. While Larry and Bob felt their nerves tightening and their brains scrambled for opposing arguments Sargasso dashed to the entrance.

"Well, if it isn't 'Quid and the Sycophants'," he shouted at the soldiers.

The men were momentarily frozen with surprise; then they ran towards Sargasso drawing their swords.

Sargasso ran away quickly and then made a sharp turn around a stuffed swamp beast. Torth put his huge hands on Larry and Bob's shoulders and held them back out of sight of the soldiers. The strength of the grip helped to steel their resolve and hold them against the overwhelming urge to run. The infuriated guards launched themselves towards Sargasso and away from their post. As the guards emerged from the confines of the hallway into the trophy room Torth attacked. The first soldier was knocked off of his feet by a blow that Larry could feel in his boots.

The guards went from bloodlust pursuit to unbridled fear in the beat of a heart. They came to an abrupt stop and tripped over their own feet in attempting to get away from the giant.

The gentle man that Larry had known in his travels was gone, replaced by a horrific berserker. Torth grabbed men and broke them like kindling. He hit men and their faces would disintegrate. Their arms were broken as he hurled them aside. The guards

321

rained attacks upon him. Sargasso joined the fray. Larry and Bob stood ready to strike but they didn't know how to engage the battle. Sargasso retrieved a fallen sword and now suitably armed attacked with confidence. Torth's eyes raged red like a bull's and spittle and snot spewed from his face. A guard attacked him from the side while he was engaged with another and sank his sword into Torth's leg. Torth raged with pain and turning on the man the sword was ripped from his hands by the force of the turn. Torth struck the man with a hit to the neck and shoulders dropping the man while the sword still stuck out of his bleeding leg. Another soldier saw his chance and lunged towards the giant. But Bob and Larry were upon him before he could reach their friend. Bob tackled the man while Larry grabbed at the soldiers leg. Larry struck at the struggling man while Bob struggled to hold the man down. The soldiers kicked and struggled. Larry felt abstracted from himself as he hit the man. It felt so awkward to try and hurt a person. He felt uncoordinated and like he couldn't direct his destructive energy.

The clang of swords broke Larry's momentary confusion and he looked up to see Sargasso deftly fighting off two of the soldiers. Sargasso laughed heartily while he skillfully parried and thrust. A soldier was flung into the two Sargasso dueled causing them to stumble and Sargasso dispatched them quickly. Torth stood looming over the bodies of moaning soldiers.

"That is all of them," he said between gasping breaths. His face was still glowed hot with blood but his eyes were calm. "Go on!" shouted Torth with a voice that sounded as big as him. "I'll make sure they won't get through, do what you need to do!"

Sargasso slapped Torth on the back and handed him the sword, "Okay, we will see you in a while."

Sargasso, Larry and Bob slipped down the hallway and into the caverns of Bander's private chamber.

Chapter Thirty-Seven

Bander quivered inside his new skin. He slid his oily tongue over his fangs and marveled at their size. He didn't attempt to move for several minutes as he acclimated to his new body. He could see! The world looked different from these eyes. He looked past his scaly snout and the spiky whiskers that jutted into the lower part of his vision. He was still inside his cage but he knew where the inner release was located and as he worked his massive limbs to open it he was thrilled with the sheer force of his muscles. The lid clicked open and he threw it aside and gracefully climbed out of the cage.

Gone were all his ailments; gone was the frailty of an old sorcerer. He was vital! He was reborn.

His former body lay bleeding on the stone floor. The sight held his thoughts, a moment of mourning for what he was. He felt pangs in his new stomach and felt his mouth fill with saliva. The instincts of the Gour were apparently intact and the sight of the carcass triggered a feeding response in him. He ignored it. This body was his now and he made the decisions. He moved over to the table and then thrashed it. He swung an arm across the table's face his claws ripped through the hard wood without resistance. He opened his maw and his tongue lulled out. Frothy saliva bubbled between his teeth. On the inside, Bander was laughing.

*   *   *

Larry hesitated as the cavern they followed opened into an underground hot spring. Carved stone steps led to the various pools.

"So this is the bath house," said Sargasso trying to lighten the mood.

"Maybe he's gone or maybe we are too late," said Bob.

"I doubt it," said Larry. "I don't have that kind of luck."

"I can't believe we are doing this," said Bob. "We have no plan, nothing, and yet still we walk deeper into this mountain."

"I like to think that things will work out all right," said Sargasso.

"Well so do I," said Larry, "but that's not necessarily rational."

"So maybe this is the end," said Sargasso grinning.

"Bring em on!" said Bob kiddingly aggressive.

"Yeah, brin,b,br,br, bring em on," said Larry quietly.

The spring boiled around them and the air hung humid and hot. The slime-covered rocks were slick with moisture.

"Over here," said Bob from between two stalagmites. " I found the passageway!"

Larry and Sargasso joined Bob at the opening into the rock. They stared at it quietly for a moment. The opening patiently stared past them through the ages.

"It looks kind of dark," said Bob.

"Maybe this is the wrong cave," said Larry.

"Yeah, this couldn't be the path to some unimaginable ancient magic. It looks too scary and foreboding," said Sargasso sarcastically.

Talking about it was making it worse and like a plunge, they stepped inside.

They heard the occasional 'chink' as Torth kept the soldiers back and they tried to hurry in case he couldn't hold them permanently. How would they get past them on their way back out of the keep, thought Bob. Apparently, this was a one-way mission, no one mentioned getting away again. Larry felt sick. This whole journey had been one long fall and now he was about to hit bottom.

And then there it was. The tunnel opened into a circular room. The statues of two stone dogs in its center, their snouts raised in a howl to some eternal moon. A dozen feet into the room, writhed the black coils of Tock. His massive reptilian frame undulated and his thick head slid back and forth while his purple-black tongue darted in and out.

The men froze at the entrance to the room. Behind Tock were the two statues and behind that was the most terrifying beast the men had ever seen. It was huge. It was covered in thick green scales and patches of spiky black hair. Its claws were ridiculously long. And its eyes were red. It sat back on its haunches and when it saw the men, it rose to its full height and made a guttural shrieking growl noise.

Larry, Bob, and Sargasso quivered, paralyzed with fear. Tock paid no attention to the monster behind him and kept his black swaying head focused on the men in the doorway. After the Gour finished screaming it looked from one man to the other and then with complete confidence it walked up to the ancient vases. Its claws sounded like someone was grinding bone against a whetstone as they slid over the stone floor. The beast slid its forearms into the gaping maws of the stone dogs. The dogs came to life and for a moment their eyes bulged in viscous anger and their teeth clamped down on the monsters arms.

"No!" shouted Larry. Bob and Sargasso didn't move their eyes off of Tock. "That's Bander! We've got to stop him! He is going in!"

"What do you mean that is Bander? Bander is a man," said Sargasso.

The beast howled in pain while the wolves bit into its flesh and then the dogs turned stone again and the beast was gone.

325

Larry moved towards the right of the room and Tock lunged towards him. Bob quickly moved into the room on the left and Tock turned back towards him, stopping short of Larry. Bob waved his arms to get Tock's attention. The giant snake had positioned itself well. If either man moved any closer into the room Tock would be able to strike.

"What are we going to do?" yelled Larry. " We have got to stop Bander!"

Sargasso stared at the death in front of him. All of his life he'd taken care of himself. Nothing was worth more to him than himself. Now as he watched his two friends lunge and feint at the serpent everything came into focus for him. All his fear left and he felt quiet. Sargasso ran into the room straight away and threw himself directly onto Tock.

The snake had to retreat slightly at the unexpected attack and in that moment Larry and Bob were past it.

Sargasso flailed inside Tocks coils, he fought desperately to keep every appendage moving and thrashing to give Tock little to strike at, while trying get a grip around the giant snakes neck.

Larry and Bob ran straight to the spot where Bander disappeared and without looking at each other thrust their arms into one of each of the stone dogs. Again the dogs came to life and their fangs tore into the brother's arms. They both screamed in pain and then they disappeared.

*   *   *

Bander stood at the base of an ancient pyramid. He stretched his fur-covered legs sinking his claws into the gravel at his feet. He arched his neck backward inhaling the scents around him. His tongue wormed out licking the dust off of his snout. The air had no smell. Bander had hoped to take advantage of his newly acquired Gour nostrils but apparently it would not help him here. The pyramid towered overhead. It was made of row after row of square stones stacked atop each other. Each row of stones was twelve feet tall and twelve feet deep until the next row started. A normal man would need climbing equipment to ascend each step. Bander would not.

He crouched and then sprung up landing atop the lowest row of stone. His black hairy frame and the pads on his feet allowed him to land almost silently like a cat.

"The first level," Bander relished the thought. Of course the creators would design the battleground like this. It forced the challenger to always climb from the lower ground.

Bander looked to his left and then his right. It appeared to be clear. He contemplated jumping up to the next level but reminded himself that all previous challengers must be defeated to claim the prize. So he began to circle the pyramid searching for his first opponent.

As Bander neared the corner of the pyramid his ears pricked at low melodic humming. He hastened backwards in preparation. His haunches tight like coiled springs. His yellow eyes narrowed to slits their goat like pupils scanning for danger.

The humming grew louder. Abruptly an old man rounded the corner.

"Oh be what kind of nasty are you?" the man exclaimed upon seeing Bander. Bander hesitated a moment sizing up his opponent.

"So you came to steal my magic?"

Bander nodded affirmatively.

"Well you've got a long way to go. With each new challenger the pyramid gets one level taller and they all start with me."

Bander stayed where he was. Age had taught him things aren't always as they appear and the casual way the old man regarded him seemed out of place.

"You are pathetic," the old man chided Bander. "All teeth and claws, probably no brain." The old man took off his shirt revealing his skinny frail body. "I guess I'll have to knock you back over the side," the old man advanced on Bander. Bander didn't like the apparent weakness of his foe but his, or rather the Gour's instincts, were kicking in. His mouth began salivating and his blood pumped hot. The old man continued toward him. Bander sprang. He caught the man with a front paw in the face. Bander's weight knocked the man backwards off of his feet and before the man's back hit the ground Bander's back feet tore open the man's chest cavity. Bander's claws sliced through the rib cage eviscerating him. The attack took only an instant and Bander bounded off of the corpse. He turned to look at the destruction his new body was capable of. The old man lay sprawled on his back his intestines wormed out of him. Blood spread around the body. Bander's black fur dripped with the man's blood. Bander turned to the ledge and prepared to leap up to the next level when he felt it. Heat, stinging heat. Wherever the man's blood spattered on Bander it was searing. Bander frantically tried to wipe the blood off but it was too late, the blood burst into flame. Bander roared in pain and frustration as the blood burned itself out taking with it patches of fur and skin. Bander's belly and legs blistered where the blood burned. The old man's corpse burst into flame as the phosphorus in his blood dried in the atmosphere. Bander watched the body burn and then he took a step back, his body lurched as the pain in his haunches cased him to limp. Bander forced himself onto his back feet and raised his front legs high into the air. He howled a blood chilling cry.

The designers had done a good job of protecting the magic. The first combatant was meant to die and thus weaken the challenger. He had fallen for it this time. He would be more prepared the next.

*   *   *

Larry and Bob looked up at the pyramid. Above them the sounds of Bander and the old man wafted down. They caught glimpses of the fight and felt sick as Bander won. They watched as Bander's snout and legs burst into flames. Then Bander slipped out of sight.

"It looked like Bander was going to be alright," said Larry. "Those flames went out pretty fast and he is tough."

"Well," said Bob. "At least there isn't a monster on the first level of the pyramid anymore."

"Yeah but there are about fifty levels above the first one,"

"Well we could always stay one step behind Bander. You know let him defeat one and then climb up after. We can wait until he is tired out before we attack."

Bob bent down and clasped his hands together offering a step to boost Larry up.

"Very funny."

"Allow me,…I insist," said Bob smiling.

"Oh fine," conceded Larry.

"Bander already jumped to the next level so it should be safe," offered Bob.

Larry stepped onto Bob's hands and was boosted up onto the first level of the dusty pyramid. The level was bare. There was a burnt patch where the man burned up. Larry looked up towards the next level of the pyramid. Bander was up there somewhere preparing to fight someone else. Larry peered back down at his brother and was in the motion of dropping onto his knees to offer Bob a hand up when the same old man that Bander had just killed rounded the corner.

"Two in one day, that's one for the ages," the old man exclaimed.

Larry's mind tried to make sense while the old man continued walking towards him.

"You must be some kind of wizard or something," the old man continued. "You certainly don't come across as intimidating, no offense."

Larry was reminded of his friend Torth and wished he was here with him.

"Well no use dragging this out," said the man while taking off his jacket. Larry wasted no time, he dropped to the ground and swung his feet over the side of the pyramid so that he was hanging above Bob and then he dropped down to ground level leaving the old man up top.

"Where are you going?" shouted the man peering down at the brothers. "No one has ever gone back down the temple. It's always been up and onward towards the prize.

Seeing that the old man wasn't about to jump down to pursue them, Larry and Bob relaxed.

"We don't want the prize," Bob stated.

The old man scratched his ear as if he had never seen anything so strange as the two brothers that ran away from little old him. Then an expression of grand understanding swept across his face. "You're slaves! Of course, now it makes sense. You are builders, just like me."

Larry didn't understand what the man was talking about.

"I haven't seen slaves since we built this thing. It feels like a hundred lifetimes ago. Anyone seeking the magic would climb, not retreat. Well if there's no challenger I fade to wait. If you're going to protect the magic be sure to use the slave's entrance."

Then the man faded away and left Bob and Larry staring up at nothing.

"Well there goes my idea about following Bander up the pyramid," said Bob.

"It's like a dream," said Larry. "Bander didn't really kill the old man."

"Course not. They were all defeated in the past that is why they are stuck here."

Something screamed above them and a cloud of dust kicked over the edge and rained down on them. Larry caught a glimpse of Bander's black hairy form launching itself up to a higher level.

"We are running out of time," said Bob flatly.

"I know," replied Larry. "We can't chase him up the pyramid we will get killed. Let's find the slaves entrance."

Larry and Bob began circling the structure looking for another way in. The ground was sand and dust. They left shuffling footprints behind them. Bob noticed that there was no sun in the sky, another reminder of where they were. There was no entrance anywhere on the base of the structure.

"You know Larry," said Bob scratching his nose. "The builders of this were pretty smart."

"How so?"

"Well it just seems so symbolic. Every different layer to climb gets you closer to your goal, each level guarded by its own particular challenge and every failure adds a level, its kind of like life, its like every accomplishment leads to a more precise ending.

"Yeah well if we don't hurry up Bander is going to get to the top."

*　　*　　*

Bander licked the blood from a wound on his leg. It wasn't deep. He pressed on, circling this new level looking for the next fallen champion. It didn't take too long. Bander's animal instincts sensed the danger before seeing anything and he crouched down and listened. His fur moved in a breeze and his yellow eyes darted back and forth.

A voice echoed inside Bander's head. "You can't see me creepy crawly,"

Bander's hairs stood on end.

"I see you though," the voice continued.

Bander backed up a step.

"Turn around."

Bander felt his body react to the command and before he could protest he turned around. There, a few paces away, stood a little girl. Her red hair tied back behind her ears. Her skin was covered with red freckles. She looked like any other little girl except that her eyes were yellow.

"Let's see," the voice in Bander's head intoned. The little girl's mouth didn't move but Bander knew it was her voice inside his head. "What kind of crawly are you? Stand up!"

Bander, to his horror, felt himself standing tall obeying her command.

"You nasty beastie. You want my treasure. If I can't have it no one can."

Bander didn't move, his body felt rigid. The girl's command had triggered some instinctual response in the Gour he inhabited. Bander wiped the doubt, the shadow of fear, from his mind and calmly took over his new body again. He lowered himself back onto all four legs. The girl taken aback screamed in his head.

"I said stand!" Bander felt his body shudder at the command but he held fast. "I am master of this body," Bander snarled to himself. The girl tilted her head to the side apparently confused that he was not obeying her. Her face contorted with rage and she lifted her hands in front of herself. Bander felt a tremor in the stone at his paws. Suddenly from out every crack or hole in the pyramid poured rats. White ones with pink eyes and hairless skin tails clamored over each other in a race to get to Bander. Thousands of vermin surrounded him launching at him biting and scratching anywhere they could. Bander swiped at them with his claws but his body was ill suited for battling small numerous attackers. On they came. Bander's legs dripped red with blood. Bander launched himself into the air to shake off the mad little vermin.

The girl, he must kill the girl. He forced the thought to the front of his mind and he charged at her. The surge of rats blocked his path and almost succeeded in knocking him over. A ripple of fear coursed up his spine at the thought; if he lost his footing amongst the throng of vermin he would never regain it. The girl's snarl turned to a smile. Bander stopped thrashing at the rats. He calmly hunched down and let the hoard climb all over him. Within seconds he was covered with biting rats, his black fur mostly hidden under their white. Then he launched. The speed of the attack caught the girl by surprise. Bander shed rats as he flew through the air. He landed on the girl, knocking her down, his back legs kicking downward and his back claws raking into her torso. Her guts spilled out of her and rats slipped and scurried in her blood.

Bander ripped her head off with his front claws and the rats bolted back into the cracks and divots from which they came. Bander's lungs heaved from the exertion as he stood there over the corpse. His body was covered with bloody bits and scratches. All his wounds were only cosmetic. They were of little consequence to what he must do. Although he didn't yet realize it, the damage was far greater then he thought. His body might be fine but his mind would soon be compromised.

The thousand tiny wounds had infected him with rabies.

*   *   *

Larry and Bob finished circling the pyramid.

"There has got to be another way in," said Larry. "We are running out of time!"

"The entrance would have to be hidden to keep others out," said Bob calmly rubbing his cheek. "But it would need to be functional. After all, building one of these would take years and hundreds of people."

Larry's arm had been itching ever since they chased Bander here. He could see a faint outline on his forearm in the spot where Dubla and her sisters flicked that liquid on him back in their lair. It looked like a burn mark, but it itched like crazy.

"The witches," said Larry mostly to himself. "Come on!" he said pulling at Bob. "We need to get farther away."

"Okay," said Bob. "I guess a new perspective couldn't hurt."

The brothers marched away from the pyramid with Larry leading the way. When he was satisfied at the distance he stopped and turned to face the now distant pyramid. Bob stared at the structure, trying to figure out how this helped. "What now?" he finally asked.

"We circle it again," said Larry.

"I don't know…" Bob began.

"And you let me find the way in silence."

Bob shrugged his shoulders and motioned to his mouth meaning he buttoned his lip. The two began the circle with Bob in tow. Larry scrunched up his eyes. Bob thought to himself there was something different about his brother he was more decisive, more capable.

"There!" Larry exclaimed rushing ahead and pointing at the ground in front of him. Bob hurried after but saw nothing. Larry turned his smiling face to him. "Don't you see?" asked Larry pointing at the ground.

"See what?"

Larry carefully brushed at the sand and dust to reveal scratch marks in the ground.

"Scratches?" asked Bob confused.

"That man thought we were slaves. The slaves that built the pyramid. That got me trying to think like a slave."

"I don't understand," said Bob.

"Well if I was a slave the first thing I would be worried about is how to drag all the huge rocks to the building site. Then I realized that somewhere, even if they were concealed near the pyramid, there would be signs of dragging huge rocks."

"Brilliant, I should have thought of that. But just because we find the old rock trail how does that help us find the secret entrance?"

"If you had a huge slab of stone wouldn't it make sense that you would drag them the shortest distance possible?"

"Of course…a straight line."

"A straight line. If we walk from here directly to the pyramid I'll bet we walk right to the hidden entrance."

Larry and Bob looked to the pyramid and carefully walked straight towards it.

"How did you find those ruts?" asked Bob.

"I used the trick the witches taught me, I concentrated. It's way more useful that I thought it could be."

As the brothers marched straight back to the pyramid they caught glimpses of Bander; flashes of light indicated that some sort of magic was happening. Even as they let themselves fantasize that one of the defenders would strike Bander down, their hopes collapsed as they watched the dark from of Bander spring to yet an even higher level.

"We've got to hurry!" Bob urged Larry on. The brothers ran. Now back at the base the brothers looked for the entrance. It looked just like the rest of the structure, smooth rock, no entrance.

Larry reached out to put his hand on the surface. He stumbled forward as his hand met no resistance.

"What? This is it!" exclaimed Larry. Its only an optical illusion. It's the entrance!" Bob and Larry shuffled forward with their hands outstretched. The opening was the size of one of the building blocks that formed the pyramid. After six feet in the tunnel turned sharply to the left. Within one step the outside world disappeared and they were enveloped in near darkness.

*   *   *

Bander blinked blood out of his eyes. The cut on his head was but another irritation. He was getting close. Only four or five levels separated him from ultimate power. He shook a buzzing from his ears, his head cleared. He climbed another level.

He was barely over the edge when the sword struck his face. The blade slid off of his forehead and cut into his snout. Blood filled his mouth and he choked.

He slashed in every direction unaware yet of his attacker's position. Bander finished clamoring over the edge and got to his feet. His attacker was upon him again but this time Bander jumped backwards a dozen feet and saw his opponent.

The man, Kinto, was known to Bander. Kinto was the greatest swordsman in memory. Folk songs still spoke of Kinto's blades.

The slice of steel

Regret's appeal

Kinto never strikes a bone

His force, his will

Meets no resistance home.

Kinto stood no taller than an average man. His dark beard hid most of his face. The tendons in his arms moved like fins on a fish and his eyes seemed to take in everything. He held a sword before him and it looked weightless in his grip.

Bander readied himself. His tongue hanging out of his mouth dripped coppery blood. His instinct to charge was hard to suppress. The Gour he inhabited lusted to kill. Bander however was in charge. To charge a swordsman is to die, especially one with skills like Kinto. Bander kept Kinto in front of him and the two began to circle each other. Kinto took small quick steps; he was ready to lunge in any direction. Bander growled baring his blood-soaked teeth. His mind felt clouded. Only the adrenaline kept him focused. He knew that it would only take one well placed cut with that sword to end him. Kinto knew it too.

Bander slashed at kinto's sword like an animal would do, testing the waters. Kinto carefully kept just out of reach and waited for his opportunity to strike. Bander continued batting at the sword with increasing confidence. Kinto prepared for the rush that was coming, ready to slide his sword through the throat of this beast. Bander charged and Kinto thrust his sword. However, Bander was not a mindless beast. He was not charging to attack Kinto. He was charging to avoid the sword and at the last instant he dropped his shoulder down in front of his throat and chest. The sword struck home. It buried itself deep in the meat of Bander's shoulder but not in a vital spot. Bander rolled forward in a summersault ripping the sword out of Kinto's hand. Bander's claws tore through Kinto's flesh. Bander maniacally ripped Kinto apart with the sword still sticking out of his shoulder.

*　　*　　*

Larry and Bob stood side by side with their heads tilted back. The inside of the pyramid should have been dark but it was fully lit. It was much smaller than the outside, the thickness of the walls ate up most of the space. Wooden scaffolding clung to the ancient rocks like spider webs.

"The slaves must have been amazing architects," said Bob in awe of the size of the project.

"I d, dd don't th, think they b, built it themselves. They were slaves to somebody remember. I bet that is who designed it." said Larry.

The stone walls were etched with thousands of images. Men, women, and children stared down at the brothers. There eyes pleading for mercy. Their faces sunken and callow.

"I think those were the slaves," said Larry pointing at the etchings. "I wonder if that was why they erected so much scaffolding in here so they could etch their own likeness into the stone."

"They look so sad."

"Well of course they're sad, they were slaves. They probably got whipped and starved their whole lives," said Bob.

The brothers pulled their eyes off of the macabre walls and scanned the room.

'Now what are we supposed to do?" asked Bob.

"We climb."

"Then what?"

"The universe will provide." said Larry stepping onto the lowest scaffolding and hoisting himself up.

The ancient wood creaked under his efforts and dust filled in around him. Bob followed.

*   *   *

Bander knew something was wrong. His thoughts were unfocused and his heart beat too fast. Somewhere along the ascent he had been poisoned. He could feel its effects. His mouth gaped open in a heavy pant. His fur felt unnatural. Focus. His entire life, this pursuit,… he would not be denied now. He was too close. Bander climbed to the next level, the last level. From here he could see the shining cap of light atop the pyramid. One last foe and he could reach out and take it. He would do it, nothing could stop him now. All the years of amassing power, honing his skill, led to this.

He almost lost himself staring at the glowing magic. A sound of bone sliding across stone brought him back to the task at hand. Bander turned to the sound. His eyes locked in on the figure approaching. The sight of the dead grey eyes froze the air in Bander's lungs. This man was an abomination. A thing of the past, a thing long since dead. Bander longed to flee, but his body had shut down. The smell of death grew strong as the specter approached him. The dead do not walk; whatever was inside this corpse — whatever controlled the movements — was not from the realm of man. It was unnatural and Bander knew in his bones that he could not defeat this. Bander's aspirations to master the taking of life were helpless against that which existed in the world of the dead. He strained to run, to throw himself over the edge but his body refused.

The specter's ashen skin clung to withered muscles like moss on a tree. Its dead eyes saw nothing. It worked its jaw to speak.

"You greatest of fools. Welcome," the decayed tendons crackled in its head with every word.

"Welcome to the edge."

*   *   *

Inside the pyramid Larry and Bob struggled to climb the ancient scaffolding. The wood was decaying but it had been black walnut, a good strong wood. Bob admired the strength of a section of railing that he hefted.

"Isn't that amazing. I wonder how old this is and I still can't hardly bend it. The guys that built this sure knew what they were doing."

"I know, I kn, kn, know," stammered Larry. "We've got to hurry. I, I, don't even know what we are doing."

Bob looked over at his brother and saw the look of desperation on his face. "We are doing what we can." he said. "We can climb, so we climb."

Larry nodded approvingly.

The higher they reached, the more the edges of the pyramid leaned into them. This brought the murals on the walls in like an approaching band of warriors. The walls were covered with depictions of the slaves in their tattered clothing. Their knees and hands rubbed raw while they toiled to pull slabs of stone. The ribs poking through their emaciated bodies bespoke of the cost they were paying to complete their tower. They could be wild humans — almost beastlike — except for their eyes. The eyes were painted with an intensity of purpose that was exceptionally human.

"It looks like they are coming after us, doesn't it?" asked Bob.

"Yeah, there must be hundreds of them. What are they all stretching towards at the top?"

"I can't see that far, but I have a feeling that's where we'll find Bander."

The soot kicked by Larry's shoe fell over the scaffolding and drifted towards the dirt floor it fell for four seconds before hitting. They were a long way up. The brothers continued to climb the shaky old wooden structure with the faces of the damned glaring at them from all sides. The top of the pyramid revealed itself in dramatic display. All of the slaves were stretched out to lift the figure of a dead child centered at the point of the pyramid. The scaffolding stopped short and Larry and Bob outstretched their arms to point at the child. Larry and Bob could go no farther.

*   *   *

Bander's skin crawled on his frame. He could feel the specters cold breath move his fur. He could smell the dirt of a grave in the puffs of air.

"You made a mistake," spoke the ghost.

Bander remained frozen with fear. Unable to break away and run.

"The child, though he is fallen, is not of the world of man."

The apparition's voice chilled Bander's blood. Bander fought against his fear. His heart pounded against his chest. The ghost mocked him.

"The Fallen Star isn't for... What would you do with it anyway?" The ghost's voice rose until it shrieked at Bander. Bander recoiled like a child. "you're the wrong hands!" The ghost ranted at Bander waving its arms like a madman. "Heed me!"

Bander shuddered. The spirit touched a part of him on a primordial level. But the pull from the magic drove him. Reaching down into his mind to where he maintained control Bander took a stride towards the apparition and the magic. The ghoul shrieked and charged him. Its eyes rolled back into its skull exposing the yellowed whites. Its mouth gaped in a madman's scream.

Bander backed up. The spirit charged him. Bander shut his eyes and steeled himself against the attack. He forced the fear down into his bones and found the calm his logic commanded. A ghost is not physical and shouldn't be able to harm him as long as he kept his wits. But when the apparition reached out to him Bander felt the wet coldness of its touch. It was solid and it could hurt him. He recoiled but the creature was on him. Grabbing at his face with its icy dead hands. Bander brought up his hind legs and raked at the ghost but his claws, though they tore gray-dead flesh from the thing, did not slow it down. Bander's fur turned white where the thing grabbed at him. Its touch sucked something out of him he felt life slip out of his skin and the thing relentlessly attacked. Bander's mind converted to a primal instinct, something more than survival, something like revulsion. Revulsion of the unnatural, the living dead. His Gour-body fought ferociously but each snap of his jaws tore but chunks of already dead tissue from a corpse. The thing attacked ferociously and Bander responded savagely like an animal. Back and forth they parried. The corpse was shredded from Bander's claws with gaping chunks of flesh hanging from its frame. Yet still it attacked. Bander felt it each time the thing grabbed him some of his life was leaching out of his bones. He would not last long. The ghost latched onto Bander's shoulder and flung itself around and onto his back. Bander thrashed around his claws were useless he couldn't get to the apparition. He felt its teeth sink into the back of his neck and the pain surged through him. In desperation, Bander trudged forward toward the glowing light of the Fallen Star and with his arm outstretched he lunged for its power.

*　　*　　*

Inside the pyramid Larry and Bob caught glimpses of the battle above. Bander's large form cast a shadow near the opening where the glowing orb rested. Larry yearned to stop Bander but there was nothing left to do. His outstretched hand pointed to the orb and while he watched, Bander also stretched out his hand to grasp the prize. The scaffolding they were standing on shook. The entire inside of the pyramid shuddered. Bob and Larry almost lost their footing but were able to grab onto each other. All around them began a deep ancient chanting. It seemed to come from the rock or from the ground. The sound grew louder and louder. At first it looked like a fog was growing from the ground towards the brothers but as it got closer they saw that it was the forms of hundreds of men. Ghosts of the slaves that built this monument. They climbed out of the ground and on top of each other. Their numbers seemed to be never ending. Their writhing mass of smoky bodies rose up quickly filling the entirety of the tomb.

Bob felt their cold hands on his legs first. He recoiled but they hoisted him off of the scaffolding. Next Larry was lifted. The eyes of the dead all fixed upon the fallen star. It was their god. They were summoned to its call and they lifted the brothers towards it. Larry instinctively fought against their grasp but found he was no match for their supernatural strength. Within seconds the mass of ghosts had lifted Larry and Bob to the glowing orb.

Larry felt his arms worked by the hands of the slaves. They forced him to grab the orb and once he had it, they pulled him and Bob back down into the pyramid.

Bander reached the spot the orb had moments earlier occupied. He stared down into the small opening in the top of the pyramid and into Larry's eyes. Bander opened up his teeth filled maw and screamed. Larry and Bob fell away into the arms of the dead.

*   *   *

343

Their eyes came into focus on the stone floor of the chamber. Bob realized that his arm remained inside the mouth of the stone wolf. He slowly pulled it out revealing bloody punctures where the statue's teeth had gripped his arm. Larry also was shaking off the fog and extricated his arm from the other twin wolf statue.

"Did we do it?" Larry asked weakly.

"I don't know," said Bob tending to his arm. A thought came streaming back upon them; Sargasso.

Larry felt a wash of cold as his eyes found Sargasso's still body. He lay stretched out on the floor in front of them. Tock's inky black body lay stretched right beside him, also still. Bob shuddered and turned to Larry whose face hung like tattered sails.

Then Sargasso moved. It could have been a trick of the light but his weak voice quietly filled the chamber.

"Welcome back, girls."

"Sargasso!" the brothers moved quickly over to their friend who was now trying to get up. "You killed Tock?"

"Well lads," Sargasso said while rubbing at his throat. "I think the spell that forced Tock to hunt you for all his days also prevented him from killing himself. Every time he had a chance to sink his teeth into my flesh, which was often, he stopped short on each strike. I don't think he was allowed to bite into a thing as poisonous as me! How is that for irony? I finally got my grip around his neck."

"Let's get out of here," said Bob.

"What if Bander gets out? Maybe we should try to break these statues," said Sargasso.

"I don't think he will get out, look," said Bob pointing at the mural on the wall. The mural had changed. Now at the end of the procession chasing the elusive golden orb stood Bander frozen in time like all the others that had come before him. His clawed hands stretched out ahead of him and his eyes bulged with mad desire. On

344

his back clung the visage of death. It looked like a ghostly rider atop a monster. Larry felt the hatred in Bander's eyes which seemed to follow him around the room.

"Let's get out of here," said Larry.

Larry felt discombobulated as the group wound its way back to where they left Torth. The big man stood ferocious over piles of broken soldiers. He turned quickly at the sound of their approach and his shoulders relaxed at the sight of his friends. He wiped blood from his left eye and greeted them.

"That didn't take too long," he said.

"Torth, you are really hurt!" said Larry.

"Oh, this is nothing that a little dandelion wine won't fix," said Torth with a smile.

"Well, lets get on that order," said Sargasso. "Let's get out of here."

But Larry insisted that they return to the dungeon to attempt to free Dubla. Torth put up a brief argument, but time was of the essence so they rushed back down to the dungeon. It was easy to find. They just took every turn that led down into the depths of the Keep. The soldiers seemed to be avoiding them, if there were any that Torth hadn't dispatched already.

Dubla sat hunched in the shadows but she brightened when she saw the men.

"You did it?" She seemed overjoyed. "Bander is dead?"

"Well, I don't think he's dead but he isn't in this world anymore," said Bob.

"The Tetheroot withered away. I was sure he must be dead," she said.

"Why didn't you escape?" asked Sargasso.

"I was waiting to see if it was a trick. It would be just like Bander to give me false hope before torturing me. We've got to go."

Dubla opened the cell and stepped into the open with the men. She seemed a little shorter to Larry. It was a good thing Dubla was with them because her magic caused any guards they ran into to look the other way as they passed.

Once outside of Bander's Keep, they felt like sailors upon first regaining the land after a long voyage. They zigzagged their way through the crowded streets to avoid the guards. Dubla's magic seemed to be camouflaging them from the soldier's eyes.

"Sargasso," whispered a voice from behind a bunch of wooden crates nearby. The whole party turned poised ready to fight. There stood a beaten-up old man with a middle-aged woman and two children. It was Stip.

"Stip!" Sargasso said surprised. "What are you doing?"

"I'd like you all to meet my family," said Stip proudly. They exchanged pleasantries and decided that they needed to hurry up and get out of the city. Since Stip and his family were on the run they decided to accompany Bob and Larry to Agea Hills. It seemed as good a place as any and Stip insisted that he guide them back to their home in appreciation for their help.

At the edge of town Dubla turned to Larry and took a hold of his hand "My sisters and I will welcome you back anytime you want Larry. Sargasso, Bob, Torth, the world owes you a huge debt." And then she turned to walk away but Larry said, "Dubla, what is this marking on my arm? You know... from that one night."

"Larry that mark brands you as a very special man. Your powers are just starting to grow," and then Dubla walked away.

Chapter Thirty-Eight

The journey back to Agea Hills was a joyous one. Torth practically carried Stip's children the whole way on his shoulders. Bob and Larry and Sargasso went over everything that had happened and took turns embellishing their bravado and making jokes about each other. When they finally made it back to their homes everyone in the group was the best of friends. The first thing they did when they got into town was go to the bar where they had spent so many happy nights. The world felt like a warm blanket. They expected all their friends to be surprised to see that they were alive and well. But they didn't expect to see Grento sitting at the bar surrounded by town folk.

"Oh, Larry, Bob, it's about time you got here," said Grento over a glass of ale.

Larry, Bob, Sargasso, Torth and even Stip beamed huge smiles at the old man and his salutation.

The townspeople all welcomed the brothers and were fascinated by the strangers. Grento had apparently been there for a while and had prepared the town for Bob and Larry's arrival and described Torth to them so they were prepared for the giant. When everything settled down, and much ale had been enjoyed, the travelers sat and talked quietly of their adventures.

"Grento," began Larry. "What I can't figure out is what was the orb. I could feel something from it, like it was calling to me. After we fell it was gone. But for a second I had it, and for a second it felt like it had me."

"The magic only calls to certain people," said Grento. "Bander ached for the magic but your indifference to it may have allowed you to return. That magic seems to trap the most dangerous men of each age."

"Well I'm glad I'm not dangerous," said Larry thoughtfully.

"No, of course you're not," said Sargasso loudly.

The group spent the next few days meeting Bob and Larry's friends in town and resting and drinking. After about a week the group decided to go its separate ways. Torth and Sargasso left together and Sargasso promised that they would visit often. Sargasso left them shouting heartily, "Next time I see you lads we can go look for my elusive treasure!"

Grento and Stip and his family, decided to go to a Gelk village. Grento shook the brother's hands and said, "Well the long trick is finally over, take care."

Bob and Larry walked back to their little houses and their quiet lives.

The End

Paul Amdahl's other books include;

Vince's Workshop

Henry's uncle Vince disappears leaving only his wheel chair behind. There is absolutely no where Vince could have gone. He hasn't been able to move his legs since he was a kid and that was a bazillion years ago. Henry explores Vince's workshop searching for answers and most importantly, Vince. You'll never guess where he finds him or what else he finds at the same time. Let's just say there is more to this workshop than anyone would guess.

The Barefoot Fisherman; a fishing book for kids

The book explains the fundamentals of fishing as if the author were your older brother. Amdahl does not preach; he shares. The book reads like a pirate's treasure map as each chapter tugs the young reader deeper into the seaside caves of angling. The Barefoot Fisherman does not discuss entomology, advanced knots, or difficult casting techniques. Instead, it focuses on the aspects of fishing that kids love: raising earthworms, catching crawdads, making dough-bait. Try to find a grownup book that considers tomato worms as bait. The author's contagious love of the sport and gentle humor will probably create many new fishermen. But even adult anglers will pick up some tricks and tips.

All books are available at Amazon.com and eagerly await your book reviews.